'Fowler shocks and frightens, while making us laugh out loud . . . original, erudite and exciting'
Good Book Guide

'Fowler's fresh and unusual characters breathe new life into an established genre in which it's getting harder and harder to find anything genuinely fresh'
Booklist

'Madcap mystery . . . crazy and great fun for it'
Los Angeles Times

'This most unusual and impressive detecting duo . . . Fowler's wit and visual acuity combine for entertaining and thrilling results'
Chicago Tribune

'Christopher Fowler has offered his readership so much beyond a well-crafted British crime story . . . [he] will stretch your mind and leave you with a feeling of accomplishment after the final page is turned'
The Mystery Reader

'Places Fowler in the first rank of contemporary mystery writers'
Publishers Weekly

'Wartime London is conjured up with unique skill . . . Fowler's powers of description are enviable'
Independent on Sunday

Also by Christopher Fowler

Novels
ROOFWORLD

RUNE

RED BRIDE

DARKEST DAY

SPANKY

PSYCHOVILLE

DISTURBIA

SOHO BLACK

CALABASH

BREATHE

FULL DARK HOUSE

THE WATER ROOM

SEVENTY-SEVEN CLOCKS

TEN-SECOND STAIRCASE

WHITE CORRIDOR

THE VICTORIA VANISHES

BRYANT AND MAY ON THE LOOSE

Graphic Novel
MENZ NSANA

Short Stories
CITY JITTERS

CITY JITTERS TWO

THE BUREAU OF LOST SOULS

SHARPER KNIVES

FLESH WOUNDS

PERSONAL DEMONS

UNCUT

THE DEVIL IN ME

DEMONIZED

BRYANT & MAY
OFF THE RAILS

Christopher Fowler

BANTAM BOOKS

LONDON · TORONTO · SYDNEY · AUCKLAND · JOHANNESBURG

TRANSWORLD PUBLISHERS
61–63 Uxbridge Road, London W5 5SA
A Random House Group Company
www.randomhouse.co.uk

BRYANT & MAY OFF THE RAILS
A BANTAM BOOK: 9780553819700

First published in Great Britain
in 2010 by Doubleday
an imprint of Transworld Publishers
Bantam edition published 2011

Addresses for Random House Group Ltd companies outside the UK
can be found at: www.randomhouse.co.uk
The Random House Group Ltd Reg. No. 954009

Typeset in 11/14pt Sabon by
Kestrel Data, Exeter, Devon.

10 9

Penguin Random House is committed to a sustainable future for
our business, our readers and our planet. This book is made from
Forest Stewardship Council® certified paper.

Printed and bound in Great Britain by Clays Ltd, Elcograf S.p.A.

For Peter Chapman

ACKNOWLEDGEMENTS

Every Bryant & May novel is self-contained, and each a separate pleasure to write. This latest volume reflects my crowded city life and the happiness of chance meetings. I'd like to thank the London Underground staff who found the time to answer my dumb questions while patiently helping the millions of commuters who use the system every day. I don't know how you remain so calm and clear-headed. My Transworld editor Simon Taylor clearly knows the secret, because he maintains the same kind of grace under pressure, which entirely eludes me.

In life everyone needs a good teacher, a good doctor and a good lawyer. To that I would add a great agent, and would like to thank Mandy Little once again for her practically perfect patience and positivity. Kate Samano has a talent for making these books better, so my respect goes out to her, and to Lynsey Dalladay and the rest of the Transworld team.

A thumbs-up too to everyone who has posted suggestions on my website about Bryant & May (and all my other books), a number of which eventually find their way into print. Join us on my blog at www.christopherfowler.co.uk, which is somewhat different to usual author sites in that you can add entirely irrelevent thoughts or simply get into a fight with strangers.

'Youths green and happy in first love,
So thankful for illusion;
And men caught out in what the world
Calls guilt, in first confusion;
And almost everyone when age,
Disease or sorrows strike him,
Inclines to think there is a god,
Or something very like him.'

Arthur Hugh Clough

The Old Warehouse
231 Caledonian Road
London N1 9RB

THIS BUILDING IS NOW OCCUPIED BY THE PECULIAR
CRIMES UNIT UNTIL FURTHER NOTIFICATION FROM
THE HOME OFFICE

STAFF ROSTER: MONDAY

Raymond Land, Acting Temporary Unit Chief
Arthur Bryant, Senior Detective
John May, Senior Detective
Janice Longbright, Detective Sergeant
Dan Banbury, Crime Scene Manager/ InfoTech
Jack Renfield, Desk Sergeant
Meera Mangeshkar, Detective Constable
Colin Bimsley, Detective Constable
Giles Kershaw, Forensic Pathology
Crippen, staff cat

STAFF BULLETIN BOARD

Clipping from the Police Review:
'King's Cross Executioner' kills PC, escapes custody

A hired killer who left his beheaded victims on building sites in the
King's Cross area would have fatally undermined public confidence in

13

the multi-million-pound project to reinvigorate the former red-light area if he had not been identified, said an official Home Office report last week.

However, the report went on to castigate the unit bosses for failing to provide adequate security checks at its temporary headquarters, an oversight which resulted in the escape of the suspect.

The investigation had been conducted by London's Peculiar Crimes Unit, a little-known police division created by academics in 1940 to handle serious crimes that could be considered a threat to public order and confidence. As a secret wartime department, the PCU was allowed to develop many innovative (and questionable) investigative techniques. In the 1950s the unit fell under the jurisdiction of the Metropolitan Police, and was later absorbed into the British Military Intelligence department MI7 to handle cases involving domestic and foreign propaganda. In the last few months, the PCU has found itself increasingly mired in controversy after being placed under Home Office jurisdiction, and the principles upon which it was founded have been called into question.

Ministers accused the management team of failing to follow accepted procedural guidelines. But its senior detectives, Arthur Bryant and John May, remained determined to operate on the London streets using investigation methods unauthorized by present-day government officials. As a result, they successfully brought in a suspect known only as Mr Fox, who admitted carrying out the King's Cross murders for financial gain.

However, what should have been a cause for celebration turned to tragedy after Mr Fox succeeded in breaking out of the unit's holding cell and stabbing the officer on duty to death. PC Liberty DuCaine lost his life after being attacked by the accused, who then found his way back to the street. To date, the killer has not been recaptured.

Despite their ultimate exoneration by an independent judicial body, the PCU's future is looking less secure than ever before in its contentious history.

From the Desk of Raymond Land:

Is it necessary to remind staff NOT to provide the press with information about the escape of the so-called 'King's Cross Executioner'? We don't want to give tabloid hacks a reason to go through our dustbins for the next six months. DON'T SPEAK TO ANYONE. If you're in any doubt, talk to me first.

A word of warning about PC Liberty DuCaine's funeral: his family don't want any of you lot going anywhere near them this morning. They already had the Mayor creeping round for a photo op, and sent him away with a flea in his ear. Send flowers if you want, but stay away from the service.

I have to acknowledge the resignation of our Liaison Officer April May from the unit, effective immediately, for health reasons. April is planning to spend some time with her uncle in Toronto, following the recurrence of her agoraphobia. I'm sure you all join me in wishing her well for the future. I thought we should have a whip-round to get her something nice. By the way, when April said she'd like a gift voucher for a couple of hours in a flotation tank she was, in fact, joking.

As of this morning we now have fully functional computers and phones. You have John May to thank for this. I don't know how he did it. No one tells me anything.

Older members of the PCU will recall a pair of utterly useless workmen who sat in our former offices at Morning Crescent for months, brewing endless pots of tea instead of getting on with their work. You'll be thrilled to know that another pair of layabouts, two Turkish gentlemen both called Dave, will be arriving today to restore the electrics and plumbing, while no doubt offering unsought-for advice on the policing of the capital. Don't complain, their quote came in a lot lower than anyone else's. I daresay we'll find out why in due course.

By the way, there's a hole in the floor in Mr Bryant's office. Don't go near it.

If anyone sees Crippen, can they please butter his paws before letting him out? We don't want him getting lost in this neighbourhood. He's put on a bit of weight lately, and there are a couple of dodgy takeaways on the Caledonian Road that look like they could use the meat.

1

A PRIVATE FEUD

FROM: LESLIE FARADAY, HOME OFFICE SENIOR POLICE LIAISON

TO: RAYMOND LAND, ACTING TEMPORARY HEAD, PECULIAR CRIMES UNIT

CONFIDENTIAL

Dear Raymond,

With regard to your apprehension of the hired assassin operating in the King's Cross area, this so-called 'King's Cross Executioner' chap, thank you for acting so quickly on the matter, although it's a pity he subsequently managed to give you the slip. I had a bit of trouble opening your report because, frankly, computers have never been my strong point, but the new girl in our office seems to understand these things and printed out a copy for me.

Following the judicial review we decided to scrap the idea of holding a press conference, but we're speaking to our key contacts today, so we'll have some idea of the coverage that's likely to run in tomorrow's papers. Always talk to the press, I say, even when you've got nothing to tell them. We're hoping that a bit of publicity might flush him out. I'm trying to discourage sensational references to his nickname, without much luck, I'm afraid, but when a little boy finds a human head while fishing for eels in a canal, you can expect the press to react strongly.

I have passed your amendments and conclusions on to my superior and other concerned department heads, and will return with their reactions in due course. I also have to acknowledge the receipt of an additional report on the case from one of your senior detectives, Arthur Bryant, although I must admit I was only able to read portions of this document as his handwriting was extremely small and barely legible, and pages 23 to 31 had some kind of curry sauce spilled over them. Furthermore his account is opinionated and anecdotal in the extreme, and on several occasions positively offensive. Could you have a word with him about this?

Naturally we are all sorry to hear about what happened. It is always with great sadness that one hears of a police officer's demise in the course of his duty, especially in this case when the officer in question was so highly regarded, with such a bright future ahead of him.

Although the tribunal was reasonably satisfied that no member of the PCU could be held responsible for the unforeseen events occurring on your premises, we do not feel that full autonomy can be returned to the unit until a series of regulatory safeguards have been put in place to ensure that the impossibility of such an incident—'

'Oh, for God's sake get on with it,' Arthur Bryant complained at the page, balling it up and disdainfully throwing it over his shoulder as he skipped to the concluding sheet. He had filched the report from Raymond Land's mailbox and was vetting it before the acting chief arrived for work.

'Let's see – "inadequate safeguards", *yadda yadda yadda*, "irregular procedures", *yadda yadda*, "unnecessary risk factors" – all predictable stuff. Ah, here's the bit I was expecting – "because the perpetrator of these crimes was allowed to escape and is still at large, he remains a potential menace to society, therefore we cannot consider fully reinstating the PCU until he is apprehended." In other words, catch him but don't expect us to help you with additional resources. Bloody typical. Oh, listen, you'll like this bit. "Due to the financial reorganization of the Home Office's outsourced operations units, you have until the end of the week (Saturday at 6:00 p.m.) to conclude this and any other unfinished investigations in order to qualify for annual funding." So he wants us to achieve the impossible in one week or he and his ghastly boss Oskar Kasavian will cut us off without a penny. "Your Obedient Servant, Leslie Faraday." Who signs their letters like that any more? Anyway, he's not our Obedient Servant, but I suppose he couldn't sign it Sad Porky Timeserver or Snivelling Little Rodent.'

With increasing age the grace notes of temperance, balance, harmony and gentility are supposed to appear in the human heart. This was not entirely true, however, in Arthur Bryant's case. He remained acidulous, stubborn, insensitive and opinionated, and was getting ruder by the day, as the byzantine workings of the British Home Office sucked away his enthusiasm for collaring killers.

Bryant started to screw up the rest of the memo, then remembered he wasn't supposed to have seen it, and flattened it out imperfectly. He fished the other pages out of the bin, but now they were smeared with the remains of last night's takeaway.

'I don't know why you get so het up, Arthur. What did you honestly expect?' John May carefully pinched his smart pinstriped trousers at the knee and bent to give him a hand picking up the pages. 'A man kills three times, is arrested by us, breaks out of a locked cell, stabs a police officer in the neck and vanishes. We were hardly going to be rewarded for our efforts.'

'What about the innocent people we protected, the deaths we prevented?' Bryant asked, appalled.

'I think they're happier counting the millions of pounds we saved them.' May rose, twisted his chair and flopped down, stretching himself into a six-foot line. 'Just think of all the companies that would have pulled out if we hadn't been able to secure the area.'

'What a case for my memoirs,' Bryant muttered. 'Three mutilated bodies found on the mean streets of King's Cross. Murders committed solely for financial gain, by a slippery, adaptable thief who's grown up in the area around the terminus, a small-time crook propelled to the status of murderer when a robbery went wrong. You know what's happened, don't you? For the first time in his life this Mr Fox has been made to feel important, and the escalation of his criminal status from burglar to hired killer has increased his determination to stay free.'

There was a darkness at the heart of this chameleon-like killer that the members of the Peculiar Crimes Unit had underestimated. For a while it had felt as if gang war was breaking out in the area, but by getting to the root of the crimes, the detectives had managed to allay public fears and reassure investors that the newly developing region was still open for business. In the process they had lost an officer, and had been unable to stop their quarry from escaping back into the faceless crowds.

Bryant pottered over to the sooty, rain-streaked window and tapped it. 'He's still out there somewhere,' he warned, 'and now he'll do one of two things. Having had his fingers so badly burned he'll either vanish completely, never to be seen again, or he'll returneth like a dog to vomit, just to taunt me further. Proverbs 26:11.'

'I don't understand,' said May. 'Why are you taking this so personally?'

'Because I'm the one he's after. DuCaine just got in the way.' Bryant had never exhibited much empathy towards his co-workers, but this struck May as callous even by his standards.

'Liberty DuCaine's parents have just lost a son, Arthur, so perhaps you could keep such thoughts to yourself. Don't turn this into a private feud. It concerns all of us.' May rose and left the room in annoyance.

Bryant was sorry that the lad had died – of course he was upset – but nothing could bring him back now, and the only way they could truly restore order was by catching the man responsible. With a sigh he popped open his tobacco tin and stuffed a pipe with Old Arabia Navy Rough Cut Aromatic Shag. His gut told him that Mr Fox would quickly resurface, not because the killer had any romantic notion of longing to be stopped, but because his anger would make him careless. His sense of respect had been compromised, and he was determined to make the police pay for cornering him.

I'll get you, sonny, Bryant thought, *not just because I owe it to DuCaine, but to every innocent man, woman and child out there who could become another of your statistics. You'll turn up again, soon enough. You've tasted blood now, and the need to let others see how big you've grown will drive you back out into the light. When that happens, I'll have you.*

Unfortunately, Bryant tried to avoid reminding himself, it would need to happen this week.

2

CHOREOGRAPHY

DC Colin Bimsley and DC Meera Mangeshkar were watching the station. They had no idea what their suspect might look like, or any reason to assume he would suddenly appear before them on the concourse. But Mr Fox knew his terrain well and rarely left it, so there was a chance that even now he might be wandering through the Monday-morning commuters. And as the St Pancras International surveillance team was more concerned with watching for terrorist suspects following a weekend of worrying intelligence, it fell to the two detective constables to keep an eye out for their man. At least it was warm and dry under the great glass canopy.

Each circuit of the huge double-tiered terminus took between twenty minutes and half an hour. Bimsley and Mangeshkar wore jeans and matching black nylon jackets, the closest anyone at the PCU could come up with to an official uniform, but Bimsley was a foot taller than his partner, and they made an incongruous pair.

'Down there,' Meera pointed, leaning over the balustrade, 'that's the third time he's crossed between the bookshop and the florist.'

'You can't arrest someone for browsing,' Bimsley replied. 'Do you want to go and look?'

'It's worth checking out.' She led the way to the stairs. Colin checked his watch. Eight fifty-five a.m. The Eurostar was offloading passengers from Brussels and Paris, the national rail services brought commuters from the Midlands and the North, trains were disgorging suburbanites and reconnecting them to the Tube. Charity workers were stopping passers-by, others were handing out free newspapers, packets of tissues and bottles of water, a sales team was attempting to sell credit services, the shops on the ground-floor concourse were all open for business – and there was a French cheese fair; tricolour stalls had been set out down the centre of the covered walkway. Travellers seemed adept at negotiating these obstacles while furling their wet umbrellas and manhandling their cases through the crowds. But was a murderer moving among them?

'There he goes again,' said Meera.

'You're right, he just bought a newspaper and a doughnut, let's nick him. Uh-oh, look out, he's stopped by the florist. I'll make a note of that; considering the purchase of carnations. Well dodgy.'

'Suppose it's Mr Fox and you just let him walk away?'

'You want to call it? I mean, if we're going to start stop-and-search procedures down here, we'd better have some clearly defined criteria.'

'You can come up with something later – let's take him.' Meera paced up through the crowd, then stopped by the French market, puzzled, looking back. 'Colin?'

'What's the matter?'

'Something weird.' She pointed to the far side of the concourse, where half a dozen teenagers had suddenly stopped and spaced themselves six feet apart from each other. Bimsley shrugged and pointed to the other wall, where the same thing was happening. 'What's going on?'

All around them, people were freezing in their tracks and slowly turning.

'They're all wearing phone earpieces,' Meera pointed out.

Now almost everyone in the centre of the station was standing still and facing forwards. Beneath the station clock, two young men in grey sweatshirts and hoods set an old-fashioned ghetto blaster on a café table and hit 'Play'.

As the first notes of 'Rehab' by Amy Winehouse blasted out, they raised their right arms and span in tight circles. Everyone on the concourse copied them. The choreography had been rehearsed online until it was perfect. The station had suddenly become a ballroom.

'It's a flash mob,' Meera called wearily. The internet phenomenon had popularized the craze for virally organized mass dancing in public places, but she had assumed it had passed from fashion a couple of years ago.

'I took part in a freeze in Victoria Station once,' said Bimsley, watching happily. 'Four hundred of us pretending to be statues. It's just a bit of harmless fun.'

'Well, our man's using it to cover his escape.'

'Meera, he's not *our man*, he's just a guy catching a train.'

The diminutive DC did not hear. She was already haring across the concourse, weaving a path between the performers. The song could be heard bleeding from hundreds of earpieces as the entire station danced. The song hit its chorus and the choreography grew more complex. Colin could no longer see who Meera was chasing. Even the transport police were standing back and watching the dancers with smiles on their faces.

As the song reached its conclusion there was a concerted burst of leaping and twirling. Then, just as if the song had never played, everyone went back to the business of the day, catching trains and heading to the office. Meera was looking through the crowds, furious to find that her target had disappeared. But just as Bimsley started walking towards her, someone grabbed at his shoulder.

Colin turned to find himself facing a portly, florid-faced businessman who was slapping the pockets of his jacket and shouting to anyone who would listen. 'Hey, calm down, tell me the problem,' Bimsley advised.

'You are police, yes?' shouted the man. 'You look like police. I have been robbed. Just now, I am crossing station and this stupid dancing begins, and I stop to watch because I cannot cross, you know, and my bag is taken from my hand.'

'Did you see who took it? What was the bag like?'

'Of course I did not see, you think I talk to you if I see? I would stop him! Is bag, black leather bag, is all. I am Turkish Cypriot, on my way to Paris. The takings are in my bag.'

'What takings?'

'My restaurants, six restaurants, all the money is in cash.'

'How much?'

'You think I have time to count it? This is not my job. Maybe sixty thousand, maybe seventy thousand pounds.'

'Wait a minute,' said Bimsley. 'You're telling me you were carrying over sixty thousand on you – in notes?'

'Of course is notes. I always do this on same Monday every month.'

'Always the same day?' Bimsley was incredulous. How could anyone be so stupid?

'Yes, and is perfectly safe because no one knows I carry this money. How could they?'

'Well, what about somebody from one of your restaurants?'

'You tell me I should not trust my own countrymen? My own flesh and blood? Is always safe and I have no trouble, is routine, is what I always do. But today the music start up and everybody dance and someone snatch the bag from me. Look.' The irate businessman held up his left wrist, dangling from which was a length of plastic cable, neatly snipped through. 'I want to know what you will do about this,' the man shouted, waving his hairy wrist in Bimsley's perplexed face. 'You must get me back my money!'

Meera came back to his side. 'What's going on?' she asked.

'Nothing,' Colin sighed. 'Another bloody Monday morning in King's Cross.'

3

PARASITICAL

Bryant stared down into the sodden streets. It was hard to detect any sign of spring on such a shabby day. At least the doxies and dealers had been swept out of the area as the fashionable bars moved in. Eventually the raucous beckoning of hookers would only be recalled by the few remaining long-term residents. Such was life in London, where a year of fads and fancies could race past in a week. Who had time to remind themselves of the past any more?

Maybe it's just me, thought Bryant, *but I can see everything, stretching back through time like stepping stones, just as if I'd been there.*

No one now remembered Handel playing above the coal-shop in Clerkenwell's Jerusalem Passage, or Captain Kidd being hanged from the gibbet in Wapping until the Thames had immersed him three times. Thousands of histories were scrubbed from the city's face each year. Once you could feel entire buildings lurch when the printing presses of Fleet Street began to roll. Once the wet cobbles of Snow Hill impeded funeral cortèges with such frequency that it became a London tradition for servicemen to haul hearses with ropes. For every riot there was a romance, for every slaying, a birth; the city had a way of smoothing out the rumples of the passing years.

The elderly detective tossed the remains of his tea over the filthy window and cleared a clean spot with his sleeve. He saw coffee shops and tofu bars where once prophets and anarchists had held court.

The recent change in King's Cross had been startling, but even with buildings scrubbed and whores dispatched, it had retained enough of its ruffian character not to feel like everywhere else. Bryant belonged here. He basked in the neighbourhood's sublime indifference to the passing of time and people.

A week to solve a case. Well, they had risen to such challenges before. Carefully skirting the alarming hole in his office floor, Bryant donned his brown trilby, his serpentine green scarf and his frayed gabardine mackintosh, and headed out into the morning murk. At least it felt good to be back in harness. As he left the warehouse which currently housed the Peculiar Crimes Unit he almost skipped across the road, although to be fair he had to, as a bus was bearing down on him.

Arthur Bryant: have you met him before? If not, imagine a tortoise minus its shell, thrust upright and stuffed into a dreadful suit. Give it glasses, false teeth and a hearing aid, and a wispy band of white hair arranged in a straggling tonsure. Fill its pockets with rubbish: old pennies and scribbled notes, boiled sweets and leaky pens, a glass model of a Ford Prefect filled with Isle of Wight sand, yards of string, a stuffed mouse, some dried peas. And fill its head with a mad scramble of ideas: the height of the steeple at St Clement Danes, the tide tables of the Thames, the dimensions of Waterloo Station, and the methods of murderers. On top of all this, add the enquiring wonder of a ten-year-old boy. Now you have some measure of the man.

Bryant jammed the ancient trilby harder on his bald pate and fought the rain on the Caledonian Road. Typically, he was moving in the wrong direction against the elements. He seemed to spend his life on an opposite path, a disreputable old salmon always determined to head upstream.

As he marched, he tabulated life's annoyances in escalating order of gravity. He was sleeping badly again. He had forgotten to take his blue pills. His left leg hurt like hell. He had six days in which to close the unit's cases, and no money to pay his staff. He was likely to be thrown out of his home any day now. A good officer had died in the line of duty. And he had a murderer on the loose who was likely to return and commit further acts of violence. Not bad for a Monday morning. With a gargoyle grimace, he looked up at the rain-stained clouds above and muttered a very old and entirely unprintable curse.

Everyone talks about the unpredictable weather in London, but it has a faintly discernable pattern. At this time of the year, the second week in May, caught between the dissipation of winter and the failed nerve of spring, the days were drab, damp and undecided, the evenings clear and graceful, swimming-pool blue melting to heliotrope, banded altostratus clouds forming with the setting of the sun. You can forgive a lot when a dim day has a happy ending.

On this Monday morning, though, there was no sign

of the fine finish to come. Bryant made his way to the threadbare ground-floor flat in Margery Street where their escaped assassin, Mr Fox, had been living.

The building was a pebble-dashed two-storey block set at an angle to the road, possessing all the glamour of an abandoned army barracks. Dan Banbury, the unit's Crime Scene Manager, had already been at work here over the weekend, tying off the apartment into squares for forensic analysis. Bryant stepped over the red cords in his disposable shoe covers, but managed to lose one and dislodge a stack of magazines on the way.

'Just sit over there on the sofa, can you?' Banbury demanded irritably. 'Stay somewhere I can see you. You're supposed to wear a disposable suit.'

'I am. Got it from a second-hand stall on Brick Lane.'

'At least put your hands in your pockets. There's meant to be a constable on guard to log visits but Islington wouldn't provide one. Dispute over jurisdiction.'

'You're an SCO, you can let in who you want. Have you had your ears lowered?'

'Oh, my nipper came back from school with nits and wanted his hair cut off, but he wouldn't let me do it until I'd tested the electric shaver on myself. I went a bit too short.'

'Wise lad.' Bryant stuck his hands in his coat and found a boiled sweet that was probably a barley twist under the pocket fluff. He sucked it ruminatively, looking around. 'Still using pins and bits of string? I thought you could do it with a special camera now.'

'That's right. Buy me the equipment and I'll mark out the grid electronically. I think it's about seven grand.'

'Point taken. Bagged much up?'

Banbury sat on his heels and massaged his back. He had been staring at biscuit crumbs and dead flies for the last half hour. 'There's no physical evidence to take.'

'Don't be daft. There's always evidence.' Bryant picked a bit of fluff off his barley sugar and flicked it on to the floor.

'Not in this case.'

'Have you started on the bedroom?'

'Not yet. But if you're going to poke around in there, please don't – you know – just don't.'

Bryant was infamous for his habit of traipsing through crime scenes and fingering the evidence. He had begun his career at a time when detectives had been trained simply to observe with their eyes rather than to illuminate body fluids with blue lights and Luminol reagents. These days, specialist equipment came with specialists who charged by the hour. Many routine cases of criminal damage and assault were dumped simply because it was too slow and expensive to send off samples.

Bryant stood at the head of Mr Fox's single bed and studied the room. No books on display. Hardly any furniture. A framed photograph of a blue-eyed girl with long blonde hair, vacuous to the point of derangement. It was the photograph that had come with the frame. Mr Fox was a human sponge, a magnet for the knowledge of others, but he had no interest in real human beings and therefore possessed no real friends. He couldn't trust himself in any relationship that demanded honesty.

According to the Council's rental records, their murderer had lived here for almost ten years under the name of Mr Fox. Yet there was no character to be found in the rooms, nothing that would reveal his personality traits or give any clue to his real identity. Most people's hotel suites offered up more than this. To Mr Fox the flat was a place to sleep and visit periodically for a change of clothes, but even here he had been careful not to leave spoor.

'Fox,' said Bryant aloud. 'Dictionary definition: a wary, solitary, opportunistic feeder that hunts live prey. Good choice of a name. No real sign of who he is, I suppose.'

'Nothing,' Banbury called back. 'It's really odd. You and John met the man. You interviewed him at length. You didn't get anything at all?'

'We did, but it was all lies. Our mistake was taking what we saw at face value. He played us beautifully. I don't understand how he disarmed me. I'm usually so suspicious.'

Bryant felt that he understood very little about serial killers. Demonstrable motivation was the keystone of criminology, and just as altruists made the best benefactors, murderers were at their most comprehensible when it was possible to see what they gained from their actions. This chap was a total cipher.

Mr Fox should have been easy to find. After all, he had initially killed for gain, not because he derived pleasure from it. But, Bryant wondered, would he *have* to continue killing, now that he had discovered the taste?

A parasite, he thought. *He takes and takes without giving anything back, and remains in place until the host is dead*. He studied the lair of his quarry, and felt an ominous settling in his stomach that warned him of imminent danger – although it might have been germs on the barley twist.

4

THE VOID

'A serial killer,' said Banbury, standing up to stretch his aching calves. 'That's what I reckon we've got here. We've not had many of them at the PCU, have we?'

'Not proper saw-off-the-arms-and-legs-boil-the-innards-put-the-head-in-a-handbag-and-throw-it-from-a-bridge jobs, no.' When it came to fathoming the private passions of serial killers, Bryant felt lost. What were their most notable attributes? Solitude and self-interest. The rest must surely be conjecture. Novels and films were filled with the abstruse motivations of intellectual murderers – they carved designs into corpses according to biblical prophecies and hid body parts in patterns that corresponded to Flemish paintings – but the reality was that the act of murder remained as squalid and desperate as it had always been, the province of the spiritually impoverished.

Bryant dug out a none-too-clean handkerchief and noisily blew his nose. 'Why do you think he's a serial killer?'

'Well, here's the thing, Mr Bryant. It's very hard to

completely hide your personality. I know when my boy's been in my room, no matter how hard he tries to cover his tracks.'

'The poor little bugger's got a forensic scientist for a father. How can he ever hope to pull the wool over your eyes?'

'And we always know where you've been – we follow the smell of your pipe, the mud and the sweet wrappers. It's easier if you've no personality there to begin with. And serial killers suffer from a sort of moral blankness. There was a case in America, a young couple, Karla Homolka and Paul Bernardo. They were known as the Ken and Barbie killers because they were middle-class WASPs. In the trial notes, the prosecution asked Karla how she could take breaks to sit downstairs in the lounge reading, while her husband murdered a young girl upstairs. Do you know what she replied? "I'm quite capable of doing two things at once." Blankness, see? And they go about things in the wrong way. Karla was worried that she'd leave behind evidence, so she shaved a victim's head. It really confused the profilers, who thought it must be a psychosexual signature, but she'd done it so she wouldn't have to throw away the rug that the corpse was lying on. She was more concerned about the rug than the murdered girl.'

'And you can see something like that here, can you?' Bryant could not appreciate the silence of empty souls; his passions were too rich and various. They included Arthurian history, anthropology, architecture, alchemy and abstract art, and those were just the As. He let his partner handle the messy human stuff. While he appreciated the biological intricacies of the heart, its spirit remained forever encrypted.

An absence of personality. Banbury's right. Mr Fox takes alienation to a new level. He examines others as if they're circuitry diagrams. Bryant studied the murderer's cold, bare little bedroom in wonder. *He sees this weakness as a skill, but we have to make it the cause of his downfall.*

The room was as dead as an unlit stage set. *Ten years,* he thought. *That's how long you've been hiding your true nature. When did you come to realize you were different? What happened to make you like this? Do you even remember who you once were?*

Bryant knew that the man they were looking for had befriended several local residents. They had visited him, and Mr Fox had socialized with them in order to use their knowledge of the area. Had he let them inside the flat? Why not – he had nothing to hide here. He was an actor who adopted personalities and characteristics that he thought might prove useful. Actors were good at doing that. How many books had been written about Sir Alec Guinness without ever revealing what he was truly like?

'When you report in to Janice, get her to circulate Mr Fox's description to acting schools, would you? There are several in the immediate area,' said Bryant. Banbury threw him an intrigued look as he repacked his kit. 'This ability to deceive might be rooted in some kind of formal training.'

Bryant could only sense his quarry in the broadest of sweeps. There were people out there who were touched by nothing. The damaged ones were the most dangerous of all. He needed concrete facts about his quarry. But even the people who had been befriended by Mr Fox seemed to recall nothing about him. In a world of streaming data, how could one man leave behind so little?

'Dan, can I borrow your brains for a minute?' Banbury was good at repopulating empty rooms; he could put flesh back on the faintest ghosts. Everyone at the unit knew that Banbury had been a lonely child, overweight and socially lost, locked in his bedroom with his flickering computer screens. Perfect PCU material in training, as it turned out.

Banbury dusted powder from his plastic gloves with an air of expectation. Bryant had a habit of asking questions that weren't easily answered.

'What can you tell me about Mr Fox from this room? I don't mean on a microscopic level, just in general. There must be something. I can't read much at all.' Bryant looked around at the IKEA shelves, the cheaply built bed, the bare cupboards.

'You met him, Mr Bryant, you know what he looks like.'

'That didn't tell me a lot. He stuck to answering questions, gave us facts without opinions, avoided bringing himself into the conversation. He's very clever at not sticking in the memory, especially a memory like mine.'

'Well, give me your impression.'

'I don't do impressions. Let me think. Slight but muscular. About five ten. Smooth, unmemorable face, like a young actor without make-up. Fair complexion. Grey eyes. Not much hair, although I have a feeling he shaved his hairline. I wish we'd had a chance to photograph him. I got one interrogation in before going to brief the others – entirely my fault; I was anxious to get down the details of the case. We should photograph them on arrest, the way they do in America. John took a picture on his mobile, but the room was dark and it didn't come out very well.'

'OK, so we don't have an ID for him, but there's a piece of face-recognition software that might pick up his main features from your shot and find a match. That's assuming he has a record.' Banbury took a few steps forward, pinched his nose, leaned, peered, scratched at his stubbly head. 'I've already had a good look around, of course—'

Of course you have, thought Bryant. *Natural curiosity got the better of you. We all want to know about the kind of man who can kill without thinking twice.*

'I think he's probably lived here since his late teens, which makes him just under thirty. A loner from a broken home. Very closed off about the past. Something bad happened there that he doesn't go into very often – there's usually some kind of family trouble in the background. We know that his friendships are cultivated for their usefulness, and any emotions he expresses are meticulously faked. The habit of never presenting his true self to anyone is probably so ingrained that he wouldn't be able to reveal himself now if he tried. A classic user, unemotional and unrepentant. You tell 'em they've done wrong and they look at you as if you're speaking French. This really does place him in the serial-killer category. Clever planning, no witnesses, no evidence; it's a pattern. I bet he hasn't used his real name for so long that he's almost forgotten it. Probably has OCD. A fantasist, a reinventor, but it has all come out of necessity.'

'Where are you getting all this?'

'Oh, the belongings, mainly.' Banbury waved a hand across the shelves. 'A few other points of interest. The picture on the wall there.' He indicated an evenly lit photograph of an empty red metal bench against a white tiled wall. 'You couldn't get much more sterile than that, could you? He doesn't do people. Except his grandparents

– there's an unframed photo of an old couple on the bedside table. We'll see if we can get anything from it. There are only two types of items here: the stuff he owned as a child, and recent acquisitions. In the former group you've got the alarm clock with the chicken on it beside the bed, and that little grey metal animal – an armadillo, I think. The clock's from the early 1950s so I'm guessing it was purchased by the grandparents. Anything that ugly would have to have sentimental value. The armadillo figurines were popular in Texas in the mid 1970s, but were available here. Maybe it reminds him to keep a tough shell. Might have been a gift from his father.'

'That's a bit of a leap.'

'The trick is not to look at anything in isolation. Whether they mean to or not, most people continually reassess their belongings, adding and subtracting all the time to keep everything in balance. So I add the picture, the clock and the armadillo to that book over there.' He pointed to a single hardback in an alcove beside the bed. *Founders of the Empire* was a volume on great British explorers. 'It's signed with a message from his father. No names, unfortunately.'

Banbury picked up the book and showed Bryant. He wasn't about to let the detective touch it without gloves. 'See, he's written on the flyleaf. "An independent man makes his own way in the world – Dad." Hard to imagine a more impersonal note. I guess he wanted his kid to grow up self-reliant and disciplined. No sign of a mother anywhere. Kid's stuff here, near the bed – adult stuff over there. The teenage years are missing. Then we jump to a few recent purchases in the cupboard: the paperback copy of Machiavelli, psychology manuals, the fiction choice suggesting that he likes reading about villains more than heroes – *American Psycho*, *The Killer Inside Me*, damaged people. He's interested in learning how to control others. He's probably disdainful of ordinary folk, despises their weakness, thinks of them as lower life forms. The books and magazines are arranged thematically and alphabetically. Four separate volumes on the great disasters of London; maybe he enjoys reading about other people's tragedies. He's obsessive-compulsive because at first it was the only way to protect himself and keep his real feelings hidden, and now it's an unbreakable habit.'

Banbury walked around the bed. 'Check out the wardrobe drawers. His clothes are neatly grouped into different outfits for the personalities he wants to project. Grey suit, white shirt, blue tie; jeans and grey T-shirt. Grey, white, blue, the colours of sorrow, austerity, emptiness. The brands are H & M, Gap, M & S. No choices that reveal any sign of individuality. The bed linen's been washed so there aren't even any fabric prints to lift. One plate and one mug – he certainly wasn't planning to have anyone over to stay. He lives here and yet he doesn't.'

'What do you mean?'

Banbury scratched his nose and thought for a minute. 'Some people have no sense of belonging, because they live inside their heads. They carry themselves wherever they go. They're complete from one moment to the next. Most of us, if we were told we had to board a plane in the next couple of hours, would need to head home first. We like to tell others what we're doing, where we're going. We go online, make calls, form connections. He doesn't. No phone, no mail, no laptop, no keys, wallet, money, bills or passport. He always makes sure he's got everything he needs on him.'

'But he had nothing on him when he was arrested.'

'Then he has a place to stash stuff. Obviously he'd be tagged at any airport.'

'I don't think he wants to leave the country,' said Bryant, 'or even leave the area. Something is keeping him right here.'

'Then what are we missing? Don't touch that, it's not been dusted yet.' Banbury pulled out a camel-hair brush and twirled it between his fingers. 'It's complicated. He's living off the grid, old-school fashion, face contact only. He stays in this block because it's Council-owned but cared for by the residents, which means the cops aren't as familiar with it as they are with the Evil Poor Estate up the road.' The so-called Evil Poor Estate was home to multi-generational criminal families whose recourse to violence and destruction was as natural to them as going to the office was for others. Such estates formed modern-day rookeries around London.

'Have a look at this,' said Banbury. 'There are stacks of local newspapers in the cupboards, articles starred in felt tip – he's fascinated by London, particularly the area in which he lives. Plenty of neatly transcribed notes about the surrounding streets and Tube stations. He has abnormally strong ties to his home. This is interesting because it contradicts all the other signifiers. To me, it's the only part of his behaviour that's outwardly irrational.'

'An emotional attachment to the neighbourhood. Why would you stick around if you'd killed someone?'

'Killers do. But it's usually the disorganized, mentally subnormal ones who stay on at the location. The organized ones use three separate sites: where the victims are confronted, where they're killed and where they're disposed of. Then the killer leaves the area. So we have a contradiction.'

41

'Hmm. Anything more from the newspapers?'

'He's earmarked the obituaries of people who live around here. Maybe he was planning identity theft.'

'Think he'll come back to the flat? Is it worth keeping someone on site?'

'He's got no reason to return. There's nothing worth taking.'

'Come on, Dan, give me something I can use.' Bryant impatiently rattled the boiled sweet around his false teeth.

'OK. His name. I've bagged one of the notes you might find interesting, some research about a dodgy pub that used to exist nearby called The Fox At Bay. He's clearly a local lad, born in one of the surrounding streets. Maybe he took his name from the pub. He won't have become friendly with anyone else in the building, but maybe someone knew his old man. I think at some point Mr Fox lost contact with his family, maybe when his folks split up. He cuts his own hair, is capable of changing his appearance quickly. But he's cleaned his electric clippers so that there's not so much as a single hair left behind. He's bleached everything. He left home fully prepared to travel, because there's nothing of value here, only the two changes of clothes and one pair of knackered old shoes. No one else's fingerprints but his own, and he hasn't got a record so we can't match them. No foreign fibres so far, nothing to link him to the murders beyond what we already have. We could try the National DNA Database, but less than 8 per cent of the population is recorded on it, so if he's managed to keep himself out of trouble and away from hospitals it's of no use. He keeps his dirty work off the premises. Hair dye in the bathroom cabinet, and a pair of steel-rimmed spectacles with plain glass in them. Not exactly a master of disguise, but you do feel he enjoys the power that accompanies deception. No sign of a woman anywhere. He's the kind of man who visits prostitutes. He can't risk getting close to anyone. He wouldn't trust them.'

'Well, I'm disappointed,' Bryant complained. 'I thought you were going to provide me with some genuine revelations instead of a load of old guesswork.'

Banbury blew out his cheeks in dismay. 'Blimey, Mr Bryant, I thought I was doing quite well.'

'Let me tell you something about this man. He doesn't see himself as damaged. The cities are our new frontiers; it's here that the battles of the future will be fought, and he's already preparing himself for them. He knows that the first thing you have to do is chuck out conventional notions of sentiment, nostalgia, spirituality, morality. There's no point in believing that faith, hope and charity can help you in a society that only wants to sell you as much as it can before you die. Mr Fox has divested himself of his family and friends, and he's taking his first steps into uncharted territory. He considers himself as much of a pioneer as, oh, Beddoes or Edison.'

Banbury stared in bewildered discomfort at Bryant, who was cheerfully sucking his sweet as he considered the prospect.

'You think he's some kind of genius, then? Sounds like you admire him.'

'No, I'm just interested in the way people protect themselves in order to survive. It's an instinct, but he's turned it into an art. And this solipsism ultimately blinds him. Ever had dinner with an actor?'

'No.'

'Don't. All they ever talk about is themselves. They

never ask questions, never bother to find out who you are. They're not interested in anything but getting to the truth of their characters. And in most cases there isn't any truth, just an empty, dark, faintly whistling void. The serial killer Dennis Nilsen was so incredibly boring that he actually sent his victims to sleep.'

'Blimey.'

Bryant broke the unsettling silence. 'I had an aunt once who appeared in drawing-room comedies. She was doing a Noel Coward at Richmond Theatre – *Hay Fever*, I think – when a man in the front row dropped dead. She was very put out, because there was a practical meal in the second act and they had to halt the show while the St John's Ambulance Brigade carried the body out, so her food got cold. Heartless and selfish, you see. Do you want a gummy bear? They're a bit past their sell-by date but that just improves the flavour.' He seductively waved a paper packet at Banbury.

'No thanks. I'm going to close up here, then.' He stopped in the doorway and looked back. 'It's incredible that someone can operate as a lone agent in a city this size. You wouldn't think it possible. We've got four million CCTVs beaming down on us, rampant personal-data encryption and local-authority surveillance, and he can still make himself invisible.'

'Urban life has an alienating effect on all of us, Dan. When was the last time you got a smile in a shop or talked to someone on the Tube? Mr Fox has learned to adapt and embrace the new darkness. He has the tools to control it. His life unfolds inside his head. I need to know what he's planning next.'

'I don't know how you can find that out. He's a murderer,

Mr Bryant. He's separated from everybody else.'

'Maybe he always has been. What happened to create the void in him? There's a danger that when you pack up from here, tape the front door shut and leave, we may never see or hear from him again, do you understand? I can't let that happen.'

'I've done my best, but I can't work with what isn't there.' Banbury shrugged.

'We're supposed to specialize in finding out what isn't there. Find me something.'

'Some people – ' Banbury sought the right phrase, ' – don't have a key that unlocks them. But if Mr Fox does, I'm willing to bet it'll be in his formative years, between the ages of, say, seven and twelve. It won't tell us where he is now, of course—'

'Maybe not, but it's a place to start,' said Bryant. 'Keep looking, and leave everything exactly where it is, just in case he decides to come back. I'll see if we can run surveillance for a few days at least.'

Bryant was about to leave, then stopped. Inside the open bathroom cabinet he could see a small white plastic pot. Removing it, he checked inside. 'He wears contacts. The case is still wet, and there's what looks like an eyelash. Can you run this through your DNA Database?'

'Depends on whether the saline solution has corrupted the sample, but I'll give it my best shot.'

'You'll need to. We don't have anything else.'

'Do you think he's insane?'

'We're all mad,' Bryant replied unhelpfully. 'That chap Ted Bundy was working as a suicide-prevention officer while he was murdering women. In 1581, the test of legal insanity was based upon an understanding of good

45

and evil. A defendant needed to prove that he couldn't distinguish between right and wrong. But what if he could, and still committed atrocities? The insanity ruling was amended to allow for those who couldn't resist the impulse to kill. Nowadays, that clause has been removed because serial killers don't fit the legal definition of insanity. They accumulate weapons, plan their attacks, hide evidence and avoid detection for years, so it's clear they should know right from wrong. They certainly appear to be making informed choices. Voices in the brain? Perhaps. Something in the darkness speaks to them.'

'I thought you didn't know anything about serial killers,' said Banbury.

'I don't,' Bryant replied. 'But I've seen the things that make men mad.'

5

TROUBLE

Detective Sergeant Janice Longbright was not exactly the tearful type. She had been around police stations all her life, and it took a lot to upset her.

When she was seven years old she had been sitting in the public area of the old cop shop in Bow Street, waiting for her mother to come off duty, when a distressed young man walked in and cut his wrists with a straight razor, right in front of her. The scarlet ribbons that unfurled from his scraggy white arms were shocking, certainly, but she was fascinated by the trail of blood splashes he left as he walked on through the hall, because she had been seeing their pattern for the previous two weeks whenever she shut her eyes. His death seemed to clear the problem, and her sleep that night was deep and dreamless.

Longbright's mother had often brought copies of case notes home with her at night. Gladys was always careful not to leave them lying around the flat, but her daughter knew exactly where to find them. Shootings, stabbings, men 'going a bit mental' – political correctness had been thin on the ground back then. No diversity training, no child-trauma services, nothing much to comfort the beaten and bereaved beyond a cup of strong tea and a comforting chat. And somehow, perhaps because she was used to the subject of death being introduced at the meal table or between Saturday-night TV shows, young Janice had remained a well-balanced child.

Gladys had discussed the mysteries of human behaviour with her daughter in a kindly, dispassionate manner, as if they were stories that could only damage the sensibilities of other, less robust families. Janice had grown up tough enough to survive the defection of her father and the loss of her beloved mother. She had spent eleven years with a partner whose nerve had ultimately failed him when faced with commitment. There was a core inside her as firm as oak, inherited from a long line of strong women, and nothing could chip it away.

But by God, she was sorry to lose Liberty DuCaine.

Friends for four years, lovers for one night, they would probably have proved too similar to grow their relationship further, but the chance to try had been snatched away from her. So she sealed his death inside her head, somewhere at the back with the other sad things, and told herself she might look back one day in the future, but not yet. There was too much to do. Her colleagues probably all thought she was a hard cow, but it couldn't be helped. There was a time to cry, and it was not now.

First things first; if they were really going to clear up all outstanding work by the end of the week, they needed to get organized. The offices were a dirty, dangerous disgrace. The unit hadn't had a chance to catch its breath since it moved in. Crates were piled in the hall, taps leaked, light fittings buzzed and smouldered, the floors were strewn with badly connected cables, doors jammed shut or opened by themselves. The detectives' files were a hopeless mess. Bryant kept hard copies in cardboard folders, May kept his on hard drives, and neither knew what the other was doing.

She had hoped April would help her sort everything out, but the poor girl had declined into her former agoraphobic state after DuCaine's death, and could not be persuaded to return to the unit. Janice was annoyed with her for giving in to her demons. Her departure had handed another small victory to Mr Fox. *She's gone and it's a shame, but there's work to do*, she thought, rolling up her sleeves and filling a bucket.

The PCU's new home was situated on the first and second floors of an unrenovated warehouse on the corner of Balfe Street and Caledonian Road, sandwiched between a scruffy Edwardian residential terrace and a traffic-clogged arterial road. The detectives' room overlooked the latter, and despite the detective sergeant's best efforts, they had so far resisted rehabilitation.

A little chaos had always suited the elderly detectives. The world was an untidy place, Bryant always told her, and he had an innate suspicion of those who tried to keep it too neat. John May was, of course, the exact opposite. His white apartment in Shad Thames was eerily immaculate, and only the burbling presence of a small television, left on a rolling news channel whenever he was at home, disturbed the sense of orderly calm. But here in King's Cross, their chaotic offices defied order.

Longbright looked over at the two Turkish Daves. One

was drinking tea and the other was reading Thackeray's *Vanity Fair*. 'Are you two going to do any work?' she asked.

'We're waiting for the wood,' said one.

'Can't do anything without the wood,' said the other.

She snatched away the mug of tea and the novel. 'If you're reading this for tips on British society, it's out of date. These days, pushy little bitches like Becky Sharp end up working in the media.' They looked blankly at her. 'It doesn't matter. Go and get the wood or you'll get the boot.'

'No good,' said one. 'We got no cash.'

Longbright dug a roll of notes from her pocket and tossed it over. 'Buy the wood, bring me the change and get a receipt or I'll break your nose.'

The workmen left, muttering under their breath.

Longbright wondered if she could get away with throwing out some of Bryant's rubbish. He would notice if the bear's head table-lamp went missing, but perhaps his collection of Great Western railway timetables 1902–1911 could be quietly dumped in the skip at the back of the building. She hoisted up a mouldy carton.

'I'll kindly thank you to return my railway timetables to where you found them,' said Arthur Bryant, poking her in the back with his walking stick.

'You can't possibly need all this stuff, Arthur.' She dropped the carton back on his desk with a cloudy thump.

'It's not all timetables, you know,' said Bryant, pulling off his overcoat. 'Remove the top volume.'

Longbright did as she was told. Underneath was a dog-eared copy of *Greek Mausoleums: Their History and Meaning*.

'You see?' Bryant declared triumphantly. 'You'd have felt a bit silly throwing that away.'

Longbright wrinkled her nose. 'It's even less useful than the timetables.'

'Wrong. The sculptor Scopas carved mythical figures with the features of humans, not gods. He was the first artist to notice that hidden muscles shaped the face, which was square rather than oval. He taught us to see what was hidden. In that sense, he was the first detective.'

'All right, but we've moved on a bit since then. We've got forensic psychology and seriology, DNA testing – '

'You're missing the point, enchantress. A body is more than mere meat and fluids. Its humours are ultimately unknowable. Why do people behave as they do? Every book I own adds a tiny piece to the puzzle.'

'But books don't hold the key to people.'

'They hold the key to society, and if we ignore that, we know nothing. Now put everything back in the same order.'

'There was no order.'

'*Exactly*,' said Bryant mysteriously.

'What about these then?' Longbright held up a set of tattered blue volumes. '*Conjuring & Tricks with Cards*, volumes one to six. What are they going to teach you?'

'I'll show you. Over there in the corner you'll find a small blackboard.'

Longbright picked up the board, which was divided into nine panels.

'Stand it on the shelf behind John's desk,' Bryant instructed, pulling out a pack of cards. 'Now pick one of these. Look at it, then pick eight more.' Longbright drew the three of spades, and added eight further cards. Bryant gave her a handful of drawing pins. 'Shuffle your cards and pin them face down on the squares of the board.'

'I've got better things to do with my time,' the DS complained. She completed her task and turned to find Bryant pointing a gun at her. It looked like a Colt Single Action Army revolver. 'Where did you get that?'

'Evidence room. Get out of the way. You don't know which square holds the card you picked, do you?'

'No. Are you sure this is safe?'

'Of course. It's a Victorian parlour trick.' Bryant aimed randomly, squeezed his eyes shut and fired the gun. The explosion made their ears ring. 'Check the board,' he instructed. Longbright found a bullet hole in the centre of one card. She unpinned it and turned it over.

'Is that the card you chose?'

'No. I picked the three of spades. This is the nine of clubs. What did you do?'

'You were meant to pick the nine of clubs. An identical card with a bullet hole was pinned to the back of one of the board's squares. The square is on a pivot. When you pressed the card on to it, you activated a timer that flicked the square over. Persistence of vision covered the switch. The gun was loaded with a blank, obviously.'

'Well, if you'd forced the right card it would have worked,' said Longbright encouragingly.

Just then, Raymond Land came storming into the office. 'What the bloody hell is going on?' he demanded. 'Someone just fired a gun!'

'That was just a blank,' Longbright explained. 'Mr Bryant was showing me a trick.'

'Blank my arse. The bullet came straight through my wall. You could have killed me! It missed my ear by about two inches and exploded Crippen's litter tray. Gave him the fright of his life. Look.' He held up a squashed slug.

'My mistake,' Bryant apologized absently. 'I'm sure I gave you the nine of clubs. I think I'll just step out to my verandah for a smoke and a ponder. Behave appropriately while I'm gone.'

'Wait, come back, you've got no right—' Land began, but Bryant had slipped out.

After all this time he's still trouble, thought Longbright. *I like that in a man.*

Land was looking for someone to blame. 'And you, the way you encourage him,' he said, shaking a finger at her.

'Don't look at me, boss. Mr Bryant's teaching himself magic.'

'Well I'll teach him how to disappear if he's not careful,' Land concluded ineffectually, returning to his room.

Longbright replaced the books in their rightful places, but the dust was setting off her hay fever. Checking her watch, she noted that Liberty DuCaine's funeral would soon be starting. Although the unit had been warned to stay away, she felt that someone should be there. Reaching a decision, she donned her jacket and set off.

6

BEST BOY

At first glance, the City of London crematorium appeared to be nothing more than a pleasant London park. There were a great many rose beds neatly arranged like ledgers, and a variety of clipped English trees: elm, walnut, chestnut, beech. On closer inspection, Longbright noticed the small rectangular plaques set at ground level in the grass. An aquamarine sky released soft patters of rain, accentuating the landscape's greenness, releasing the fresh smell of spring leaves.

Feeling guilty because she had forgotten to change from her PCU staff jacket, Longbright turned up her collar and headed for the chapel's ante-room. She could hear an organ recording of 'From Every Stormy Wind That Blows' coming to an end.

The doctor at University College Hospital had told her that if Liberty DuCaine's neck wound had been a centimetre lower, it would have been over his jawbone. The tip of the weapon would have been deflected and prevented from going into his brain. Instead it had slid straight up, tearing into his temporal lobe. Longbright had spent the weekend trying to imagine what she could have done differently. But there was no use wondering, because they were all at fault; they had fatally underestimated the capabilities of their suspect.

'What do you think you're doing?' asked a large Caribbean woman, watching her from the damp archway.

'I was just reading the tributes on the flowers,' said Longbright, straightening up.

'We don't want the police here. Did you even know my son?'

'I worked with him for a while.'

The woman examined the badge on Longbright's jacket. 'He wasn't at your unit for very long.'

'No, but we brought him in on a number of special investigations before he joined full-time.' Longbright held her ground. She had heard about Liberty's mother, and knew what to expect. 'I'm sure you'd rather not have anyone from the PCU here, Mrs DuCaine, but I counted myself a close friend.'

'How close?' Mrs DuCaine gave her a hard stare before approaching the floral display with a weary sigh. She bent with difficulty and tidied the tributes with the air of a woman who needed something useful to do. 'If you want to be here, I suppose I should accept with grace. There's too much bad blood in the world.'

'Thank you.'

She stood with a grimace, sizing Longbright up. 'I'm as much to blame as anyone. I encouraged Liberty to enter the force. We all did. But I didn't want him joining that crazy unit of yours. Most of his friends were against it. They said it would damage his career, that it wasn't even part of the real police.'

'There's a lot of prejudice against us, Mrs DuCaine. We don't operate along traditional lines.'

'Then what *do* you do?'

'We look after cases of special interest. Sometimes people commit crimes that can cause . . . unrest . . . in society.'

Mrs DuCaine waved the thought aside with impatience. 'I don't know what you mean by that.'

Longbright tried to think of a good example. 'Suppose two people were killed in your street in one week. People would think it was a bad neighbourhood.'

'We already live in a bad neighbourhood.'

'Well, in such a situation our unit would be called in to find out if the deaths were connected, or if it was just coincidence. We would try to lay public fears to rest. A lot of people live and work in this city. Someone has to look after its reputation. Your son was invited to help us do that. Not many people are good enough to be asked.'

'Is that supposed to make me feel better? He ended up getting stabbed in the neck.'

'It could have happened to him anywhere, Mrs DuCaine.'

'As soon as I heard the doorbell, I knew.' She reached past Longbright and delicately replaced a card on top of a spray of yellow roses. 'It was the stupidest thing. My mother had a plate, a big Victorian serving plate with scalloped edges, covered in big red roses. I dropped it. We never use that plate, it stays in the dresser and nobody touches it. But that day I used it. I remember looking at the pieces of china on the floor and thinking something must have happened.'

'We're going to catch this man. I don't know how long it will take, but we will. He's dangerous. He hurts people for money, and has no feelings for anyone except himself. But we're going to take him off the street.'

Mrs DuCaine studied the array of flowers. 'When someone in the police force dies, his friends are supposed to rally around him, aren't they? No one from Camden even called. His workmates deserted him because he told them he was moving to your unit.'

'I know.'

'Well then.' Mrs DuCaine studied the flowers with dry eyes. 'There's nothing more to say.'

Longbright knew she was being dismissed. She turned to leave.

'Take one of the yellow roses,' said Mrs DuCaine. 'It was his favourite colour.'

Longbright selected a rose and turned to see two horribly familiar figures looming out of the misty rain. With the arrival of Bryant and May, it became obvious that a police presence at the crematorium was not a good idea. One officer was acceptable, but three looked defensive. The rest of DuCaine's friends and relatives were emerging from the chapel into the cramped ante-room and a demarcation line quickly developed. DuCaine's father fired a baleful stare towards the detectives, who retreated on to the porch.

'I thought you weren't going to come today,' said Longbright, displeased to see them.

'We knew him for years,' May reminded her. 'We couldn't just stay away.'

'And I thought there was a chance *you know who* might turn up to gloat,' Bryant added, 'so I made John come with me.'

'All right, but please don't say anything to the family.' She knew only too well how Bryant's condolences had a habit of turning out.

Bryant thrust his hands deep into his pockets and watched as DuCaine's relatives moved slowly between the wreaths, reading the cards, rearranging flowers, conferring in low tones. 'You know as well as I do that every arrest contains an element of risk,' he told his partner.

'We should have covered all eventualities,' said May.

'You know that's impossible, John. The lock on that door should have been strong enough to hold him.'

'But it wasn't, and that's an oversight on our part.'

Mr Fox's weapon of choice had been a slender sharpened rod that left virtually no trace of use. Using a skewer to pick the lock of the holding room and attack DuCaine had seemed bizarre at first, but the more Bryant thought about it, the more expedient the method became. Their killer had been raised on the streets of King's Cross, where carrying a knife was still considered a necessity for many. But knives were carried to provide a display of defence, not for efficiency of attack. Mr Fox had streamlined the concept, making his weapon easy to hide. The effect of punching the skewer through the neck into the brain was swift and lethal, like causing a stroke. In this case it had worked despite the fact that their officer's sharp reflexes made him a difficult target.

May watched as DuCaine's mother leaned heavily on her husband's shoulder, staring down at a wreath from the

PCU. 'They'll come over if we stay any longer,' he whispered to his partner, leading him away. 'We have to go. The rest of the family's coming out.'

Emerging from the chapel were Liberty DuCaine's grandparents, several aunts and uncles, his brother Fraternity, and his attractive young sister, named, with a certain amount of grim inevitability, Equality.

'Presumably she doesn't actually call herself that,' Bryant mused.

'They call her Betty – apparently it was her grandmother's name.' The pair could replicate Holmes and Watson's old trick of picking up each other's unspoken thoughts. After so many decades together, it was second nature.

'Look out, the family's finished, let's get out of here,' said Bryant, heading for the crematorium car park. 'One tough old Caribbean bird in my life is more than enough, thank you.'

'You'd be lost without Alma and you know it,' said May. Bryant's former landlady was currently spending her days at the town hall, where she was defending the pair's right to stay in their Chalk Farm home. The building was scheduled for demolition. Bryant was meant to have gone with her, but he'd had his hands full for the last few days. The unit's investigations were rarely finite; many had loose ends that dragged on long after the cases had been officially closed. As a consequence, Bryant had been staying late through his weekends. There were times, May knew, when his partner used work to avoid his other responsibilities.

As they stepped back on to the rain-swept tarmac, DuCaine's mother appeared around the corner and waved an enormous rainbow-striped umbrella at them. Bryant tugged his trilby down over his eyes in an attempt to render himself invisible.

'Mr Bryant,' she called. 'Do you have a minute?'

'Oh Lord, she's going to beat me with that umbrella,' he warned, forcing a smile. 'Ah, Mrs DuCaine.'

She planted herself squarely in front of him, blocking the route to May's car. 'I need the answer to a question, and no one has been able to give me a satisfactory explanation. Can you tell me why my son was left alone to guard a dangerous criminal?'

'The criminal was locked in a holding room,' Bryant replied. 'We've already been through this.'

'A holding room – not a proper cell.'

'We'd been forced out of our old offices, Mrs DuCaine, and were short-staffed. We were having to make do. We'd taken every precaution—'

'No, you had not. If you had, my boy would still be alive.' Her tone was firm and fair, but there was no simple answer to her complaint. 'I could take this much further, you know that. But Liberty thought the world of you both. He never stopped talking about you and the unit. And all the complaining and compensation in the world isn't going to bring back my boy.' She peered out at them from under the great umbrella, seeking a kind of closure the detectives were not equipped to provide. 'I lost my best boy,' she said simply. Bryant saw a tremble in her features, a brief ripple that, if it was allowed to stay, would shatter into public grief.

'If you need any help,' he offered, 'we have a system in place that can—'

'We can provide for ourselves, we don't need your money or your sympathy,' Mrs DuCaine snapped. 'Every policeman knows about the dangers involved, isn't that right?' Her tone softened a touch. 'We were just so proud of him. And the move made him happy. But I want the pair of you to promise me something.'

'We'll do whatever we can,' May promised.

'You have to find this man and bring him to justice. None of us can rest easy until we're sure that everything possible has been done to catch him. You know you owe it to Liberty.'

'I'm very aware of that,' Bryant replied. 'I won't be able to rest until he's been made to pay for his crimes.'

'That's all I ask.' She turned to go, then stopped. 'There is one other thing you could do.'

'Name it, Mrs DuCaine.'

'His brother, Fraternity, wants to follow in Liberty's footsteps. I said no, but he won't be talked out of it. He did his officer training at Henley last year and got good grades, but they still failed him. We don't know what happened. He won't tell me, and nobody ever explained anything to us. I want you to find out what went on up there. If he wasn't good enough, that's fine – but my boy is convinced he should have passed, and was still turned down. I don't want this to have been about the colour of his skin.'

Bryant scratched at his neck, thinking. 'I'll have a poke around in his files and see what I can find out, but I can't guarantee it will make any difference.'

May cut across his partner. 'Don't worry, Mrs DuCaine, we'll get to the root of the matter.'

They watched Liberty's mother as she rejoined the family, leading them to the limousines. 'A good woman,' sighed Bryant. 'No one should lose a child.'

'If we're going to honour her wishes, we need a plan of attack.'

'I don't think anyone at the Met or the Home Office will be able to give us any help,' replied Bryant, tugging at his hat. 'Come on, let's get out of here before the brother comes over. Head down, don't look back. He's a big bugger.'

7

FALLING ANGEL

She was wearing a poppy-red dress. You didn't see too many women on the Tube wearing bright-red dresses. Even better, it had white polka dots on it. If the dots had been black she'd have looked like a flamenco dancer, but they matched her white patent-leather heels and her red cardigan. She was glossy-haired and pretty, and maybe she'd been ballroom dancing, except it was early afternoon and she was reading a copy of the *Evening Standard*, or at least trying to, for she was jammed between two arguing Italian teenagers with ridiculous amounts of luggage.

Time to bump into her lightly, nudging a spot between her shoulder blades.

Make sure you're quick to apologize.

She did not bother to look up.

Check your watch. 15:40 p.m.

A flooding feeling of elation. Of rising triumph.

Is it possible to dare think that this could be the end of the problem? The best chance to get rid of the ever-present fear, the terrible nagging terror that keeps me awake all night, that's been haunting my every waking hour?

Push it out of your mind, it's making you sweaty and creepy. You know you can't allow that. Concentrate on something. Study her carefully.

From the tips of her shiny white shoes to the white plastic slide in her neatly combed hair, nothing was out of place. It took a minute or two to figure out her job, but suddenly it was obvious. The scent was the first clue; they always smelled like candy. The yellow plastic bag at her feet confirmed it.

If you lean forward on the tips of your trainers, you can take a peek inside and see the free sample tubes.

She worked on a cosmetics counter at Selfridges department store.

It was all too perfect. Everything fitted. Time to move a little closer without arousing suspicion. At Warren Street the Italians got off, dragging their huge suitcases with them, and suddenly there was space. But danger, too, because now she could get a clear view.

Move to one side, but be careful not to catch her eye.

She was skimming the pages, not really reading, just involving herself in an activity that stopped her from having to look at other passengers. As the train slowed on its way into Euston, she folded the paper shut and looked for somewhere to put it.

You can't get off now. If you leave now, everything will be ruined.

The platform appeared. The train came to a halt and the doors opened. She moved a little nearer and looked out.

No, don't do it.

Was there such a thing as telepathy? Because moments

later she changed her mind and reclaimed her ground in the middle of the carriage.

As the doors slid shut and the train lurched away, it was time for the next phase.

Remove the mobile phone from the pocket of your jeans and slip it into the palm of your hand, deftly operating the buttons without needing to look.

One shot, two, three. A manoeuvre practised in the bedroom mirror for hours. No need for a flash in the bright compartment. Together the pictures scanned her entire body. Perfect.

Hands so slick that you almost dropped the mobile putting it away. For Christ's sake be more careful. She could have seen you.

Her eyes flickered over, attracted by the sharpness of the movement, but there was no thought behind her glance. A very faint smile appeared and faded.

Jesus, is that really sweat dripping from my forehead? Stay calm, you're nearly there. One more stop. She is so artificial, the make-up's so perfect, and yet she's beautiful. How long does it take to get her eyebrows like that? And her shapely figure, every girl on this train in drab jeans and a shapeless sweatshirt should be shaking with envy. Does she understand how her perfection shines through? Does she have any idea of the power she holds? She radiates so brightly that she's lighting the entire carriage, giving it purpose.

She is saving my life.

With each passing second, she restores me more and more. Maybe I'll talk to her afterwards, tell her how she came to be so important. She'd be like a sister, full of private confidences.

The announcement that the train was approaching King's Cross St Pancras brought passengers to their feet. Bags were gathered, newspapers dumped. The casual orderliness had a strange grace, each movement choreographed for efficiency without connection. No two strangers ever touched. Accidentally brushing someone's sleeve required the issue of an immediate apology. The doors opened, the carriage disgorged itself.

It was important to follow tightly behind her, right along the platform to the tiled hall and its bank of escalators. And to stand immediately behind, because it was time to take another photograph.

She never looked back, never noticed anything, her thoughts somewhere else. She stepped lightly on to the moving stairs and was borne aloft like a rising angel. She stood to the right with the middle two fingers of her hand brushing the black rubber rail, just enough to stabilize herself. Everything about her had a lightness of touch.

The banks of illuminated ad panels showed a bouncing cartoon orange. It might have been advertising a fruit drink, insurance or mobile phones. Who knew any more? Mobiles.

Fire off two more discreet shots and palm the thing back in your pocket. Remember to keep the flash off this time – you nearly wrecked everything the other day. One mistake and it's all over.

They reached the top of the escalator and she stepped off. It was a walk of less than twenty metres to the exit barriers. Her patent-leather heels were surprisingly high, and gave her an over-emphatic sashay, as if she was seeking to impress the men behind her. Women in those kind of heels learned to glide with one foot carefully placed in front of the other, if they wanted to avoid walking like farmers.

Her purse was already in her right hand, flipped open to her Oyster Card. She was ready to release herself through the barrier and climb the first bank of steps. Beyond was the semicircle of the station foyer, a great snaking queue of tourists buying exorbitantly priced tickets. She deftly avoided oncoming fleets of commuters as she got ready to swipe her card across the yellow panel. After that there would be twenty steps to the first sign of daylight, and the concourse of the mainline station. As she stepped into the light, she would unconsciously trigger the pathway to salvation. The urge to stop her and thank her for saving a pitiful human life was strong, but that would have spoiled everything.

But she didn't step into the light. Suddenly, right in front of the ticket barrier, no more than a few metres from the outside world, she stopped dead in her tracks.

Look out – you nearly piled right into her, step around! Stop beside the electronic gate and look back.

Behind, commuters were stacking up, impatiently trying to get through the barrier. What the hell was she doing?

You can't stop now. Everything's fine, keep going.

She seemed to be thinking about something. She pulled open her bag and stared into it, not seeing the contents. Then, with a smart turn, she headed back towards the escalators.

You stupid bitch! You can't do this, you're destroying everything, you're destroying me! There will never be another chance like this, you can't take it away now! I almost had you!

Surely she wouldn't go right back down into the station? The Oyster Card had to be put away again; it was necessary to see what she would do.

Sure enough, she walked back across the concourse and headed for the Piccadilly Line, but one escalator was out of order and the other had a queue of passengers, so she made for the central stairs, the static concrete ones that ran between the moving staircases, and began carefully walking down in spite of her heels, descending and wrecking everything.

There were few people on the middle stairs. Nobody liked using them.

Get further forward, come in as close as you dare behind her.

She knew what she was doing, that was obvious now. She had done it deliberately, building up so many hopes just to smash them down at the last minute. A torrent of furious filth rolled forth, silently.

I wish to God she was dead, the selfish bitch.

An anger rose up that could set fire to the world, reddening the tunnel, washing the walls in crimson flames.

She deserved to be punished, to have the life knocked from her body. It was odd to look down and see a disembodied right hand sharply rising to plant itself at the base of her spine. Suddenly she was propelled forward, just enough to throw the balance from those carefully planted high heels. She gave the smallest of gasps as she lurched forward at a startling angle, falling with surprising force and weight. She brushed against one, two other passengers on the staircase, but it wasn't enough to break her fall.

The steps were steep and the drop was long. Several times it seemed as if her descent might be stopped by the human obstacles in her way, but on she fell. She hit the bottom step face down, and by the time her body had settled to a stop, she was dead.

The yellow Selfridges bag landed beside her and burst open, rolling smashed cosmetic samples in an erratic rainbow of paint and powder around her, like a pair of iridescent wings.

8

BORN IN HELL

'I like my tea strong but this stuff's musclebound.' Bryant sat beside his partner in the Paris Café, St Pancras International Station, their elbows on the brushed-steel counter, steaming mugs folded in their mitts, listening to the rain hammering at the great arched roof. Bryant refused to go to the Starbucks down the road because he was allergic to any place that attracted children, and was bothered by the little trays of glued-down coffee beans that surrounded their counter.

John May perched straight-backed in his smart navy-blue suit and overcoat, his silver mane just touching the collar of his Gieves & Hawkes shirt. Bryant had receded so far into his moth-eaten raincoat that only his broad nose and bifocals showed above his equally threadbare green scarf. White seedlings of hair poked up around his ears like pond-grass, and there was cake on his chin. Even after all this time, they still made an oddly incongruous pair.

'There has to be a way of drawing him out,' Bryant

muttered. 'He knows we have no way of finding him. But his pathological desire to stay hidden means he's forced to keep covering his tracks. He'll get rid of anyone who comes too close. His informants unwittingly provided him with knowledge of his victims, so he'll have to surface if he wants to guarantee their silence. And that means he'll reappear in King's Cross.'

'You're saying we should just sit back and wait for him to attack?'

'No, but we know where he operates. He's tied to the area around the stations. We need to intensify surveillance. Never our strong point.'

May drained his mug. 'Well, we don't have the facilities to do it well, and we can't get help from anyone else. Come on, let's get back. I've a lot of work to get through, and I'd like to leave on time tonight.'

'That must mean you're still seeing this French woman.' Bryant refused to be hurried. He dunked his cake, but half of it fell in his mug. 'Your granddaughter told me she's very nice, for a divorced, bottle-blonde alcoholic.'

'Brigitte has gone back to Paris to see her children,' May explained as he watched Bryant fishing around for soggy icing. 'She loves red wine and tints the grey out of her hair.'

'But she *is* divorced.'

'Why is it de rigueur to have a pop at anyone who tries to have a life outside of the unit?'

'I suppose you'll be slipping more and more French phrases into your conversation from now on. Is that why you agreed to move the unit to King's Cross? So you'd be near the Eurostar?' Bryant enjoyed teasing his partner because May took so much at face value.

Bryant was the wilier of the two, but May knew how to deal with him. 'I'll bring Brigitte around to meet you next week,' he suggested, 'She works for the Paris tourist office. I'm sure she'd love to tell you all about her wonderful city, and how much nicer it is than London.'

Bryant made a face and set the last of his tea aside. 'I remember Paris, thank you, all garlic and accordions and waiters refusing to cook your meat properly. Parisians are the most argumentative people I've ever met.' He unglued errant crumbs from his dentures with a fingernail. 'The last time I was in Paris some ghastly woman threw soup over me just because I accidentally sat on her dog. They carry them around fully loaded like hairy shotguns and feed them chocolates. I don't hold with animals in restaurants unless they're being eaten. Why can't you date a London woman for a change?'

'They have a different mindset. French women argue, but English women complain. French women are thin and think they're fat, but English women are fat and pretend they're thin. French women—'

'All right, you've made your point. Come on, Casanova, I've done with my tea, let's get back.'

They were just rising to leave when a skinny boy began moving towards them through the café tables. He looked as if he was on a Methadone programme. There were scarlet spots around his thin lips, and his skin was the colour of fish meat. When he spotted the detectives at the window, he made his way through the tangle of chair legs.

'Is one of you Arthur Bryant?'

'That's him,' May pointed.

The boy dug in the back pocket of his jeans, produced a crumpled white envelope and handed it across.

'Who gave you this?' Bryant asked.

'Some bloke outside.'

'What bloke?'

'Dunno. He's gone now.'

The boy was already heading off. 'Wait, come back here,' May called.

'No,' said Bryant, 'let him go. Look out of the window. There are about a thousand people out there.' He tore open the envelope and pulled out a slip of paper. He read it, then looked up with a grunt of annoyance. 'The boy won't be able to tell us anything.'

'Let me see.' May took the slip and read.

Mr Fox was born below in Hell and now there will be Kaos.

Beneath this was a small hand-drawn symbol: long red ears, a white snout. A fox's head.

'What is that supposed to mean?' asked May. 'Chaos with a K? Born in Hell? It's like something Jack the Ripper might have come out with. There was no sign that he was religious, was there?'

'None at all. This is all we need.' Bryant's frown settled more deeply. 'I humiliated him, so now we have to play cat and mouse. This is about respect. He has to re-establish his power over me.'

'You can't be sure it's from him, Arthur. The press know about this now. It might be anyone.'

'It's his method. He uses other people, and always seems to know exactly where we are.'

May rose and went to the window. 'That means he's within sight of us. It gives us a chance of catching him.'

'No it doesn't, John, any more than you could run after a real fox and seize it. They say criminals who do this sort of thing want to be caught, but I'm not so sure. I think he's arrogant enough to assume he'll always be one step ahead of us. And coming right back here, into the station! The nerve of him.'

'The message is a bit vague.'

'Is it?' Bryant studied the letters, thinking. 'I wonder. Hell in St Pancras Station? Torment and brimstone, down below – underground . . . Underground? You don't think he's talking about the Tube, do you?'

'How can you tell? There's not enough here to go on.'

Bryant tightened the threadbare scarf around his neck. 'I haven't got any better ideas.' He pointed towards the entrance to the Underground. 'Perhaps that's where we should start looking.'

9

PUSH

'One bleeding, sodding week,' said Renfield, watching the Daves as they attempted to thread electric cable through a skirting board with a bent coat hanger. 'They're having a laugh over at the Home Office.'

'They won't be if we pull it off,' Longbright replied.

'Oi, you're doing that wrong,' Renfield told one of the Daves. 'You'll need to earth it.'

'You leave the wiring to us,' Dave answered, 'and you can get on with what you're good at – setting up innocent bystanders and knocking protestors unconscious.'

Renfield's bull-like head sank between his shoulders as he strode over and snatched away the Daves' nailgun.

'Blimey, look at this.' Longbright pulled a water-stained book from beneath Bryant's desk. 'Put him down, Jack.'

Renfield finished nailing the Dave to the wall and came over. 'What have you got?'

She turned the page around to show him a photograph of a sooty old building surrounded by a howling mob waving burning sticks. 'This place, taken in 1908. The locals were trying to burn it down. Listen to the caption: "Police were called in to disperse an angry crowd of residents attempting to incinerate the home of the Occult Revivalists' Society. According to unconfirmed reports, society members had succeeded in their attempt to invoke the Devil. Evidence of Satanic worship was found on the building's first floor (third window from right)." That's Raymond's office.'

'Can you get me down?' Dave called plaintively. 'You've ruined my jumper.'

Renfield ignored him and moved in for a better look at the photograph, although he was also enjoying standing close to Longbright. 'They summoned the Devil from Land's office?'

'That's what it says here.'

'That would explain a lot. The pentagram on the floor, for a start.'

'Maybe they succeeded,' said Longbright. 'Maybe that's where Mr Fox came from.'

A fine rain was falling with the kind of wet sootiness that stained the colours from the cityscape. Looking along Euston Road was like watching old black-and-white television, thought Bryant, like the original opening credits of *Coronation Street*, grey and grainy and out of focus.

He and May were taking the note back to the unit so that Banbury could analyse it, but Bryant was already convinced of its sender's identity. The few civilians who knew about Mr Fox had been interviewed, but their knowledge added nothing. Despite the vigilance of the anti-terrorist police and the ubiquity of the capital's camera network, it seemed he could appear and vanish at will.

'But he's shown us his greatest personality flaw,' Bryant shouted to his partner across traffic, wind and rain. 'An anger so intense that it uncouples his senses and wrecks his plans. And we know exactly where he operates.'

'Look where you're walking, Arthur, you nearly got hit by that van.'

'I have to be patient. I've stung his pride. He'll nurse the grudge until it forces him to show himself.'

'Then don't turn it into something personal, not while we need to lock down our unit status. Let's get the note examined first.'

Bryant almost got squashed between two buses, and was about to bellow a reply when the call came in and changed everything.

The new King's Cross Surveillance Centre was one of London's best-kept secrets. The underground room was accessed by an inconspicuous grey metal door, and its personnel monitored all activity above and below the surrounding streets. The local coppers referred to it colloquially as the North One Watch. Over eighty CCTV screens filled the dimly lit control room, and most of the monitors could be manually operated to provide other views in the event of an emergency. The afternoon's surveillance team was headed by Anjam Dutta, a security expert with almost twenty years' experience of studying the streets. He welcomed the detectives and led them into the monitor hub.

'One of my boys spotted something on Cam 16 at 15:47 p.m. That's the down escalator you can see here.' He swung out a chair and tapped a biro on his desk screen. From this monitor he could flip to any camera in the station complex. 'A young black woman fell down the entire flight of stairs. She died instantly. The steps are very steep, but we rarely have accidents because there's a crowd-management system in place here. Problems usually only occur late at night after lads have had a few. Most people are pretty careful.'

Dutta adjusted his glasses and peered at the monitors, pointing to each in turn. The detectives watched as passengers pulsed through the station, passing from one screen to the next.

'We switch the escalator directions according to traffic flow. At this time of the day we have more passengers coming up than going down, so there are four platform-to-surface escalators for every two descending, and over the next three hours they operate at their highest speed. If one of the escalators is out of order, customers spill over to the central fixed staircase. When that becomes heavily trafficked, we position a member of station staff at the base, where any accidents are most likely to happen.'

'What went wrong?' asked May. 'She didn't just miss her footing?'

'I don't think so. Watch this.' Dutta began playback on the disk that had recorded the event from the top of the concourse looking down. 'She's there on the right of the screen.' The detectives hunched forward and stared at the monitor, but the image was not sharp. 'What you can't see on a monochrome monitor is that she's wearing an outfit in a startling colour.'

'So plenty of people noticed her.'

'My lads certainly did. They can recognize strong tones just from the greys. The monitors are supposed to be in colour, but there's still another two months' work to do on the Victoria Line.'

'Meaning?'

'The Victoria tunnel crosses one of the station's main electrical conduits, and the power outages kick the monitors into black and white. We've completely lost some of the non-essential cameras.'

Dutta twisted a dial and forwarded the picture until it matched his disc reference. 'We can follow a single character through the thickest crowd without losing sight of them. There she goes.'

They watched as the woman tumbled, vanished, re-appeared and was lost. 'I can't tell what's going on from that,' Bryant admitted. 'Who's standing immediately behind her?'

'We don't know. There's a focal problem. The system isn't perfect,' said Dutta. 'The best cameras are stationed in all the busiest key areas. Resolution remains lower in the connecting tunnels, basically the non-essential spots. This is a good camera, but it's due for an upgrade. Plus, you still get lens smears, dust build-up, focus shifts. Escalator cameras are key anti-terrorist tools because it's easier to identify someone when they're standing still on a step. The problem with the central fixed staircase is that it's not as well covered as the main escalators. There's another issue, which is the recording speed. We primarily use the system to control flow and identify passengers, but sudden movements can be problematic. We're trained to read images and interpret what we can't make out, so I knew at once it was a fall, but here's the interesting bit.' He re-ran the footage to the moment before the woman lost her balance. The detectives saw her shoulders drop and rise.

Dutta ran it again, frame by frame. A ghost image fluttered by, little more than a dark blur at her back.

'There's the push,' said Dutta. 'Right there.'

'You can tell that?' May was surprised.

'I know a stumble, and I don't think that's one.'

'But we can't see who's moving behind her.' The screen showed a soft dark shape with the head cut off.

'It's unfortunate. A few feet further down, and we'd have got everything. The image was blocked by the people walking past to the left. By the time we get to the bottom and the rest of the commuters have bunched around the fallen woman, the suspect's already gone.'

'But you have witnesses?'

'Not really.'

'How could you not?'

'Commuting is a chore, something most people do without really engaging their faculties. When something unusual happens they only start noticing after the commencement of the event. Their attention and concern was focussed on the injured woman. And there was a train arriving. Most commuters were more worried about getting home than waiting around to help us. We've put up information-request boards.'

'Was she travelling alone?'

'Looks like it. We got a name and address from the contents of her bag. They're sending someone to her flat right now.'

'So do you have more footage taken from the bottom? Can you get any sort of a fix on who was directly behind her, anything at all?'

'No. As she fell she knocked against two other passengers, and by the time she reached the base there was chaos. It's impossible to see clearly who was walking at the back.'

'Presumably you don't evacuate the station for something like this?'

'No, that would take the setting-off of two or more alarms at the same time. A single accident can be easily dealt with. Fatalities only take about an hour to clear away, so long as they're handled by LU staff and not the Fire Brigade – firefighters like to play trains. We only call them in when we've got an Inspector Sands.'

"What's that?'

'Tannoy code for a fire alert. It's an old theatrical term, a call for the sand buckets they always kept in theatres to put out fires.'

'But I don't understand why you rang us,' Bryant admitted.

'We called Camden but they didn't seem too interested. They've got a lot on their hands at the moment, with the pub.' One of Camden's best-known public houses had burned down at the weekend, forcing the closure of a major road to the North, and the re-routing of all traffic. Camden police were being blamed for overreaction by angry shopkeepers, who were staging a protest. 'One of your former staff members is the new St Pancras coroner, and he suggested giving you a call. It sounded like your kind of thing – a problem of social disorder.'

'Do you get many actual attacks in the system?' May asked.

'Hardly ever. If gang members want to pick fights with each other they generally do it away from bright lights and other people. Besides, this lady doesn't fit the victim pattern, which is usually male and teenaged. But if she was shoved down that flight of stairs by a complete stranger, it's a pretty nasty thing to do. And if he's done it once, he could do it again, couldn't he?'

Bryant looked back at the suspended image of the flailing woman, and wondered if Mr Fox's anger had risen to the surface once more. A murderer in the Tube. He had to be dragged away from the screens when Anjam Dutta finished his report.

10

DESCENDING

'What do you know about the London Underground?' asked Bryant, who loved the Tube as much as May loathed it. He felt entirely at home in the musty sunless air beneath the streets. He could scurry through the system like a rat in a sewer, connecting between lines and locating exits with an ease that defeated his partner. If Mr Fox had gone to ground here, he had found himself a worthy adversary.

'It's the oldest in the world, the Northern Line is crap and I hate the way it makes my clothes dirty,' May replied. 'I know you seem to find it romantic.'

'You have to think of it as a mesh of steel capillaries spreading across more than 630 square miles,' said Bryant, shaking his head in boyish wonder. 'Of course, it was built to alleviate London's hellish traffic problem. Imagine the streets back then: a rowdy, smelly collision of horses, carriages, carts, buses and people. But they only dug beneath the city streets when every other method of surface control had failed. They'd tried roadside semaphore, flashing lights and warning bells, but the horses still kept crashing into each other and trampling pedestrians to death. It was a frightful mess. Thank God for Charles Pearson.'

'Who's he?'

'The creator of the Metropolitan Railway Line. He dedicated his entire life to its construction, and turned down every reward he was offered. He dreamed of replacing grey slums with green gardens, linking all the main-line stations from Paddington to Euston, and on to the City. In the process he wiped out most of London's worst slums, but he also had to move every underground river, gas pipe, water main and sewer that stood in the way. And London is built on shifting marshlands of sand and gravel. An engineering nightmare. Can you imagine?'

'No, not really.'

'An engineer called Fowler came up with the cut-and-cover system that allowed tunnels to be built under busy streets.'

'Fowler, eh? Sounds dodgy.'

'The Tube displaced a huge number of the city's poorest citizens. Naturally, the rich successfully convinced the railway to pass around them. In the three years it took to build, there were endless floods and explosions. Steel split, scaffolds were smashed to matchwood, suffocating mud poured in. At one point the Fleet Sewer burst open, drowning the diggings and burying everyone alive. The line finally opened in 1863, a year after Pearson's death. They tried a pneumatic train driven on pipes filled with pressurized air, but the pipes leaked and rats made nests inside them, so they built steam locomotives instead.'

When May stopped to buy some chewing gum and a

newspaper, Bryant began to sense that he was losing his audience.

The Tube's history fascinated him because of the way it transformed the city. The directors of the world's first Tube lines were old enemies with an abiding hatred of one another, and when the captains of industry clashed, all London felt the fallout. Streets were dug in and houses ripped out like rotten teeth, without the approval of parliament or public. The despoliation of the city provided visible proof of the monstrous capitalism that was consuming the streets. While ruthless tycoons fought over land and lines, the project caught the national imagination and threw up moments of peculiar charm; when a baby girl was born in a carriage on the Bakerloo Line, she was supposedly christened Thelma Ursula Beatrice Eleanor, so that her initials would always serve as a reminder of her birthplace. Typically for London, the story turned out to be untrue.

The Underground was Bryant's second home. He had always felt warm and safe in its sooty embrace, and loved the strange separateness of this sealed and secret world. A century of exhaust fans, ozonizers and asbestos sweepers had improved the air quality below, but the atmosphere was still as dry as Africa on the platforms for reasons that no one was quite able to fathom. Strange whorls of turbulence appeared before the arrival of a train, and tangles of tunnels could lead you back to where you started, or simply came to a dead end. The system's idiosyncrasies arose from its convoluted construction.

'You know, there are all sorts of intriguing stories about the Tube, or "the train in the drain" as I believe it was once called,' said Bryant, swinging his stick with a jauntiness that came from sensing that murder was once more on the agenda. 'There's a story that an Egyptian sarcophagus in the British Museum opened into a secret passage leading to the disused station at Bloomsbury. I don't give it much credence myself.'

'Really? You surprise me,' said May, steering his partner away from the station. They headed along York Way in the direction of the St Pancras coroner's office.

'Oh yes. The straightening of the Northern Line almost caused the demolition of a Hawksmoor church, St Mary Woolnoth, but the public outcry was so great that the railway company had to underpin it while they built Bank Station underneath. That's why the station entrance is marked by the head of an angel.'

'Well, I'm sure this is all very fascinating,' said May, 'but we've a young dead woman who's being taken to Giles Kershaw's morgue right now, and it would be a good idea if you could help me find out what happened to her.'

'You see, that's your trouble right there. You can't do two things at once. I've got a dozen different things going on in my mind.'

'Yes, and none of them make any sense.' Cutting away from the crowded thoroughfare of Euston Road, the detectives found themselves alone in Camley Street, which angled north beside the railway line. 'Do you honestly think Faraday will allow us to remain operational? We allowed a suspect to escape.'

'He's not a suspect, John, he's a murderer, and his continued freedom provides us with a reason for staying open. We're the only team likely to catch him. If anything, his arrest will trigger our closure. A cruel paradox. Let's see what Giles has got for us.'

The desolate redbrick building behind the graveyard of St Pancras Old Church was situated in one of central London's emptiest spots. It might have been built on the edge of Dartmoor for the number of guests it received.

'I wonder what the staff do for lunch,' Bryant said, looking around. 'I suppose they must bring sandwiches and sit among the gravestones.'

'You realize that every time we've been here in the last month, Mr Fox was probably watching us?' May pointed to the rowan tree where the murderer had waited for them. Mr Fox had been employed as a caretaker by the church. He had befriended both the vicar and Dr Marshall, the previous coroner of St Pancras, in order to steal secret knowledge from them.

'I know, and it gives me the creeps. You can never be quite sure what's lurking below the waterline around here.' Bryant rang the bell and stepped back. 'Look out, here comes old Miseryguts.' He waited while Rosa Lysandrou, the coroner's daunting assistant, came to the door.

'Mr Bryant. Mr May. He's expecting you.' Rosa stepped back and held the door wide, her face as grim as a gargoyle. Dressed in her customary uniform of black knitwear, she never expressed any emotion beyond vague disapproval. Bryant wondered what Sergeant Renfield had seen in her. He couldn't imagine them dating. She looked like a Greek widow with an upset stomach.

'How very lovely to see you again, Rosa,' he effused. 'You're looking particularly fetching in that – smock thing.'

Rosa's lips grew thinner as she allowed them to pass. 'She has hairy moles,' Bryant whispered a trifle too loudly.

'Dear fellows! So remiss of me not to have swung by.'

Coat-tails flapping, Giles zoomed at them with his hands outstretched. Although he had achieved his ambition to become the new St Pancras coroner, he missed his old friends at the PCU more than he dared to admit. 'Come in, we hardly ever seem to get visitors who are still breathing, there's just me and Rosa here.'

The energetic, foppish young forensic scientist had brought life and urgency into the still air of the Victorian mortuary. The building's gloomy chapel of rest and green-tiled walls encouraged reflection and repentance, but Kershaw's lanky presence lifted the spirits.

'I heard about Liberty DuCaine, poor fellow. I thought it best to stay away from the funeral. There was something grand about that man; what an utterly rubbish way to die. Have you got any leads?'

'We're running lab tests on his flat and re-interviewing witnesses, but no, we've nothing new apart from a cryptic little warning note,' May admitted.

'He grew up in these streets, didn't he? I'm keeping an eye out for him and will bring him down with a well-timed rugby tackle if spotted, rest assured.'

'You're very cheerful,' said Bryant with vague disapproval. 'What's wrong?'

'What's right, more like.' Grinning broadly, Kershaw dug his fist into his lab coat and pulled out a letter, passing it over. 'Have a read of that, chummy.'

May snatched the envelope away from his partner. He couldn't bear having to wait for the protracted disentangling of spectacles that preceded any study of writing less than two feet high. Home Office letterhead, two handwritten paragraphs and a familiar signature. 'I don't believe it,' he muttered, genuinely awed.

'What? Show me,' barked Bryant, who hated not knowing things first.

'Giles, you are a genius. He's pulled it off, Arthur. He's done something neither you nor I could achieve.'

'Let me guess. He's worked out why people who don't drive always slam car doors.'

'No, he's got the unit reinstated.' May waved the paper excitedly.

'How did he do that? Give me that.' Bryant swiped at the page.

'You're not the only one with friends in high places,' said Kershaw, pleased with himself. 'But I did owe you a favour. It cost me a couple of expensive lunches at the Ivy.'

Although he had been told often enough, Bryant had forgotten that Kershaw had once dated the former Home Secretary's sister-in-law. 'So you pulled a few strings for us.'

'Less string-pulling than back-scratching,' Kershaw replied. 'He's pleased that you recommended me for the position. The old St Pancras coroner, Dr Marshall, was a scandalous old Tory of the more-than-slightly-mad school. Got caught charging the construction of a duck pond on his expenses. They'd wanted him out for years.'

'We recommended you because you were the best person for the job, Giles. You deserved the chance of advancement.'

'Well, you're to be officially recognized once more, effective from next Monday. And you're to be allocated an annual budget. It's conditional on you clearing up this business with Mr Fox by then, but I'm sure you'll be able to do it, won't you? You might even get some new equipment out of it.'

'That's wonderful news,' said May. 'Giles, you're a star.'

Bryant slapped his hands together gleefully. 'Don't tell Raymond Land, I'll do it. I want to watch his face drop. All we have to do now is recapture London's most elusive killer by Saturday.' His irony fell on deaf ears.

'I know why you're here today. Come and meet Gloria Taylor.' Kershaw ushered them through to the morgue's autopsy tables.

Gently unfolding the Mylar wrapping around the badly bruised face of a black woman in her mid-twenties, he pulled out the retractable car antenna Bryant had given him as a leaving present and tapped the corpse with it. 'Identifying marks – well, the teeth would have given us her name if the contents of her bag hadn't. Unusual bridgework. Ms Taylor is single, lives in Boleyn Road, Islington, has a kid, a little girl of five, no current partner, that's all I know about her life so far, but I can tell you a little more about her body.'

'Why do coroners always refer to their clients as if they were still alive?' Bryant wondered.

'Well, they are alive to us, just not functioning. Her hair and nails are still growing. There's all kinds of activity in her gut—'

'Thank you, you can stop there. You'll end up giving everyone the creeps, just like your predecessor.'

'She was in pretty good shape, but she'd had an operation on her right leg below the knee. It had left this muscle, the tibialis anterior, severely weakened. It's why she wasn't able to stop herself when she fell; she knew it would hurt to throw sudden weight on it. Instinctively, she tried to protect her head but still fell badly, breaking her neck. It was all over in seconds. It didn't help that she was wearing ridiculously high heels. A terribly dangerous fashion, but women won't be told. There are the usual surface injuries you'd expect from this kind of fall, damage to the knees, hips and wrists. She slipped, went head-first, velocity kept her going all the way to the bottom. It's a pity nobody thought to grab her dress as she passed. The English stand on the right and walk down on the left. In the case of a fixed staircase like this, there are still unspoken right-and-left rules. Those on the right walk slowly, the ones on the left walk faster.'

'I imagine the weight imbalance on the treads of moving escalators is the reason why they're constantly being replaced,' Bryant remarked, inadvertently reminding the others that he was more concerned with the mechanics of death than the tragedy of its victims.

'The slow-walking people probably thought she was being rude, trying to barge past, and got out of the way. Certainly no one stopped her. I understand there weren't many on the staircase – the rush-hour hadn't started. In any event there was nothing to impede her fall and she hit the ground with a wallop. The impact was enough to tear her dress, which according to Janice is an original Balenciaga outfit from the 1950s.'

'Trust her to know. So you think it was an accident?'

'From a forensic point of view, yes. If you fall off a tall building, you reach terminal velocity at around 200 kilometres an hour and death is most likely to be instantaneous. Fallers instinctively try to land the right way up, so they fracture the pelvis, lower spine and feet. The impact travels through the body, and can burst the valves and chambers of the heart. Survivors say that time passes more slowly during a fall. This is because the brain is speeding up, trying to find ways of correcting the balance. Gloria didn't actually travel that far, but she went head-first. You can survive a considerable fall if you've got something soft to land on, or if you're drunk, because your limbs are relaxed. You're more likely to land on your head in a short, angled fall from, say, under ten metres, which is the case here.' Kershaw scratched the tip of his nose with the antenna. 'Now ask me what I think from a personal perspective.'

'What do you mean?'

'Well, say you stumble and try to right yourself. It's harder to fall downstairs – I mean properly fall – than most people think. It feels like she was launched. It's a matter of momentum. She didn't land on her knees and slide the rest of the way, as most people would – she went out and down, like a high diver.'

'How do you know? It's not on the CCTV.'

Giles ran a hand through his blond hair. 'Well, the heaviness with which she landed. The angle of injuries. I'm not sure the evidence would stand up in court. There's nothing I can directly point to. Something just feels wrong about it. Then there's this. Her doctor's records show she suffered from Ménière's Disease. She was deaf in her right ear and was supposed to wear a small hearing aid, but her colleagues say she hated having to use it. So if somebody stumbled behind her or made a warning noise, she may not have heard it.' He opened a drawer beneath his examination table and produced a plastic packet of clothes. 'Her outfit was very distinctive. Where is it? Ah, here. She was wearing this over her dress.' He held up a small red cardigan. In the middle of the back panel was a plastic sticker.

'Wait, I need my glasses.' Bryant dug out one of several pairs of spectacles that had become interlaced in his pocket.

The lenses were so scratched that it was a miracle he could see anything through them at all. He examined the orange sticker. A line drawing showed the right half of a shaggy-haired male, standing with his arm raised and his legs apart. 'It's da Vinci's figure of a man, surely, seen from the back?'

'Either somebody stuck it there or it came from the Tube seat,' said Kershaw.

'Seems a bit unlikely, doesn't it?'

'I don't know, all sorts of odd things happen on Tube trains. I've been going through my predecessor's online log book. Fascinating reading. Dr Marshall had a fellow in here, found dead on a Victoria Line Tube. His trousers were burned, and there were blisters on the backs of his thighs. Turned out a workman had stood a plastic canister filled with a corrosive chemical on the seat before him, and it had leaked into the cushion. This chap sat down, the caustic fluid went through his trousers and gave him the skin rash. The reaction raised his body temperature and caused a seizure.' He peered at the roundel, flicking his hair from his eyes. 'I don't know, maybe it was put there by the person who pushed her. But I'm pretty sure she was pushed.'

'It's not much of a starting point, Giles, but I don't think we're going to get anything more from the CCTV. Can I take this?'

'Of course. I got a partial thumbprint from it. I ran it through IDENT1's online database but drew a blank.' Kershaw carefully divorced the sticker from the cardigan and slipped it into a sample bag.

'It looks to me like a sticky-backed advert that got transferred from someone else during her journey,' said May.

'I don't think so. The only fibres on the glue are from her coat and the train seat.'

'Then we concentrate on the logo itself,' said Bryant, squinting at the symbol. 'It might stand for something.'

'What do you mean?'

'Well,' he replied, adjusting his spectacles, 'if it's Leonardo da Vinci, perhaps she'd visited a place where you might be likely to find such a sticker. A museum shop, perhaps.'

'The figure's cut in half,' May pointed out. 'You look at this and see da Vinci. I just see the letter K. As in Kaos.'

II

VISIBILITY

Mac was jittery. His old employer, Mr Fox, was out there somewhere, and was probably looking for him. He regretted ever having met the guy. He should have known from the start that it would end in trouble.

Mac had allowed himself to be picked up in St Pancras Station, and had agreed to perform a few simple, legal services – driving a van, acting as a contact for a client, nothing that would undermine his probation record. He had fulfilled his tasks and been paid well for them, but then something had gone wrong. The deal had ended in disaster. Mr Fox had screwed up, and Mac knew about it.

He chose not to look too deeply into what had happened; he suspected there had been a beating, possibly even a death. It was nothing to do with him. He didn't want to know.

He had assumed that Mr Fox was a small-time crook just like the ones you could find all over King's Cross, the ones studying their phones in snack bars and stations, who made themselves available at short notice whenever middle-class urbanites decided their dinner parties should end with a few lines of coke. But there was more to Mr Fox than that. There were shadows in him that made Mac deathly afraid. The job had ended badly, as these things sometimes did, but Mac was fearful that Mr Fox would somehow blame him and come looking to take his pound of flesh. There was a terrifying irrationality about the man, and now Mac was peering around every corner with trepidation.

But Mac couldn't get out of town, because he was working right outside the station. He'd needed to make some money fast, so he'd borrowed a monkey from a dealer in Farringdon and put it on an outsider running at Aintree because the tip was sweet as a nut, only somehow he'd got the wrong horse and it had run like a fat girl, coming in last. And now he needed to make some downpayments before he got his head kicked off his shoulders. So he had taken a couple of legit jobs, one of which was handing out copies of a daily freesheet to commuters. It meant making himself visible to as many people as possible. He knew it was the last thing he should be doing right now, but the need for cash had made him desperate.

On Monday evening, in what was already shaping up to be the wettest spring on record, he was standing on the pavement thrusting copies of the paper at pedestrians, who would take three minutes to skim it before abandoning it on the Tube, adding to the tons of rubbish and clutter no one really wanted or needed.

As he handed them out, he flinched whenever anyone brushed against him, fearing an unseen tap on his shoulder. Then, by the station entrance, he thought he saw Mr Fox watching him from beneath the brim of a red Nike baseball cap.

But he looked different. A tanned face, a black soul patch, trendy glasses, thick upper-arm mass in his short sleeves – and now Mac had doubts, because if it really was him, Mr Fox had radically changed his appearance in a matter of days. When the shades came off, though, there was no hiding from those dead eyes. Mac would have known them anywhere.

He tried to ignore the motionless figure and carried on handing out papers. He wanted to run, but couldn't move far because two other vendors were staking out the other Tube entrances, and his team leader would send him back if he tried to leave.

He stared at the great stack of freesheets on his cart, panic dancing in his brain. When he glanced back the figure had vanished, and he wondered if his fearful mind was playing tricks. He needed to get away right now.

Mac dropped the papers in his cart and took off. He was thinking fast – or at least, as fast as he could – about how to escape into the crowds.

He sent himself bouncing down the stairs into the station. Northern, Victoria and Piccadilly lines to the right, Metropolitan, Hammersmith & City lines straight ahead. Office workers, tourists and students were milling about with bags and cases. People were walking so slowly, stopping to examine maps, just getting in the way. He pushed through the ascending travellers, down the next flight of steps, and was quickly caught up in a contraflow of commuters heading for the escalator.

So many people. A distressed woman trying to manoeuvre a double-width baby buggy, a crowd of arguing Spanish teenagers, a smiling old man carrying a cocker spaniel, a couple just standing there in the busiest section of the tunnel, bewildered and lost. Mac looked around, trying to sort through the oncoming faces. Some part of him had known all along that Mr Fox was a killer. Mr Fox knew that Mac knew, and perhaps nobody else at all knew because the man pushing through the ticket barrier towards him had taken care of them all.

He was coming up behind Mac on the descending escalator.

Now he stopped and was standing on the right, in no hurry, looking straight ahead. When Mac looked back, Mr Fox failed to catch his eye. There was nothing to guarantee it was the same person, but Mac was surer than he'd ever been in his life, just as he knew that Mr Fox would some-how manage to kill him in public view and get away with it.

At the bottom of the escalator he swung right and headed to another, lower escalator. At the base he stepped beneath a cream-tiled arch that opened out on to the platform. A train was in, and the crowds were pushing forward to board it. He skirted the passengers and continued along the platform, turning off and running up the stairs towards the Piccadilly Line.

Mac's stomach was an acid bath. He glanced back and saw Mr Fox closing in, and felt sure he was being forced in the wrong direction. He knew the station as well as anyone and remembered that the foot tunnel they had entered was now out of use. It led to the long uphill subway connecting the station to the former Thameslink line, which had been closed down. *Christ, I'm going into a dead end*, he thought.

He tried to keep calm, but knew that Mr Fox meant to kill him.

There was one hope; the tunnel had a cross-branch from the Piccadilly Line which was still in use. Maybe he could turn off into the crowds once more.

He sensed Mr Fox tacking closer, seeking ways to move ahead, from left to right and back. He didn't know how it happened, but when they reached the junction the crowd was too dense and Mac was forced to continue straight across. Into the section where the tiles were already crusting with grey dust, and the CCTV cameras had been dismantled, and litter had blown in from the other tunnels; into the corridor that no longer led anywhere.

On, towards his death.

12

IN THE TUNNEL

On top of everything else, Arthur Bryant was meant to be conducting a walking tour around the King's Cross Underground system at seven p.m.

He had all but given up his little sideline lately. The anglophile tourists irrationally annoyed him with their endless questions, and were always trying to trip him up. If they knew so much about the subject, why did they bother coming along? The only other people who attended Bryant's admittedly esoteric tours were retired archivists, bored housewives or socially awkward loners filling their days with museum trips and cookery courses. His pastime required him to talk to strangers, something he had little interest in doing if it didn't involve arresting them.

When the tour company called Bryant to remind him of his obligation, he tried to wriggle out of it, but it was too late to cancel. Now he looked around at the group assembled before him and conducted a head-count, studying them for the first time, and found the usual suspects.

A pair of charming Canadians in matching fawn raincoats and pristine white trainers who were looking as English as possible, and consequently stood out from the surrounding grubbiness like clowns at a wake. A Japanese couple, neat and insular, in straight-from-the-suitcase walking outfits, who oozed such attentiveness and respect that Bryant avoided catching their eye in case they started bowing. A handsome young man of indeterminate Arabic extraction, the kind who could freeze an entire railway carriage just by reaching into his backpack. A handful of sturdy older ladies squeezing the walk in between a Whistler exhibition and a display of traditional dancing at the English Folk Society. A sour-faced man with an annoying sniff and a hiking stick who looked as if he harboured thoughts of attacking kittens with a hammer. And a smattering of invisibles, attending either because they wished to get out of the rain, or by accident.

'We now find ourselves standing in a passage that passes beneath Pentonville Road,' Bryant told the group, not all of whom appeared to be following his words. 'During the War, anti-blast walls were placed over station entrances, flood gates were erected in tunnels and trains had nets fixed over their windows to reduce injury from flying glass.'

'How could passengers tell where to get off?' asked the kitten-hammerer.

'The nets had little holes cut in them so they could still read the station names,' Bryant explained. 'The service ran normally despite the fact that many of the stations were modified to provide shelter. They had libraries and bunk beds, medical posts, play centres and even classrooms.'

'And racketeers,' said the Canadian lady. 'I heard ticket touts illegally sold sleeping spaces on the platforms.'

'The unscrupulous are always ready to profit from war, Madam,' said Bryant patiently. 'When the fighting ended, the Tube's defences were dismantled at an astonishing speed, and life returned to normal very quickly.' He had one eye on a Chinese man who was more interested in the wall tiles. Perhaps he had been expecting a ceramics tour.

'What about the flood gates?' asked the Canadian lady. 'They weren't dismantled after the War.'

'No, you're right. There was a worry that an unexploded bomb might breach one of the tunnels under the Thames, so they stayed in place.'

'But didn't they also—'

'Perhaps you'd like to take over the tour while I go and get some shopping in,' Bryant snapped. 'I'm out of milk and you obviously know more than me.'

'You've no need to be rude.'

'No, but it helps to pass the time.'

Bryant struggled on for several minutes before noticing that some members of the group had lagged behind. Now one of them came running back.

'Mr Bryant, I think you'd better come, someone's been hurt.' A young man, one of the group's more invisible members, was pointing back into a closed-off branch of the tunnel. Bryant pushed through the gathering and followed the speaker into the disused passageway. He could see the boy sprawled on the ground, face-down, a dark pool forming around his neck.

He knew at once what he was seeing; the aftermath of a stabbing, without question. The boy reminded him of the one who had come into the café with the note; he had the facial wasting of a long-term heroin addict. Blood circled his throat like a red silk bandanna. Bryant pulled back his collar, releasing an abundance of gore. His fingers could not undo the shirt buttons. Remembering that his Swiss Army knife was in his top pocket, he pulled open a blade and sawed through the buttons. The boy's carotid artery had been pierced at two points just centimetres apart. It looked as if a vampire had attacked him.

Blood was running across the sloping tunnel floor in a thin, persistent stream. Bryant tore off his scarf and applied pressure to the boy's neck. 'Did you see who he was with?' he asked.

'I heard a noise behind me. I turned around and saw this guy arguing with someone. There was a scuffle – I don't know – this one fell and the other ran off.'

'Get a good look at him?'

'No, man. It's dark down there. Look at it.' Bryant took the point. The end of the tunnel was lost in shadow. The ceiling lights were out.

'Wait here,' he called to the rest of the group. 'I just need one of you. You, Ma'am? Could you come over here?' He led the Canadian lady to the victim. 'I want you to take over from me, just press on his neck if you'd be so kind.'

'I know what to do. I trained as a nurse.'

'Excellent. The rest of you, stay exactly where you are.' He flicked open his mobile but it had no reception. 'Has anybody got a signal?' He raised his mobile, pointing, but saw only a sea of shaking heads. 'Nobody is to move, understand?'

Bryant headed for the nearest CCTV point, a dusty camera wall-mounted at the junction to the Piccadilly Line. He raised his arms in front of it, hoping that Dutta's crew was paying attention. The stairs would take him to ground level, where he could call an ambulance.

Pinpoints of sound sparkled in Mac's brain. His senses seemed to be shorting out. He was lying on his back, with something warm and wet around his neck. The dirt-streaked tiles of the Tube tunnel drifted into his vision. *Dumped out with the rubbish*, he thought without rancour. *Well, this is pretty much how I expected to die.*

Bryant got through to the London Ambulance Service. The emergency crews were always stretched on Mondays. Fewer patients were discharged by hospitals at weekends because it was harder to find staff who could assess them, so they stacked up in the wards, meaning that A & E trolleys could not be found for incoming patients, and medics were forced to slow down. Luckily, University College Hospital was close by, and their EMTs came charging down the stairs in under six minutes.

Years of heroin addiction had damaged Mac's lungs. He developed breathing difficulties in the ambulance, and started to undergo respiratory collapse just as the vehicle was pulling into the A & E bay at the hospital.

When Bryant arrived to give his report, the staff nurse told him they weren't sure whether their patient would survive the night.

13

MEMENTO

'I don't understand.' Raymond Land stalked back and forth past Bryant's desk. The floorboards nearest the metre-wide hole creaked dangerously as he did so. 'How did you manage to lose the witness?'

'I was forced to leave him with the others while I called the ambulance.' The detective had a conjuring manual open on his desk, and was attempting to shuffle a pack of cards.

'Couldn't someone else have gone?'

'I knew the EMT codes, I knew the equipment we needed, it was faster for me to go. Time was of the essence.'

'This late display of efficiency isn't like you, Bryant, but I'd be more impressed if you hadn't lost him. Any of the others in your group know this bloke?'

'They'd all just met for the first time. Most of them pay in advance, so the company has their booking details. Don't worry, Janice will find him. She's on his case right now.'

'What about an ID on the victim? Can you put those things down for a minute?'

'We're working on it, but there was nothing in his jacket or jeans.' Bryant attempted to shake out the nine of clubs. 'By the way, there was a journalist in the station when it happened. Followed the ambulance to the hospital. Got a good look at the victim, I'm afraid.'

'So what? Stabbings aren't news any more.'

'There was something unusual about the attack. The boy was hit twice in the neck. The attacker knew exactly what he was doing and punctured the carotid artery, but unfortunately the wound looked a bit like a bite mark.'

Land was even more confused than usual. 'You've lost me.'

'You do remember, I suppose, that we investigated the Leicester Square Vampire?'

'Oh no.' Land rubbed a hand over his sagging features. 'Don't tell me this hack's going to try and syndicate a "vampire running amuck on the London Underground" story. He's not, is he?'

'It's not a he,' Bryant replied. 'It's our old friend Janet Ramsey, the editor of *Hard News*. That awful Botox-faced woman who could put a frost on a cappuccino from twenty paces.' He lost control of the shuffle. One card pinged off the vase on his mantelpiece. Crippen ran for cover.

'She's on the story? What was she doing at the station?'

'Catching a train, I imagine.'

'You'll have to stop her. Wait, I'll do it.' Land punched Ramsey's number into his mobile.

'I can't prevent her from reporting the facts, Raymond, you know that. I've warned her that if she tries to foster an atmosphere of panic, we'll have her under the Public Order Act. Where's John?'

'He's gone to St Pancras Station, said you'd understand what he was up to. Really, I don't know why there always has to be an air of mystery about everything you two do. I'm surprised you don't leave each other messages in code.'

'We do sometimes. Well, I do, just to annoy you.'

'Hello? Janet Ramsey, please.' Land covered the phone. 'Could you put down those bloody cards for a second?'

Bryant set the pack aside and dug in his pocket for the parts of his pipe. Land was about to protest, but thought better of it. 'All right, you can have a smoke just this once. After all, we've got the unit back and a chance to put things right. I suppose that's something for you to celebrate.' He turned back to the phone. 'Well, when will she be out of the meeting?'

'Oh, for God's sake give me that,' said Bryant, waggling his fingers at the phone until Land reluctantly handed it over. 'Put Miss Ramsey on right now,' he bellowed into the receiver. 'Tell her it's Arthur Bryant and if she doesn't pick up at once I'll send someone around to have her arrested for obstruction. And you too. Janet, hello. Next time you get your PA to lie for you, try not to be heard in the background. You think you're speaking softly but it sounds like someone mooing through a traffic cone. Perhaps you're going deaf. Listen, if you publish a single reference to vampires or madmen running loose in the Underground I'll bring you in for questioning and keep you here for so long that by the time you get home all your house plants will be dead. Yes, I know I'm a horrible old man, but at least I'm attractive on the inside, which is more than you'll ever be, unless you become a nun.' He threw the phone back to Land. 'So, they've officially given us Gloria Taylor, the woman who was pushed down the escalator?'

'The Camden team has nothing to go on so they've turned the case over to us. It clearly falls under our jurisdiction. Risk of causing panic at London Tube stations.'

'Good news for once. You could break open that bottle of Greek brandy you keep under your desk.'

'I haven't got a desk. I have two packing crates held together with bits of duct tape. But all right, yes.'

'Excellent, it will kill some time while I'm waiting for Meera to come back with the X-rays.'

'What X-rays?'

'Sorry, *vieille chaussette*, I forgot to mention. The stab-victim, we're getting X-rays ahead of the post-mortem – not that he's quite dead yet, but he's on a respirator, and I don't suppose he's long for this world. The entry wound suggests he was stabbed with a skewer, and they should tell us if he was, which would mean that Mr Fox has resurfaced, just as he said he would.' Bryant lit his pipe and sucked pensively. On the desk before him lay the note. 'Take a look at that.'

'So this is the famous warning? Not very informative, is it?'

'It's suggestive. Foxes live underground. Hell is underground. And the misspelling of chaos, there's a sense of timeless tragedy.'

'A sense of illiteracy, more like.' Land gave a harrumph. 'Wishful thinking on your part.'

'Not at all. He's growing in confidence, but perhaps he also wants to be stopped. Something torments him. Why else would he bother to send a message like that? There's another thing. Giles thinks the sticker on Gloria Taylor's back is a letter K. Suppose it stands for Kaos?'

'Are you seriously suggesting he attacked two different people in the same Tube station a little more than two hours apart? Why didn't he use the same method for both?'

'I don't know. Do me a favour, will you, and pick a card.'

Land was so used to Bryant's odd behaviour that he accepted the card, looked at it and put it back in the pack. 'Why would he leave a sticker on one victim but not the other? It doesn't make any sense.'

'For once I agree with you. Nine of clubs.'

Raymond smoothed his straggling hair across his bald patch, a sure sign that he was attempting to think. 'I mean, what possible connection could exist between a single mum working at a cosmetics counter and a King's Cross junkie?' He gave a weary sigh. 'It was the four of diamonds. Let's hope you're a better detective than you are a magician.'

'I don't know how you can eat that,' said Meera Mangeshkar. She watched as Colin Bimsley stuffed a forkful of dripping orange noodles into his mouth. He was sitting on top of a green plastic recycling bin, grazing from a yellow polystyrene box, and didn't seem to mind the smell of rotting garbage that permeated the brick yard.

The pair were staking out the Margery Street flat from the rubbish-disposal area. It was the only place on the ground floor of the estate that could not be seen from the windows of the apartment. Half past nine on a murky, saturated Monday night. Meera was wet, cold and impatient for results. She was also annoyed that Bimsley appeared to be enjoying himself.

'I can eat anything if I'm hungry,' he told her, thrusting his plastic fork into the glutinous contents of the box. 'Chicken korma, pad thai, shawarma, fishcakes, spag bog, whelks.' He chewed ruminatively on a piece of stir-fried pork. 'Sushi, cod and chips, saveloy, doner kebab, pasties.' A tiny old woman came to throw some leaking binbags into a container and pretended not to notice him. 'Sauerkraut, pickled eggs, curried goat, fried bananas.' He air-ticked the items with his fork.

Meera grimaced. 'You're a genuinely disgusting person, do you know that?'

'No, I just come from a big family of coppers, that's all. None of them ever went home and cooked after being on duty, they were all too knackered, we lived on takeaways. The difference between you and me is that you saw the career as a way out, whereas it never occurred to me to do anything else.'

'So you want to spend your life sifting through rotting crap and doing surveillance? You don't want to better yourself?'

Bimsley spat a piece of gristle back into the box and looked at her with blank blue eyes.

'I give up with you,' she said. 'We've got nothing in common.'

'That's why it'd be a good idea for you to go out with me. I never trust those online dating questionnaires where you list all the things you like and find someone who likes exactly the same stuff. I mean, what's the point of having someone who agrees with you all the time?'

'And that's your entire philosophy for dating, is it?'

'Yeah, I ask out the least likely women. It worked until I met you.'

'If you know we've got nothing in common, why do you keep asking?'

'I figured you'd eventually crack. I thought one day I'd be talking to you and there would be this tiny noise, like – ' There was a tinkle of breaking glass. 'Yeah, like that.'

'No. Someone's got in,' said Meera.

Bimsley threw his dinner carton behind him and jumped to his feet. The pair ran around the corner in time to see a leg vanishing through Mr Fox's kitchen window.

'There's a back way,' said Mangeshkar. 'You take it. I can get through the front.' They splattered through the flooded forecourt to the flat. Meera reached the kitchen window, lifted herself to the sill and carefully climbed through. The apartment was in darkness, but she could hear footsteps in the room beyond. After dropping to the floor, she entered the hall and saw a far door closing. She padded along the hall and cautiously pushed it open.

A familiar figure was framed outside the window. 'He's already gone,' Bimsley called. 'Go back out the front.'

They met outside the block, but there was no sign of anyone. A small park backed on to the estate. Beyond that was a maze of misted sidestreets. 'How could he have gone through the flat so quickly?' Meera asked.

'He came back for something and knew exactly where to look,' said Colin. 'Call it in.'

Dan Banbury was halfway home when the message came through. Bryant wanted him to return to Margery Street and see if anything was missing. Banbury had taken photographs, but did not need to rely on them. He could always tell when something had been moved at a crime scene. As a kid he had conducted memory tests for bets.

A favourite party trick had been to divine the contents of other kids' pockets, a pastime he was now teaching to his own son.

He arrived back on the estate half an hour later, and found Bimsley waiting for him. It only took a few seconds of looking around the lounge to spot what had been removed.

'A framed photograph – there.' Banbury pointed to a small space on the wall. 'It doesn't make sense.'

'What do you mean?' Bimsley cocked his head at the rectangle of pale wallpaper.

'It was a photograph of a metal bench,' Banbury replied.

'And that's all he's taken?'

'Nothing else has been touched.'

'What kind of frame?'

'Aluminium, with a cardboard back.'

'Blimey,' said Bimsley. 'There must have been something pretty valuable hidden inside it to risk getting caught like that.'

14

THE LETTER K

John May checked his vintage Rolex for the fifth time. He was seated at the bar of the St Pancras Grand, a restaurant on the upper level of the vast, airy St Pancras Station. He was waiting for Rufus Abu. Like a pixilated image on a TV screen, Rufus was infernally difficult to keep in focus. He left a ghost-track across the city's security network, and never stayed longer than a few minutes in any public place. May had tried contacting him on every electronic device he owned, but there had been no answer. All he could ever do was send a call into the ether and wait for him to appear at a pre-arranged spot.

The police remained unconvinced that the diminutive teenaged hacker was on their side. He was still wanted for extradition by an American intelligence agency operating in London, because he had slipped under the tracking defences of a US insurance company and exposed their vulnerability to cyber-attack. The fact that Rufus had merely intended to highlight the firm's security issues revealed his greatest weakness: he was driven to try and change the world for the better, without realizing that he would always make the wrong people angry.

'Don't make me eat here.'

May turned and found Rufus standing beside him at the counter.

'Just get me an OJ. I have my own gin.'

'I knew you wouldn't stay long enough to have dinner,' May replied. He had picked the venue because there was only one surveillance camera in operation, by the door, and he was blocking its view. 'How are you doing?'

'Copacetic, John, staying fly and dry. Cotchin' down in the South Bank until the fudges pass. Buncha drag-ass cholos in old-school Pumas looking for a face-up.'

May had trouble deciphering Rufus's retro-slang, but vaguely recalled that a *fudge* was an idiot because the initials stood for low examination grades. For once the hacker was dressed like a regular teenager, in jeans and a black sweatshirt, instead of looking like a miniature version of a suburban nightclub manager.

'Sorry your 187 'scaped.'

May gave him a blank look.

'Your killer, man. He'll pop again. Listen, I need your help. Can you get me off the grill?'

'You're wanted by American intelligence, Rufus, what do you expect me to do? Maybe I could talk to someone, but you'll have to do something for me.'

'Spell it, I'm listening.'

May waited while Rufus added homemade gin to his orange juice, then took the plastic sticker from his pocket. 'Have you seen anything like this around town?'

Rufus studied the label. 'Where'd you catch it?'

'From the coat of a dead woman. There's a chance the killer might have marked her with it for some reason. We're running checks on her friends and family, going through her apartment, the usual stuff, but I don't think we'll get much. If you have a fight at home with someone, you don't wait until they're boarding a train to take a pop at them.'

'Wait, I have an IRC CyberScript giz for this.' Rufus pulled out a white plastic stick no thicker than a ballpoint pen, and extended an antenna the width of paperclip wire. He ran it over the sticker and jacked the other end into a slender white credit card. 'We 'steined this from some military defence pattern recog software – simple stuff, just creates a rolling design database.'

'"We"?' said May. 'There's more than one of you?' His question went unanswered.

'Man, this station's wi-fi is dragging. Give me a minute.' He shook the box impatiently. 'One ID traceover. It's a bar.'

'A bar? What does that mean?'

'No man, a *bar* – a drinking establishment.' He turned the screen around and showed May the logo of the Karma Bar. 'Corner of Judd Street and Tavistock Place – it's the nearest bar to UCL, apart from the college union lounge. Either your vic chilled there, or you're looking for someone who hung with her. UCL suggests a student.'

'Rufus, you're a genius, I owe you one.'

'So pay the debt. Call off the intel before they cap me.'

'I'll try, Rufus, but you know I can't promise. I'll do what I can. Don't worry, they're not going to shoot you.'

'I can't keep running, John. I'm getting too old. There are faster guys comin' up under me.'

May looked at the small-boned West Indian boy, noting

that his oversized trainers barely reached the lower rung of the stool. He tried to imagine what a faster, younger generation of computer hackers would be like, but the idea was quite beyond his grasp.

He could easily have arranged for someone else to cover it, but May headed for the bar because he had nothing better to do. He felt bad about April. His granddaughter had been doing well at the unit until the traumatic events surrounding DuCaine's death had unseated her. Refusing to talk to her grandfather, she had folded a few clothes into a suitcase and used the ticket her uncle Alex had emailed. For a girl who claimed to suffer from phobias whenever she became stressed, he thought it odd that she had no qualms about getting on a plane. *All that hard work with her*, he thought, *and I'm back where I started*.

The newly divorced Brigitte was back in Paris for the week, visiting her two sons. May wanted to stay in her rented apartment in Bloomsbury, to slouch on her ridiculous beaded floor cushions drinking fierce red wine and talking until all the street traffic had died away. He couldn't survive as Bryant did, with only his books and his disapproving landlady for company. He had long been considered a ladies' man, but now the advancing years made the idea unseemly. *There's nothing less attractive than an ageing gigolo*, he thought. *Brigitte might be the one I could settle down with, but she doesn't seem that interested. She only calls me late at night, when she's been drinking.*

So he defaulted back to work. The Karma Bar was marked by a small steel sign featuring the same logo that was found on Gloria Taylor's back. Beside the entrance, a bouncer with a head shaped like a stack of bricks stopped him and searched his bag. 'Give me a description of your granddaughter,' he suggested, 'and I'll go and see if she's inside.'

'Very funny. Let me in or I'll arrest you.' May flashed his badge.

'Right-ho.' The bouncer swung aside.

Inside the doorway, stacked with various club flyers and student special offers, were pages of the same plastic labels, eight to a sheet. May was assailed with doubt. If the design was that familiar, it was likely to be stuck on posters all over town. Taylor had probably leaned against one and inadvertently transferred it to her jacket.

May found himself in a pleasant, dark-wood barroom surrounded by counters of illuminated white glass. When the barman set his beer bottle down, digitized silver ripples pulsed out around its base. The sound system was playing 'Jazz Music' by the German funk band De-Phazz, a personal favourite, but surely an old-fashioned choice for a student bar. *We had nowhere like this to hang out when I was a kid*, he thought with a twinge of jealousy. *Mind you, we didn't have to borrow money for our education, either, so it's swings and roundabouts.*

Once his eyes had fully adjusted, he could see that the place was full of students sprawled across low brown-leather seats. Except that they didn't look like his idea of students. Monochromatically attired, calm and quiet and faintly dull-looking, they could have passed for trainee accountants. Did they still march, squat, riot, rally, fight? Or did they only communicate through screens and share their opinions with strangers? It was hard to know what the young honestly thought, because the barrier of years increasingly barred his way.

'This symbol, do you know what it means?' he asked the barman, pointing to the logo.

'I don't know, it's just a design for the bar. I don't think it means anything.'

'You get mostly students from UCL in here?'

'They get a discount.'

'Any trouble?'

The barman realized he was talking to a policeman, and imperceptibly stiffened. 'It's not that kind of bar.'

'What kind is it?'

'What is it you want?'

'One of these stickers was found at a crime scene. I'm just checking it out. Hang on.' He pulled out a photograph of Gloria Taylor. 'Ever seen this woman in here?'

'No, no one like her, and I'm on most nights. You can talk to the girl who designed the sticker, though – she's over there. The one with the hair.'

The first thing May noticed about the girl was her height. She was folded over a sofa that didn't seem long enough to contain her. Her head was close-cropped, except for an immaculate blonde centre braid that made her look like a virtual-reality version of herself. She was talking with two Asian boys who, from May's attenuated viewpoint, looked about fifteen years old. When May introduced himself, she shook his hand in a curiously genteel fashion, which made him warm to her.

'I'm Cassie Field. Can I help you?'

'I understand you designed this logo.'

'Yeah, though the brewery never paid me for the job.'

'So you're an art director, a designer, what?'

'Visual artist. If you can work in the media these days

118

everyone assumes that you have rich parents and tries to avoid paying you, like designing isn't real work. I ended up covering the print bill myself. And I don't have rich parents.' She gave a throaty laugh. 'I run this place – well, four nights a week. I split-shift with another manager. It's paying for my tuition.'

'What are you studying?'

'English Civil War documents at the British Library, they're for an educational video-game project. I can give my eyes and brain a rest here after I've been working on my laptop all day.'

'So you must know most of the regulars.'

'Yeah, it's a pretty familiar crowd.'

'I'm interested in these stickers.' May held up the one removed from Taylor's body. 'The K is for Karma, right? Not Kaos.'

She looked at him properly now, intrigued. 'Not necessarily. Show me.' She took the bagged sticker from him and examined it. 'This one's been coloured in. The man's body, see? Day-Glo orange marker. The originals are lighter.' Bryant had not noticed in the dim light of the bar. 'I've seen a few around like this.'

'In here?'

'I suppose so. I can't think where else. A lot of different tribes come in. Emos in that corner, bless 'em, Goths over there. The rest are mostly – to tell the truth, I don't know what they are any more. It evolves, you know? Mostly they're just students. Quite a few Japanese kids. All they do is talk about work. The idea was to get people to customize the stickers and put them on their bags. The bar owners told me to make sure they didn't end up on walls. It's illegal to flypost around here.'

'Since when were students worried about legalities?' May asked.

'Since their education could be cancelled,' Cassie replied tartly.

'Could you do me a favour? Keep a lookout for any stickers shaded in this fashion? I have a number you can ring if you see anything.' He handed her his PCU card, then thought for a moment. 'Actually, don't just call if you see the sticker. Call if you see anything unusual – anything at all. It might seem insignificant to you at the time, but make a note and ring me.'

'There's a group that comes in . . .' She tapped a frosted white nail against her teeth. 'They're here most nights of the week. Something funny about them. I don't know . . .'

'Funny in what way?'

'I guess they're just really focussed. They don't like to mix with anyone else. I think I've seen the orange-coloured stickers on their bags. They huddle together in the corner at night, working on their PDAs.'

'So what makes them funny?'

'I guess it's just that they're too intense, working as if . . .'

'What?'

She gave a shrug. 'I don't know, as if their lives depended on it. Hang on – there's someone here who knows them.' A tall, smartly suited young man stood at the bar rummaging in a black leather briefcase. 'Theo!' Cassie called out. 'Over here.'

'Hey, Cassie.'

'Don't you ever pick up your voicemail?'

'I was in Devon visiting my folks. What's up?'

'Mr May, this is Theo. He may be able to help you.'

John May shook Theo's hand, taking note of a tanned wrist and an expensive-looking Cartier watch.

'Theo, those guys with the red sports bags are your flat-mates, aren't they?'

'Geek Central, yeah. The loser patrol. Have they been causing you any trouble?'

'No, but Mr May is trying to track down these.' She showed him the sticker. 'They have them on their bags, don't they?'

'Yeah, I think so. Cassie gives them out here in the bar.'

'Not coloured in, like this.' She turned to May. 'Can I say who you are?'

'I'm a detective,' said May. 'Maybe I could talk to these friends of yours?'

'I think "friends" is overdoing it. We share a house. Actually, it's my house and they pay me rent. I can give you the phone number there.' He flipped out a pen – another Cartier – and scribbled on a card. 'I don't think they'll be too thrilled to hear from the police.'

'It's a long shot,' May confided. 'Right now I'm ready to try anything.'

Cassie had a killer smile. 'I'd get you a drink,' she suggested, 'if you weren't on duty.'

'I'm not,' May replied, 'and I'll have a whisky.' He wondered how much he should tell her, but figured it wouldn't do any harm to mention the case. The PCU had fewer restrictions on information than the CID. 'We have a woman who died on the Underground with one of these stickers on her back.'

'And you suspect my flatmates?' asked Theo, incredulous. 'That's brilliant. Oh, that's genius.' He started to laugh.

'What's so funny?' May asked.

Theo's smile broadened to match Cassie's. 'You'll find out when you meet them,' he said.

15

TUBE TALES

'North End.'

'City Road.'

'Down Street.'

'British Museum.'

'Lords.'

'Trafalgar Square.'

'Strand.'

'That became the Aldwych.'

It was, Arthur Bryant conceded, an unusual way to end a Monday.

Seated in the gloomy, cluttered staffroom of King's Cross Underground Station at midnight, sharing bottles of warm beer and listening to the guards who had just come off duty, he wondered about the kind of person who would be attracted by such a lightless, closed-off world. He looked around at Rasheed, Sandwich, Marianne, Bitter and Stone, who were naming stations that had been closed down over the years.

Rasheed was so impossibly thin that his uniform seemed virtually uninhabited, although he had just eaten an enormous curried beef pie in under five minutes. 'I never heard of no station at Trafalgar Square,' he told the assembly, unwrapping a KitKat for dessert.

'It was on the Bakerloo Line,' said Sandwich, who was as broad as Rasheed was slender. When he tipped back on his plastic bendy chair, Bryant half-expected the legs to buckle. Sandwich's real name was Lando – he had been named after a character in a Star Wars film, and hated it – and now he was called Sandwich, because no one had ever seen him eat. 'They got rid of it 'cause it wasn't used enough, and anyway, it's only a two-minute train ride from Leicester Square to Charing Cross.'

'Covent Garden to Leicester Square is only 250 metres,' added Rasheed. Stone nodded in agreement; he rarely spoke. Small and nondescript, he looked like an exhausted lifer who had spent too many years underground, away from sun and fresh air. Bitter – so called because that was all she drank – was heavier and healthier-looking, but didn't like joining in with the others. Everyone agreed that she had communication issues. Apparently she liked working alone at nights, coordinating tunnel maintenance work.

'Most of the central London stations are only a couple of minutes apart,' said Sandwich. 'A strange line, though, the Bakerloo. Brown and gloomy, and all them twisting tunnels, loads of them derelict and closed off. The Bakerloo stations all seem underlit to me, even Piccadilly Circus. Sort of yellowy at night, but friendly.'

'I was posted at Camden Town for a while,' said Marianne, a West Indian ticket clerk, the only one who was dressed for the surface. 'They used to change the listing on the central destination board from Bank to Charing Cross branch, just to make the commuters run backwards and forwards between the platforms.'

'I don't believe that,' said Rasheed, finishing his KitKat.

'No lie,' Marianne told him. 'And we used to get them commuter pigeons.'

'I beg your pardon?' asked Bryant, intrigued.

'Yeah, they live outside the West End and come in for the food. We used to see 'em all the time on the Northern Line, but we couldn't work out how they knew which station to get off at.'

'You're having a laugh, man,' said Sandwich. 'All right, then, here's a good one. Which is the only Tube station with a "Z" in its name?'

'Belsize Park,' said Marianne. 'Easy. Which station is the only one that doesn't have any letters in the word "Mackerel"?'

'St John's Wood,' said Stone.

'I suppose there are a lot of games you can play with the Tube map,' said Bryant.

'Oh yeah, loads. Like the one where you have to make a journey that passes through one station on each of the thirteen lines. I can tell you something weird about the District Line,' said Stone, who looked as if he hadn't visited the city's surface since the death of Winston Churchill. 'I know why the trains run quieter when they pass under the Inns of Court and the Houses of Parliament.'

'What do you mean?' asked Bryant.

'When the District Line was being built, the MPs and the lawyers all complained. Said the noise of the trains would ruin their concentration. So the railway company chopped up the bark of hundreds of trees and laid it below the tracks to cushion the carriages, just for them. Money talks, see.'

'Tell him about Bumper Harris,' said Sandwich.

'Oh, everyone knows that one,' Stone replied dismissively.

'I don't,' said Bryant, who did, of course, but wanted to hear their version.

'When they opened the first escalator at Earl's Court in 1910, everyone was too scared to use it. So they hired a bloke called Bumper Harris who had a wooden leg, just to go up and down on it all day. Passengers figured that if a one-legged man could use it safely, they could too.'

'Why was he called Bumper?'

'Apparently he lost his leg when two railway carriages bumped together.'

'When they dug out the tunnel at Earl's Court they found a seam of prehistoric oak, and six walking sticks were made out of it, with silver handles,' Sandwich added.

'Yeah, pull the other one, it's got bells on,' said Rasheed.

'It's true. My grandad had one of 'em. His missus was a Confetti Girl at Chiswick Works. She counted the bits cut out of tickets to tally the change.'

Bryant had come down here to question the staff about unusual events occurring on the Tube system, but had been sidetracked. He had not fully realized what he was letting himself in for; everyone, it seemed, had tales of drunks and madmen, gropers, flashers, con artists, thieves, buskers, fights and suicides. Yet, for the most part, it seemed that the system ran with astonishing efficiency. Nearly eighty million passengers passed through King's Cross Station every year. Sometimes, over three million journeys were made through the Tube system in a day. Bryant was surprised just how few deaths there were.

'My cousin Benny, right, he was in charge of the track-mounted flange greasers at Rayners Lane,' said Sandwich, whose whole family worked down the Tubes, 'and one morning he got the grease dosage wrong, and every train on the Victoria Line ended up skidding straight past its stations. There was a right ruckus about that.'

'So what happens if you spot something suspicious in the foot tunnels or on the platform?' asked Bryant.

'I can get the LT police there in seconds, but if there's a problem, like it's rush hour on a Saturday night or Arsenal's playing at home and the LTP are busy dealing with something else, I can issue a station code and we send our nearest team down there. Other passengers used to help out more, but they're scared to now, what with knife crime.'

'But I've heard about weird stuff at this station,' said Rasheed, hunching forward on his chair. 'Always late at night. You follow someone on one camera, you know instinctively they'll appear on the next one – only, according to some of the guards, they don't. They just vanish into thin air. There's this one bloke, I've heard about him a few times from a guard at Canonbury Station, one moment he's heading down the escalator, then he's running in the tunnel and the guard's thinking why's he running? He can't hear a train coming 'cause there's not another due for three or four minutes, then he watches the platform monitor, expecting him to appear – only he doesn't. The way this bloke tells it, he's the ghost of a dead passenger, a bloke with a broken heart who threw himself under a Piccadilly Line train a few years back.'

'I've heard about him too,' said Marianne. 'After the last Victoria Line train had gone, creeping along one of the empty tunnels, close to the floor, in a shiny black raincoat, like a giant bat. Gave my friend Shirley the willies. She saw him again a few days later, standing on the concourse at Highbury & Islington in the same outfit, surrounded by people, but nobody else noticed him. She thought she was going mad. A giant bat, just crawling through the empty tunnels . . .' She let the thought hang in the air.

'They reckon that passengers saw ghosts after the Moorgate disaster in 1975—'

'A real mystery, that was,' Sandwich interrupted. 'Forty-three dead – train overshot the platform and ploughed into the dead-end tunnel. There was nothing wrong with the train, the track or the signalling equipment. The driver was a good bloke, careful, conscientious, he just didn't apply the brakes. Hadn't even raised his hands to cover his face before the impact. He was sitting bolt upright at his post before the collision, holding the dead man's handle.'

'Must have been suicide, then,' said Stone, opening a beer. 'Bitter, do you want a bitter?' Bitter accepted the can.

'The driver had three hundred quid in his pocket when he died – he was going to put a deposit on a car for his daughter after his shift. That's not the action of a suicide. I suppose some good came out of it, with TETS.'

'What's that?'

'"Trains Entering Terminal Stations", also known as the Moorgate Control. Special stop units put in place to release the air from the train's braking system.'

'And what about the blood thrower?' added Rasheed. 'About once every couple of months, someone on the last Piccadilly Line southbound gets sprayed with blood.

They're not hurt or nothing – it's just this nutter who goes around chucking blood over people. We don't know where he gets it, and we can't catch him. 'Course, the tunnel power goes off after the last train, for the incoming workers from Tube Lines, the company in charge of the infrastructure, so maybe he escapes to the next station.'

'Can we stop now?' asked Marianne. 'All this talk's starting to give me the willies too.'

'Yeah, I'll give you the willies,' laughed Sandwich, cracking up the others. Even Bitter managed a lipless smile. 'Here, you know Upminster Bridge Station in Havering?'

'Yeah, end of the District Line,' said Rasheed.

'There's a swastika on the ticket-office floor – can't tell if it's a Nazi-type swastika or like Hindus have, you know – the reversed swastika for good luck. I used to be a home-beat officer on a council estate in West London, and when Indian families got a flat, the first thing they did was create one out of dried beans on the floor.'

Bryant studied his new friends with interest. Perhaps the London Underground system was a place where men and women could come to forget the outside world, like the Foreign Legion. Was it really only a job, or did some of them feel uncomfortable when they finally ventured out, blinking, into the sharp blue light of day?

'Come on, just one more,' said Rasheed.

Everyone groaned in protest, but he continued. 'I heard about a man who got off the train when it opened its doors by mistake at South Kentish Town. This was in 1951, and the station had been shut for years, but the train doors closed before he could get back on, right. His name was either Brackett or Green – there's different versions of the story. He used his lighter to find his way along the platform, and burned bits of old posters to provide light. The lifts were turned off so he tried to get out by climbing all 294 steps up the spiral staircase, but when he got to the top he banged his head on the boarded-over floor of the shop above, and had to go back down. He tried to flag down trains for days afterwards, but none of the drivers would stop, and eventually he became too weak to move. He was found by a bunch of gangers coming up the tunnel, but they were too late to save him.'

'There are so many things wrong with that bloody story I don't know where to start.' Marianne had a throaty, dirty laugh. 'How could he get out at an unlit station? And if he died, how does anyone know he banged his head? What do you think, Mr Bryant?'

Arthur was miles away. He was trying to understand why Mr Fox might have moved his operations underground. The Tube system was vast, and connected every part of London. But more importantly, its axis was now King's Cross, where the Eurostar linked it to the rest of Europe. Almost overnight, Mr Fox's lair had become the gateway to forty-eight countries.

But what he was doing here, and what he might be planning to do, remained a disturbing mystery.

16

CRUELTIES

'What a day. New funding for the unit and a case properly sanctioned by the Home Office. Welcome back.' John May raised his beer in salute. The two detectives had dug down into a musty sofa at the rear of the Charles I, an oaky little pub tucked away behind King's Cross railway terminal that had a fireplace, stag heads, bookshelves and an occasional willingness to continue serving behind closed shutters. It was very late, but neither of them slept much when they were on a case. May had wanted to share his discovery about the Karma Bar sticker, and had caught Bryant leaving the Underground station. He studied his pensive partner. 'What's the matter?'

'I don't like being made a fool of,' Bryant complained. 'The case would have been closed by now.'

'There's no point in dwelling on what might have been, Arthur.'

'I suppose Mr Fox picked his name because he thinks of himself as feral and adaptable. But he's a small-time conman who accidentally became a killer. The act has strengthened him, John, that's the awful thing.'

'Why do you say that?'

'He leaves bodies scattered around the neighbourhood and gets us to clear up the mess. We nail him, he kills again as he escapes – he didn't need to do that – and he immediately returns to his old stamping ground to continue. He's humiliating us. He thinks he's above the law, and that can't be allowed to happen.'

'We badly need the link between the beautician and the junkie.'

'Maybe she's a former girlfriend.'

'No. Janice interviewed Gloria Taylor's work colleagues. They say she was very strict about her partners, happy on her own, wasn't currently involved with anyone. Meera spoke to her ex and he says the same thing. They were still close; she called him two or three times a week. Never mentioned anything out of the ordinary. Had her hands full just keeping her job and looking after her little girl. The junkie, well, that's a different matter. Maybe their paths crossed on the streets around here. You can imagine Mr Fox and his victim starting out as thieves together.'

'If Mr Fox is getting rid of anyone who knows who he was,' said Bryant, 'it's because he means to go on.'

'That might explain the junkie, but not why he would shove an innocent woman down an escalator.'

'And in front of witnesses. Can they be traced?'

'We can trawl through the tags on their travel cards. If we start checking records from, say, thirty seconds before Gloria Taylor passed through the barrier, we'll be able to get all the registered user addresses. But it's a lengthy process tracking them all down. The fact that St Pancras is an international station means many of them could now be abroad.'

'Well, I'll leave the gadgetry to you and Dan. You know what happens when I touch anything electronic. I rewired one plug in the new building, that's all.'

'Janice told me you melted it to the floor.'

'Not intentionally. I've been thinking about the sticker. If that's some new part of the MO, why not do the same to the junkie?'

'Maybe he killed the woman for the sheer pleasure of being cruel.'

'But why kill both at the same Tube station?'

'It's the most crowded crossing-point in England, so that's not much of a surprise.'

'The station staff are a lovely bunch of people, they were telling me ghost stories about the London Underground. Apparently, the developers tore down an old theatre, the Royal Strand, to make way for the Aldwych station. Before the 1970s, there was an army of women who used to enter the system after the last train had run. They were called Fluffers, and their job was to remove all the dust-balls, flakes of skin and human hair that had gathered in the tunnels. They were frightened by the spectre of an actress from the Royal Strand who had committed suicide on the spot where her old dressing room had been, and refused to clean the Aldwych tracks any more.'

'Collective hysteria.' May took a swig of his beer. 'Mind you, I imagine you'd be spooked too, if you had to walk through pitch-black tunnels every night. It must have made people very jumpy in the days before they improved the lighting.'

'Did you get to meet up with that funny little boy?'

'You mustn't call Rufus a boy, he gets terribly upset,' May admonished. 'He has the IQ of an Oxford lecturer, and considers it a grave misfortune to be trapped in a child's body. The roundel with the 'K' is the logo of a bar in Judd Street. I've got a lead out of it, if you can call it that. A bunch of students – I'll go and see them tomorrow.'

Bryant gave a weary sigh. 'I miss the old cases. Things were more clear-cut when we started. Generations of robbers and professional thieves, you saw the same people year in and year out, and you could always get a lead by talking to the families. All those mothers, brothers and uncles who couldn't keep their mouths shut. It's not like that now. Death has become so random. Angry children attacking one another over issues of respect – such a terrible waste of life. And I can't categorize Mr Fox, he doesn't fit anywhere. Half a dozen people have seen and spoken to him. We've actually interviewed him, for God's sake. And what have we got between us? A pencil sketch of a nondescript man, nothing more.'

'There must be someone out there who knows what he's like. I mean, what he's *really* like, when he lets his guard down.'

'Janice is having trouble finding the witness in my tour group. She got hold of the Canadians, but they didn't remember anything significant about him.'

'Wait, you've got witnesses trying to remember another witness?'

'Well done for keeping up. I suppose we could have them hypnotized.'

'That's illegal, Arthur. Let's try and keep our noses clean this week, eh?'

Bryant was taken with the idea. 'Actually, I know someone who would do it. Old Albert Purberry, he's legitimate now, almost, and he'd be cheap.'

'What do you mean, *almost?*'

'He had some problems a couple of years back – it was nothing. A trick that went wrong, that's all.'

'What happened?'

'He was booked for a stag night and hypnotized the groom-to-be, told him he would fall in love with the first person he saw on his wedding day. Unfortunately, the first person he saw the next day wasn't his wife.'

'Who was it?'

'Barry Manilow. On the television. He drove to Birmingham, where Manilow was performing, broke into his dressing room and proposed, but Manilow turned him down. Then Manilow had to get a restraining order, and the wedding was called off and the fiancée's mother burned Albert's house down. But he's better now. I'll give him a call.'

'I'd hold off for a day or two,' May cautioned. 'If we don't find a link between the deaths tomorrow, we treat them separately. Do we have a deal?'

'Do I have a choice?' asked Bryant.

Janice Longbright was on all fours under her desk. There was something wrong with the electric socket on the floor that Dave and Dave, the two builders, had connected up. It was crackling and popping, but as Bryant had blown up the other circuit, she needed it to work. She was tired and wanted to go home, but staying in the office stopped her from thinking about Liberty DuCaine.

'Need any help?' asked Renfield, bending low.

'There's some kind of intermittent fault, the power keeps

shorting out.' She refused his offer of a hand and clambered up. 'Don't worry, I can fix it.'

Renfield folded his thick arms and regarded her sternly. 'You don't always have to be so independent, you know.'

'It comes naturally to me.' She dusted herself down. 'Was there something you wanted?'

'I'm sorry about DuCaine.' He looked awkward. 'I know you and he got . . . close.'

'We slept together once, Jack. There's no need to be coy about it. I'd be sorry for anyone I knew who got killed in the line of duty. So I'm sorry he died, nothing more.'

'Bit of a harsh way of looking at it.'

'Well, small cruelties are what get us through.'

Renfield looked uncomfortable. 'I was going to say that I'm here if you get fed up, or need to talk to someone.'

'Thanks for the offer, but I've been around the block, it's happened before. If I think too hard about it I won't come in tomorrow morning. So let's just draw a line under the matter.'

'OK. I just wanted to say . . . you know . . .'

'Can we talk about this some other time? Go home and get some rest.'

Renfield looked dejected.

She touched his arm. 'But it's good of you to think of me.'

She dropped back into her chair and pinned a stray auburn curl behind her ear. Releasing a long, slow breath, she looked around the room. *This is it*, she thought, *the other end of my rat run. It starts at my empty flat in Highgate, and descends to a derelict warehouse in King's Cross. There and back. My life in the service of the public.*

I wanted to be a burlesque dancer and ended up being a copper like my Ma.

Liberty DuCaine had given her a glimpse of the outside world. Most men seemed to smile on her in the way that they might admire an old Land Army poster, for vigour and colouring. Liberty had found more within her, and liked the very qualities other men found unappealing. She had no desire to change. She was big-boned, strong-willed, blunt, outspoken, womanly, as glamorous as a lipstick lesbian and as kind as a man's memory of his mother. In the catalogue of desirable female attributes, it felt as though she had managed to tick all the wrong boxes.

She caught sight of herself in a huge gilt mirror that stood propped against the opposite wall and knew this was who she would always be, a Diana Dors lookalike who wore a corset under her uniform and made weak men afraid. *To hell with them*, she thought with sharp finality. *If they can't handle me, that's their problem, not mine. I'm not going to change who I am now. Tomorrow I'm going to bleach the hell out of my hair and go back to being big, blonde and buxom. I reined it in for you, Liberty, because I wanted you to want me. I won't do that again for anyone.*

She stayed for want of something better to do. Paperwork smothered her desk; there were dozens of King's Cross passenger statements still to sort through. With any luck, it would keep her busy for the rest of the night. She could sleep on Bryant's motheaten sofa and start again first thing in the morning.

17

IN PLAIN SIGHT

At 11:47 a.m. on Tuesday morning, John May received a phone call from Cassie Field. 'You said to call if I saw any of the stickers,' she explained. 'Well, I saw some last night.'

'In the bar?'

'Yeah, on the backpacks of that group I told you about, the ones who spend all evening on their PDAs. They came in just after Theo left. I got talking to one of them, and got his mobile number for you.'

'Thanks. I've been trying the house phone, but nobody answers. That was thoughtful of you.'

'Not really. I fancied one of his mates and was trying to pick him up. He wasn't interested, so I thought I'd turn them all over to the police. Have you got a pen?'

'Fire away.'

'His name's Nikos Nicolau. He's taking some kind of pharmaceutical course at UCL. He started to tell me about it but he's got a bit of a speech impediment, and the music was too loud for me to hear him properly, plus he was boring. I asked him about the stickers, but he was evasive. He's kind of creepy. I thought I'd better call you.' She gave him Nicolau's mobile number.

'I'm on it,' said May, thanking her. He rang off and called Nicolau, who sounded uncomfortable about being contacted by a police officer. May arranged an appointment for 2:00 p.m. at the college and was heading out of the room when he collided with Bryant coming in.

'You will not believe this,' said Arthur, out of breath. 'He doesn't exist!'

The two Daves, who had been attempting to fit an inadequate piece of hardboard across the hole in the detectives' office, stopped work and turned their attention to Bryant. He seemed to fascinate them.

'Who doesn't exist?'

'My blithering, blasted, bloody witness. Inattentional blindness, the oldest trick in the book.'

'I have no idea what you're on about.'

'He's playing psychological games with me. Do you remember there was this perception experiment, conducted in the 1990s?'

'Strangely enough, no.'

'A researcher pretended to have lost his way and stopped people to ask for help. Each time he did so, two workmen carrying a door barged between them. One of the workmen switched places with the researcher. Over half the subjects failed to notice they were now talking to someone else, because they were concentrating on the problem at hand, not on the researcher's face.'

'Who are we talking about?' May threw up his hands helplessly. 'I'm lost.'

'I'm sorry, I forgot you exist in an alternate universe

where everything has to be slowly explained to you. The man who was on my walking tour, the one who saw Mr Fox attacking the addict? We got his ID from the tour company, but he's not the man I remember meeting.'

'Maybe I'm being dense—'

'You most certainly are and it's very simple. I did a head-count when we set off – I always do to make sure we don't lose anyone. Sometimes when I get too interesting they try to slip away. We had the same number at the end as we had at the start. Mr Fox followed his victim, forcing him into a dead-end tunnel. After stabbing him, he knew he couldn't get out of the other end, so he had to double back. It meant having to pass through my group, so rather than draw attention to himself he dismissed the person who most looked like him and replaced him. Obvious, really, just what I would have done.'

'What do you mean? How do you "dismiss" someone?'

'Who knows, maybe he gave him money or just threatened to duff him up. Took his jacket, changed his hair – I don't know exactly how he does it, but he does. To be honest, he could have switched with almost any of the invisibles in my group because I barely noticed them.'

'Invisibles?'

'It doesn't matter. Then he drew my attention to the attack, which allowed him to manipulate the situation and slip away.'

'What are you going to do now?'

'I think I have a vague idea of what he looks like at the moment. He's shortened his hair and smartened up. He's been to a tanning salon and done something to his face that makes it look different, but I can't put my finger on it. I can get out a basic description.'

'He'll change his appearance again, you know that. Keeping one step ahead is a matter of pride with him.'

'But he's tied to the area, John. I don't know what keeps him here, but that's how we're going to get him.'

'So what have we actually got? He doesn't mind being seen because he's never the same person for long. He absorbs others and uses their knowledge until it's time to change once more. The danger is knowing something about him in return. What did the victim know that placed him at risk? Get Janice to dig into the boy's background, we might get lucky and turn up something. Has anyone spoken to UCH this morning?'

'He's alive and stabilized, but not conscious. Janice is talking to his doctor right now.'

'The Taylor case gets priority treatment. You know how this goes, Arthur; a junkie's death matters less than a young mother shoved down the stairs, because if it turns out she's done nothing wrong and was pushed by a stranger, everyone is at risk, and then it's a matter of public safety—'

'—and a case for the PCU,' said Bryant impatiently. 'Yes, I appreciate that. But if we keep a watch on the Tube station, we can tackle both problems at once.'

'It's a big place, I don't see how we can cover it with only a handful of staff. Dan, wait.' May collared Banbury as he passed the doorway. 'I heard you applied for a priority DNA check – anything from the contact lens case in the apartment?'

'Nothing from the eyelash,' said Dan. 'The saline had corrupted it. But there were fingerprints on the exterior of the case, and they match Janice's ID of the victim lying in UCH.'

'She's got an ID? Why didn't I know this?'

'Only just happened. Tony McCarthy, aka Mac, small-time crook, recovering heroin addict, a known face in the dodgier King's Cross pubs. He's got an impressive string of convictions. He pulled down a couple of years in Pentonville for dealing.'

'Looks like Mr Fox slipped up,' said May.

'It's not like him,' Bryant insisted. 'He's too careful for that.'

'If he's addicted to changing his appearance, he probably wears coloured contacts. And Mac was a junkie. If Mr Fox invited him over and left him alone for even a minute, it's likely he'd go through his host's bathroom cabinet looking for something to steal or swallow. He picked up the lens case, checked it out, put it back somewhere different, and Mr Fox failed to wipe it clean.'

'OK, we've been handed McCarthy, but if there's something in his past that connects the pair of them, Mr Fox must know we'll find it. He wants me to try and stop him. Wouldn't you want to measure your opponent's strength? See how close he's likely to get?'

'What kind of man thinks like that?' asked Longbright.

'It's about power, Janice. There are some men who use everything as an opportunity to prove their superiority. Life is a perpetual dare for them. This is his work, and rather than shift from his location he'll hide in plain sight until one of us is forced to make a move.'

'Killing people is not normal work, Arthur,' May pointed out. 'I don't think it's a good idea for you to act as if you admire him.'

'Of course I don't.' Bryant's watery blue eyes rolled behind his bifocals. 'I think he's horrible. But if something wriggles under a rock, don't you want to pick the rock up and take a look? I wouldn't be much of a criminologist if I wasn't intrigued.'

'Then I shall leave you to your intrigues.' May searched around for his coat. The two Daves were standing by with screwdrivers raised, listening with interest. 'I'm going to try and throw some light on why an innocent woman died. Perhaps you'll give us the benefit of your intelligence by doing the same.'

'I have my suspicions about her death,' Bryant told his partner's retreating back, 'but you're not going to like it. You never do.'

'You're not going to win this one by ploughing through a bunch of old books, Arthur,' May called back. 'It'll come down to modern detection techniques. I'm willing to put money on it.'

'So am I,' said one of the Daves. 'Twenty quid says he proves the old codger wrong.'

'Make it fifty,' said the other, 'and you've got yourself a bet.'

18

LUNACY

Rain was sifting through the office ceiling. Everyone looked up as a piece of plaster divorced itself and fell into a bucket with a plonk. They dragged their attention back to the acting head of the unit.

'Words fail me,' Raymond Land continued, despite the fact that they clearly did no such thing. 'What more am I supposed to do, for God's sake? You get your old positions back, we might finally be allocated a decent budget, thanks to Giles Kershaw's old school network, our enemies at the Home Office have heard the news and are wandering around with faces like slapped arses, we even get a case that fits our public remit, and what happens? I ask you, what happens?'

Ask he might, but there was no response. The assembled staff of the PCU looked at one another in puzzlement. Outside the door, one of the Daves was using a spanner to hit a pipe with the desultory air of a Victorian nanny beating a child. Land pressed his eyelids together and waited for the workman to finish.

'Exactly. Nothing. Twenty-four hours is a bloody long time in this area, and the trail has wiped itself clean. I walk around the office – if that's what you can call this doss-house – hoping to see someone in the throes of a revelation, or at least bothering to fill in their paperwork, and what do I see?'

'Is this going to take very long, sir?' asked Meera.

'You'll stay here until I've finished, young lady.' He tried to take his eyes from her and failed. 'What . . . what is all that stuff on your face?'

'Lip gloss and blusher, sir. Janice gave me some make-up tips. I had a makeover.'

'During your duty hours? What the hell is going on here?'

'Not here, at Selfridges, in the cosmetics department where Gloria Taylor worked. I got more out of her colleagues that way, catching them while they were working. Taylor caught the same train home every night. She was in perfectly normal spirits when she left, looking forward to seeing her daughter because she was going to take her to the cinema for the first time, to see an old Disney film they had just reissued at the Imax, *The Lion King*. She'd bought the kid a stuffed lion from the Disney Store, but hadn't taken it home with her. It was still in her locker. I filed my report and emailed it to you.'

'Oh, well, I suppose that's all right. But the rest of you . . .' His attention fell upon Colin Bimsley, who was reading a cookery book. 'I assume that's not a police manual in your hand?'

'No sir, it's aubergine and mozzarella parcels. I'm thinking of taking a course in Italian cuisine.' He had found the book in one of the bins while he was staking out Mr Fox's apartment, and had decided it was about time to learn a new skill. John May encouraged them all to do so whenever they were inundated with paperwork, to keep their brains sharp. Besides, Longbright had tipped him off that Meera liked Italian food.

'What about the requisition forms I asked you to handle? You can't have finished those already.'

'They've all gone off. John created online spreadsheets for us so we wouldn't have to print hard copies any more. But I ran out some sets for you and Mr Bryant because I knew you'd prefer paper. They're on your desk.'

Land wasn't keen about being yoked with Bryant. 'I know how to open a spreadsheet, thank you, I can do that. I do know about computers, Bimsley, you don't have to patronize me.'

'Good, because I didn't fix your printer utilities, so I guess I can leave you to upgrade the file manager for—'

'Fine, fine, whatever, and I suppose the rest of you have completed your duties for the day?'

'No, sir,' said Banbury. 'Obviously, we won't have done that until we find out who was standing behind Gloria Taylor. I've been through every second of the CCTV footage covering the escalator, but we have no clear shots of her falling. The movement is just too fast. I've sent some frame grabs out for enhancement. I'm just waiting for them to come back.'

Land was starting to suspect that he had been set up. 'Then where has John got to? I'm supposed to be informed whenever anyone goes out.'

'He's interviewing a student at UCL,' Longbright told him. 'Following up a lead on Taylor.'

'Well, somebody should have told me. What about you?' Land pleaded. He turned to Bryant in desperation. 'What do you expect to find in that huge filthy-looking book?' He pointed at the leather-bound volume wedged under the arm of London's most senior detective.

'This? Glad you asked. It's a copy of the asylum records from Bedlam, after it moved to St George's Fields, Southwark,' said Bryant, happily holding the book up for Land's perusal.

'You can't tell me that this has something to do with the case.'

'Actually I can. The sticker found on Taylor's body is a reinterpretation of a design used by the hospital. As you can see here, the patient's arms and legs are held apart by iron rods which are then chained to the walls.' He pointed to the inked symbol within the pages. 'At first I thought the drawing was taken from Leonardo Da Vinci, but then I noticed the thin black bands on the wrist and the ankle, see? The illustration here is described as "an unspecified method of coercion for violent lunatics and proponents of unwarranted anarchy, 1826". Gloria Taylor told everyone she was twenty-three, but she was younger. She became pregnant at the age of sixteen and suffered a nervous breakdown two years later. Her parents tried to have her sectioned. It's probably just a coincidence that the symbol somehow became attached to her, but I thought you'd want us to investigate all avenues.'

'I suppose you all think you're very clever,' Land ended lamely. 'I'm sure you imagine you can run this place without me, but I'm here to make sure you can't. Because you don't think of everything, you know. There are two work-men brewing up tea on a primus stove in the hall, both apparently called Dave, and they don't seem to have been given any instructions about what to do.'

'That's because they're your responsibility, old sausage,' Bryant reminded him. 'You specifically said you wanted to take care of them, remember? I imagine you don't, otherwise you'd have arranged a work schedule for them. OK, someone deal with the Daves for poor old Raymondo here, I'll put the kettle on and let's all get back to work.'

Having returned the acting temporary chief to his usual state of incandescent frustration, Bryant strolled out to the balcony for a smoke, but Land followed him.

'And there's another thing I've been meaning to talk to you about,' he hissed. 'Your memoirs. You can't be serious.'

'I have no idea to what you are referring, *mon vieux tête-de-navet*.'

'You should do. I found a manuscript of the first com-pleted volume when I was unpacking one of your boxes yesterday morning. What the bloody hell do you think you're playing at?'

Bryant regarded him innocently. 'I'm writing down histories of our cases at the unit precisely as I remember them.'

'That's the problem – you don't remember anything pre-cisely.'

'Oh, I have a system for that.' Bryant screwed up an eye and peered into his pipe-stem. 'When I remember two facts but can't recall the event that connects them, I use the bridge of my imagination.'

'All I can say is it's a bloody long bridge. You wrote up a full account of your first case—'

'The business at the Palace Theatre, the crazed killer who struck during a rather saucy production of *Orpheus in the Underworld*. You read it?'

'Yes I did, and I've never read such a pile of old rubbish in my life.'

'Obviously I had to make a few changes to protect the innocent.'

'A few changes? You say it took place during the Blitz, for God's sake! I know for a fact that you didn't meet John until the 1950s.'

'Yes I did.'

'No you didn't. You met when you were working out of Bow Street Station.'

'No we didn't.'

'Yes you did. Apart from anything else, if your account was true you'd be in your late eighties by now, whereas you're clearly not.'

'Yes I am.'

'No you're not. Don't be ridiculous. I'm not denying the basic facts – I've seen the official case notes – but you've moved the whole investigation back by about fifteen years.'

'No I haven't.'

'Yes you have. Stop contradicting me!'

'I'm not. You only think I am.'

'I don't.'

'You do.'

'Just stop it! I know what I'm talking about. The unit was founded in September 1940, but you weren't in it then. I've read the Home Office file on the place. It was called the Particular Crimes Unit at that point. It didn't become Peculiar until you came along.'

'That's not how I remember it. And if that's not how it happened, it's how it *should* have happened. Far more colourful background material.'

'What, so the Palace Theatre murderer was killed by a bomb while escaping, instead of getting banged up in Colney Hatch Asylum until finally being carried out in a box?'

'Poetic licence. If I wrote down your days exactly as they happened, my readers would be asleep in minutes.'

'Well, I hope we're not going to be treated to revised versions of all our cases.' Land had a sudden frightening thought. 'And I hope I'm not featuring in any of these lurid fabrications?'

'Oh, I'm weaving you in all the way through, dear chap.' Bryant patted him consolingly on the shoulder. 'My publisher said I should make it as amusing as possible, so I shall be popping you in whenever my readers are in need of a cheap laugh.'

He closed the balcony doors behind him and lit up a satisfying pipe.

19

NIKOS

As John May descended the basement steps and entered the University College Cruciform Library on Gower Street, he realized he had no description of the man he was there to meet. He needn't have been concerned, as Nikos Nicolau was waiting for him.

May knew it was wrong to judge by appearances, but it seemed that Nicolau had gone out of his way to appear unprepossessing. He had been put together wrongly: his head was too large, his back slightly hunched, his eyes protuberant. Thinning hair was slicked across a broad expanse of skullbone, although he couldn't have been more than twenty-one. He was wearing a crumpled baggy T-shirt bearing the slogan *A Joy To Have In Class*, which seemed unlikely as he didn't smell very fresh. The senior detective was fastidious about personal grooming, and it bothered him to admit that he was adversely influenced by its lack in others.

'Mr May? There's a corner over here where we can talk.'

Nicolau led the way to a pair of red sofas screened off from the central part of the library. 'I have trouble working down here because there's no natural light. I have a melatonin imbalance, and get very claustrophobic, but it's necessary for me to be here because they have good pharmacological reference tools, and that's my study area.' He spoke with the clipped North London accent of a transported Greek, but sounded as if he had trouble with his sinuses.

'I appreciate you making the time to see me.' May seated himself and extracted a notebook. 'Cassie Field gave me your details. She works for the Karma Bar just behind here?'

'Oh, the *babe*.' Nikos gave a snort of delight and was forced to wipe his nose. 'She knows who I am?'

'Well, she must do, because she gave me your number.'

'I give out my number all the time, but people don't usually . . . especially . . .' He could see how that was starting to sound, and killed the rest of the sentence. 'How can I help you?'

May produced the sticker in its clear plastic slipcase. 'Seen one of these before?'

'Yeah. They're from the bar.'

'Were you aware that it's an early Victorian symbol denoting lunacy?' He had promised Bryant he would ask.

'No, I had no idea. Interesting.'

'This one's hand-coloured. Like the one on your bag.' May pointed at the satchel between Nicolau's boots.

'Yeah, I coloured it in.'

'Any others like that?'

'A few of us have them, I guess.'

'Are you some kind of a group – a club?'

'Just friends, some of us started on the same day.

Three guys are doing urban planning, I'm in biochemical engineering, ah – ' he scrunched his eyes shut, thinking, ' – someone's doing computational statistics. A bunch of us share the same house.'

'I can't imagine you would have that much in common, all doing different courses.'

'The bar. We have the Karma Bar in common. It's a good place to meet girls and just hang out. There are a few pubs nearby but they get too crowded with suits in the evening, and they screen football. None of us are very interested in sport.'

'So – what? Miss Field gave each of you a sticker, or did one of you hand them out to the others?'

'I don't remember, but I can tell you why we put them on our stuff. Nearly everyone who goes in there is carrying a laptop bag. They get piled in a heap by the bar, and many of them look the same, so one evening Ruby coloured the stickers, so that we'd be able to find our gear when we were leaving.'

'Ruby?'

'She's Matt's girlfriend. He's in the house as well. I don't really know her well, she just came along one evening. It may even have been her idea.' He settled his glasses further back on the bridge of his nose. He was sweating heavily. 'Can I ask why you're so interested?'

'One of these was found on a dead body.' May waited for the idea to sink in. 'In an investigation of this kind you check anything that's unusual, or even just a little bit different.'

'If I can give you a suggestion? People often chuck their coats on top of the bags – maybe it got transferred.'

'You're probably right.' There didn't seem to be

anything more May could glean which might be of use. 'Well, it was a point worth covering. Thanks for your time.' He rose to leave. 'Tell you what, though. In case I need to check any further, I don't want to disturb you. Perhaps you'd give me contact details for this girl – Ruby?'

'Sure.' Nicolau seemed relieved. He scribbled something on a scrap of paper. 'Ruby Cates. Here's her email address.'

May left, but somewhere an alarm had been triggered. The harder he tried to focus on what was wrong, the less sure he became. *Leave the thought*, he told himself, *it will surface when it's ready*. The uneasy feeling stayed with him all the way back to the unit.

Then he remembered. It was something Cassie Field had said. *Too intense*. Nicolau had been trying hard to convince. The look of relief on his face when May had switched his attention to the girl had been palpable.

20

FALLING IDOL

Panic was setting in now. What if it was too late? But there was no point in thinking about what might already have happened, and anyway, here was Matt in his crazy old rainbow-striped coat and brown woolly hat, raising a hand in greeting from the other side of the bar.

'I'm really sorry I'm so late, I don't know where the time went.'

'That's OK.'

'I bumped into an old pal from Nottingham, and we had some catching up to do. Hit a few bars together, I'd forgotten how much he could drink. Then I spent ages on the phone, and you know how that goes, right? It's like I can't do anything to please her. I'm like "If you don't want to go out with me, just say so," right? Can I get you a drink?'

'No, let me get you one.' The smile must have looked painfully forced. The barman was summoned and a drink was poured. 'Did you have a lecture this afternoon?'

'Yeah, the architect from Bartlett, the one with the stoop, it was meant to be about traffic restructuring in the late 1960s, but it was so data-driven that he lost most of us about halfway through. And I still have a hangover from last night. Then I got the nagging phone call and wasn't allowed off the hook until she'd described everything that's wrong with me in huge detail.'

'Did you tell her you were coming to meet me?' The obviousness of the question caused an inward cringe.

'No, you know I didn't, you told me not to. Anyway, if she thought I was meeting up with you she'd accuse us of conspiring against her. A toast to my good fortune.'

'To winners.'

'Damn right. We've got the skills that pay the bills. Just in time, because I'm seriously broke. Here's to money, the root of all evil.' Matt downed his vodka cocktail in one. He was drinking something that was a spin on a Smith & Wesson – vodka and coffee liqueur with a dash of soda. His version added an oily sambuca to the mix.

Matt looked even messier than usual. His tumbleweed hair needed a wash and there were violet crescents beneath his eyes. Everybody knew he was on his way to becoming a serious alcoholic, but tonight it was important that Matt drank at least another two or three doubles, otherwise the plan wouldn't work.

'You're always good with advice. I don't know what I'm going to do about her. I just think I'm a little too wild for her, right? She always wants to do the kind of things her parents do – go to Suffolk and see the rest of her family, go hiking, stuff like that. I don't know what she's going to do with a degree in urban planning. I don't think she knows, either. She says she wants to become a member of the Royal Town Planning Institute, like her old man, but she's doing it for his sake.'

'You have to stop worrying about it so much, Matt. Take things as they come.'

'I can't this week, you know that. There's too much at stake now. Look at me, I'm shaking.'

'Let me get you another cocktail.'

They drank until the bar became too noisy and crowded. When Matt slithered down from his stool to weave his way towards the bathroom, it was obvious that he was trashed. The rising temperature and the accelerating beats had conspired to increase the pace of their drinking.

OK, while Matt's gone you've got less than a minute to dig into his backpack and see what's there. Evidence, evidence – mobile, laptop, what else has he got? Now put everything back before he reappears. Done it – did he notice anything? No, he looks out of it.

'It's getting late, let's get out of here.' Matt jammed his hat back on his head.

The cold air outside was a sobering shock. It was important to get Matt into the warmth of the station before he became too sharp. They tumbled down the steps into Liverpool Street Tube and made their way to the Circle Line.

There were no empty seats, so they sat on the platform floor to wait for the train.

Matt tried to focus. 'I've got to stop drinking Smith & Wessons, nobody knows how to mix them properly. They're meant to taste like a liquidized Cuban cigar.'

'Yes, you told me that before.'

Matt massaged his forehead. 'My brain's banging against

the sides of my skull. If I still feel like this in the morning I'm going to cut my first lecture.'

'It's your call, I suppose, but you seem to be missing an awful lot of them lately.'

The train arrived and they lurched to their feet. Inside, unable to sit, they stood jammed against the curving doors of the carriage. Racing through the uphill tunnels towards the King's Cross interchange, it was necessary to keep a surreptitious eye on Matt. The thought came unbidden: *why did you ever put up with him?* The amazing thing was that everyone seemed to idolize the guy. He was a walking disaster, yet the scruffier he looked and the more chaotic his life became, the more they hung on his every word. Especially other girls, the ones from outside the group, they couldn't get enough—

A buzz emanated from Matt's backpack.

'Damn, that's my phone.' Matt swung the bag from his shoulder and started rooting about inside it.

'You've got reception down here?'

'God, where have you been for the last two years? There's mobile reception everywhere west and south of here now. Hampstead and . . .' a long pause while he tried to frame the thought, 'Old Street, still a problem because of the tunnel depth or something. I dunno. Where the hell . . .' The contents of his bag were tumbling over people's feet: a dirty ball of stained T-shirts, some books with loose pages, half a dozen plastic pens, his mobile—

'Here, let me give you a hand.' Together they started shovelling everything back into the bag. Matt helplessly attempted to pick up the fluttering pages. Then the train was slowing and they were arriving at King's Cross.

'Come on, you have to change here. Zip up your bag.'

Matt followed, lurching from the carriage and along the platform.

The scabrous, half-retiled tunnel led to stairs, but Matt baulked before climbing them. 'Give me a minute,' he protested, holding back in an attempt to steady himself, like a sailor in a storm. His chest was wheezing. Three teenaged girls passed them, heading towards the exit. A few tourists were dragging cases; a smartly dressed young couple and a drunk middle-aged man passed; after a few more seconds, there was no one else.

'Hang on, I have to tell Ruby—'

'You don't, you're fine.'

'No, have to do it . . . always letting her down . . . promised to say when I was on my way.' He rummaged in his bag for his mobile and still managed to fire off a text in record time. The effort of concentrating so hard nearly made him fall over.

'It's OK, I've got you. Wait, wait.' It was time to produce the inhaler. 'Here, you left it in the bar. You should be more careful. You know how Ruby gets when you've been smoking and drinking.'

'Yeah, she can be a pain,' said Matt, compliantly opening his mouth and sticking out a furry tongue.

'Put your tongue in. Come on, Matt, you know how to do this.'

'OK.' He was finally ready. 'God, it tastes like—'

'That's because you've been hammering the cocktails tonight.' Anyone coming? No, the coast was clear. 'Look, I have to get you home.'

'I'm meeting—'

'I know, I heard. Don't worry, I can fix that.'

'The train—'

'Come on, concentrate on the stairs, you can do it.'

There was the depth-charge rumble of a train arriving, the last southbound Piccadilly Line trip of the night. A plug of warm air pulsed in the tunnel and lifted a newspaper. Pages drifted past as if brought to life.

Something was happening to Matthew Hillingdon. He felt himself rising, moving. *Everyone likes me*, thought Matt. *It's so great that everyone wants me to succeed, but they don't know my secret. The secret is that I can't help myself.* Everything he ever did was because others told him to. Even when he could sense that their advice was hopelessly misguided, he followed it. He was like a stick in a drain, swirling around and heading for the gutter, but someone was always there to pull him out in time. *She's always there for me*, he thought. *Girls are great, they'll give you, like, six or seven chances at least, if they really like you.* Lately, though, events had been shifting beyond his comprehension. You had to trust your friends, though, didn't you? Otherwise you had nothing.

He was having trouble lifting his legs. Now his right arm was tingling. He'd drunk more than this before without losing control of his limbs. Weird.

The feeling got worse. Was this what dying felt like? *My neurons are being deprived of oxygen*, he thought. *It just feels like I'm falling very gently. Swirling around and around, towards the gutter.*

I'm one of life's naturally lucky guys, he told himself. *What a charmed life I lead, there's always someone there to catch me when I fall. I think I'm falling faster now. And there's someone right here to catch me again. How perfect is that?*

21

ALPHA MALES

Wednesday's dawn was fierce and raw, low crimson light splashing the sides of the glass offices in Canary Wharf. A turbulent sky of sharp blue cloud unfurled over the frothing reaches of the river. John May leaned against the railing of his steel balcony on the fourth floor of Shad Thames, and drew in the brackish smell of the tide. As a child, he had played on the shore below these windows. *I haven't strayed very far from home in my life*, he thought. *How we love to tether ourselves.*

Leaning over the rail, he looked down at the pebbles stained with patches of verdigris, wondering if the sand beneath held the memory of his footprints. His mother had once lost a bracelet while chasing him along the shore. Was it still buried in the mud, another layer of London's history? Although the embankments had been transformed, the cranes and wharves giving way to boxy riverview apartments, the shoreline had hardly changed at all. It seemed strange that he and the other kids had once swum here. Surely the water was cleaner now, free of tyres and trolleys and iridescent lumps of tar? His sister Gwen had never joined them. Fastidious and superior, she had always sat on the river wall to wait, smoothing her patterned dress, ignoring their yells, biding her time.

He smiled sadly at the thought. Gwen, happily living in Brighton with her extended family, was the only one to have survived unscarred. A strong sense of self-preservation had protected her, but the rest had all suffered in some way. His wife Jane, fragile and disturbed, in Broadhampton Hospital; his daughter Elizabeth, dead; his grandchildren at war with their own devils; and now a new woman in his world, the beautiful, haunted Brigitte, who had called him a few hours ago, drunk again. If he had not been able to help his own family, how would he ever be able to help her?

He listened to the city. A few minutes earlier it had been virtually silent, but almost on the stroke of seven a low, steady roar began and grew, like the sound of factory machinery starting up. It was the hum of engines, the turning of pistons, of voices and vans and coffee machines, of peristaltic traffic and disgorging trains. The sound of London coming to life.

He used the last of his cold coffee to wash down a statin designed to tackle his high cholesterol. As he stood above the water, his thoughts turned to Gloria Taylor's uncomprehending daughter, and his fingers brushed the cotton of his shirt, over the ridged scar on his heart. A five-year-old girl left without a mother. The wound opened by the loss of a life could never be fully healed, but it was the PCU's duty to find a way of restoring balance. He had not been able to save those closest to him, but perhaps he could make a difference in the life of a stranger.

He knew it was what his partner would be trying to do, in his own mad way. Tonight, long after the others had gone home, the top-floor lights in their King's Cross warehouse would be burning as Arthur worked on, driven less by a sense of injustice than the need to solve a puzzle. At least they would work towards the same end. The city was a blind, uneven place where injustices could never be fully righted, just smoothed out a little. With its funding returned, the unit stood a chance of making a difference. If it failed in its first case, the fragile faith it had newly engendered would be destroyed.

He took the circular sticker from his pocket and traced the outline of the figure with his forefinger. It wasn't much to go on, but anything with a connection to the case, no matter how tangential, was worth exploring.

Ruby Cates rented an apartment on the second floor of a house in Mecklenburgh Square, in the back of Bloomsbury. The square, built on the grounds of the Foundling Hospital, had been named in honour of Queen Charlotte. The damage it had sustained in World War Two had been tidily repaired, but the grand square and its spacious roads were little-used and overlooked. At the centre was a high-railed garden filled with mature elms and plane trees, shadowy and vaguely mournful, in the way that empty London squares could feel damp even in high summer.

Ruby answered the door in a sweat-stained red Mets T-shirt, with a white towel knotted around her neck. She was pleasant-faced, but too thin and fiercely blonde, with an intensity in her deep-set eyes that put May on his guard. Having emailed her first thing, he had received an instant reply providing her address and the time she would be at home. She held open the door and started explaining the moment he stepped inside. May saw that the lower half of her left leg was locked in a grey plastic cast.

'I went up to Camden police station but they said I have to wait until tomorrow. I told them there couldn't be any mistake but they weren't interested in listening to me, so I went down to the Tube to check for myself.' Her voice had a soft country burr, Dorset perhaps.

'Come through. This is my kitchen, but the others tend to turn up here for coffee. It's not really fair because they have bigger bedrooms. There's another kitchen upstairs but they use it as a storeroom. There's a mountain bike in it no one's ever ridden. I've learned one thing: never be the only woman in a household of men.' Ruby's kitchen was overflowing with dirty crockery, newspapers, magazines and books. A heavy blue glass ashtray pinned down wayward paperwork. There was a faint smell of tobacco, as if someone had been rolling it from a pouch.

'Under normal circumstances I would have run back up here. I run everywhere. I finished the marathon last year. Not going to do it this time, though.' She knocked on the plastic cast.

'What happened?'

'I was training. Really stupid of me, I slipped off the kerb outside the house and fell badly. I didn't even feel the bone break. I'm working out every day, trying to keep the muscles strong. It should be off soon. I didn't leave details about Matt at the station, so I suppose you're going to take a statement now?'

'I'm sorry, I think we're at cross purposes. This is a routine inquiry about an accident.'

'You're not here about Matthew Hillingdon?'

'No, a chap called Nikos Nicolau gave me your email address.'

'So you haven't spoken to the police at Camden? That's really weird.' Ruby shook the idea around in her head. 'Well, it's good you're here.'

'Why?'

'Because Matt is missing – I reported him missing.'

'Ah – no, I'm not connected with that. I'm tracing a set of these things a girl called Cassie handed out at her bar.' He passed over the plastic sachet containing the sticker.

'But you must have known something. Matt has one of these things on his computer bag.'

'I think you'd better start from the beginning,' said May, sitting down.

'Matthew Hillingdon is a friend of mine. Well, maybe a bit more than a friend – I've been seeing him. He lives here.' She paced awkwardly to the window and back, unable to settle. 'We study together at UCL. We were supposed to be meeting up last night, but he never showed.'

'And you went to the police?'

'As soon as he failed to appear. I know, I know, you're going to say I was overreacting – that's what they said – but I had my reasons. I haven't heard from him since.'

'But if it was only last night . . .'

'He texted me just as he was entering King's Cross Station and said he'd be on the last train, OK? He'd been out drinking at some bar in Spitalfields.' She dug her mobile from her pocket and showed him the message. '*At KX just made last train C U 2mins*'. The call register showed that the text was sent at 12:20 a.m. 'He was probably pretty pissed.'

'What makes you say that?'

'He has a habit of texting me when he's had too many, because if he calls I'll hear him slurring his words, and he knows I don't approve of him getting wasted when he's got a lecture the next morning.'

'Does he get drunk a lot?'

'Yes, lately. He's under a lot of pressure. He's got money worries. And he's finding the course difficult.'

'Did he tell you who he was drinking with?'

'No, one of his classmates, probably. But look at the time of the call. He always catches the Tube, so he'd have come on the Circle, Metropolitan or Hammersmith & City Line, and changed on to the Piccadilly at King's Cross. We both know that the last train goes at 12:24 a.m. I was waiting by the exit at the next stop, Russell Square. The train only takes two minutes, and came in at 12:26, but he wasn't on it.'

'Maybe there's another way out of the station.'

'No, I've waited there often enough, there's only one exit and I was there, right at the barrier, as always.'

'Then he must have missed it.'

'He'd have walked down to me. It doesn't take long.'

'He could have chosen not to catch the train for some reason.'

'In that case, why would he bother to call and tell me he'd be on it?'

'The London Underground is the most heavily monitored system in the world,' May said. 'There are some things we can do to establish where your friend went. But before I start that process, I need you to be absolutely sure about the facts.'

'If you knew me, Mr May, you'd know I'm sure.'

'One thing at a time. Tell me about the sticker.'

'I don't know anything more. It was on his bag, that's all. They're from the Karma Bar. All the geeks have them. I said I wouldn't call them geeks, but it's just that they hang out together so much and they never stop working.'

'And you also have one.' May pointed at the label on Ruby's backpack.

Below them, the doorbell rang. 'Excuse me for a moment,' said Ruby.

'Do you want me to get it? Your leg . . .'

'I can manage.'

May walked over to the kitchen table and thumbed through a paperback. He heard the slam of the front door, followed by thumping footsteps on the stairs.

The wild-haired Indian student who appeared in the doorway did not bother introducing himself. He was trying to prevent a fat stack of papers from sliding out of a plastic wallet, which was splitting under several loose items of shopping. 'Have you seen Theo?' he asked Ruby.

'I think he had a meeting with one of his tutors. Why on earth didn't you get a bag?'

'I forgot. Don't start. I don't know what he's bloody playing at. Did Matt leave me any money?'

'He didn't turn up last night. I'm really upset, actually. Are you making toasted sandwiches?'

'You know I am, I don't know why you always have to ask.' The boy stamped off up the stairs.

'That was Rajan,' Ruby explained, 'he has the room above this one.' She did not seem pleased to see him.

'Who else lives here?' May asked. He had forgotten the

peculiar atmosphere of urgency, languor and confusion that could be detected in student digs.

'Apart from Matt, there's a guy called Toby Brooke, then there's Nikos Nicolau and the guy you just saw, Rajan Sangeeta. Theo Fontvieille has the top floor because his rich parents own the building, and we pay his family the rent direct, so it gets kind of feudal around here just before rent day.'

'And you,' May reminded.

'They gave me the attic at first. I wanted to change rooms so I wouldn't have to go up and down the stairs all the time, but of course I'm a mere girl, so my vote didn't count until Theo stepped in and supported me. We have too many alpha males living under one roof. The competitiveness drives me crazy sometimes.'

'Are you in the same field of studies?'

'Toby, Theo, Matt and Rajan are all taking social engineering together.'

'That sounds rather Nietzschean.'

'It's a branch of urban planning, they're happy to explain it to anyone who listens. Nikos's aiming for a degree in biochemistry. The rest of his family owns restaurants, and they're very anxious to ensure that he passes. Theo's in line to inherit his parents' fortune and doesn't have to study, so he's just doing it for fun.'

'Why were you meeting Matthew Hillingdon at Russell Square Tube?'

'We were going to go to the Horse Hospital. I mean, it's not a horse hospital any more, although it's still got cobblestones and there are horse ramps inside. It's a club, stays open until two. My leg was hurting like hell, but I wanted to spend some time with Matt. Have you got a cigarette?'

'I don't smoke. So you're at the same college?'

'I'm a second-year research student, doing bioinformatics.'

'I'm afraid I have no idea what that is.'

'It's mostly about searching databases for protein modelling and sequence alignment.'

'How long have you been seeing Mr Hillingdon?'

'He's missing – you don't need to know about our private lives, do you?'

'No, but I might find something you haven't thought of. Please.'

'Well, we've been dating about four months. He's very sweet, a bit helpless. Probably needs a mother more than a girlfriend. I met him at the Karma Bar. Some of the stuff he's studying crosses over with the others, which is how they met. He specializes in the analysis of pedestrian traffic flow in urban areas. He's very goal-oriented, works long hours.'

'And sometimes forgets about meeting you?' added May.

'It's happened before. But not this time, I'm sure of it. When I spoke to him, he was definitely catching that train.' She checked her watch. 'I'm due at a class.'

'I'll walk down with you.'

The sound of The Avalanches playing over the roar of an engine outside sent Ruby to the landing window. 'Here's another one,' she told May. 'Theo's probably the richest guy in the whole of UCL. His father owns, like, half of Hertfordshire or something.'

'That would explain the car,' said May, impressed. Fontvieille was driving a new red Porsche Carrera, a beacon of conspicuous consumption branded with the numberplate THEO 1. He was unfolding himself from the driver's seat as May arrived back on the street.

'Theo, this is John May. He's from—'

'The Peculiar Crimes Unit,' May explained, holding out his hand. 'We've met.'

'I thought you were a little too old to be a foot soldier. Peculiar Crimes Unit? What's that?' The surname might have been French, but he had no trace of an accent. Although he shook hands, Fontvieille was clearly keen to get inside.

'It's a specialist detection unit.'

'I don't understand, why are you here? Ruby, what have you been up to?' Although he could have been no older than twenty-one, Fontvieille had the patrician air of some-one mature, confident and secure in his wealth. Tanned and moisturized, his long black hair sleekly groomed, he was dressed in a grey hooded top and jeans too well cut to be confused with the kind generally worn on the street. His clothes were bookended with a red silk scarf and red leather trainers that perfectly matched his car. He might have been a model or a city executive, except that there was a discordant note in his appearance that May couldn't nail down.

'This young lady has lost a friend,' he said.

'What's he talking about? Ruby, who have you lost?'

'Matt's been missing since last night.'

'You know he doesn't always come home.'

'He was supposed to be with me.' She was clearly uncomfortable arguing about a mutual friend in front of May.

'You've got to give the guy a bit of room to manoeuvre, he's really stressed out at the moment.'

'That's easy for you to say, Theo, you never get worried about anything. You don't have to worry.' It sounded like a put-down. *She's wrong*, thought May, who had pinpointed what was bothering him. Theo Fontvieille looked as if he had not enjoyed a good night's sleep in a week. Beneath his smooth tan were fault-lines and shadows.

'I've got to get going,' said Theo. 'I'm meeting Rajan, running late. Is he up in his room?'

'God, you guys hang out together every night – don't you ever get tired of each other's company?' She sounded jealous.

'Ask me in five years' time, when we're running the country. Nice to meet you again, Mr May – and Ruby, when you find Matt tell him he owes me fifty quid.' Theo swung a smart red leather case on to his shoulder and bounded up the stairs.

'Not the bookish type?' May suggested.

'I'm sure he only attends UCL to annoy the rest of us, he makes it all seem so easy. He'll go to an all-night party, then come back and knock out a paper that will have his lecturers mooning over him for weeks.'

'No Karma Bar logo,' May noted.

'Theo wouldn't be seen dead sticking a cheap club advert on his fine Italian leather. I fear our common ways don't appeal to him.' *She hates him*, thought May. *Just because of his money, or is there something else? Perhaps that's not hatred in her eyes but something quite the opposite.*

'All right,' he said, 'I'll cut a deal with you. Keep your eyes open for any more of these stickers, and I'll see if I can get you some information on Mr Hillingdon's whereabouts today, to save you waiting for the regular police.'

'You could do that? I'd be really grateful. I wouldn't have gone to the police if I wasn't worried.' She shook his hand. 'He has . . . a history . . . of being found in unlikely places, rather the worse for wear.'

Strange, thought May as he walked away along the rainy street, *she showed little interest in why I had come to see her. She didn't ask me anything. Presumably too preoccupied with the missing boyfriend. But then there's the book.*

He had seen a bright-yellow paperback on her kitchen table, packed with bookmarks and Post-it notes. It had set him wondering if she had deliberately chosen to tell him lies.

May looked back up at the house, and thought he saw Ruby's face at the rain-streaked second-floor window, staring blankly down at him. A moment later, it was gone.

22

THE GHOST SYSTEM

Late on Wednesday morning, the two detectives stood in their usual positions, side by side, leaning on the balustrade of Waterloo Bridge, looking into the heart of the city. The clouds moved like freighters, flat-bottomed and dark, laden with incoming cargoes of rain. Bryant had ill-advisedly washed his favourite trilby after venturing into snowdrifts in an earlier case, and its brim had lost all shape. With his hands stuffed in the voluminous pockets of his ratty tweed overcoat and the backs of his trouser bottoms touching the pavement, he appeared to be vanishing entirely inside his clothes. It seemed that a breeze might come along and blow what was left of this bag of rags into the river.

May, on the other hand, stood with his back erect in a smart navy-blue Savile Row suit, his blue silk tie knotted over a freshly pressed shirt, his white cuffs studded with silver links. As rain began to fall, he unfurled a perfect black umbrella and held it over them. Whenever May felt that his life lacked order, he redressed the balance by sprucing up.

It had commonly been noted that anyone becoming involved with one had to accept the priority of the other. This fact had resulted in two lifetimes of dissatisfying romantic attachments, but could not be helped. To remove either would have been like cutting away a supporting vine, and would have created a sense of misfortune in both that no woman would have been able to forgive herself for.

'Sorry to drag you down here,' said Bryant. 'Old habits die hard. I needed to come and do some thinking. I was going to try the Millennium Bridge, but there are too many tourists.'

'That's OK.' May leaned forward to watch a police launch chug under an arch. 'Brigitte called late last night. She wants me to come and visit her in Paris.'

'I bet she was drunk.'

'She was, a bit.'

'I hope you told her you're in the middle of an important investigation.'

'I said I'd go if we could close the case and stabilize the unit. But we're not getting anywhere fast, are we, and unless something breaks . . .'

'It will. If we fail the Taylor woman, we'll have struck out twice in a row. There won't be a third chance. How did you get on with your student?'

'She thought I'd come to visit her because she'd reported her boyfriend missing,' May explained. 'Reckons he disappeared at King's Cross Station early this morning.'

Bryant's ears pricked up. 'Strange coincidence.'

'Most of the other students in the house had the same

altered sticker on their bags. And I saw something in her flat that bothered me.'

'Oh, snooping around, were you?'

'Hardly. It was on the kitchen table, in plain sight. A pocket guide to the haunted stations of the London Underground called *Mind the Ghosts*, with her name pencilled inside. It resonated a little too much with what she was saying. I swiped it. Here.' He pulled the dog-eared paperback from his pocket and passed it to Bryant. 'Take a look at Chapter Six. She's bookmarked a section about the ghost of a girl called Annie Evans.'

'This is more my territory than yours. I'm impressed you'd think of it.' Bryant dug out his reading glasses, wound them around his ears and found the passage. 'Says here "a sickly child, imprisoned, starved and beaten to death by the woman who employed her, in 1758". I'm not entirely with you.'

'If you look at the next page, it explains that her ghost is supposed to haunt Russell Square Tube Station between midnight and one a.m. The guards hear her running along the platform, but as soon as she boards a carriage she vanishes. The girl I saw, Ruby Cates, said she had been waiting at Russell Square for her boyfriend under identical circumstances.'

'So you think she read this and concocted the story?'

'I really don't know what to think. I mean, what would she have to gain by doing so? And why bother to report him missing at all?'

'You know, you're finally starting to think like me. Leave me the book and I'll see if there's anything you missed.'

'Be my guest.'

'Students,' Bryant sighed. 'They're all so impatient to get on with their careers now. Why can't they go back to smoking pot and talking rubbish like in the good old days?'

'At least they're not scruffy any more.'

'Oh, you think anyone who doesn't wear a tie is scruffy. Your mother started your toilet training too early. I've watched you in restaurants, lining up your knife and fork with the edges of your napkin. And that new flat of yours, so bare that it looks like the furniture delivery van took a wrong turn and never found the place.'

'I can't abide clutter, you know that. Rooms reveal the inner workings of the mind. I just thought it was odd that she had left the book out, that's all.'

Bryant perused the chapter. 'I say, listen to this – the section has been underlined. "Thirteen-year-old Annie Evans, a child of sickly nature, locked in a cupboard for three years, left unfed and repeatedly beaten by her employer with a broom handle. She escaped twice but was sent back to the house both times. Died from infection and multiple fractures, compounded by malnourishment. Her maggot-filled body remained in the attic for two months, because her employer feared it would provide clear evidence that she had been brutalized. The property stood on the site of Russell Square Tube. Parts of her burned body were found in Chick Lane gully-hole by the nightwatchman, and were taken to the coroner. Her employer was brought to trial at the Old Bailey and was found guilty, after being turned in by her own daughter. On certain nights, just past the hour of midnight, the ghost of Annie Evans still appears in the last train at Russell Square Station, only to vanish just as suddenly."'

'The house where Ruby's boyfriend lives is full of students studying public-transport systems and traffic control,' said May. 'Funny how everything keeps coming back to the London Underground.'

'Not really,' Bryant argued. 'This guide has a UCL library tag. It's a bit of light reading for anyone studying transport systems. Besides, you can't help but be aware of the tunnels beneath your feet when you walk around the city.' He thumped his walking stick on the pavement. 'I always think that the system operates as a kind of ghost London, just below street level. Its routes mirror the streets, which in turn follow the hedgerows marking out the city's ancient boundaries. So you could say that the Underground provides us with a kind of spiritual blueprint for the passage of London's residents.'

'No, I'm not buying that,' May declared. 'There's nothing at all spiritual about the Underground railway, just tunnels full of mice and dust.'

'But it's also a closed system filled with dead ends and unrealized plans, and that makes it fascinating. All the stations that were excavated and never opened, the platforms that were used to hide art masterpieces in the war, follies like the theatre train that only ran in one direction. And of course there's a lot more Underground than just the Tube network. I heard tell of a huge shelter beneath Clapham where the authorities chose to leave all the *Windrush* passengers.' The *Empire Windrush* ship had docked in June 1948, carrying nearly five hundred West Indian immigrants, ready to start new lives in the UK. Their arrival sparked a national debate about identity, and exposed deep prejudices. 'Supposedly, the families were fed up with being forced to live in the shelter, and came above ground to make Brixton the strong ethnic enclave it is today. You can't hide people away; they find ways to blossom.'

'You know your trouble?' said May. 'You're a hopeless romantic. You see a bit of old tunnel and imagine it's a secret passage to another world. Nothing's ever straightforward with you, it always has to have a hidden meaning. You have too much imagination. You don't believe in filling out a tax form, but you believe in ghosts.'

'Of course. What about all the lives lost and changed below ground?' Bryant's rising passion changed the colour of his nose in the cold air. 'I honestly believe that the rules are different down there. The suicides, the crash victims, the missed liaisons, the romances and betrayals, the lovers parting or rushing to meet each other. Don't you think something of them has been left behind within those curving tiled walls?'

'The only things they leave behind are bits of dead skin and the odd newspaper,' said May. 'You know how many deaths there are on the Underground every year?'

Bryant peered out from beneath the ridiculous brim of his hat. 'I've no idea.'

'Well neither do I, but I bet it's a lot, and no reasons ever come to light about why these things happen – they just happen, and that's all there is to it. Now you've had me standing here in the freezing rain for ages – let's head back to the Tube.'

'The station guards I went to see might be able to help us,' said Bryant, clattering his stick against the railings like a schoolboy as they walked. 'They can pull up camera footage of the entrance hall, the escalators and the platform, and form a sort of visual mosaic that shows the boy's movements.'

'Fine, give me your contact there and I'll call them now, get them ready for our arrival.'

'This lad Matthew, he's not been missing for very long.' Bryant pushed up his hat and fixed his partner with an aqueous blue eye. 'He'll turn up at a friend's flat with a flaming hangover. We have to concentrate on closing up the Taylor case.'

'Giles Kershaw isn't prepared to write it off as misadventure. He's convinced she was pushed.'

'He has no hard evidence for that.'

'Well, it must have been a complete stranger, because it's not someone from her past. Taylor was ostracized by her family because of the pregnancy, but was on good terms with the father. She overcame the problems caused by her breakdown. Everyone at work liked her. There's no one else. All we can do is keep on tracking witnesses.'

'Gloria Taylor couldn't see her attacker, but the killer was also denied the satisfaction of eye contact with his victim. It was the act of an angry coward who simply wanted to maim someone.'

'I imagine it's a bit too mundane for you,' said May. 'Not weird enough, a woman falling down some stairs. The sticker on her back was the only mark of interest. You were secretly hoping it was a sign that she belonged to some kind of secret society.'

Bryant pursed his lips, annoyed. 'No,' he said, 'I was hoping it was a sign that her killer does.' He gave his partner an affectionate pat on the back. 'Come on, a quick cup of tea first, then we'll see if we can find your student.

You're right, of course. We should concentrate on clearing up one mystery at a time. But the missing boy and the book of ghosts, they're – well, suggestive.'

May could not resist asking, 'Of what?'

'Oh, of an entirely different direction,' said Bryant, and he would not be further drawn.

23

LAST TRAIN

'I didn't think we'd get you back so soon,' said Anjam Dutta, the security expert at North One Watch, the King's Cross Surveillance Centre. The luminescent monitors surrounding him showed such long queues building up at the ticket windows that temporary barriers had been installed to filter passengers. Dutta saw them watching the screens.

'We've got a new office building just opened this month and two new blocks of student accommodation, totalling an extra 2,200 potential passengers, and they're nearly all Tube users. Usually it wouldn't make a difference but a couple of trade fairs just opened on Monday, one at the Excel Centre, the other at Earl's Court, and there are a lot of visitors staying in the nearby hotels. We can regulate the number of people entering the station by reducing surface access, but we've already had to shut off the escalators several times this week because of passenger overload. The system works on the probability ratio of a certain number of travellers per day, and has trouble coping with unexpected demand.'

'I noticed you're renovating some of the platform and tunnel walls as well,' said May. 'How do you cope with that?'

'The equipment is stowed during Tube working hours, but it means a couple of the monitors are disengaged. When you've only got four hours a night to find an electrical fault, it can take several days to sort out. What can I do for you gentlemen today? Is this about the escalator footage?'

'No, it's a new problem that may be related. We've lost someone. He was supposed to catch the last southbound Piccadilly Line train last night. A student called Matthew Hillingdon.'

'It would have passed through here at 12:24 a.m. The service was good last night. There's a Northern Line train three minutes later and then that's your lot until the next morning.'

'Ridiculous that we don't have a twenty-four-hour system,' Bryant complained. 'We know he called his girlfriend from – what's the nearest point to the trains that still has mobile reception?'

'That would be the lower hall.'

'Below the escalators?'

'He'd get general coverage until about halfway down the final flight of stairs, but some networks have transmitter points on the Piccadilly. Who was he with?'

'Virgin,' May remembered.

'He would have been able to transmit as far as the interchange, but not on the platform.'

'He texted her from King's Cross at 12:20 a.m., a bit the

worse for wear. He'd been out with a mate and was heading for Russell Square Tube.'

'It's only a two-minute journey.'

'I know, but he never made it. I need to find out whether he got on the train. If he didn't, perhaps we can see which exit he used from the station and collect witnesses from that point.'

'OK, give us a couple of minutes. Everything's digitally backed up 24/7, so it shouldn't be hard to nail. Most of the cameras are recording constantly. As you pointed out, a couple of tunnels are being retiled, so they're not fully covered, but we can pick up action on the platform overheads.'

The detectives seated themselves in the darkened room and watched the screens around them. 'Look at all these passengers. Why do people have to move about so much?' asked Bryant irritably. 'Everyone would get a lot more done if they just stayed in one place.'

'You're a fine one to talk,' May replied. 'You can't sit still for a minute.' He looked back at the screens. 'They're like blood cells pulsing through an artery.'

'That's what they are. They're feeding the city with energy. There's no pushing or shoving; it's so orderly and purposeful. Rather beautiful to watch.'

'OK, we have this now.' Dutta punched a series of illuminated keys on what looked like a studio mixing board, and footage speckled through one of the monitors. 'I'm starting it from 12:17 a.m. The left screen is the camera footage covering the interchange tunnels from the Circle to the Piccadilly Line. I've got another one covering the main entrance, but from what you're saying there was no reason for him to leave the station. There are two ways of switching lines, depending on which end of the platform you're coming from. The main problem is that one of the tunnel cameras was out, and one currently has restricted vision.'

'That's not very efficient, is it?'

'Not our fault. Health & Safety carried out a junction install that's affected some of the camera sightlines. We're waiting to get the mountings re-sited. That's not public knowledge, though, so we're pretty well covered. The cameras are still up there. As long as people think they're being watched, they behave themselves. What does your man look like?'

May passed over a photograph showing Matthew Hillingdon in a brown woollen hat and a long grey overcoat sewn with thin rainbow stripes. 'He was hardly ever seen wearing anything else,' he explained.

'Well, it's distinctive.' Dutta's nimble fingers tapped at the speed controls as he checked the images. 'The Tube is still busy up to the minutes just before the last train, then it empties fast. Most Londoners have a pretty good idea how late they can leave it to get home. Is that him?'

'Too short,' said May.

'How about this one?'

The images in front of them fractured into blurred squares, then slowed and restored themselves as a man in a dark raincoat entered from the right of the camera field.

'Similar – but no, I don't think so.'

Dutta tried again. 'How about this one?'

'That looks like him.' May tapped at the rainbow coat.

May checked the screen's time readout, which had ticked to 12:21 a.m. The boy wavered at the far side of the screen. He was putting his mobile away, but appeared to be having trouble finding his pocket. Now they could clearly see the top of his brown woollen cap. Hillingdon had trouble staying upright as he staggered towards the stairs. There was a brief dark blur to his left.

'Wait, is there somebody with him?'

Dutta dialled the speed down to single frames. The blur vanished. 'If there was, they knew how to stay out of the shot.'

'He's very drunk. Can you get him from another camera?'

'No, that's the one that's out.'

Hillingdon had passed beyond the camera's range now. The scene showed the shadowed empty arch of the half-tiled tunnel.

'There are two more cameras between the boy and the train,' Dutta explained. 'One is situated in the short stairway leading to the platform, the other is on the platform itself.'

The detectives watched the deserted staircase, waiting for Hillingdon to appear. The time readout said 12:23 a.m. Suddenly a drunken figure burst into the frame, striped coat-tails flying. He virtually fell down the steps in his rush to get to the platform.

'Hillingdon's got less than a minute before the train is due, so can we assume he heard it approaching through the tunnel?' asked May. 'Do your guards stop people boarding trains when they're plastered?'

'If they look like they're a danger to themselves,' said Dutta. 'Hillingdon's borderline. We get much worse. I don't think there was anyone in the immediate area. More crucially, it probably wasn't picked up on the monitors. It'll be easy to check and see who was on duty.'

The screen was empty now. The stairwell's fixed camera could only catch a figure passing through. Dutta switched screens, searching the tiled labyrinth.

'Now this last camera is moveable and has a large wide-angle lens. It's in the centre of the roof above the platform, and we can see everything that's going on. It slowly pans back and forth to build a picture of the level as a whole. Plus, we can zoom in and pull off detailed shots, but they're quite distorted. It's really for general surveillance. Our clearest ID shots all come from the barriers rather than the platforms.'

He twisted a dial back and forth, and the image of the platform shifted from one end to the other. The time readout was now at 12:24 a.m. There were four other passengers waiting for the train: a middle-aged Chinese couple and two young black girls.

'Would it be hard to get witness traces on them?'

'Not if they used Oyster cards. They can't be tracked if they just bought tickets, although we might get general descriptions from the counter staff. But only tourists use the windows.'

'Here it comes, right on schedule.'

They watched as the silvered carriages slid sleekly into the station. The camera had lost Hillingdon. The doors opened. Dutta panned the device back along the platform. At the last moment Matt Hillingdon's striped overcoat and woollen hat shot into view. He was moving with dangerous speed. It clearly required a superhuman effort to jump the gap into the carriage, but he made it just before the doors closed. In fact, the door shut on the tail of Hillingdon's coat, trapping it.

'I'm annoyed about this,' said Dutta. 'Somebody really should have cautioned him.'

They watched as the student pulled at the tail of his coat, which remained trapped in the door. A moment later, the carriage doors opened again while he was still pulling, so that he fell over, vanishing from view.

'If you ever see me that drunk,' said May, 'shoot me.'

'The train remained here a little longer than usual. The last one of the night often does that, to pick up the last few stragglers,' said Dutta, accelerating the footage. He slowed it down once more as the Tube doors opened and closed, and the train started to move out.

'If Hillingdon got on the 12:24 a.m. he could have fallen asleep and missed his stop,' May suggested.

'The stations are only a couple of minutes apart,' said Bryant. 'If he knocked himself out when he fell, we'd have heard about it by now. I think it's more likely that your Miss Cates lied. She might be playing you for a fool.'

'She seemed sincere enough.' May frowned, puzzling. 'I don't see what she would have to gain by making up the episode.'

'To throw you off the track of something else?' Bryant suggested. 'You said she'd been reading about vanishing passengers. It looks to me like they're in it together.'

'Then where did he go?' asked May.

Bryant pulled his sagging trilby back on to the crown of his head. 'Next stop, Russell Square,' he replied.

24

PHANTOM PASSENGER

Shiny red arches, leaf-green corridors: the Tube stations of London had once sported a uniform look, just as the roads had been matched in neat black and white stripes. In the 1980s they received a disastrous cosmetic makeover. Ignoring the fact that the system was coming apart at the seams, lavish artworks were commissioned and left unfinished, stations were closed instead of being repaired, and only a handful of the oldest remained unspoiled. Russell Square was one of the few that survived. Similar in style to the Tube at Mornington Crescent, the frontage of crimson tiles, the blue glass canopy and the arched first-floor windows remained intact. The station was largely used by tourists and students staying in the nearby hotels and hostels, so the entrance was always crowded with visitors consulting maps.

Mr Gregory, the stationmaster, was a thin, peppery man with a face that, even in repose, made him look as if he was about to sneeze. He greeted the detectives with a decongestion stick wedged up his right nostril. 'I'm sorry,' he apologized, 'my passages get bunged up in dusty atmospheres.'

'You picked the wrong job, then, didn't you?' said Bryant with an unsympathetic laugh.

'It's not the station, it's pollen from over there.' Mr Gregory pointed to the tree-filled square that stood diagonally across from them. 'Too much bloody fresh air coming in.' He led the way behind the barriers, ushering them through. 'Can I get you anything?'

'A cup of tea and a Garibaldi biscuit would hit the spot.' Bryant looked around the monitoring station, a small bare room with just two monochrome monitors on a desk, one focussed on each of the platforms. 'You don't have a camera over the entrance door?'

'No, someone's always here keeping an eye out. It's an old-fashioned system, but I find it works well enough. LU Head Office wasn't happy, but I told them not everything has to be high-tech. That's an original Victorian canopy. I don't want dirty great holes drilled through it.'

'A man after my own heart,' Bryant agreed, finding a place to sit.

'A Mr Dutta from King's Cross called and told me you were on your way. He said you wanted to see the arrival of yesterday's 12:26 a.m. It'll take me a few minutes to cue up the footage. Our regular security bloke isn't here today, he's up before Haringey Magistrates' Court for gross indecency outside the headquarters of the Dagenham Girl Pipers.'

'So you're not fond of fresh air, then,' said May, changing the subject with less fluidity than he'd hoped.

'Not really, no.' Mr Gregory sniffed. 'My lungs can't cope.'

'Only people usually complain about the poor air quality down there.'

Mr Gregory looked aghast. 'That's rubbish. Travelling on the Tube for forty minutes is the equivalent to smoking two cigarettes, so I save a bit on fags. Plus it's about ten degrees warmer on the platforms in winter. I've worked for London Transport for over twenty years, and I've got a lot of mates down the tunnels. There's the casual workers, your economic migrants who're just doing it for a job, like, and then there's your tubeheads. It's a place where you can forget the rest of the world.'

'So is the Foreign Legion, but that doesn't make it a good thing,' Bryant pointed out.

'I hold the world record for visiting all 287 stations in one go, you know,' Mr Gregory told them. As a conversational gambit it was chancey at best. 'I did the entire network in eighteen hours, twenty minutes.'

'Is that a popular sport?'

'Oh yes.'

'You do surprise me.' Bryant pantomimed stifling a yawn.

'People have been beating the time since 1960. There's a set of rules laid down by *The Guinness Book of Records*, but that's just the start – we also hold the annual Tube Olympics, and there are all sorts of challenges.'

'Really,' said Bryant flatly.

'Oh yes, like the ABC challenge – that's where we have to visit twenty-six Tube stations in alphabetical order. The current record for that is five hours twenty minutes. And the Bottle challenge . . .'

'What's that?' asked May, trying to show an interest while they watched for the footage.

'Look at the centre of the Underground map,' Mr Gregory instructed him. 'The lines form the shape of a bottle on its side. That's the circuit. My aim is to beat the record of two hours thirteen minutes.'

'This is all very riveting,' said Bryant, 'but might we get back to the matter in hand?'

'Here we go. The train came in just under a minute late.' The station-master clicked off the lights, and the trio watched the screen.

The monitor revealed an angled shot of the silver carriages pulling into the platform. 'Can you home in on a specific carriage?' May asked.

'Which one do you want?'

'The third from the end.'

'Which end?'

May decided not to point out that there was only one end to a train arriving at a station, for fear of sounding pedantic. The stationmaster expertly panned along the train and settled the screen on the correct carriage. The shot was just wide enough to include all three exit doors, which now slid open. Inside, all was bright and bare.

'I don't believe it,' Bryant exclaimed. 'The damned thing's empty!'

'There must be some mistake,' May told the stationmaster. 'This can't be the right train.'

Mr Gregory tapped the numerals at the bottom of the screen with his forefinger. 'That's the time-code, 12:27 a.m., right there. There's no tampering with that.'

'You're sure this is yesterday?'

'Definitely. And it's the last train through. The journey took two minutes fifty seconds.'

'We saw him get on,' said Bryant. 'Could the train have stopped anywhere on the way?'

'No, there's no junction at Russell Square, it's a straight line without any branch-offs. Even if it halted for some reason, the doors wouldn't open. Nobody could have got out. You can interview the train driver if you want, but he'll tell you the same thing.'

'What about between the carriages? The connecting doors are kept unlocked, aren't they?'

'That's right, but they only open into other carriages, so no one could get off. Let's see who alighted here.' Mr Gregory panned along the entire length of the train. 'There you are, only two passengers.' He zoomed in on them. One was a small elderly man laden with plastic shopping bags, barely five feet tall, and the other was an overweight, middle-aged Nigerian woman.

'I don't suppose he could have disguised himself?' asked Bryant. 'In order to give his girlfriend the slip?'

Mr Gregory zoomed the camera in, first on the old man, then on the Nigerian woman. Even a master of disguise would have been unable to transform himself into either of these characters.

'Could he have let himself into the driver's cockpit somehow?'

'Not a chance, it's dead-bolted.'

'Then he must simply have stayed on board the train.'

Mr Gregory reversed the footage and panned along each of the carriages while the train stood with its doors open. They zoomed in on all of the few remaining passengers, but there was no one in a striped coat and woollen cap. 'See for yourself. I don't know where you think he could have gone, unless he found a way of tearing the seats up and hiding inside them.'

'You're telling me a six-foot-tall student vanished into thin air on board a moving train?' Bryant complained.

'No,' said Mr Gregory, 'you're telling *me*.' He shoved the inhaler back up his nose and snorted hard.

On their way back out of the station, the detectives passed a neat row of 'K' stickers that had been stuck on the tiled walls. 'Oh, those,' said Mr Gregory, when they were pointed out. 'Bloody anarchists.'

'It's advertising a local bar, isn't it?'

'It might be now, but those stickers have been around for donkey's years. They're a bugger to get off.'

Bryant picked at one with a fingernail. 'How do you know they're anarchists?'

Mr Gregory shook his head in puzzlement. 'Actually, now I come to think of it, I don't know. Somebody must have mentioned them before. It's a local symbol, like. Been up on the walls since I was a nipper. My old man used to bring me here. I'm sure it's something to do with wanting to bring down the government. Someone must have told me. Hang on.' He called across the station forecourt to a guard. 'Oi, Aram, them stickers along the wall, what are they for?'

'Anarchists, innit,' Aram confirmed. 'Bash the rich an' that.'

'Ah, a psychogeographical connection.' Bryant perked up. 'Leave this to me.'

'No,' May replied. 'There's no time left for your pottering.'

'I'll have you remember that my "pottering", as you call it, caught the Fulham Road Strangler.' Bryant had discovered that their suspect was a collector of Persian tapestries, and had matched a fibre left on one of his victims. Tracking him to an antique shop, May had wrestled him to the ground while Bryant crowned him with the nearest object to hand, which unfortunately proved to be a rare seventeenth-century ormolu clock. The killer's sister had sued the unit.

'It was a horrible clock anyway,' mused Bryant. 'Let me potter for a few hours and I might surprise you.'

May wearily pressed a thumb and forefinger on the bridge of his nose. 'We're already looking for an invisible passenger and an anarchist,' he said. 'Let's not have any more surprises today.'

25

LATE-NIGHT CONVERSATION

Bryant spent the next few hours in a dim basement library you could only access with the possession of a special pass and a private knock. For the other members of the PCU, Wednesday dragged past in a grim trudge of paperwork, legwork, statements and interviews. Colin Bimsley and Meera Mangeshkar were now resigned to being yoked together, but the paucity of leads made it feel as if there was barely a case to resolve. Meera felt guilty for thinking so, but it was certainly not the kind of investigation upon which reputations were built, not unless there was a racial or political motive for the attack. What did they really have to go on, other than a couple of hunches and the vague sensation that something was wrong?

Just after noon, one of the Daves took the curl out of his hair by cutting through a power cable, which darkened the offices and killed the computers.

At 2:15 p.m. Crippen managed to locate the packet of butter that had been used on its paws and ate the whole thing, regurgitating his lunch into Raymond Land's duffel bag.

At 4:45 p.m. the other Dave, now differentiated from his colleague by the lack of singeing in his extremities, removed some plaster from a wall in order to locate a pipe, and in doing so uncovered an amateurish but alarmingly provocative fresco of naked, overweight witches cavorting in a devil's circle. It was further proof, if any more was needed, that the warehouse had once been used for something damnably odd. Land had immediately demanded to know what the witches were doing there, and was not satisfied with Bryant's suggestion that it might be the foxtrot.

By 8:30 p.m., having exhausted all existing avenues of enquiry, the worn-out investigators reached a dead-end and were sent home, leaving only Bryant and his favourite Detective Sergeant at King's Cross headquarters.

DS Janice Longbright pulled the cork from a bottle of Mexican Burgundy with her teeth and filled two tumblers. 'The trouble with you, Arthur,' she began, with the cork still in her mouth.

'Any sentence that starts like that is bound to end with something I don't want to hear,' Bryant interrupted. 'Take a card.' He held out the pack in a hopeful fan.

'The trouble with you is that once you get the bit between your teeth you can't be shifted. Two of diamonds. Like this thing with Mr Fox. Take a look.' She spat out the cork and threw a page across his desk. 'It's a screen grab from your security-wallah, Mr Dutta.'

'You weren't supposed to tell me what the card was.' Bryant fumbled for his spectacles and held the page an inch from his nose. The blurred photograph showed Mr Fox and his victim walking side by side outside King's Cross

Station. 'Well, that's just what I told you. He followed McCarthy into the Tube and stabbed him.'

'Come on, even I noticed this.' She threw him another sheet, the same scene a few frames later, as the pair moved into clearer view.

'Oh, I see what you mean,' said Bryant. 'That looks like Mr Fox in his earlier incarnation, before he shaved his hair closer to his head.'

'Because it was taken ten days ago. Concrete evidence that they knew each other. You were right, Mr Fox was taking care of business, getting rid of an unreliable junkie who had something on him.'

'Any news from the patient?'

'Nope, he's still unconscious. There's a staff nurse on duty outside his room, making sure nobody tries to get in. She'll call us if and when he comes around.'

'Has anyone tried to see him?'

'He's had no visitors at all.'

'I wonder if Mr Fox thinks he's dead. You'd better check and see if anyone's been talking to the ambulance crew. Take another card.'

'Do I have to?'

'Humour the meagre amusements of a frail old man.'

Janice threw him an old-fashioned look and withdrew a card.

'Remember it and put it back.' After she had done so, he threw the pack at the wall. One card stuck. Grunting, he reached across and turned it over. 'Nine of clubs.'

'No, it was the queen of spades.'

'Bugger. You know those television detectives who put themselves in the minds of killers? I've never been able to do that. I never have the faintest idea what killers might be thinking. But I would imagine Mr Fox would like to make sure Mac never opens his mouth again. He'll be watching the hospital, or asking around.' Bryant tasted his wine. 'This tastes like that bottle of Chateau Gumshrinker I meant to throw out when we moved.'

'There was nothing else in the kitchen. Try not to let it touch your teeth.'

'It doesn't matter, they're made of plastic. Did you get a chance to look into Mrs DuCaine's claim that her other son was turned down for the force?'

'I put in a couple of calls to Hendon, but Fraternity's file appears to have gone missing.'

'You think there's been some funny business?'

'Not sure,' said Longbright. 'I spoke to a guy called Nicholson, who'd been one of his examiners. He says Fraternity was a good bloke, fully expected him to pass with flying colours, doesn't know what happened.'

'A bit odd. Not like them to be evasive. Who was he under?'

'That's the funny thing – nobody could tell me. If I can find out the name of the team leader, I might get somewhere. Nicholson remembered that the regular officer had been taken sick, so they had a replacement for a few days.'

'Sounds like someone took a dislike to Fraternity and put the boot in. Keep trying, will you? It's the least we can do for his mother.'

Longbright sipped some wine and winced. 'I heard Raymond was upset about one of the Daves uncovering another creepy painting in his room.'

'The waltzing witches?' Bryant released a hoot of laughter. 'Poor old Raymondo is spooked because he thinks there was some kind of Satanic secret society operating out of this place. He says he keeps hearing strange noises at night. Doesn't fancy being left alone on the premises.'

'Was there really a secret society here?'

'Oh, absolutely. That's why the estate agent had trouble renting it. The Occult Society of Great Britain conducted a series of legendary experiments in this very building in the 1960s. The society was closed down after one of their rituals resulted in a death.'

'How do you know about this?'

'Maggie Armitage still has the press clippings. She never throws anything away.' Bryant's old friend was the white witch who ran the ailing North London branch of the Coven of St John the Elder. 'She reckons the occultists chose the property because it was built on one of London's strongest ley lines, which runs from the Pentonville Mound to Sadler's Wells, passing right through the centre of this building. Of course, John thinks I chose the premises just to wind Raymond up.'

'Do you think he's fully recovered from his operation? He seems a bit . . .'

'He's fine,' said Bryant, dismissing the idea that anything might be wrong with his partner. 'He's had heart problems before. His doctor has started bleating about retirement again, but we both know where that would lead. I've just finished reading John's notes on the Mr Fox investigation, and I'm starting to think he's right after all. The deaths can't be connected. Perhaps it's wrong of me to try and forge a link between them.'

'So our priority is still to find Gloria Taylor's attacker.'

'You'd better copy Mr Fox's updated file, the one with the new photos, get it over to Islington and Camden, and let's hope the plods at the Met manage to pick him up on their rounds. You know how they think: if he gets rid of a few thieving junkies, it might be better to let him continue clearing the streets.'

Longbright sat back and allowed herself to relax. 'I've reached a dead end with the witness statements. Nobody remembers who was walking behind Taylor on the stairs. If it had happened on the escalator they'd have been standing still, not concentrating on where to place their feet, and someone might have noticed who was there.'

'Maybe Giles is wrong and it was just an accident. But the man has good instincts. I keep asking myself, how could it have been murder? There are simply too many variables. First, there was the risk of being seen and blamed. Then, the chance that someone else would catch her or merely get in the way and break her fall. Even pushing an old lady down her stairs at home doesn't guarantee that she's going to die. It's best to test these things out with physical experiments. I tried it once before with a pig.'

'What happened?'

'It was very upset, jumped over the banisters and landed rather heavily on an occasional table. Alma was furious. I should have used a dead one, but I was minding it for a friend.'

'I notice Taylor's death didn't warrant a mention in the press today. It's been written off as an accident. And Janet Ramsey didn't pick up on Mac's vampire wound.'

'I'd probably be inclined to think it was accidental if I didn't share John's puzzlement over these students,' said Bryant. 'If you were going to attempt to take someone's life in such a damned awkward manner, you wouldn't risk drawing attention to yourself by whacking a label on your victim's back. Why leave a clue at all? And once you've pushed her, then what do you do? You can't fight your way up the staircase when everyone's coming down, so you have to carry on walking to the bottom. Too much of a risk.' Bryant wiped his lips and set down his tumbler. 'It's no good, I can't drink any more of that. Is there really nothing else?' He tipped the remains into Crippen's bullet-punctured litter tray.

Longbright poked about in one of the crates. 'There's half a bottle of Merlot here. You try it.' She unscrewed the top and tipped some in his glass.

The bouquet forced his eyes shut. 'Well, it's got a bit of a bite. It would probably burn quite well.' Bryant examined the label. 'Produce of Morocco. Why was it in the crate?'

'Old evidence.'

'Not the Lewisham Poisoner? Give me a top-up.'

'When you think about how crowded the Tubes get it's amazing there aren't more accidents.' Longbright kicked off her heels and put her feet up on Bryant's desk, crossing her nyloned ankles.

'The guards were telling me that drunks tend to fall down the stairs or on to the tracks further out of town, away from the West End stations, because the alcohol is kicking in just as they arrive at their destinations. There are very few deliberate assaults, though. I suppose it's the proximity of others, the lighting and the CCTV system. No, I think we have to assume the Taylor death is a one-off. Hillingdon's disappearance is bloody odd, though. You can't vanish on a moving Tube train in the two minutes it takes to travel between stops. He'll probably turn up with some silly-ass explanation.'

'I hope you're right.'

'As far as I know, there's never been a serial killer with such a random MO, even in the Forties, when entire neighbourhoods slept down on the platforms during the air-raids. Once you go down those stairs, it seems as if there's a separate unwritten code of manners in place.'

'The peer pressure of the crowd,' said Longbright. 'Everyone has a go at you if you do something wrong.'

'It's like all these freesheets they give out at the stations. There's an understanding that you can leave your paper folded on the back of the seat when you leave because someone else will read it – a form of recycling that's acceptable. And this thing with the litter bins.'

'What thing?'

'Well, there aren't any. Not around the station anyway, because of terrorist threats. So people tuck bottles and coffee cups in every little corner of the street. They can't be bothered to take stuff home, but they don't want to leave the place untidy either. What strange creatures the English are. We make up our own rules, despite the politicians trying to control us. Remember when the Mayor banned booze on the Tube and everyone had a huge party in the carriages the night before it came into effect? I love a bit of anarchy, so long as it doesn't harm the undeserving.'

'Absolutely. It's a bloody good idea to frighten Whitehall once in a while.'

'Funny about the stickers being a symbol for anarchy. The mad are often seen as being free instead of prisoners.'

'I had the same logo on an old Vivienne Westwood T-shirt, back in the 1980s.' Longbright emptied the last of the bottle into their glasses. 'This takes me back to the old days, when the three of us would take on lost causes, the cases no one else believed in, like your Deptford Demon, the Oxford Street Mannequin Murderer, and that business with those glamour models, the Belles of Westminster. You should put them in your memoirs.'

'I will if I ever find the energy,' Bryant promised. 'There are so many projects I'd like to embark on, I can't imagine finishing them all. I sense a gathering darkness, Janice, not just in me but in the world outside. Perhaps it's something everyone of my age feels. But I do wonder if anyone really cares about the same things any more. Who honestly wants to know about the history of pubs or hidden waterways, or mysterious goings-on underneath the streets? I have no conversation about diets and celebrities or the bad habits of television personalities. Just once I'd like some bottom-feeding media slug to be caught in a criminal situation more imaginative than one involving call-girls and drugs. Their world is too predictable and mundane for me, but it's what everyone else seems to be interested in.'

'You can't blame people for being fascinated by their own species,' said Longbright.

'That's where John comes in. He's the human half of the team. I think I'm more of an ideas man. But I do care.' He removed his glasses and smiled at Longbright with suddenly smaller eyes. 'I know it seems he and I disagree about everything, but we don't about the important things. He has very sound instincts. I believe in him. And in you. I remember when you used to come to Bow Street with your mother. She'd leave you to play with us while she was on duty, and I used to threaten to lock you up when you became annoying. Once I even marched you down to the cells. I had every intention of leaving you there because I've never been able to abide children. But even then you knew how to wind me around your little finger. I'm so sorry you lost him.'

'Oh, Liberty. I'm sorry for him, not me. I'm still here. Don't start getting sentimental in your old age.' She made a show of looking stern.

'I know everyone thinks I'm difficult. It's just that as I've got older I've become less gullible. And that makes me harder to control. I don't listen to my peers any more, but that's because most of them are either dead or have gone mad, so now I'm free to explore anything I want.'

'Then why not apply a bit of free thinking to this case?' Longbright suggested. 'What's the most unlikely thing you can come up with?'

Bryant studied the cracks in the ceiling for a minute. 'The most unlikely thing? That Gloria Taylor was deliberately targeted and attacked by someone who thought he could get away with it,' he said finally.

Longbright flourished her palms. 'Then that,' she announced, 'should be your starting point.'

Their conversation was interrupted by a crash from above. 'There's no one else in the building, is there?' Bryant asked.

'You stay here.' Longbright jumped up and headed for the stairs. Bryant listened to the creaking floorboards over his head, and the chill memory of the attack on Liberty DuCaine crept up on him. He was sure they were the only ones left in the old warehouse, but it had sounded as if someone was walking directly above.

Longbright returned with a frown on her face. 'There's nobody,' she said, puzzled. 'I definitely heard someone, didn't you?'

'You don't think Raymond's ghost is putting in an appearance, do you?' he asked, lightening the moment, but it wasn't enough to remove her anxiety. Longbright was also remembering the murder of a police officer on the floor above.

26

ANARCHISTS

Thursday morning. With the arrival of bitter blasts from the north-east, the temperature plunged, and the office roofs of central London were pearlized with late frost. In the PCU's warehouse, Arthur Bryant had cleared away the evidence of last night's drinking session, and was buried within a tottering fortress of soot-encrusted ledgers.

'How are you getting on with the anarchists?' asked May, tossing his elegant overcoat on to the armchair that sat between their desks.

Bryant had enjoyed less than three hours' sleep. He peered over the printed parapet and rubbed at his unshaven face. 'I've found a link with the missing boy, but I don't think you're going to like it.' Reaching down to pull a bundle of straw from a crate, he unloaded another ledger and blew the dust from it.

'You'd better tell me while I'm still in a good mood. We can't keep all of those books in here. Where are you getting them from?'

'Don't worry, they're on loan from the London Metropolitan Archive. They're going back after I've done with them.' Bryant raised his watery blue eyes to his partner. 'I was having another look through the patient files for the Royal Bethlehem Hospital, Moorgate, 1723–33.'

'As you do.'

'Ah, well, yes. You see, back in the early 1700s some anarchists were arrested and labelled "incurables" because they wouldn't renounce their beliefs. These are the ones who were banged up in Bedlam and left to die, attached to the cell walls with rods and chains. You see where I'm going here.'

'The sticker.'

'Precisely. The London Anarchists was a society formed to avenge the Bedlam Martyrs. It survived for half a century, then died out.' He tapped the bright-red paperback in his hand. 'This is the *Time Out Guide to Alternative London, 1971*. Gosh, we did a lot of marching in those days, didn't we? There's an article in the Agitprop section here – imagine, political agitation had its own section! – all about the revival of the London Anarchists, one branch of which was a protest group called Bash the Rich.'

May maintained his patience with dignity. 'We had a few punch-ups with them at Bow Street, if I recall.'

'That's right, rather a sad little gang, not much of a threat to the established order. Their rallies rarely involved much more than some synchronized chanting, the odd scratched Mercedes and a few broken windows in a wealthy neighbourhood. I always felt we were instructed to come down too hard on them. But they used the same logo. So now we have an active symbol of anarchy with virtually a three-hundred-year history attached to it.'

'The bar designer probably found it in a copyright-free book, liked the look of it and adapted it for commercial use.'

'No. I took the liberty of calling Miss Field. The symbol was suggested by someone in the bar who knew its meaning. She liked the anarchy connection and added it to the existing lettering. But she can't remember who suggested the idea.'

'This is really clutching at straws, even for you.'

'All right, but in turn the symbol gets used by a group of students who all live in the same Bloomsbury house, one of whom is now missing. Have I got it right so far?'

'Yes, but as is so often the case, I don't quite see the point you're trying to make.'

'Have you considered the idea that they might belong to a revived society of secret anarchists?'

May felt his tolerance level start to slip. 'What is it with you and secret societies? These young people hang out – along with hundreds of other students – in the same bar because it's the cheapest and nearest watering hole outside the university. There are no underground organizations, satanic sects or secret societies any more, OK?'

'That's where you're wrong. There are terrorist cells.'

'I met Theo Fontvieille, one of the flatmates, and I can tell you that the only private club he's likely to belong to is one that serves vodka martinis on a Soho roof terrace. The girl, Ruby Cates, is so focussed on her future career that the only way she can relax is by running marathons. Nikos Nicolau looks like he's been locked in a windowless library for the past ten years. Students have changed, Arthur. They're more focussed now, more concerned with personal growth.'

'I was never a student,' Bryant admitted. 'I was chucked out to work at fourteen, so perhaps I feel an affinity with London's rowdier residents. The city has an extraordinary history of anarchy, you know. In the eighteenth century it was virtually ruled by rioters. The mob was referred to as the fourth estate in the constitution, because it decided which laws would be enforced.'

'And I suppose you'd like to return to those times.'

'Heavens, no. The lower classes specialized in public disorder, perhaps because they lived so much of their lives on the streets. They expressed violent opinions at every level, kicking pregnant women in their stomachs for begetting illegitimate children, exposing the private parts of enemies. Attacking someone's nose in public was considered an act of defamation because you were suggesting they had a sexually transmitted disease – it was where syphilitic infections became most visible. And of course the city was filled with small businesses that existed on credit, so if you humiliated a merchant in front of his customers, you could ruin him. The crowd, the so-called King Mob, could destroy reputations. It must have been a fascinating time.'

'Well, Gloria Taylor worked for a shop.'

'She sold cosmetics. How angry would a woman have to be to shove her cosmetician down the stairs?'

'I don't know, Janice tells me she gets pretty annoyed when they don't have her eye-liner in stock.'

'Most of us tend to limit ourselves to verbal assaults these days. But in some ways, the cities of the past weren't much different from the present ones. The main thoroughfares were just as noisy. Imagine the processions and pageants, the duels, cockfights and boxing matches, crowds jeering at prison-carts, public hangings, floggings, and everyone having their say.'

'Hmm. I can see you at a public hanging.'

'The point I'm making is that they were there.'

'What? Who? Where?'

'Do try to stay in the game. The anarchists, they shared a house in Bloomsbury. And these students of yours . . .'

'You're not going to suggest they're living in the same building.'

'No, but they were in the same street. Right next door, in fact. And back in 1725, the two buildings might have been one.'

'So you think a bunch of students are running an organization of secret anarchists just because they're living on the same spot? Everybody in central London is living where someone else lived. That doesn't make us adopt their habits.'

'I'm not saying they're all anarchists. Perhaps only one, for reasons of his – or her – own. And somehow it involves the taking of life.'

'I can guess where you're going with this, Arthur, but you're way off track. These students don't look like anarchists. I imagine they do a little ethical shopping and wear a badge or two, but they're more concerned about their future prospects. A fall down some stairs and a missing lad, that's everyday life in the city, not a criminal conspiracy. Don't you have any better ideas?'

The ringing of Bryant's old Bakelite phone made them both jump. May answered the call and listened for a minute. 'Tony McCarthy's off his respirator,' he announced.

'What, dead?'

'No, it sounds like he's going to be OK.'

'A witness. Hallelujah. Can he talk?'

'Nurse says we'll be able to see him late this afternoon.'

'Why not now?'

'He's just had a tube down his throat, Arthur, and he's heavily doped up. She doesn't want him seeing anyone before 5:00 p.m. at the earliest.'

'Book us in,' said Bryant. 'As long as he survives, he'll remain a threat to Mr Fox. I stayed up late last night thinking about everything. I'm starting to see a way forward, but it will require diligence, nerve and a complete lack of scruples. Best not to tell Raymond what we're up to.'

'What are we up to?' May wondered.

'Let's see the boy first. Make sure nobody else goes near him. Meanwhile, perhaps Janice could arrange a little informal gathering of your students for me in about an hour. I want to meet them alone. I don't care where they are or what they're doing; have her find them, pull them out of class, but get them waiting for me at their house.' Bryant bared his false teeth in an approximation of a grin. 'You know how I always enjoy meeting young people.'

27

PERSONAL SPACE

'Some of you met my partner, John May,' said Bryant, fumbling in his voluminous coat for a toffee éclair and searching for somewhere to sit.

'Yes, he was very nice,' said Ruby, clearing an armchair for him.

'Well, I'm the other one.' Unable to locate the sweet, he pulled out one half of his pipe and waved it about. 'Mind if I smoke?'

'Yes, we do actually,' said Nikos, with a censorious look.

'Ah. Only I saw the ashtray . . .' He pointed to the side table.

'We use it as a paperweight,' said Ruby hastily.

'Odd that it has ash in it, then.'

'I'm the only smoker, but I use the balcony.' She indicated the others. 'This is Nikos – '

'I met your partner at the library,' said Nikos. 'He was asking me about some stickers. I couldn't help him.'

'You gave him my email address,' said Ruby with a trace of indignation.

'Theo Fontvieille,' said Theo, jumping forward to pump Bryant's hand.

'That must be your car outside,' said Bryant. 'You're very lucky to have such a beautiful motor.'

'Yes, it's funny,' said Theo, 'the harder my parents work, the luckier I seem to get.' He threw himself back in his armchair with an annoying laugh. 'It's a reward for getting good grades, Mr Bryant, it has nothing at all to do with luck.'

'I meant no offence. You'll know when I do.' He glanced at the slender Indian boy sitting beside Fontvieille. 'And you are?'

The student looked about himself theatrically. 'I am what?'

'Your name. It was simple enough English.'

'Well, that's not my nationality.'

'We seem to have got off on the wrong foot. Let's try again. My name is Arthur Bryant. What is yours?'

'You don't have to talk to me as if I were a child. My name is Rajan Sangeeta.'

'And you live here as well?'

'I pay my rent like everyone else in this room,' Sangeeta bristled.

'You seem very aggressive.'

'I don't like being questioned by the police when I've done nothing wrong.'

'Oh don't worry, the police can always find something wrong.'

'Mr Bryant is here to help us, Rajan,' said Ruby. 'He and his partner are trying to find Matt.'

'Which just leaves you,' said Bryant, pointing to the only person in the lounge who had not spoken. He had an impudent, friendly face, a stepped haircut and a broad baby nose. He had seemed keen not to draw attention to himself, but now he uncurled from the seat and held out his hand. He looked a year or two younger than the others. 'Toby Brooke.' He brushed Bryant's hand and drew back, casting his eyes downwards again, his dirty trainers drawn up beneath him.

'Tell me about Mr Hillingdon. Does anyone know anything that might be able to shed some light on his disappearance?'

The assembled students glanced at each other but remained silent.

'Let's keep it simple. Where is he from originally?'

'What does it matter where a person is from?' said Sangeeta. 'What relevance does that have?'

'He's from somewhere in Hertfordshire,' Ruby offered. 'He's got a sister and a step-brother. He doesn't get on with his parents.'

'And he's always broke,' added Theo. 'Entirely unambitious, finds his studies a struggle—'

'Theo.'

'Well he does, Ruby. Whereas the rest of us are concentrating on making our first million.'

'You've spoken to his tutors?'

'First thing I did,' said Ruby. 'They haven't seen him.'

'All right, let's find out a bit about you lot.'

'Why do you want to know about us?' Sangeeta complained. 'If something's happened to Matt, we're not automatically suspects. The burden of proof can only be fulfilled by the provision of evidence.'

'Ah, we have a budding lawyer in our midst,' said Bryant cheerily. 'You're going to love this part. I'm going to fingerprint you.' He pulled out Banbury's kit and set it up on the table to a chorus of complaint and disbelief.

'You can't do that!' stormed Sangeeta.

'That's the best part – I can. Because I may be about to transfer the burden of proof to one of you.'

'But for what?' asked Ruby.

'Murder, young lady. You see, one of the uniquely hand-coloured stickers you plaster over your bags was found on one of our corpses, and it contained a partial thumbprint.' Bryant was moving on to extremely shaky ground and knew it. But he was counting on peer pressure; everyone would be keen to clear themselves of blame. He looked around the room and waited for someone to turn him down. 'I'm being overdramatic,' he explained, opening the ink pad. 'We detectives are prone to that. We'll probably have to test everyone who uses the Karma Bar, but I thought you'd like to eliminate yourselves while we're all here. Especially as I have an inducement. I'll find Matthew Hillingdon for you, and I'll keep the prints out of the national database.'

'What if I refuse?' asked Sangeeta, suddenly less aggressive.

'I think you know the answer to that one. Get a lawyer.' *And risk looking suspicious to everyone else*, he thought, praying that no one would do it.

'I'll go first,' said Theo, breaking the deadlock.

'Excellent. And while he's doing that – Toby, why don't you tell me about yourself.' He needed to keep them talking, and to do that it made sense to start with the one who least wanted to join in the conversation.

'W-why me?' Toby stammered. 'There's nothing much to tell.'

Suddenly, Bryant realized, the subject of class had crept into the room. He had accidentally picked the working-class boy. Toby sounded as if he was from one of the rougher boroughs south of the river.

'Ah, a Londoner like myself.' Bryant deftly took the first prints, then passed Theo a tissue. 'Whereabouts?'

'Deptford.'

'I caught the Deptford Demon there, you know. There was quite a hoo-ha at the time. Your parents probably told you about it.'

'No.'

Bryant was disappointed. He liked to think he'd achieved local fame, at least. The borough of Deptford had always been poor and troubled. The detective had spent many a night there as a kid, sitting on the steps of the Royal Albert pub, waiting for his father to finish drinking with his sister Nell. Most Saturday nights had ended with a fight.

Bryant studied each of them as they stepped up to the pad. One Indian, one Greek Cypriot, two from the Home Counties, one working-class Londoner – and one missing. Not exactly the dog-on-a-rope brigade.

'So, Toby, you're also in the same field as . . .' he glanced over at the piece of paper May had given him, 'Mr Hillingdon and Mr Sangeeta. Social engineering? It sounds rather sinister.'

'It's more like learning confidence tricks,' said Toby, examining his inky thumb nervously. 'It's as much about people as anything. They have cognitive biases you can expose and use. The term is used a lot by hackers, but we're studying it in conjunction with architectural urban planning.'

'How does that work?'

'At its most basic level, you know people have a habit of unconsciously walking on the left side of a pavement because we drive on the left? When you're designing entrances for a building you have to put them in places where everyone expects to find them.'

'As usual, Toby, you're being hopelessly over-simplistic.' Theo sighed and made a show of sitting down and slumping in boredom. Clearly, he was used to owning the conversation.

'Please,' said Bryant, 'go on.'

'Well, before you plan a building, you have to take into account the way people behave. A lot of our research is about pack mentality, leader establishment, group behaviour. For example, the distance you stand from someone is your way of establishing your relationship with them. There are several scientifically defined zones of proximity.'

'Such as?'

'Well, public space is an ideal measurement, placing you three metres from another person. It's what you see on architects' CAD plans of new buildings. Beneath that there's a social-consultative zone of between three metres and 1.2 metres. That's ideal for bars, restaurants, recreation areas. You can talk in comfort but you still own your space. Personal space is the half-metre to 1.2-metre zone that surrounds you, so when you're designing an office this is your minimum space between chairs. And private space is when you're less than half a metre from another person.'

Bryant pressed another thumb into his pad. 'But what about the London Underground? People are forced into much closer proximity during rush hour.'

'Which is why they get so uncomfortable,' Rajan cut in.

'The proximity thing is OK when the train is moving, because social convention dictates the necessity of this travel mode, but when it stops and everything goes silent we feel threatened. Our behaviour becomes more protective. That's why drivers now make frequent public announcements.'

'So, imagine you're walking down a public staircase, and somebody near you slips and falls. What's the reaction of the people standing nearby?'

'That would be dependent on a more practical problem,' said Toby. 'The people behind would see the accident but couldn't physically help, because it's taking place ahead of them, lower down, and those in front would have a similar problem because it's happening behind their backs, and they'd receive no warning.'

'Interesting.' Bryant made a show of looking at everyone in the room, but while Toby seemed interested in the practicality of the question, no one else showed any response.

'I suppose we'd better get to the subject in hand, your missing flatmate.' Bryant dug out a notepad and pen.

'I thought you said you weren't going to keep anything on file,' said Rajan.

'I won't, Mr Sangeeta, these will be purely for personal use. It seems Mr Hillingdon boarded the train he told you he'd catch, Miss Cates, but he never alighted from it.'

'He must have done,' said Ruby. 'Where else could he have gone?' She shifted the weight of her plastic cast, trying to find a comfortable place to rest it while she had her thumb inked.

'We checked the camera footage at the station and couldn't find him. I thought perhaps he'd slipped and fallen between the carriage and the line, but we've had Tube workers walk the entire length of the tunnel between King's Cross and Russell Square, and they've found nothing. So it appears we have a rather peculiar mystery on our hands. Perhaps it would help if you told me a little more about the poor lad. Now, how did you all meet each other?' Bryant hoped he wasn't laying the avuncular act on too thickly; he sounded fake even to himself. At least they had been distracted from worrying about the prints. He closed the lid of the pad and discreetly slipped it back into his pocket.

They were politely waiting for each other to speak. 'We met him when he moved in, about four months ago,' said Ruby finally.

'So when did you two start dating?'

'Around about that time.'

Theo snorted. 'She didn't even let him get his coat off. You know how desperate some girls get.'

Ruby shot him a glance that could have cracked a wine glass. 'I felt sorry for him. He didn't know anyone. He'd just arrived here from Nottingham.'

'And you all got on with him? No problems, nothing at all unusual in the way he behaved?'

Silence, shrugging, vague looks of embarrassment.

'We advertised the room on the UCL student site,' Rajan explained. 'We interviewed him, then put it to the vote, and it was carried three-to-one.'

'Who voted against?' asked Bryant, intrigued.

'I did.' Theo raised his hand. 'I thought we could do

better. He was rather desperate to be accepted, although nowhere near as desperate as Toby, obviously.' He laughed alone. 'I know, Toby, you're doing better academically than any of us, but you must admit you've got more to prove.'

'Leave him alone,' said Rajan. 'Everyone's equal here.'

'Do you really think so?' Theo drummed his foot impatiently against the table, looking amused by the proceedings.

'Mr Hillingdon was out with friends on Tuesday night,' Bryant stated. 'Who exactly?' The group looked blankly at each other. 'Well, someone must know. It's important.'

'We don't check with each other before going out,' said Rajan hotly. 'This isn't a police state.'

'Where was he before he went missing?'

'I have no idea,' Ruby admitted. 'He didn't tell me. In a bar. I asked around at college but nobody knows.'

'Does he use drugs? Is he on any medication? Drink so heavily that he forgets what he's been doing? Was he upset about anything? Has he any particular habits you think I should know about?'

Ruby looked to the others for approval. 'Well, he's asthmatic. He carries an inhaler. He drinks way too much. Smokes – you know – but doesn't do *drug* drugs. Nothing else that we're aware of.'

'You've checked with his family?'

'I called his parents in Nottingham. They haven't spoken to him in weeks. He had tickets for a band playing at the Bloomsbury Theatre last night, but he never showed to collect them. I'm out of ideas.'

'Did he ever shop at Selfridges?'

Puzzlement showed around the room.

'OK, what about the rest of you? He hasn't called anyone here? Have you tried his mobile?'

'Of course, that was the first thing we did. It's switched off.'

Silence descended again. Theo was watching Bryant with interest. Nikos was rubbing ink from his thumb. Toby still stared anxiously at the floor. Rajan looked more irritated than ever. Only Ruby seemed comfortable.

'So, if none of you were out with him, what were you doing on Tuesday evening? Why don't you start, Mr Sangeeta?'

'Why me? It's typical that you picked the non-Caucasian to go first.'

'I'd rather talk to you than to the chip on your shoulder, Mr Sangeeta, if you don't mind. You happen to be sitting nearest.'

'I don't have to answer any more questions. I know my rights.'

'Fine. This inquiry's still informal, so I'll just make a note that you didn't wish to cooperate with the police. Then if it becomes necessary we'll place things on a more formal basis.'

Rajan saw that he had been outmanoeuvred; the others would cooperate, leaving him looking like the only one with something to hide.

'I was in the Cruciform Library until seven, then I went and had something to eat.'

'Where?'

'At Wagamama, in the Brunswick Centre.'

'By yourself?'

'Yes, alone, all right?'

Great, thought Bryant, *now I've made him look like Nobby No-Mates*. 'Then what did you do?'

'I came back here to work.'

'See anyone when you came in?'

'No, I went straight to my room and sent some emails. You can look at the log on my laptop if you don't believe me.'

'I'd rather not get all my information from a computer if I can avoid it, Mr Sangeeta. Technology doesn't provide all the answers.'

'That's what Luddites always say,' Rajan scoffed.

'I'm not a Luddite,' said Bryant. 'I don't smash up computers because I think they're stealing my job. Perhaps if you spent less time in front of a computer you wouldn't be so quick to make assumptions. Or be so out of shape. Mr Fontvieille, how about you?'

Theo stretched and yawned. 'I went to the Buddha Bar on the embankment with Cassie Field, the girl your pal met in the Karma Bar. The UK arm of the company's planning a design makeover. She wants to pitch for part of the work, and I'm helping her to draw up a business plan.'

Bryant noticed that Ruby was glaring at him.

'So you drove there?'

'The assistant manager let me leave the car right by the door. Stupidly, I managed to lock the keys inside.'

'How long did you stay?'

'We had the meeting, then Cassie went back to the Karma and I stayed on with some friends. Eventually the place filled up with suburban trash, so I left, came back here and got the spare keys. If you want to check, you'll find at least a dozen people who saw me. I drove back at about half one.'

'I can vouch for that,' said Ruby. 'I saw him come in.'

'OK. Mr Nicolau?'

Nikos looked around at the others. 'I looked in at the Karma Bar around eight to see if there was anyone I knew. Cassie hadn't arrived, but she'd texted one of the barmen to say she was on her way. After that I was up in my room, defragging my hard drive. It took all evening, and it still isn't working properly.'

'I hope you backed up your work,' said Theo.

'I think I got most of it, but there are a few—'

'If we could stick to the subject,' said Bryant sharply. 'Did anyone else see Mr Nicolau?'

'You'll be able to check from the log on my laptop's webcam. I was on Skype talking to some friends in Athens.'

The atmosphere in the lounge had changed. Bryant's questions were forcing the residents to justify their actions. He wondered how he could push them further.

'Which just leaves Miss Cates and Mr Brooke.'

Ruby spoke first. 'I went for a quick drink at the Karma Bar with two girlfriends. You can talk to them if you want, they'll vouch for my whereabouts.'

'You didn't see Mr Nicolau?'

'Maybe we were there after him. We didn't get there until nine, about the same time Cassie arrived.'

'And after that, Miss Cates?'

'I came back here for a while, then went off to meet Matt. As you know.'

Toby cleared his throat. 'I, uh, went to see a film in Leicester Square.'

'Which film?'

'A horror movie, *Buried Alive*.'

'Oh, how was that?' asked Nikos, perking up.

'It was pretty rubbish. I fell asleep, don't even remember what it was about.'

'The film would have finished at, what, ten fifteen, ten thirty? What did you do then?'

'Ten fifteen or thereabouts. I just came back here.'

'Toby, you didn't get here until just before two,' said Theo. 'I heard you come in.'

'What did you do in the meantime?' Bryant asked.

Toby shifted uncomfortably. 'It wasn't that late.'

'I wouldn't swear to it, mate, but I think you'll find it was,' said Nikos.

'I went for a beer, then walked back here. I wasn't in any rush.'

'Where did you go for a beer?'

'A pub on the way, I don't remember.'

'Nobody really hears who comes in when we've got our doors shut,' said Ruby, in an effort to ease the tension. 'Not unless someone's really drunk and noisy.' She shot Theo a look. 'Why don't we show you Matt's room?'

Bryant climbed the stairs to the second-floor landing. Ruby went ahead and pushed open the door in front of him. 'I haven't touched anything.'

'Give me a minute. I just need to look.'

'Sure.' Ruby looked uncertain, and remained on the landing chewing a nail. Bryant wished he had brought Dan Banbury with him. He saw a mess of a bedroom: towers of books on an unmade bed, three pizza boxes, old newspapers, clothes strewn across the floor. It was impossible to know where to start. In order to arrange a meeting with his mysterious friends, Hillingdon could have used his mobile, which he probably still had on him, his laptop, which was here, or half a dozen other food- and beer-stained communication devices. Then again, he might simply have bumped into an acquaintance at college. *London might be the surveillance capital of the world*, thought Bryant, *but running a trace can be just as tricky as it's always been*. He had a good rummage in Hillingdon's bedside table, then poked through the clothes in his wardrobe.

This year's student trends appeared to involve tiny grey cardigans and slim-fit check shirts that made the wearer look like a premature grandfather. *Perhaps my clothes are finally fashionable*, he thought without much conviction. There was nothing illegal or even vaguely interesting to be found here. He considered impounding the laptop, but needed to get Hillingdon officially registered as a missing person first. Disappointed, he was about to leave when he saw a Post-it note stuck on the back of a book entitled *Future Paths: Urban Development and Public Transport*. It read, 'Pay Toby back'.

'Is this Mr Hillingdon's handwriting?' asked Bryant. Ruby came back in and checked the note.

'I think so.'

They descended to the front room, where the group was breaking up. 'Just a moment,' cautioned Bryant. 'Mr Brooke, why did Matthew Hillingdon owe you money?'

Toby Brooke could not have looked more guilty if he'd been caught drowning a bag of puppies. 'I lent him some,' he said lamely.

'How much exactly?'

'I can't remember.'

'Try to hazard a wild guess.'

'Seventy-five quid.'

'Did he say what he needed it for?'

Brooke would not meet his eye. 'No.'

'Go on then, bugger off,' snapped Bryant. 'But I know you're lying, and I'll be watching you.'

28

___

OBSERVATIONS

'You did what?' said May, incredulous.

'I fingerprinted them,' said Bryant, pleased with himself.

'Why would you do that? They're not even suspects.'

'A student vanishes from the Underground system – more specifically, he vanishes in the same station where we suspect that a psychotic killer may be hiding out – and those closest to him can't come up with a single reason why this could have happened. Mr Fox doesn't select victims at random. I haven't been able to find any link between Gloria Taylor and Matthew Hillingdon, but if either of them had a connection with Mr Fox and was unfortunate enough to run into him in the Tube, we'd have cause and effect. And perhaps those students hold the key to his disappearance. Plus, we might get lucky from the partial. Dan's running it right now.'

'Hmm.' May was far from satisfied. 'How did they react to you?'

'Oh, the usual bluster, deflection, sarcasm and showing off. Underneath the displays of bravado they're just your average annoying college students. Their alibis aren't exactly watertight, either. Fontvieille's the only one I'll be able to verify. Sangeeta ate alone, Brooke was at the pictures, Nicolau swears he was in his room and Cates was waiting by herself at Russell Square Station. Oh, and I saw another book similar to the one you showed me, called *Haunted Underground*. It was lying on the table by the window, but nobody seemed to know who it belonged to. Ruby didn't recall seeing it before, but it has her name written on the flyleaf. There was something else, something I couldn't quite put my finger on . . . an atmosphere of tension. It felt as if somebody in that room was keen on keeping certain bits of information hidden from me.'

'Are you sure it wasn't just your natural suspicion of the young?'

'I delight in the young folk, as you well know.'

May tried not to show his amusement. Bryant would have more easily been able to describe and date the architectural details of their house than recall anything about the five students he had just spent an hour with.

'Well, come on then. I don't suppose you did any better. What did you spot that I missed?'

'Specifically? OK, here are some of the notes I made. It's just the group's emotional background.' May produced the little black leather notebook Bryant had given him for Christmas and opened it. 'Ruby Cates may well be dating Matt Hillingdon, but she's in love with the rich boy, Theo Fontvieille. Her pupils dilate every time she looks at him. She knows more than she's telling. Then, as you say, there are the highly suggestive books.

'There are other undercurrents. Rajan Sangeeta feels the same way about Ruby. She's the only one he's not defensive with, and he always backs her up. Perhaps he made his feelings known and she rebuffed him; it might explain his spiky attitude. The rich boy is also worshipped from another quarter: Toby Brooke lowers his eyes whenever he speaks to Theo, and meekly accepts his criticism. This is probably a class issue, because Toby is constantly being reminded that he's the only working-class member of the household, and looks up to Theo even when he's being insulted. He has a chip on his shoulder almost as large as Sangeeta's. Theo doesn't care about breaking hearts. He looks after number one. He used to date Cassie Field, but now they're just friends. He still uses the bar with the others, which hurts her.'

'Well, that's very impressive—' Bryant began.

'I haven't finished yet. Nikos Nicolau is obviously besotted with Cassie Field, but she's repulsed by him. By the way, according to him, Ruby is so competitive with the other flatmates that it's making her bulimic. She gives herself away by making elaborate excuses for her disappearances after mealtimes. The household is in debt – there's a stack of unpaid final demands in the kitchen. Presumably Theo could help everyone out and lend them some cash, but he chooses not to, so everyone borrows from Toby, who appears to have suddenly come into money in the last few days. He's entirely dressed in new clothes, the price tags for which are in the kitchen wastepaper basket. He's also sporting a brand-new laptop that only went on sale at the Apple Store at the beginning of this week.'

'You got all that from one fifteen-minute visit to their flat?' Bryant was staggered.

'They interested me,' said May simply.

'Hmm,' harrumphed Bryant.

'Is that all you've got to say?'

'No. I suppose you were very thorough, in your own way.'

'What's that supposed to mean?'

'Nothing. You're like some kind of gossip columnist. I don't notice stuff like that. And you missed a very interesting piece of evidence.' Bryant enjoyed knowing something no one else had picked up.

'All right,' sighed May, 'out with it.'

'Well, there's the business of the Oyster cards. Travel passes are oddly personal things. If you're a student and keeping an eye on your money, I imagine you know exactly how much you have left on your card. I took a look around Matt's bedroom. In a household where there are six students sharing the same lounge and kitchen you might have your own shelf in the fridge, but you keep the important stuff somewhere close to your bed.'

'I can see that. What's your point?'

'Matthew Hillingdon was travelling back from Spitalfields to meet Ruby. So why was his Oyster card in Toby Brooke's bedroom?'

'How do you know it was his?'

'He'd written his initials, MSH, across the top in felt-tip.'

'I hope you didn't take it.'

Bryant opened his hand to reveal the card. 'Of course I did. Let's find out where he went.'

29

NIGHT CRAWLER

They seemed to be spending more and more time below ground, as if the labyrinthine network of Victorian tunnels was drawing them down from the surface, away from cold natural light, into musty foetal warmth.

The detectives found themselves back in King's Cross Station, in the dimly lit guards' staffroom with Rasheed, Sandwich, Marianne, Bitter and Stone. The station was between rush hours, but to the untrained eye the concourse traffic seemed just as populous as ever. Sandwich had taken a reading from Matthew Hillingdon's travel card and was now checking the codes. 'Here you go, he used it on Tuesday night at 6:25 p.m. to go from Euston Square to Old Street,' he told the detectives.

'He'd been researching at the UCL library, so his nearest Tube would have been Euston,' Bryant told his partner.

'It was used again at Liverpool Street, 11:57 p.m., but it wasn't swiped out.'

'He changed at King's Cross – that's where he texted Cates – and should have used the card again to exit from Russell Square. He has to be in the Tube system somewhere.'

'I told you, the night shift covered every foot of the tunnel between here and Russell Square, but found nothing.'

'What about the terminus – did someone examine the train at Uxbridge?'

'It was a Heathrow train, so it stopped at all five flight terminals. It'll be an expensive business checking all the logs.'

'We know he got on board, and disappeared some time before its next stop.'

'But it's imposs—'

'Don't.' Bryant pressed his eyes shut and held up a warning forefinger. 'Just don't say that.'

'He went drinking in the East End with someone,' May reminded them. 'We could search the station footage at Old Street and Liverpool Street, see who he was with.'

'There's no reason to assume he was accompanied on the train journey,' said Bryant. 'He came over to King's Cross, changed platforms and went down to the Piccadilly Line to go to Bloomsbury.'

'Then how did his travel card mysteriously reappear in his house? We've got enough to bring in Toby Brooke for questioning. You said yourself Brooke's alibi doesn't hang together. Suppose they went drinking, had a fight and Hillingdon got concussed, woke up with amnesia somewhere? Brooke could have lifted his pal's card to prevent his exit from the Tube system being registered.'

'Surely he would have thrown it away rather than hang on to incriminating evidence?'

'Maybe he didn't know something was going to happen to his friend. Maybe Hillingdon went off with another girl and Brooke was helping him to hide the indiscretion from Ruby Cates.'

'Matthew Hillingdon called his girlfriend moments before running for the train!' Bryant all but shouted.

Anjam Dutta attempted to defuse the situation. 'I sent Rasheed here to go over the footage again,' he said, 'and the platforms were all empty within moments of the last train going. But there's something—'

'Me and Marianne, we told you about the man in the tunnels who looks like a crawling leathery bat,' Rasheed gabbled, 'and I know it was just a story an' that, 'cause there's no such thing as giant bats in the Tube system . . .'

'Are you all right?' said Bryant, almost concerned. 'Perhaps you should eat less sugar.'

'It was a silly story about something the guards said they'd seen in the tunnels, Mr Bryant,' Marianne reminded him.

'Yeah, we got something that looks like proof now, from two nights ago, the night your bloke went missing.'

'Wherever there's darkness there are ghost stories,' Bryant conceded. 'So what are you saying, that you've actually seen this creature for yourself?'

'Better than that,' Rasheed told him. 'We have footage. Mr Dutta was going through the hard drive checking it again and he found this.' Rasheed searched beneath the burger wrappers on the desk. 'Where did you put it, Sandwich?'

'Sorry, mate, I was using it as a coaster.' Sandwich pulled the disc box out from beneath his tea mug. Rasheed wiped it down and inserted the disc in the optical drive beside his desk.

'The footage is very dark because half of the lights are out,' he apologized. 'When the old Thameslink station shut down and moved over to St Pancras, they left the tunnels open because the maintenance crews still need access to the trunking at night. Most of the CCTVs have been decommissioned because there's no one down there any more. A couple are still used for fire prevention, but they're pretty dirty and have no burned-in timecode. We know the footage was shot late on Tuesday night, though, because the cameras are still programmed to record at set times, and there's an electronic log. Here we go.'

Rasheed hit Play, and they all watched the screen. At first it was difficult to make out what they were seeing. 'That's the tunnel wall, on the right,' said Rasheed, tapping the screen. 'Now watch the floor.'

On the monitor, a white flap tumbled and fluttered. 'That's just a sheet of newspaper. You feel the wind in the tunnels more at night.' In the murky brown corner of the screen, something appeared to be crawling slowly along the floor.

'See it?' asked Rasheed. 'It's too big to be a dog or anything like that.'

A tingle ran across Bryant's skin. The thing was scuttling like a crab, trying to claw its way up the wall, only to fall back. It had a shiny black carapace like an enormous wrinkled beetle, but there was no way of making out any details. 'What on earth could it be?' he asked, leaning forward.

Bitter suddenly spoke up. She opened her mouth so rarely and spoke so softly that everyone found themselves listening intently. 'It's the Night Crawler,' she said. 'People say it's the ghost of a dead man, but it's not.'

'Then what do you think it is?' asked May.

'A tramp. When we turned off the electrical supply to the tunnels, we created an ideal hiding place for outcasts. There are people living down there, but you'll never find them. Not without a guide. We can't cap off the tunnels, see.'

'It makes no sense,' Bryant insisted. 'Why would a bright, successful student with a great future ahead of him stage a disappearing act to live in an unlit network of tunnels with a load of homeless people?'

'If that's what he did, he must have been very frightened of something,' said May. His finger traced the crawling creature on the screen as it twisted and evaporated. The pixels split into rainbow prisms and the screen crackled into darkness once more.

30

LOST TRIBE

The asymmetrical complex of towers, gables, dormers, chimneys, spires and angled arches that comprised the old redbrick Cruciform Building had been abutted by the vast white façade of the University College Hospital. Together, the two medical centres, one Victorian, one millennial, dominated the streets around Euston. Meera Mangeshkar and Colin Bimsley arrived on the hectic third floor just before 5:00 p.m. Naimh Connor, the duty nurse, took them to Tony McCarthy's bed.

'How's your arm, Meera?' asked Connor. 'Fully healed? Only you didn't come back to get signed off.'

'I took the sutures off myself,' said Mangeshkar. She had recently received a minor injury in the course of duty, and regarded anything less than twenty stitches as not worth mentioning. 'How's he doing?'

'He's on heavy medication for pain management. I'd be in favour of keeping him that way, to be honest. He's nothing but trouble when he comes off his methadone programme.'

'You've had him in before?'

'He's turned up on my A&E shift a few times.'

'Is he ever with anyone?'

'Gentlemen with anger-management issues like Mr McCarthy here don't have too many friends,' said Connor. 'No one's tried to see him. You can have a word. Hope you get more out of him than I do.'

Mac was propped on a stack of pillows with a white plastic oxymask fixed to his face. His right wrist was strapped to the bed-guard to prevent him from pulling out his saline drip. He yanked down the mask when he saw the officers. 'I need to get to a private ward,' he told them. 'One with a door.'

'Sure,' said Mangeshkar. 'Give me your credit card and I'll have you moved this evening.'

'I don't feel safe in an open ward, man.'

'You think he's going to come after you again?'

'You don't know what he's like.'

'Tell us. We may be able to help you.'

Mac leaned up on one yellow bony elbow. He'd been washed, but still looked grubby. 'He's a crazy man. He hired me to do a bit of work, right, nothing shifty, make a delivery, drive a van, only he goes and . . .' Even in his doped-up state, Mac realized he was about to incriminate himself.

'Kills someone,' said Mangeshkar. 'We know all about Mr Fox.'

Bimsley pulled his partner to one side. 'And if he admits he does too, it could make him an accessory to murder,' he whispered. 'We have to tread carefully.'

'We want to stop him before he gets to you, Mac,' said Mangeshkar. 'He tried once, he'll probably try again.

You're safe and secure in here. But once you step out of those doors, we can't protect you. Why did he attack you?'

'Because I know what he did – I know who he killed. I saw it in the paper.'

'So did everyone else in London,' said Bimsley. 'So why'd he single you out? Just because you performed a few legals for him? Doesn't make sense, mate.'

'It's not that. Other stuff.' Conflict twisted Mac's face.

'What other stuff?'

'If you don't tell us, we can't protect you,' Mangeshkar repeated.

Mac's eyes flicked anxiously from one officer's face to the other. 'I know who he really is,' he said finally.

'This was an ordinary street crime until you interfered,' claimed Raymond Land, somewhat unfairly. 'Now it's turned into the pair of you chasing some kind of supernatural being through the London Underground. I simply cannot sanction this. I can't have you creeping through the tunnels of the subway system looking for a giant bat, placing yourself and everyone else in danger.'

'I knew we shouldn't have told him,' mouthed Bryant, rolling his eyes.

'Apart from anything else, it is not under your jurisdiction. The transport police have their own division for this sort of thing.'

'We've spoken to them,' May explained. 'They have no record of anyone living rough in the system. 'I quote: "They used to have this sort of problem in New York, but it's never happened here." But if the boy is in hiding and there really are people down there, don't you think they might have taken him in?'

'They could be holding him against his will,' Bryant added, more for dramatic effect than anything. 'All right, perhaps I shouldn't have mentioned the part about the Night Crawler, but we know this creature was in roughly the same area when the boy disappeared.'

Land folded his arms in what he hoped was a pose of determination. 'You might as well tell me the boy's been eaten by cannibals or strung up inside a giant web by aliens. I'm simply not going to buy it.'

'All right, but Hillingdon is missing and may already be dead. Somebody in that house knows something, because a travel card used by Hillingdon on the evening he went missing has mysteriously reappeared in one of the student's bedrooms.'

'How do you know that?' asked Land. 'You didn't search the place without a warrant, did you?'

'No need for a warrant, old sock. I used my legendary charm and discretion. And my light fingers. Hardly any of his friends can properly vouch for their movements on Tuesday night.'

Land massaged the centre of his brow. He was starting to get a migraine. 'You usually come to me with some kind of theory that makes a sort of distant, twisted sense, but this is the first time you haven't even bothered with that. First you let Mr Fox get away, then you take it upon yourselves to start questioning a bunch of innocent students who obviously have nothing to do with the case I've put you in charge of. I sometimes wonder what I'm here for.'

'Don't worry, old sausage, we all wonder about that.

Look, we've got evidence pointing in at least two directions and we think someone in Hillingdon's group knows where he is, so why don't we keep a discreet eye on them?'

'And how are you going to do that?' asked Land suspiciously.

'Well, there are five students, so we send Janice, Meera, Colin, Dan and Jack out to log their movements, see where they go and what they get up to. Meanwhile, John and I can search the Tube system.'

'Don't you think you're a bit old to be climbing down into tunnels?' Land scoffed.

'At least I'll be able to move at my own rate. I can't be expected to trail a fit young student all over town, not with my legs.'

'Fair point.'

'So we'll do it and report back.'

Land suddenly realized he'd been tricked into letting London's most senior detective team go underground to look for some kind of lost tribe. He dreaded to think how this would look on the report to the Ministry.

'Don't be so glum, chum.' Bryant gave his acting superior a friendly tap. 'Detection is not an exact science. It's not like you see on the telly, all mitochondria samples, antibacterial suits and slash-resistant gloves. Most days we're lucky if I can manage to locate the murder site on my *A–Z*.'

'That's because it was printed in 1953,' said Land. 'You are not filling me with confidence.'

'Look, if we're wrong about the giant bat, I'll simply blame my medication.'

'I'm the one who has to carry the can for the unit's mistakes,' Land complained.

'Then we'll tell the Home Office you've been under a lot

of stress. We'll say you had a nervous breakdown after you found out about Leanne.'

'My wife? What has she got to do with this?'

'Oh. Er, nothing.' Bryant offered up an unreassuring smile. 'Right, let's get cracking.'

31

INTO THE TUNNELS

May was sceptical about the idea, but Bryant would not be dissuaded. The pair would personally search the tunnels for any sign that Matthew Hillingdon had been abducted.

This time Raymond Land had insisted they do everything by the book. Before photo passes could be issued along with their Personal Protection Equipment, the detectives had been required to sign a liability register and read the health and safety regulations, which covered everything from the danger of discarded syringes to Weil's Disease in rats, and the risk of being bitten by the Tube system's unique breed of mosquito.

Now, dressed in lemon-yellow reflective vests, goggles and steel-capped workboots, the pair waited at the bottom of the King's Cross escalators for their guide. It was 1:00 a.m. and the Tube lines were closed for the night. An army of maintenance personnel had moved in to replace tiles, remove fire hazards, renovate paintwork, fix water damage and rewire cable boxes. They had just four hours to get everything done; all adhesive, paint and cement had to be touch-dry before they left, all equipment repacked and stored away.

'I'm Larry, your SPIC,' said the Site Person In Charge for the evening, Larry Hale. He solemnly shook each of their hands in turn. Their guide was a barrel-chested black man in his late forties with pugnacious features and gold ear studs. 'We've only got a couple of lads repairing some lights down here tonight, so you won't be in anyone's way. I say lads, but there's more women than you'd expect. Good workers.'

'How many are there on a team?' asked May as they walked towards the platform.

'Depends on the size of the job. We had nearly two hundred at Piccadilly Circus for the refit,' he told them. 'When we add electronics, the new systems run in tandem with the old ones for two weeks, to iron out bugs.'

'I've heard there's a second set of tunnels, too,' said Bryant, 'built for emergencies on sensitive sections of the line.'

'Don't know anything about that,' said Hale, and Bryant sensed he had stumbled upon an area of secure information. 'There's storage behind here, but that's not ours.' He indicated a rampart of blue-painted plywood. 'Licensed by the London Fire Brigade. There are other control and server rooms down here, as well as the giant vents. You're looking for a place a lad could hide, yes?'

'Or somewhere he might have fallen,' said Bryant.

'There are a lot of dead areas in the system,' said Hale. 'Whenever platforms get rebuilt, the old layouts get left behind. The dead tunnels are capped but not filled in. The old City and South London Line's still there, and parts of the Northern Line that fell out of use, plus there are all the connecting staircases. Many have got access doors, but we keep them locked, so he wouldn't have been able to get in. Mind you, even I don't know where all the accesses are, and I've been down here seventeen years. My missus says I spend more time here than at home. You'll have to keep your eyes peeled.'

'Does the air ever get to you?' asked Bryant.

'It's no worse than what's up on the surface,' Hale replied. 'There's a story going around that the air down here can cure anorexia, but I don't believe that. There used to be plants pumping ozone into the system, but it didn't seem to make much difference to the smell.'

Resculpted in scaffolding and blue plastic sheeting, the platform looked very different now. 'What's all the chicken wire for?' asked May, pointing to the metal mesh that ran along the platform roof.

'We can't take all the panels off every night when we're installing electrics, so some of these are ongoing repairs. Don't worry, nobody could get behind them. OK, the power's off now. It's safe to come down on to the tracks.' He dropped below the platform edge and helped Bryant down. 'Don't panic if you hear something that sounds like an approaching train. It's just the wind in the tunnels.'

'That's a relief.'

'Our biggest problems are caused by trespassers, idiots who've decided to do a bit of potholing through the system. They try to get in from the so-called 'ghost stations' like Aldwych, and leave litter on the line. There are a couple of dozen disused stations, and many more abandoned ones. Security's a big issue now, of course. Your lad, what was he doing down here?'

'Catching a train, so we thought,' said May.

'Well, he wasn't a jumper. We'd have found his remains by now. I've seen a few fried on the positive rail and it's a sight you don't forget. Keep your eyes on your feet – there are a few transverse cables here.'

They were moving out of the light now, into the gloom of the tunnel. The smell was different here, both sharp and musty, with a hint of electrical ozone.

'The section to the south-east of the main station was closed off when the old Thameslink terminal shut,' Hale told them over his shoulder, 'but the disused platforms and the tunnel network can't be bricked up because we still need drainage access.'

It had grown surprisingly warm. May loosened his collar. 'Are you all right, Arthur?' he called. He had noticed that his partner was lagging behind.

'Don't worry about me, I'm fine. I was just watching a family of mice trying to drag a fried chicken leg home.' Bryant caught up with them, his overcoat flapping in a sudden rogue breeze from the tunnel.

'We're now entering the closed-off part,' said Hale. 'Not too many lights down here, I'm afraid. The power's off, so it's best to switch your torches on.'

May was carrying his Valiant, the old cinema torch he had used for years on investigations. The curving walls were crusted with necklaces of soot. Fibrous brown matter like carpet fluff coated the floor. 'Skin flakes,' said May. 'Dan would have a field day down here.'

They had passed beyond the territory of the cleaners. Hale led them between a set of flimsy red and white plastic barriers, into the connecting tunnel that linked the two stations.

'I haven't been along here since the station was shut,' Hale admitted. 'You can't cover everything.'

'When you think about it,' said Bryant, 'there's a strong link between the LU network and civil defence facilities. Didn't part of the Piccadilly Line become secure accommodation for the Electricity Board during the Sixties?'

'That's right. The old Brompton Road Station was the Royal Artillery's Anti-Aircraft Operations Room, and part of the Central Line was turned into a sterile production unit for aircraft during the War. Safe from the bombs, see. That's why the National Gallery stored its paintings on the Tube during the Blitz.'

The darkness was almost complete now, and oppressive. May was feeling distinctly uncomfortable. A smell of burned dust filled the air. Bryant seemed entirely in his element.

'Wait.' May's flashlight illuminated Hale's raised hand. 'I heard something.' They came to a halt and listened. Beneath the faint sussurance of the tunnel wind they heard a snuffling, shuffling sound. 'There.' Hale pointed. The detectives converged their light beams.

Ahead, at the point where the tunnel broadened out into the edge of the closed station, they saw a bundle of rags shift inside walls of dirty brown cardboard.

Hale moved in and knelt down. 'Come on out,' he said firmly. 'Let's have a look at you.'

A tousled head appeared above the box. The boy was in his late teens, wrapped in a blue nylon hooded jacket several sizes too large for him. He peered blearily at the trio, waiting to be given grief.

'It's OK, we're not here to turn you out,' said Bryant.

'We bloody are,' said Hale.

'I just want to ask you a question. Did you see a young man down here on Tuesday night, shortly after midnight?'

'No.'

'You were here then?'

'Yes.'

'Think hard. Are you sure there was no one else?'

'I don't know, we hear a noise.' The boy had a strong Eastern European accent.

'How many of you are there down here?' asked Hale. 'You know you're not supposed to be in this part of the station.'

'What did you hear?' Bryant asked.

'I don't know – somebody fall down. We hear him shout.'

'Can you tell us where?'

A second head appeared beside the boy's, a girl who was equally sleepy. 'Over there.' She pointed off into the dark.

'What's down there?' asked Bryant.

'It's a short service tunnel. We used to store cleaning equipment there until H & S made us move it,' Hale explained, turning back to the sleepers. 'I'm afraid you two can't stay here.'

'We only stay one week, no more,' pleaded the boy. 'We have job cleaning buildings in London, near . . .' He consulted the other. 'Where is it we must go?'

'Aberdeen,' said the girl hopefully.

'I'll leave you to sort this out,' Bryant suggested. 'John, come with me.'

'Don't go far,' Hale called after them. 'I'll be with you in a minute.'

The detectives carefully made their way along the track.

'Why would he have come along here?' asked May, not happy about wandering off into the darkness.

'We're still not far from the main Piccadilly Line platform,' Bryant answered. 'I bet it's not more than a few hundred yards. It just seems further because you're dawdling.'

'It's a wild goose chase. If he'd suffered some kind of *petit mal*, or was simply in a state of intoxicated confusion, he'd have gone up, not down.'

'Not if he was physically too weak to climb the stairs. What's that over there?' Bryant pointed ahead.

'You can barely see in daylight, I don't know how you can spot anything down here,' May complained, but he went to look. The green plastic bin was the size of a man and missing its lid. It lay on its side between the tracks. As he approached, Bryant shone his torch inside.

It was hardly surprising that no one had discovered the body. Matthew Hillingdon was curled up within, as if, in pain and desperation, he had sought the warmth and solace of an artificial womb.

32

IN MEMORIAM

The only way to avoid thinking about Liberty DuCaine was to keep busy. Janice Longbright finished unpacking the last of Bryant's crates and loaded May's computer with witness statements, then sat back to regard the chaotic room. No amount of organization would turn it into a decent centre of operations.

The Daves had nailed cables along the skirting boards to provide extra juice, but the walls were rotten, and there seemed to be a real danger that the hole in the floor might suddenly expand and send them all down to the basement. They were planning to lay new floorboards, but could not agree how to go about it. Everything was lopsided, as if a wartime bomb had shifted the building slightly off-kilter, jamming windows in their frames and causing doors to gouge grooves in the floorboards.

While the workmen argued, Longbright called in the detective constables and impatiently listened to their report. 'Tony McCarthy doesn't know if this is the real name of the man who employed him,' said Meera, 'but he's given us our first solid lead. Mr Fox taught English at Pentonville Prison two years ago. He was employed by the former head of educational services, but she died of cancer last year. Fox was registered in her files under the name of Lloyd Lutine, and McCarthy confirms this was the name he used.'

'That must be an alias,' said Longbright.

'Why?' asked Meera, puzzled.

'The Lutine Bell is in the Lloyds building, in the city. It used to be rung to announce news of an overdue ship, once for bad news and twice for good. Here it is.' Longbright walked around Bryant's cluttered desk and located a miniature brass copy of the original cracked ship's bell. 'Arthur used to ring it whenever a new murder case came in.'

'Couldn't the name just be a coincidence?' asked Colin.

'Come on, Lloyd *and* Lutine? I can't believe he got security clearance on a moniker like that.'

'He must have been confident that no one would get the connection.'

'Multiple killers have a kind of arrogance,' said Longbright grimly, thinking momentarily of her mother's death. 'Don't worry, when we get him this time, we'll put him on the national DNA database. I'd like to see him fake his genetic code. Got anything else?'

'Yeah. He made a friend at the prison. A history teacher. We've got her address.'

'Go home, I'll go and see her.'

'We could do it first thing in the morning,' Colin offered.

'No, let me see if she's up for a visit tonight. I'm not tired.'

It didn't take Longbright long to walk to the Finsbury address. Georgia Conroy had the evasive eyes of a gentlewoman living in humbled circumstances. Her pale, lined face was designed for disappointment. 'Please, come in,' she offered, drawing her dressing gown against the cold air and stepping back from the door. 'I'm afraid the place isn't very tidy. I was about to go to bed when you called.' The flat was perfectly neat, but smelled of damp and loneliness. Longbright accepted an offer of tea, knowing that interviewees were more relaxed when they had something to do. Kitchens were places for confidences.

'Of course, I knew the name was false the moment I heard it,' said Georgia, rinsing a teapot. 'Either that, or his father had been a sailor with a sense of humour. Our time at the prison overlapped by about eight months, but we were on different shifts. He took me out for a drink a couple of times, said I reminded him of his mother – not much of a compliment. I felt a bit sorry for him.'

'Why?'

'He didn't seem to have any friends.'

'Did he tell you much about himself?'

'Only bits and pieces. He was very guarded about his private life. Hated the job. Couldn't wait to leave. I thought we got on quite well, but one day I came in and they told me he'd resigned. He never even came back to clear out his locker.'

'Here's my problem – '

'Georgia, please.'

'Georgia. Mr Fox has killed a number of times since he left his job at Pentonville, but we're having a hard time getting any leads. If there's anything you can remember . . .'

'He was obsessed with graveyards,' she said without hesitation. 'Apart from the mother thing, that's what put me off him. When we went for a drink it was all he talked about.'

The information fitted with Longbright's knowledge that Mr Fox had worked as a gravedigger in St Pancras. 'Did he ever explain why he was so interested in them?' she asked.

'Not really. But I got the feeling it was connected with his family. Some damage in the past . . .' She dried the pot thoughtfully. 'That's it. He wanted me to go and visit his father's grave with him, but I thought it was a weird thing to do with someone you barely knew, so I said no.'

'Did he tell you where his father was buried?'

'Oh yes, Abney Park Cemetery, in Stoke Newington. I remember the family name, too – Ketch – because it made me think of Jack Ketch, the executioner employed by Charles II. I'm a history teacher,' she added apologetically.

'If Lloyd Lutine was a pseudonym, how did he explain that his father had a different name?'

'He told me he was adopted. When it came to answering questions he was pretty glib, almost as if he'd rehearsed the answers.'

It had gone midnight by the time Longbright reached Stoke Newington's neglected cemetery. The gravestones seemed incongruous in their setting, surrounded by the terraced houses of a shabby North London town. Once, Isaac Newton had sat here composing hymns. Now, the graveyard was wedged between betting shops and fried-chicken outlets.

Longbright knew she shouldn't have worn stockings

and heels, but old habits died hard. The paths were muddy and half-buried in brambles. Sulphurous light fell from the distant streetlamps, but did not penetrate the knotted undergrowth to any depth. *I must be mad*, she thought. *I'm not going to find anything useful here.*

There had been one lucky break; the night caretaker had explained that only those who held plots bought before the cemetery company closed in 1978 could still be buried on the land. He directed her across the site, past the derelict non-denominational chapel that could have passed for a set in a Dracula film, to a neglected corner swamped by nettles and briars. The lights from a row of houses supplemented her torch-beam as she searched the overgrown plots.

The small plain memorial was notable for its newness; the remainder of the headstones in the area were more than a hundred years old. She leaned closer and scraped away some kind of parasitical weed that had clamped itself to the stone. Using her mobile, she took a shot of the inscription:

IN MEMORIAM
Albert Thomas Edward Ketch
Died 47 Years of Age
We Are Born in the Wilds of Darkness and Die
on the Pathway to Enlightenment.

The inclusion of his middle names meant that she should easily be able to track him through the electoral register.

She was just clipping her pen to her jacket pocket when she heard a scuffling noise behind her. Turning slowly, she found Mr Fox standing motionless with his legs set wide apart in the undergrowth, his hands at his sides. He was dressed in black jeans and a black hooded sweatshirt, and was staring back at her as if trying to make sense of a particularly abstract sculpture.

Longbright assessed her position. After dark in a secluded cemetery, less than ten feet from a man who had shown enough confidence to commit murder on a crowded thoroughfare. There was no point in playing dumb; they knew each other well enough. Mr Fox wore a black woollen hat that possessed more character than his face; if asked to re-create his image, she knew she would literally draw a blank, but still she tried to memorize the arrangement of his features.

She guessed he had continued to watch them all, tracking her from the unit to the teacher's flat to the cemetery, just as she knew that she was now in the greatest danger. Here was something he could not afford to have exposed, a piece of his past that would give them the key to his nature. He remained quite still, watching her and waiting, but a single sliver of streetlight flickered through the trees and caught the silver skewer as it slid gently down from the sleeve of his jacket, into his waiting fist.

Did he think she hadn't seen it? She had not taken her eyes from his; her peripheral vision had picked up the movement. Unit members were not licensed to carry weapons, but back in the days when she had carried a handbag, Longbright had always kept a housebrick in it. She wished she had it with her now.

She realized she was in a narrow corner where two high walls met. It was almost as if the grave had been designed to trap her. There was no way back, only forward past him. Absurdly, the warbling song of a thrush rose in the branches above her to end on a high, watery trill. She looked up and saw the boughs extending beyond her reach to the wall.

In the moment she glanced away he moved, passing through the brambles without making a sound. Did he reckon she was going to jump and somehow clear him? *He obviously doesn't know how much I weigh*, she thought, stepping back on to his father's grave, raising her heel on to the headstone and lifting herself straight over the wall behind as he suddenly grabbed at her left leg.

Too late, though – she was over, dropping into a back garden of sheds and ponds, stone swans, a heap of children's toys in circus colours. But he followed her over as she ran for the next garden, and suddenly they were performers in a bizarre suburban steeplechase, clambering over one garden fence after the next, stumbling, falling, rising again.

This should be the other way around, she thought, *me bloody chasing him*. But she had seen the damage the skewer could inflict, and had not been taught any manoeuvre that could beat its speed and dexterity.

He was at her heels, faster, lighter, and suddenly straight ahead was a garden fence that could not be climbed because it was buried within an immense juniper bush, and there was nowhere else to run.

She saw his arm lift and his fist arc towards her throat, and moved just enough for the skewer to stick in her padded jacket, slicing the kapok and stinging the flesh of her shoulder. But it was easily removed to use again, and as he did so she realized she was stuck, her heel wedged into the soft lawn, anchoring her to the spot. She felt sure she was about to die.

But Mr Fox had stopped too. Frozen, he was looking past her with something akin to horror in his eyes.

She turned to witness the same sight: a father surrounded by a rippling skirt of children, flooding out of the patio doors with murder in their eyes. And as the shout went up, 'What the bloody hell do you think you're playing at?', she realized his worst fears of attention and exposure had surfaced.

Even as she called back 'I'm a police officer,' she knew they would not catch him this time, because he had already spotted an escape route across the roof of a shed, into the alley beyond, and she was calling after him as she ran, the tables turned as she transmitted to any unit in the area, *Anyone come in, help.*

But he was fleet-footed and light – then gone.

Too late, she knew, *too damned late, even if someone picks up the call right now. He's away. This won't be over until he's tried to spill more blood.*

She stopped and dropped her hands to her knees, fighting to regain her breath as the excited children appeared and swarmed around her.

33

ACCIDENTAL DEATH

Back in King's Cross, underneath the closed Thameslink station, Dan Banbury was wedged inside the green plastic bin, grunting and complaining while Bryant and Hale trained their torches on him.

'No signs of violence on the body from what I can see, not that I can see anything. They haven't got an extension lead long enough, can you believe it? We need to get him over to Camley Street. Giles is waiting for the delivery. He wasn't thrilled about being dragged back to work at this time of night. Don't come any closer if you're not suited up. I don't want your leavings all over my site.'

'Oh stop complaining,' grunted Bryant, flicking off his torch to leave Banbury floundering about in the dark. 'What the hell did Hillingdon think he was doing, playing silly buggers down here? John, where are you?'

'Over to your left,' May called. 'The dust's thick and undisturbed in this part. We've got a single set of footprints. Looks like he was alone.'

'So he boarded the last train by himself, somehow managed to pass through a number of solid walls, and wound up wandering about in a disused tunnel, whereupon he fell asleep and died for no reason.'

'That's about the size of it,' called Banbury. 'I've got his mouth open. There's a strong trace of alcohol, and something else on his skin that I can't place. Might be aftershave, I suppose. At least the mice haven't been at him. The body position is suggestive. I'm wondering if he crawled in here just to stop the room from spinning. Come on, give me a hand out.'

'What are you saying, the booze made him haemorrhage?'

'There's no blood or vomit that I can see. Perhaps he simply suffocated. Or suffered some kind of delayed allergic reaction to an ingredient in a cocktail. Anaphylactic shock. It happens. His hypostasis appears normal, which means he wasn't moved after death. I'll need to take samples and do the shots tonight, so I'll be a while.'

'Come on, is that all you've got?' Bryant complained. 'You're telling me he couldn't handle his drink? How am I supposed to fit that in with my theories?'

'You know the trouble with you, Mr Bryant?' Banbury called back.

'Why does everyone want to tell me what the trouble with me is?'

'You don't communicate with other people. You develop these so-called theories and keep them all to yourself. How do I know what to look for if you don't give me a clue about what's going on in your head?'

'I don't wish to make suggestions about what you should be finding,' said Bryant testily. 'If I do that, the investiga-

258

tion is compromised. I want you to make deductions I can corroborate without twisting the facts to fit.' He had been accused of forcing his theories on others in the past, and wasn't about to make the same mistake again.

'I'm just here to assess the crime scene, if that's what it is. At the moment I'm looking at a verdict of accidental death, although maybe some decent lighting will reveal something I'm missing at the moment.'

'Any money on him?'

'Why?'

'He could have been mugged earlier, suffered some kind of a stroke and lost his bearings down here.'

'He's got a few loose coins. No mobile, no asthma inhaler.' Banbury passed a wallet out to them. 'Take a look at that, if you're wearing gloves. It was in his jeans. No money in it, no credit cards, so maybe it was a robbery. He's not wearing a jacket.'

Bryant flicked open the wallet and pulled out a handful of paper scraps, reminders to go to the bank and collect shopping, nothing of use. 'Matthew Hillingdon is supposed to be in Russell Square, not the arse-end of King's Cross.'

'Gloves,' Banbury reminded, 'are you wearing them?'

Bryant ignored him. 'I want this lad tested for drugs. Nice middle-class boy, he's bound to have dabbled. His medical records were clean, no fits or dizzy spells, no history of seizures, nothing. No enemies, everybody liked him. Something wrong with that, for a start.'

'You're a cynic, Mr Bryant.'

'If you live long enough, you will be too.' Bryant pulled his scarf over his squat nose. 'There's a bad smell down here. Standing water. And I speak as one who knows.'

'Ah yes, your little adventure through the city sewers,' said Banbury. 'I'm amazed you didn't get sick.'

'I've built up plenty of antibodies by eating Alma's cooking. Do you need a hand getting him out?'

'No, Mr Hale and I can bag him and move him as far as the platform. Then we'll need the med team to stretcher him. I'll get some of these fibres off to Portishead, and bung out the dabs off.'

'Can we afford it?'

'Only if it turns out to be murder, so we'll have to take a gamble. They should have finished running a match on your students by now. Why don't you go back up?'

'Come on, John, let's get out of here.' Bryant pulled at his partner's arm, but May remained in place, staring at the body that lay face-down in the bin. 'What's the matter?'

'He reminds me of Alex when he was a student,' said May quietly. 'I've lost them both, haven't I?'

'I know you and your son never saw eye to eye, but Alex moved to Toronto to follow his work. Staying with him will be a healthy change for April. She isn't taking sides against you. She'll come back when she's ready, you'll see.' Bryant was no diplomat, but he could recognize the problem from both sides. May's granddaughter had little chance of leading a normal life while she worked at the unit. She needed to be at peace with herself. 'Come on, let's see if we can find a pub that's still open.'

May lingered near the corpse of the student. 'We can go for them now,' he said at last. 'Hillingdon's misplaced travel card is just cause for a full property search. Let's come down hard on the students. Get their phone records subpoenaed and their emails opened. I'll want their laptops, mobiles, hard drives, PDAs, anything else they've got. If one of them is responsible, we'll find something that doesn't make sense.'

'If you're dealing with someone smart,' Banbury called back, 'he'll be using a pay-as-you-go phone and keeping his texts and emails clean of evidence.'

'They're college students,' May replied, nettled. 'One of them will slip up. They won't all manage to corroborate their stories. They're already under stress. We need to light a fire beneath them.'

As they walked towards the surface their mobile-phone reception returned and they received Longbright's message, informing them that she had encountered the sharp end of Mr Fox's silver skewer.

34

SURVEILLANCE

Early on Thursday morning, London was buffeted by storm-winds from the east bringing ever darker threats of rain. Three days now remained before the unit had to present its caseload closed and ready for audit.

Meera stood outside the Tottenham Court Road coffee shop and watched as, on the other side of the glass, Nikos Nicolau consumed yet another breakfast, this time a toasted cheese-and-tomato sandwich. So far he had searched three locations for discount computer software, purchased a new mobile and stopped at three different coffee shops. While he ate, he fired up the new phone and discarded its packaging on the floor. He seemed to shed litter wherever he went. At least he was totally absorbed by his tasks and took no notice of his surroundings. That made him easier to follow.

Meera was bored and cold. Usually she could find a way to enjoy surveillance, but Nicolau was an uninteresting subject, and she had not dressed warmly enough. In between snacks, the student wandered, mesmerized, around the software shelves. He seemed in no hurry to get to college, or anywhere else for that matter. The only other stop he'd made was at the Karma Bar, where he cupped his hands over the window and peered inside, looking for someone.

She huddled down in the doorway next to the Mac World store, and waited for him to finish stuffing himself. Nikos did not look as if he was capable of murdering anyone, but he was certainly on some kind of mission. Every now and again he extracted a pen from his top pocket and scribbled urgent notes on a scrap of paper. He had screwed the first pages up and shoved them in his jacket pocket.

Nicolau wiped his mouth and rose to leave, stepping out of the detritus he had created as if shucking off an old skin. Meera raised her collar and dropped back into the shadows as he passed. *Boring and obnoxious*, she thought, *but not a killer.* Even so, the intense look she caught on his face as he passed disturbed her.

Further up the road, Rajan Sangeeta threaded himself quickly and nervously through the morning crowds. He had attended an early lecture on 'Light Density Retail Building: Creating Urban Downtowns', before heading for the British Library. But he had then stopped dead in the middle of the deserted library square to take a phone call. Colin Bimsley, who had been following a few paces behind him, was brought up short and had to hastily divert behind a tree; being inconspicuous had never been his strong point. He tried to listen as he passed, but caught only a few words: '. . . it just feels wrong . . . more careful in future.' Taken out of context, the phrases sounded sinister. He strained to hear, but a refuse truck drawing up outside the library gates drowned out the rest of the conversation.

Sangeeta headed for the library coffee shop and worked on his laptop, but there were flickers of anger within him. At one point he suddenly screwed up his eyes and pressed a palm across them, as if to try to relieve a pain he knew he could not control. Bimsley ordered a coffee and settled himself, knowing he was in for a long wait.

Longbright's shoulder was sore, but the dense padding of her jacket had prevented the skewer from penetrating more than a couple of centimetres. She had cleansed and swabbed the small wound, and was now staking out Theo Fontvieille. He, too, had attended the 'Urban Downtowns' lecture – Longbright had spotted Bimsley outside the college – but he had left and was standing on the corner of Gower Street and Torrington Place, obviously waiting to meet someone.

She wasn't surprised when Ruby Cates turned up. After all, the pair were sharing a house. But the lingering kiss that followed changed the nature of their relationship, and sent Longbright's thoughts in a new direction. Everyone assumed that the killer was a man, but suppose Ruby had told Matthew Hillingdon she was breaking up with him? What if he had taken it badly and threatened her? What if she had needed to get rid of his attentions?

Theo was smiling, holding her eyes with his. Ruby didn't exactly seem to be in mourning for her missing lover. They talked, and as Longbright watched from the doorway of the Japanese restaurant opposite, she sensed something else: anxiety darted across Theo's face. It seemed he had said something that Ruby felt strongly about, because now they were sniping at each other, and this quickly turned into a full-blown argument.

Suddenly, Ruby Cates didn't seem so friendly and helpful. She looked downright lethal.

It was raining hard, but neither of them seemed to notice. Ruby stabbed her finger at Theo, who tried to laugh off her anger, and now he was asking her to please come back as she stormed off along the pavement with damp shoulders and furiously dark eyes.

Longbright was about to go after Theo when she saw Dan Banbury in the next doorway, from where he had been watching Ruby. 'What was all that about?' he asked, coming over.

'I've no idea. Has she been seeing both of them? Quick, go after her, you'll lose her.'

Banbury chased after Ruby, and Longbright headed off into Bloomsbury behind Theo Fontvieille.

Meanwhile, Sergeant Jack Renfield was running surveillance on Toby Brooke. The problem was that Toby knew he was being followed. Renfield had no idea how he knew. He'd been careful, keeping well back as Brooke headed to the UCL canteen, drank tea, exited and searched the Gower Street Waterstones bookshop, emerging with a book in a plastic bag. But Brooke knew he was there all right. He caught sight of the sergeant in several store windows, and even seemed to be waiting for him.

When the rain started falling hard, Toby unfurled a rainbow-coloured golfing umbrella and continued on in the direction of the house in Mecklenburgh Square. But when the traffic lights changed between them and Renfield briefly lost him, Brooke waited for the sergeant to catch up. At the gates of Bloomsbury Square he seemed to be toying with the idea of actually coming back to talk.

I'll make it easier for him, thought Renfield, cutting off the corner of the square and beating Brooke to the fountain at the centre of the park. He stopped in Toby's path, bringing them both to a halt.

'Hi,' said Toby awkwardly. 'You've been following me for over an hour. Aren't you soaked?'

'Part of the job,' said Renfield. 'How did you know I was behind you?'

'I just had a feeling. So, what happens now?'

'Yeah, that's a bit of a problem, my cover being blown,' Renfield admitted. 'I used to be better when I was still on the beat. Desk copper, y'see, you lose the knack.'

'Matthew,' said Toby suddenly, his face changing oddly.

'Mr Hillingdon, yes.' Renfield knew the detectives had found the boy's body beneath the Thameslink station, but was aware that the other students had not yet been told. He wondered if he should break ranks and raise the subject. Better to let Toby speak first; he looked as if he had something to get off his chest. Renfield waited. The rain lashed at them both. Toby finally broke.

'I'm not . . . safe.'

'What do you mean?'

He looked up into the dark sky, and for a moment Renfield was sure he was fighting back tears. 'I've had to hide things. I can't control myself. I know it's nobody's fault but my own. I'll deal with it, OK – but it has nothing to do with any of you.'

He turned and ran off, dashing through the puddles on

the path. Moments later he had turned a corner and there were only wet trees and veils of falling rain.

How the rain fell.

Looking out across the garden square, the dripping plane trees, the buckling plumes of the wind-battered fountain, the few passers-by fighting to control their umbrellas, it was easy to think *I hate this city and everything it's driven me to.* The fear had begun as a small but insistent pain, gnawing and nagging like an ulcer, but it had grown each day and now consumed every waking hour.

They're watching us, and if anything else breaks now the game will be up. I have to be stronger than I've ever been before. This will soon be over.

It was like a cracked pipe that was leaking under pressure, and the more the crack grew, the more attention it drew to itself. You had to treat it like any other emergency: seal it off, mend it quietly and invisibly, then get as far away as possible. There was still a chance to do that, wasn't there?

The nightmare that had begun on Monday afternoon seemed as if it would never end. It made you want to screw up your eyes and scream with the pain of it all. How much could you age in a single week?

The cliché is true, money really is the root of all evil. If I hadn't been so broke and desperate for cash, if I hadn't needed status and respect so badly, none of this would ever have happened. It's my own fault, all of it, and now I have to grow some balls and see it through.

The thought of more violence to come was sickening, but it was too late to turn back.

One more day should do it. I can still get out of this in one piece. Stupid of me to give the game away like that.

Sometimes I don't think clearly – that's when I behave like an idiot. I can cover the damage, but I have to stay ahead of the others and hold my nerve.

Some children splashed past on the path, shrieking and howling, without a care in the world. *This time next week I'll be like that*, said the voice inside. *I'll be laughing about what a nightmare it all seemed. I just have to get through the next twenty-four hours.*

Even though it means killing again.

35

CONSPIRACY TO MURDER

Kershaw welcomed Bryant and May into his autopsy room as if ushering a mistress into a box at the Royal Opera House. It was obvious that Giles was going the way of the unit's previous incumbent, who had begun as a normal medical student only to become a social outcast, reeking of body fluids and avoided by women. Enthusiasm for the job was all well and good, but too much gave people the creeps. Kershaw was virtually dancing around them in excitement, and that was how Bryant realized he knew how Matthew Hillingdon had died.

'Come on then, out with it,' he said wearily. 'I'm old and tired. I could die at any minute. I don't have time for pleasantries. If you know what killed him, just say so.'

'I might have an idea,' Kershaw teased. 'And it's all thanks to you and your filthy habits.'

When Bryant frowned, his forehead wrinkled alarmingly. Right now he frowned so hard that it looked as if his face might fall off. 'I don't have any filthy habits. Everyone else makes too big a fuss about cleanliness. We need a few germs to keep us healthy. Wipe that grin off your face, and show some respect for the dead while you're at it.'

'I'm sorry. Rosa keeps warning me about that. I examined the boy, Matthew Hillingdon. Do you want to see?'

'Not particularly.' TV coroners always seemed to have bodies lying about on tables, slit open from sternum to pelvic bone. In reality, Bryant found that their real-life counterparts kept death filed away under lock and key, to be drawn out only in the most pressing circumstances.

'Oh, very well.' Kershaw was disappointed at being denied a chance to poke about with his retractable antenna. 'He's an asthma sufferer, dodgy lungs, liver's a little enlarged, otherwise in good health. There were no unusual external marks on the body, so my first thought was alcohol poisoning.'

'That was Dan's prognosis.'

'Yes, I spoke to him. It seems the boy was alone in the Underground Station. There were no other tracks, except where you managed to walk all over the crime scene, of course. The obvious conclusion is that he went down there in a state of confusion, perhaps thinking he was heading towards the surface. That fits with alcohol poisoning, as the breath-rate drops and dizziness sets in. Hypoglycemia leads to seizures, stupor turns to coma, blue skin colour, irregular heartbeat. Victims choke on their own vomit or their hearts simply stop. Binge drinkers can ingest a fatal dose before the effects catch up with them. I wondered if that was the case here.'

'According to the girlfriend, he usually only texted her when he was too drunk to speak, so we can assume he'd been hammering the booze that night.'

'I was thinking perhaps he had knocked back a bottle and thrown it aside somewhere in the station, but Dan didn't turn up anything. Still, the thought was planted, you know? So I made a list of other kinds of poisons that could have had the same effect.'

'I can't wait to hear how I fit into this,' muttered Bryant.

'Simple. I could smell something else on the boy apart from alcohol, and remembered your horrible old pipe. Tobacco. *Nicotiana tabacum*. Simple, but incredibly effective. He has all the signs: excess saliva, muscular paralysis, diaphoresis—'

'What's that?' asked May.

'Excessive sweating. His shirt was creased across his back as if it had been ironed into place.'

'Only one thing wrong with your diagnosis. Hillingdon wasn't a smoker.'

'He didn't need to be. The stuff used to be readily available as an insecticide until its lethal properties were recognized. It's easy to make a tea out of rolling tobacco. There are plenty of recipes for it on the internet because dope growers use it to kill mites on marijuana plants. He'd have suffered dizzy spells, confusion, tachycardia, low blood pressure, with worsening symptoms, leading to coma and death. The stuff's all over his face and the collar of his shirt. I think it's possible that somebody sprayed him with it. You could empty out a perfume sampler, like the ones they give you in department stores, and fill it up.'

'Gloria Taylor sprayed perfume samples on customers at Selfridges.'

'Then I'd say you might have found your link.'

'Are you definite about the cause of death?'

'One hundred per cent.'

'Well, you reached a solution without having to show me the inside of his colon, for which I thank you,' said Bryant. 'Although I'm not sure this brings us any closer to finding a culprit. How easy is it to transfer?'

'Liquid tobacco? Pretty easy, but it also washes off. The smell's harder to get rid of. Do you have any suspects in mind?'

'That's the trouble,' said Bryant glumly. 'We have half a dozen of 'em. Nikos Nicolau is apparently studying biochemistry, but he also suffers from claustrophobia. Every suspect also has a reason not to be one. I think this time I might need to employ modern crime-detection techniques.'

'A victory for the scientific community,' laughed Kershaw. 'John, you should be pleased.'

'I'm relieved,' May replied. 'I've banned Arthur from trying to wrap up the investigation by esoteric means.'

'Did you mean that?' asked Bryant after they had thanked Kershaw and taken their leave. 'You really want me to play it by the book this time?'

'Yes, I do,' said May with determination. 'And I don't mean the book of witchcraft, or the ancient myths of England, I mean *The Police Operational Handbook*, 784 pages of sound, solid common sense. You want us to survive, don't you? Well, that's how we'll do it.'

It was time to return to the house in Mecklenburgh Square, where they could break the news of Matthew Hillingdon's death and commence the property search. That was when Banbury's call came in.

'The partial from the sticker,' he said, 'we've got a match. It's Toby Brooke.'

'No.'

'Don't tell me no. I've got the results on the screen in front of me. As I said, it's a partial, but enough to bring him in.'

All the housemates were advised of their rights, and were ordered to be present on the premises. If they hadn't taken the detectives seriously before, they would have to now.

Bryant was thinking about the tobacco in the ashtray, and Ruby Cates admitting that she was the only smoker.

'You know those old Agatha Christie whodunnits where you get the butler, the chorus girl, the aunt and the Lord into the library, then Poirot goes through their motives before accusing one of them?' he said to May as they walked. 'I feel like him, except for one small detail. I'm sure it's not Toby.'

'You just don't want to believe it's him because you feel a kinship with working-class kids,' said May.

'It probably is his thumbprint, I just don't think he's the type to commit murder. He seems scared of his own shadow. If the sticker was on one of the bags or had been picked up from the bar and left lying about the house, any of the others could have touched it. The trouble is, I haven't the faintest idea how they could have killed Hillingdon. Out of the five, only Theo Fontvieille has an alibi that checks out. Meera found at least eight witnesses who saw him at the Buddha Bar, and at the end of the evening his car was still outside the club with the keys stuck inside it. Of course, Ruby Cates has her leg in a cast, which pretty much rules her out. There's no way she could have fled from the scene of a crime. Have you seen how long it takes her to get up a flight of stairs?'

'What about the others?'

'Renfield tracked down the callers who spoke to Nikos Nicolau via video link, and they're willing to swear that it looked as if he was calling from his bedroom. They could see his furniture and posters in the background. Plus, we have the log showing the exact time he made the calls. The waitress at Wagamama doesn't remember serving Rajan Sangeeta, so his movements remain unsubstantiated, and Toby Brooke's account of his whereabouts is particularly dubious, but that sort of rules in his favour. He's a bright lad, I'm sure he could come up with a decent alibi if he wanted to.'

'Why shouldn't it be a woman?' May wondered. 'Neither of the deaths required any strength or dexterity – just a push and a spray. Besides, we know that Ruby is strong.'

'I was thinking less about dexterity than visibility. Someone would have recalled a pretty girl with her leg in a cast.'

'Perhaps it's time to add Cassie Field to our list of suspects.'

'Why? Good heavens, we've enough already.'

'It turns out that Ms Field has a history of secret anarchy. She's the girl who threw yellow paint over the Minister for Agriculture last year. Janice received a call from Leslie Faraday at the Home Office. He knows we interviewed her. She's got a very impressive arrest file. That's why she came up with the anarchists' symbol for the bar. She used to meet there with her urban warrior pals.'

'But you're forgetting – she has an alibi. She was seen at the Buddha Bar, then half an hour later she arrived at the Karma Bar and spent the rest of the evening there, with the exception of a ten-minute break a little after midnight when she went out for a cigarette. The station's not far from the bar, but to get there and back she'd have to be a marathon runner.'

'Then we have to bring in Toby Brooke.'

'Do we? I'd rather keep an eye on him for a while. Can we do that?'

'If he makes a run for it we'll be blamed.'

'I'll make sure he stays put,' Bryant promised.

'I spoke to Renfield a few minutes ago. He blew his cover and was forced to have a very strange conversation with Brooke. It seems the lad started to admit his guilt about something, then ran off.'

'Sounds like he's close to confessing.'

'Perhaps, but I want to do this the traditional way, with a formal interview. Go into Brooke's background and wear him down by sheer persistence. We have to interview them all again anyway, so we'll make it part of that process. The others shouldn't know what we have on him. Meanwhile we take the house apart, try and establish a link between Taylor and Hillingdon.'

'I'm going to leave this to you, then,' said Bryant. 'You've always said I have no understanding of the young. I remember interviewing those horrible schoolchildren who saw the Highwayman committing murder and I still get chills down my spine when I think of them. There's something wrong with today's youth; they have faces as blank as Victorian dolls and the morals of Balkan gangsters.'

They had reached the house. May rang the ground-floor bell. A lopsided thumping sounded in the hall, and Ruby Cates opened the door. *It must be tiring for her, getting about with that leg*, thought Bryant.

'Both of you at the same time?' she enquired, raising an eyebrow. 'This must be serious. You'd better come in.'

As Bryant had joked, the group were gathered around the edges of the sitting room, although they failed to resemble any of Miss Christie's characters. Most affected boredom, a pose adopted to mask apprehension.

May decided to seize the bull by the horns. 'I must inform you that Matthew Hillingdon has been found dead in a disused tunnel beneath King's Cross,' he began. 'His next of kin have been notified, and—' But suddenly everyone was talking at once. Only Toby raised his hand.

'How did he die?'

'We're not at liberty to discuss the details of the case, but I can tell you we believe he was murdered. Furthermore, you'll appreciate that as you were among the last to see him alive, we need to conduct certain examinations that may shed light on—'

'You suspect us!' said Rajan Sangeeta, genuinely outraged for once.

'We have to explore every avenue of inquiry, and that starts with searching your rooms.'

'You can't do that without a warrant.'

'Actually, we can if we suspect that there's evidence on the premises. I'd prefer your permission to act, but it's not a legal requirement. I'm afraid that's just the start. I'll need to impound all electronic communication devices, including mobile phones, laptops, PCs and so on, so I'll need all your passwords.'

'We need them for our work,' said Ruby. She sounded numb.

'I appreciate that, so we'll be supplying you with alternative computer access, and I can confirm you'll be able to request specific study documents, which we'll copy on to a separate hard drive exclusively for your use.'

'That's a bit over the top,' said Theo. 'It could throw my studies off-track.'

'Christ, Matt's dead and all you can think about is your bloody schedules,' Toby complained.

'It's all right for you, poor boy, you're going to fail anyway,' Theo barked back. He turned to the detectives. 'What can we do to get through this as quickly and painlessly as possible?'

'Our forensic team will be arriving in a few minutes to begin conducting searches of your rooms,' said May. 'You can take what you need, provided it's under supervision from a member of the unit. We'll detail all property removed from the site, and make sure it's returned to you as soon as we can. If anyone has any concerns or objections—'

'I don't want you searching my room,' Nikos blurted. Everyone turned to look at him.

'I'm afraid you have no choice in the matter,' said May. 'If you have nothing to hide, you have nothing to worry about. There are a few further things I want to bring up. Our assistant, Detective Sergeant Longbright, will need to update her statements from you all concerning your whereabouts on Tuesday night, with names and addresses of everyone who can confirm your whereabouts.'

'Why should we help you?' asked Theo. 'I mean, if you already have the powers you need?'

'A fair question, but I'd like to think you would want to do it for Matthew, to help us for his sake. We have no motive for his death. We need to find out who he was with that night. I'm sure I don't need to warn you about obstructing the due process of what is now an official investigation. Miss Cates, I understand you and Mr Fontvieille had a falling out—'

'Have you been following us? Who the hell do you think you are?'

'We're a specialist department under the control of the Home Office, and you are civilians. Trust me, you don't want to fall into the hands of the Metropolitan Police. What did the two of you argue about?'

'We need to borrow some money to pay the rent and electricity,' said Ruby. 'I asked Theo to cover the bills and he refused. I just thought he should agree to help us through a rough patch.'

'It's a matter of principle,' said Fontvieille. 'If we can't manage our bills now, how can we be expected to construct and run entire social environments which might one day involve millions of pounds? Think it through, Ruby.'

'Anyway, I borrowed the money from Toby,' Ruby replied.

'Ah yes, you're quite well off at the moment, is that right?' May checked his notes.

'An aunt died and left me some money,' Toby muttered. The lie was so blatant that it hung in the air, a balloon of falsehood waiting to be punctured.

'Well, you can give our Detective Sergeant all the details on that. Mr Fontvieille, I understand you used to date Cassie Field, the manager of the Karma Bar, is that true?'

'It's common knowledge,' said Theo airily.

'Not to me, it's not,' Ruby snapped back.

'What does it matter? It was, like, a whole eight months ago.'

The temperature in the room was rising fast, but in this

case May knew that a confrontational atmosphere could pay off; the housemates were becoming upset and dropping their guard.

'We see that two of you have had trouble with the police in the past,' May continued. 'Mr Fontvieille, assault; Mr Nicolau, sexual harassment, was it?'

'I got into a fight outside a nightclub in Richmond,' said Fontvieille. 'Fairly normal behaviour for a Thames Valley boy, wouldn't you say?'

'And you, Mr Nicolau?'

'He was caught upskirting,' said Sangeeta.

'A load of us were doing it at the time,' Nicolau admitted. 'Kind of embarrassing to think about now.'

'Is this a youngsters' term I'm not familiar with?' asked Bryant, confused.

'It's the rather grubby little practice of holding a camera under a girl's skirt in public places – when she's on a Tube escalator, for instance – then posting the shot on the internet,' May explained.

'Oh, charming.' Bryant grimaced. 'Is there nowhere a lady is safe these days?'

'Where did they find you two?' asked Theo. 'You're like something out of a display case at the Victoria & Albert Museum. Incredible. If this is going to take ages, do you mind if we order in pizzas?'

'You're not taking this very seriously, are you?' There was a thread of danger in Bryant's voice. 'You don't seem to appreciate that all five of you are under suspicion of conspiracy to murder. That is, an agreement between two or more persons to commit an illegal, wrongful act by sinister design, to use a rather archaic definition.'

The overheated room exploded into fits of bad feeling

279

and sour temper, like a series of slightly disappointing fireworks going off. There were indignant complaints and toothless threats, declarations of rights and talk of lawsuits. It was the perfect time for Longbright, Banbury and Renfield to arrive.

Soon all doors had been flung open, all drawers emptied, wardrobes cleared, computers unplugged, belongings tagged and bagged, and the fight had gone out of the five students who watched forlornly as their lives were dissected before them. It seemed the quintet had finally realized that this was no longer a mere inconvenience, but something much darker and more devastating in its consequences.

36

EMPTY-HANDED

Law-abiding citizens are hard to trace. Albert Thomas Edward Ketch existed, of that there was no doubt, but he was unknown to the police. The DVLA had a clean driving licence on record, the borough of Islington listed a name on their electoral register, Barclays Bank had a closed account, and a former address in a St Pancras council block yielded nothing but statistical proof that Mr Fox's father had once been alive.

Longbright needed to put a face to the name. If Mr Fox's father remained intangible, at least Camden registry office had a marriage licence on file, which presented her with a partner. Ketch had wedded one Patricia Catherine Burton, who provided the registrar with an address in Wembley. She had moved the same year, presumably to live with her new husband, because the marriage certificate was posted to a different North London address. Her son had been delivered less than six months later at Hampstead's Royal

Free Hospital, and had received health checks for the first four years of his life at clinics in the area. After that, the trail went cold.

'I'm running out of ideas,' she told Renfield as they finished filling in evidence forms for the Mecklenburgh Square house. 'I've got a little on the parents but nothing on the boy.'

'See if he was registered as a Young Offender under the name of Ketch,' Renfield suggested. 'A tenth of all the kids in London commit a serious offence at least once. If something happened to Mr Fox in his childhood, he might have gone AWOL and turned up on Islington's books, or Camden's.'

'Thanks, Jack. I should have thought of that. I'm tired. I haven't been sleeping well.'

'Hardly surprising. I'm going to grab a bite. Want me to pick you up something?'

'No, I'm fine. I want to get this lot sorted out.'

'You can't go off your grub and get all moody on me. Tell me you don't fancy a sausage sandwich smothered in brown sauce.'

'Strangely enough, I don't.'

Renfield headed off to the shops. She watched from the window as he strutted along the wet street with nothing more than food on his mind. *I should learn to be more like Jack*, she thought, returning to her paperwork.

'Ah, there you are,' said Bryant, ambling into the room. 'I was going to stroll back with you from Mecklenburgh Square but you'd vaporized. Those students may dress like a Gap advertisement but you should have seen the state of their fridge. Oswald Finch used to keep his cadaver drawers in a better state. Having said that, I did once leave a beetroot salad in with one his corpses, and he mistook it for—'

'Arthur, I'm not in the mood,' said Longbright. 'I'm sorry.'

'No, I'm the one who should be sorry.' He removed his hat and dropped into the battered armchair Longbright had installed for his visits. 'In my usual clumsy way I was just trying to cheer you up. Unfortunately, most of my conversation involves death, ancient history or mad people. No wonder I've never been very popular with the ladies. What did you think of our students?'

Longbright rose and blew a newly dyed blonde curl from her eye. 'A pretty ordinary bunch: a health freak, a geek, a jock, a wide boy and a nerd.'

'I love the way you categorize, it's all so simple for you. Think they're hiding any secrets from us?'

'Of course. They wouldn't be human if they didn't. I just think they'll turn out to be pretty mundane.'

'What do you mean?'

'Oh, crushes, alliances, jealousies, money worries.'

'Hatreds?'

'Strong word. Dislikes, perhaps. Toby Brooke isn't too keen on Theo Fontvieille.'

'Theo needles him about his background. According to John, the rich boy dated the girl from the Karma Bar, then dumped her, but he's so thick-skinned that he takes other girls to her establishment without realizing that he's upsetting her. Dear Lord, I'm sounding like a gossip columnist.'

The idea made Longbright smile. 'That's OK, they're just like any dysfunctional alternative family.'

'I don't believe it's a conspiracy. They wouldn't be able

to organize a tea party without getting on each other's nerves, let alone kill someone and hide the evidence. If this was something they'd planned, they would never have left Matthew Hillingdon's travel card in the house, where it could be found.'

'Right now that and the partial print are the only pieces of incriminating evidence we have,' said Longbright.

'I'm convinced that the murderer is operating alone, without the knowledge of the others. That damned sticker links Taylor to the Karma Bar and Toby Brooke. I wonder how John's getting on with him.' Bryant watched Longbright wince as she lifted a box from the desk. 'How's your shoulder?'

'Not so bad. It didn't even need a stitch.'

'Let Colin take over from you when he gets back. He and Dan are going to go through the impounded evidence.'

'I'm fine,' Longbright promised. 'I'm much happier working.'

'OK, then you can carry on following the Indian chap all over town, if you wouldn't mind. I don't like the cut of his jib. I want all five housemates tailed over the weekend. We shouldn't let any of them out of our sight. I'm counting down the hours until the unit is pulled from service. I can't see us making an arrest in time, but let's keep watching them.' Bryant tapped his fingers beneath his beady eyes. 'All five, all weekend, everywhere they go.'

Bimsley and Banbury arrived back at the warehouse, and spent the next three hours searching the hard drives of the five housemates' laptops. They turned up little of interest. Only Ruby Cates kept her financial details on record, along with an online diary that confirmed her obsession with 'The Rat', who was easily identified by his customized Porsche. Theo had a few dodgy gambling sites bookmarked, Sangeeta had too many photographs of Ruby in his photo library, Nikos had similar photos of Cassie in the bar and an awful lot of porn, Cates had posted some cryptic remarks on Facebook, and Toby had worked hard at erasing details of the sites he visited. Their computer tracks seemed unusually guarded and cautious. To Dan's suspicious mind it was proof that the students knew they were being watched, but Colin thought they were merely being security-conscious.

All five had extensive music libraries of bands that had become popular over the last few years. All five had infringed copyright laws by file-sharing movies, but that seemed to be the extent of their illegal activities.

The iPhoto files from Matt Hillingdon's laptop yielded some odd photographs that looked like colourful knitted versions of radio interference, so Bimsley forwarded them to Bryant's mobile, hoping that he might be able to figure out what they were – once he had managed to open them.

At 6:00 p.m. John May returned to the unit with bad news. He and Meera had just finished interviewing Toby Brooke. Unprompted, the student had shown them a sheet of altered stickers that had been left lying about the house, and had admitted to handling them. Their evidence was compromised.

It was now Friday evening, and the case had once more stuttered to a halt. Bryant was forced to admit that it was by far the most infuriating investigation he had ever undertaken.

It was time, he decided, to take more drastic steps, starting with a visit to North London's resident white witch.

37

BAD AIR

'What more can I do?' asked Bryant. 'We're back to one piece of evidence and five less-than-ideal suspects. John has banned me from using any of my more *outré* routes of investigation. And I have this ragbag of notions in my head that don't seem to connect – a red dress, some strange patterns from Hillingdon's laptop, a missing mobile phone, the way people move on the Tube . . .' He paused to take a good look at his old friend Maggie Armitage. 'What happened to you?'

The Grade IV White Witch and leader of North London's Coven of St James the Elder was spattered in pink paint – not a nice pink either, but a shade that could best be described as Tired Marshmallow. 'I was preparing a philtre for Dierdre,' she explained, 'because her sex life has taken a turn for the worse again. She met a Polish bus driver with a habit of calling round at 3:00 a.m., but the trouble is he's on nights, so he'd park a bus full of passengers outside her house while he came in.'

'That must have been inconvenient.'

'Not really. His route goes past her house.'

'I meant for her.'

'Oh, yes, that was the problem. She'd wanted to meet a man with his own transport, but technically of course he doesn't.'

'Doesn't what?'

'Own it. So I needed fennel for the potion. And Cheese and Onion crisps.'

'You put crisps in a love potion?'

'No, I was just hungry. So I put some bacon into the eye-level grill and went to the shops.'

'Why did you do that?'

'Well, you layer crisps on either side of the bacon and it makes a wonderful sandwich.'

'No, I mean why did you leave the grill unattended?'

'You know how my concentration has been since I fell off my bike.'

'No, how?'

'It wasn't a question. Well, when I came back the kitchen was on fire. Luckily I'd left a plastic washing-up bowl full of water on the rack above the grill, and when it melted it put out the flames.'

'That *was* a piece of luck,' said Bryant with heavy sarcasm. 'Just think, things could have turned out quite badly.' He surveyed the dripping, blackened remains of the kitchen.

'Well, they did,' said Maggie. 'He went back to his wife. And some of his passengers tried to sue him.'

'I don't think you should make any more love potions.'

'Oh, it wasn't a love potion. It was something to make him sleep so he'd go back on days. Unfortunately, it worked too well. He fell asleep at the wheel and went through the window of a lapdancing club in Liverpool Street. Which is why I'm painting the room pink. Because I can't get the bacon smoke off.' She raised the chain of her spectacles and squinted at him through polka-dot lenses.

Talking to Maggie was like using some kind of malfunctioning space communicator. Bryant decided to get to the point and keep it simple. 'I know you've got a memory like a sieve, but I did ask you on the phone whether you knew anything about odd happenings in Underground stations. I can be more specific now. Magnetism.'

Maggie peered over the top of her paint-spattered spectacles and frowned at him. 'Oh, you know about that, do you?'

'No. That's why I'm asking you.'

'No, I asked Yu.'

'Me?'

'No, Mrs Yu. I asked her to pop round. She's in the garden.'

Maggie's garden was a makeshift pet cemetery with a few desperate bluebells thrusting out of cracked paving stones. The goldfish had shuffled off its mortal coil in an earth-filled chimney pot, and the budgie had gone towards the light in a coal scuttle. Bryant looked out of the kitchen window and got a fright. For a moment he thought the moon had come out. Mrs Yu had a perfectly round white face and was peering in. She looked frozen.

'Sorry, love, I didn't realize I'd locked you out,' said Maggie, opening the door.

'It's bloody perishing in your yard,' said Mrs Yu. Although she was very Chinese in appearance, she had a strong cockney accent. 'I was chatting to your dog.'

'Her dog's dead,' said Bryant.

'Yes, he's buried under the fishpond. Bolivar says he's very happy, but he's not so happy about being so near Happy.'

'I'm sorry?' said Bryant. Things were becoming confused again.

'Happy was my cat,' Maggie explained. 'She's buried near the dog. Mrs Yu knows a lot about atmospheric disturbances, so I invited her over. Plus, I wanted her to return my wok.'

Mrs Yu laughed a lot. She tittered at the end of every utterance. When she wasn't laughing she was at least chuckling, and even when the chuckles faded she was still smiling. She plumped her big round frame down in the widest, most comfortable chair and elucidated. 'So you want to know about magnetism. There was a story going around a few years ago about the Tube. The guards started saying that the addition of extra metal flood gates throughout the system created some kind of supercharged atmospheric whirlpool. It was only supposed to happen when trains passed through the tunnels with great frequency, during the rush hour. See, before that, electrical particles ionized the atmosphere and escaped upwards on the air currents. But the iron flood doors slowly became magnetized, creating differences in pressure that made passengers feel sick and dizzy.'

'I'm not sure I put much store in that,' said Maggie. 'I mean, electrical whirlpools, it sounds a bit like those adverts for shower gel with ginseng extract to wake you up. You know, pseudo-science.'

'That's good, coming from a woman who believes you can find water under the ground just by wandering about with a stick.'

'Dowsing is scientifically proven,' Maggie insisted. 'I can always find water.'

'Of course you can,' said Bryant. 'You're a Londoner, it's impossible to get away from the bloody stuff. So, no likelihood of someone becoming disoriented and passing out in the Underground due to magnetic forces, then? Because I've heard there are powerful ley lines passing through King's Cross.'

'That's true,' said Mrs Yu, 'but there are other hidden powers at work under London. Wherever all four elements interact, you create conflict. King's Cross is one of the very worst sites . . .'

'What are you talking about?'

'The electric trains and power cables – fire. The underground rivers and pipelines – water. London clay – earth. The winds in the subway system – air. There are storms down there that disrupt the psychic atmosphere.'

'Meaning what exactly? You get headaches? You catch the wrong train? You start seeing dead people?'

Mrs Yu happily wagged a finger at him. 'Ill humours are not such a crazy concept. The Victorians believed germs were transported through miasma – the air itself. That's why they built Victoria Park in Mile End, as a barrier to protect the city's rich property owners from working-class diseases. They thought the germs would float across to them on the breeze.'

'Yes, but they were wrong, weren't they? John Snow discovered that cholera was water-borne. You think there's such a thing as bad air?'

'Well, we know that electromagnetic disruption can actually make people ill, and the jury's still out on radio masts, isn't it? There's still no air conditioning in the

London Underground system. Back when the trains were pulled by steam engines, the engineers tried everything to clear the air. They built ventilation shafts that came up behind fake house-fronts in Bayswater. Later, when the Victoria Line was built, a structure called the Tower of the Winds was constructed in a garden square up in Islington. It was meant to introduce cool breezes into the tunnels, but wasn't much more successful.'

'I was just reading about plans to chill the subway system during heatwaves by using water from the lost rivers,' Bryant interjected.

'Nothing ever works,' sighed Mrs Yu. 'The air beneath King's Cross remains old and stagnant. It's polluted with all kinds of toxins, and its composition changes all the time.'

'Well, here's my problem.' Bryant seated himself wearily and helped himself to a ginger biscuit. 'My problem is – dear Lord, it sounds so absurd. How can I explain this? Some of our most successful prosecutions have been built around a tiny shred of evidence: a piece of broken glass, a bootprint, an overheard phrase. This investigation hangs on a sticker, a travel card, a few odds and sods, and a bad feeling, nothing more. They'll hang me out to dry if I get it wrong this time.'

'Then let me see if I can help,' said Mrs Yu.

Bryant set out his case. 'A student died of tobacco poisoning in the Underground. But even though – as you say – the air in the Tube is bad, there's been no smoking down there for years. My coroner says someone sprayed him with the stuff. According to his medical records, he suffered from asthmatic attacks. We didn't find an inhaler on him, so I'm thinking that the killer substituted his inhaler for one containing poison, then took it away. But

I also have to look into the possibility of accidental death. You don't suppose certain toxins – heavier than airborne ones – could have sunk to the bottom of the system and poisoned him, do you? Through these whirlpool things? We tested the air and found nothing.'

'That's hardly surprising,' said Mrs Yu. 'Every time a train rushes past it displaces the air and transfers it to another magnetic collection point.'

'Surely it would be easier to accept your coroner's theory about the spray?' asked Maggie. 'I don't know why you're making life difficult for yourself.'

'It's what I do,' said Bryant glumly. 'If his death was an accident, then Gloria Taylor was also an accident, and suddenly there's no case. Which would be wonderful, because it would mean no one else is in danger. The alternative is to look for a clever, calculating killer who murders randomly, without remorse, and who leaves no trace.'

'Well, it seems to me that you're caught between two worlds, Arthur, the one that lies beneath London, and the hidden world in which this person you seek moves and connects. For once, you must try to think like a civilian and not like a policeman. I think the investigation is testing your powers in new ways. The Tube network isn't the only ghost system in operation – there's an entire world of invisible connections we never normally get to see. It's just a matter of finding the key. Let's consult the cards.'

She pulled a key from her crimson coiffure, unlocked a drawer in her kitchen table and brought out a packet of tarot cards. 'These are my special "Black Ace" Russian Tarots. I keep them locked up because they're dangerous in the wrong hands.' Maggie shuffled and Mrs Yu snickered.

'I hope they're more accurate than your attempt to read teabags,' said Bryant.

'Take a card.' She offered him the pack.

Bryant withdrew one and looked at it. 'Oh for God's sake, that's the nine of clubs,' he exclaimed in annoyance. 'I can never find it in a normal deck.'

'Oh, that shouldn't be there.' Maggie snatched back the card. 'Deirdre and I were playing poker last night. Choose five more and turn them over.'

He set down the five lurid pictures: a man being struck by lightning, a baby being bitten on the face by a cobra, a pair of Siamese twins being sawn in half, some lepers burying a screaming man alive and a skeleton on a drip. 'Oh, charming,' said Bryant. 'I take it my future well-being is under question.'

'You mustn't take them literally,' said Maggie. 'They're filled with codes and symbols. I'll tell you what I see. Six suspects, three deaths, and a desperate flight through tunnels of darkness. Do you want a piece of cake?'

'No,' snapped Bryant, 'give me a brandy. Listen, there's something I wanted to show you, but I can't get it to work.' He emptied the contents of his overcoat pocket on to the kitchen table, pulled a Liquorice Allsort off his mobile and handed the phone to Mrs Yu. 'Can you get it to the section with photos in?'

Mrs Yu flicked open the photo file with practised ease and examined the contents. Maggie peered over her shoulder. The screen showed a series of brightly coloured patterns, mostly diamonds and zigzags, like the backs of playing cards. Mrs Yu shrugged and snickered. 'You want to know what these are?'

'Yes, one of our detective constables forwarded them to me from the dead man's laptop. What are they?'

'You should know, you see them all the time.'

'Well?' It irritated Bryant when others took pleasure in knowing more than he did.

'They're Tube train seats,' said Mrs Yu, chortling away. 'Different livery patterns in different colour combinations. Thirteen pictures for the different London lines.'

Bryant grimaced in annoyance. 'Why would anyone want to take pictures of those?'

'You're the detective,' said Mrs Yu, as her giggles erupted into bubbling laughter.

38

ON THE LINE

It was now 11:15 p.m. on Friday night, and the surveillance teams were still working across London, hoping to break the case.

To keep things fresh, they had swapped their subjects. Longbright had followed Nikos Nicolau to the Prince Charles cinema, where he sat through a double bill of lesbian vampire movies before returning home. Banbury kept tabs on Rajan Sangeeta, but lost him in between two nightclubs in Greenwich. Bimsley was close by Toby Brooke, who was now drinking alone in a crowded bar on Brick Lane. Mangeshkar took Theo Fontvieille because she could pace him on her motorcycle, and he had now pulled up in Mecklenburgh Square. Renfield was covering Ruby Cates, first at the college, then at the Karma Bar and finally back to the house. For the most part, the PCU staff had managed to stick to their targets like shadows.

But there was a flaw in the plan. Nobody was running

surveillance on Cassie Field. And Cassie was alone, on a deserted, rainswept railway station in South London.

'I just don't bloody believe it!' Theo shouted, hammering up the stairs of the house. 'Look out of the window.'

'What's the matter?' Ruby swung her grey cast to one side and rose from the table, where she was making notes on the rubbishy laptop that had been supplied by Dan Banbury.

'Take a look, dammit. Down there in the street.'

Ruby thumped her way to the front window and opened the curtains. 'What's the matter? I don't see anything.'

'Exactly. Someone's stolen my bloody car! I only left it a minute ago.'

'All right, calm down. Could it have been towed away?'

'What, at eleven o'clock at night? I'm outside restriction hours, and anyway, I have a parking permit.'

'You know how Camden traffic wardens are.'

'No, it's been stolen. I knew it. You can't keep anything nice in this city without some dickhead resenting you. I'm going to kill someone.' He stormed up and down the room in a rage.

'OK, the first thing to do is to ring the Jamestown Road car pound, just to make sure it hasn't been towed.'

Theo was pulled up short. 'How do you know where the car pound is?'

'I can drive, I just can't afford a car at the moment. Then call the police, or better still, get over to the station and fill in the necessary forms. If it has been stolen, you won't be able to claim on your insurance without a case number. You didn't leave the keys in the ignition again, did you?'

'No of course not, I only—' He patted his pockets. 'Oh

no. I don't understand. Someone must have been watching the house and waiting for me to return, standing there in the bloody rain – I only just got out of the bloody thing.'

'And you did it again. You should never have had the car customized. Come on then.' She stuck her hands on her hips defiantly. 'Do something about it, instead of just standing there feeling sorry for yourself.'

Bimsley had lost him. A couple of minutes ago, he had watched Toby Brooke heading back to the packed Brick Lane bar, where he had ordered himself a Kingfisher, but the student had vanished. Bimsley tried the toilet, but it was empty. The dive had been constructed on the ground floor of an old carpet warehouse, and, he now discovered, had a rear exit along a corridor on the far side of the building. Brooke had given him the slip. Furious with himself for having made such a fundamental error, he called Longbright and explained what had happened.

'I'll tell the others,' said Longbright. 'We need to know that the rest are all accounted for.'

'I'm sorry, Janice. It was my own stupid fault.'

'Don't beat yourself up. You could try the Tube station.'

'No good. We're halfway between Aldgate East and Liverpool Street.'

'Then you've got a fifty-fifty chance of finding him. Put in a call to the house and see if he's gone back there.'

Banbury was having similar trouble keeping tabs on Rajan Sangeeta.

A few minutes ago the Indian student had received a call on his mobile, and had immediately conducted a search of the bar where he was drinking. Someone had clearly tipped him off that the housemates were being followed.

If a call had gone out, it meant that the others were attempting to slip off the radar too. Sangeeta waited until the bar had become severely congested, then pushed away through the crowd, leaving Banbury trailing far behind. Only two members of the PCU – Longbright and the late Liberty DuCaine – had received surveillance training, so when the student made his move Banbury found himself in trouble. Longbright had told him to fix the height of his target in his mind, but the room was being strafed with rotating rainbow lights, and Sangeeta had already slipped out through the throng.

Banbury was furious at being tricked. He called Longbright. 'Has anyone else made a run for it?'

'Toby Brooke's done a bunk, the others all seem to be accounted for,' the DS replied. 'There aren't enough of us to go around the clock. Go home, Dan. Get some kip. Nothing's going to change tonight. I'll see you in the morning.'

Banbury took one last walk around the pulsating bar and wearily abandoned his search.

Cassie Field was waiting for her train on Westcombe Park Station. She shivered and stared at the truculent downpour as it sluiced and slopped from the roof, and told herself once more that she had thrown away the evening. She had sought advice from an old schoolfriend, but had arrived at Sophie's Greenwich apartment to find her drunk and weepy. Sophie had been dumped by her creepy estate-agent boyfriend and was consoling herself with her second bottle of bad Burgundy. Cassie had been hoping for some prudent advice about her own love life, but instead had spent the evening listening to Sophie's increasingly slurred complaints about men, before having to hold her head over the sink. Feeling alone and friendless, she headed back to the station and just missed a Charing Cross-bound train.

Cassie retied her acid-pink jacket and watched the yellow carriage lights recede into the distance, as the train swayed and sparked towards the city. There was nothing to hear now but the sound of falling rain.

She wanted to talk to someone, but most of her friends regularly visited the Karma Bar, and there was a good chance that her confessions would reach the residents of Mecklenburgh Square. Her best bet was to try Sophie again, once she had sobered up and cleared her hangover. What a mess. Cassie's jacket was stained with rain and red wine, and the high heels she had chosen to wear had blistered her feet. The station platform was deserted; the overland line was used less frequently now that the Underground reached down into South London.

There was a grey shadow behind the steamed-up, grafittied glass of the waiting room. She couldn't see who it was, but the figure's body language was vaguely familiar. She wondered if she should go and look, but the pinging of the rails told her that there was a train approaching.

She walked to the edge of the rain-soaked platform and wondered how long it would take to get back indoors, where it was warm and dry. There was a sound behind her as the waiting-room door opened. She glanced back, but there was nobody there now.

She looked for the train, and saw that it was coming in fast. Typically, she had chosen to wait at the wrong end of the platform. Beyond the tracks, the ice-blue lights of the city glimmered in melancholy relief. She had never felt so alone and in need of a friend.

Cassie was still wondering if there was anyone else in whom she could confide when a pair of boots slammed into her shoulder-blades, barrelling her forward on to the tracks, right in front of the arriving train.

39

FLYING

By the time Dan Banbury and Giles Kershaw arrived, Greenwich police had cordoned off the platform and covered the body with a yellow plastic tent. 'Ghastly mess,' said Kershaw, checking under the tent flap. 'Her name's Cassie Field. She had John May's card in her wallet, so I take it she's involved with the case. Massive head injuries, so at least it was quick. What did the driver see?'

'He just caught a glimpse of her flying through the air, doesn't really know what happened,' said Banbury. 'He's in the waiting room. He's pretty shaken up.'

'The officer over there told me she jumped.'

'He only got here a few minutes ago, he's going by what the guard told him.'

'Where was the guard?'

'On the opposite platform, texting his girlfriend on his mobile, useless plonker. I'll try and get some more lights rigged up. They need some decent overheads on this platform. What a miserable bloody place to die.'

'She reeks of wine, and there are red-wine stains on her shirt. Very high heels. I know it's the fashion, but they can't be easy to wear. She could have been drunk and wandered too close to the edge. The platform's somewhat on the narrow side.'

'The driver said she was "flying". Ask him yourself. Like a trapeze artiste, he reckons, as in she either jumped or was pushed. He certainly doesn't think she slipped.'

'A couple of fresh bruises on her back,' said Kershaw, carefully turning the body over and raising her jacket. 'Are you getting this?' Banbury was operating the unit's camcorder, from which he would later pull stills. 'Neat little crescents. They look like heel marks, but they can't be. Too high up her back, as if she was kicked on to the line. Mind you, if they were we might get a boot match from them.'

'Flying,' repeated Banbury. He climbed back up on to the platform and looked around, thinking.

'Sorry Dan, what did you say?'

'I said *flying*. As in propelled. Like Gloria Taylor.' Banbury headed for the waiting room, where he stopped to examine the doorway. 'Giles, come and take a look at this.'

Kershaw left the police team and clambered back up, joining the coroner. Banbury was standing on tiptoe, running a penlight along the top edge of the waiting-room doorway. The room was a free-standing box constructed of steel struts and scratched plexiglass. The CSM pointed upward. 'Eight little channels in the dirt up there, four and four, a couple of feet apart. Any ideas?'

'I might have,' said Kershaw cagily. 'Have you?'

'Yes.'

'Go on then, you first.'

'Fingers. The killer climbed up on to that row of seats, stood on their backs, swung on the metal lintel to get momentum, then just let go. She wouldn't have seen or heard a thing, with the train approaching. The boots smacked hard into her back, the killer dropped down and ran off. How mad is that?'

'It'd take some nerve.' Giles flicked wet blond hair out of his eyes. 'Can you get prints from them?'

'I'll try, but it looks like the dust got pulled off in the process, leaving smears. The whole thing probably only took three or four seconds. No cameras at this spot to pick up her final moments. No one else on the platform. They're going to hold a couple of the passengers for witness statements, but my guess is that the windows of the train would have obscured their vision – it's been chucking it down for the last couple of hours, and the platform's shockingly underlit. If the killer was wearing something dark to blend in, no one would have even seen them.'

'Two deaths from the same household. Your old man's going to go crazy.'

'He's not my old man,' said Banbury with a grim laugh. 'You're still seconded to the unit, matey. Don't worry, though, from what I hear we've got the whole of tomorrow to work out what happened before we're kicked back out on the streets. At least you've got somewhere to go. I'll be down the Job Centre again.'

For the next half-hour they worked quietly beside each other in the falling rain, while the local police had loud arguments with each other about infringement of jurisdiction.

'Always the same with the Met,' Banbury muttered,

searching the wet ground for evidence. 'They're more worried about who gets the case than that poor girl on the tracks. Hang on a minute.' He took his Maglite to the waiting room, crouched down and carefully picked up something he had seen on the floor, bagging it. 'What does that look like to you?' he asked Kershaw. Raising the bag into the light, he displayed an inch-long sliver of curved grey plastic.

'No idea. There's a fragment of raised lettering on the inside, very small,' said the coroner. 'Let me see.' He took out Bryant's old magnifying glass and read: *rty UC*.

'Pretty clear to me,' he decided. 'Property of University College Hospital. Standard NHS typeface. Looks like a piece from a plastic leg cast. Keep looking around.'

Banbury climbed over the platform fence and conducted a search of the gorse bushes behind the waiting room. A few minutes later he re-emerged covered in mud and brambles, carrying a dark bundle. 'You're going to love this,' he told Kershaw. 'I think the overcoat got discarded before the killer carried out that little trapeze stunt.'

'Can you identify it?'

Banbury unfurled the rainbow-striped material. 'It looks like the one Matthew Hillingdon was wearing the night he was killed.'

'You're telling me Miss Field was pushed under a train by a girl with a broken leg and a dead man?' said Kershaw. 'Bryant's going to love this.'

40

CONFLICTING EVIDENCE

The warehouse on the Caledonian Road was a good venue for a wake, which was just as well, as the PCU's Saturday-morning debriefing session had virtually turned into one.

It was 7:30 a.m., and the team looked beaten. No one had had more than three hours' sleep. The thought that Cassie Field's death should have been prevented nagged at them all. Arthur Bryant had another worry. Each death brought a new level of confusion to the investigation. Especially as it seemed that the manager of the Karma Bar had been kicked under a train by Ruby Cates.

'As soon as this meeting is over, you're going back to the house in Mecklenburgh Square to make an arrest,' Raymond Land warned. 'I want that woman brought in and held here until we can make the charge stick.'

'We have to be sure first,' said Renfield, speaking for everyone. 'I saw her go into the house just after 10:00 p.m., and she didn't come back out.'

'She could have left through the back door and climbed

over the garden fence into the street behind,' said Land. 'She's an athlete, isn't she?'

'Yes, and her broken leg is in a cast.'

'Did you look to see if it was really broken when you matched up the fragment?'

'No, I didn't have to take it off. I could see the piece fitted perfectly.'

'That's not the point.'

'I've warned her not to leave the house until we return.'

'I'm going to let you chair this, John.' Land rubbed his tired face. 'I don't know where we're going any more.'

May rose to his feet. 'OK, let's go through alibis and evidence, taking into account what happened last night. We're not here to lay blame or assess performance. We need to put everything else aside and advance this very quickly.'

He and Longbright read the statements from the Mecklenburgh Square housemates and the Greenwich witnesses, ploughing through the pathology reports together and reconstructing what they knew about the deaths. Timelines were drawn across three whiteboards at the rear of the room. The low murmur of discussion sporadically burst into heated argument. The pipes ticked as the boiler struggled to warm the building. Meagre items of evidence were laid out and discussed, but after an hour they were no further on. Somewhere out in the surrounding streets, a killer watched and waited.

'What I see is that you're building a case against Toby Brooke here,' said Meera hotly. 'He has no proper alibi for the night Hillingdon was murdered. He went missing again last night at the time Field died. But just look at him — common sense should tell you he wouldn't hurt a fly. And what if it's not someone from the house at all? All you've

307

got is a travel card swiped through at Liverpool Street Station on the night Hillingdon died. He might not even have used it himself.'

'They all deny returning it to his bedroom, but they swear no one else has been in the house,' May remarked.

'Well of course they'd deny touching it,' said Bryant, 'because that would implicate whoever claimed to have returned the damned thing. Dan, where are we on physical evidence?'

Banbury consulted his notes. 'The CCTV footage on Gloria Taylor and Matthew Hillingdon – completely unhelpful in Taylor's case, but I'm trying some new frame-enhancement software on Hillingdon's footage. There might be something before the end of the day on that. Nothing else new except the bootprints on Field's back and the piece of plastic found in the waiting room, which we now know matches Cates's leg cast. Giles and I carried out a re-enactment, and we're pretty certain how her bruises got there. No prints on the travel card or the rest of the stickers, but the initials on the card are definitely in Hillingdon's handwriting. Mr Bryant and I knocked up a rudimentary tobacco spray. It was ridiculously easy to make.'

'What about their technology?'

'OK, no surprises on any of the laptops, except that Toby Brooke has been buying a lot of expensive stuff on the internet lately. We checked all the call registers on the mobiles – nothing untoward there. For all we know they might have had a few pay-as-you-go handsets knocking about. We know there was a spare house mobile for use in emergencies, but no one can find it now. Theo Fontvieille remembers seeing a couple of others at the house, one with a Hello Kitty doll attached to it. Nobody will back him up on that.'

'Anything else?'

'Yeah, the books about haunted Underground stations might have had Cates's name inside, but she swears it's not her handwriting, and it turns out they were taken out from UCL's reference library by Toby Brooke. A set of twelve photographs from Hillingdon's laptop appear to be close-ups of the seats of different Tube trains. Oh, and somebody stole Theo Fontvieille's Porsche last night.'

'Mr Fox,' murmured Banbury. The others looked at him. 'Oh, it's just that he had a photograph of a Tube station bench on his wall, then it was gone.'

'I thought we'd decided that the two cases weren't linked,' said May.

'We had,' Bryant reassured him. 'Don't worry. Let's go on.'

'Can we go back to the motives?' asked Longbright. 'According to the interviews, Gloria Taylor's workmates insist she had no enemies. But maybe she had something on her mind, because she forgot to take home her daughter's birthday present on the night she died. Hillingdon had no dodgy connections either. He was dating Ruby Cates, although it now appears she's been having casual sex with Fontvieille for a while.'

'Wait, how do you know that?' Renfield demanded.

'Simple, Jack. I asked her. We still don't know who Hillingdon drank with on Tuesday night, because most of the Spitalfields bars were rammed to the gills, and none of the staff recall seeing him. Plus, there are about a hundred of them. Cassie Field was positively adored. Nobody has a bad word to say about her.'

'I hate to raise this again,' said Renfield, 'but what if the deaths were random?' Everyone groaned. 'No, listen to me. Suppose one of the housemates has psychotic episodes and just – lashes out? So, a stranger on the Tube is attacked, and Field is literally kicked under a train.'

'Doesn't work,' said May. 'Hillingdon's death was premeditated, and if you're assuming it was a housemate, following Field to Westcombe Park Station in order to kill her means someone was waiting for an opportunity to get her alone.'

'Can I just bring in Tony McCarthy?' asked Bryant, as another groan went around the room. 'If you remember, the junkie is the only one who can identify Mr Fox. UCH is releasing him at noon today because they need the bed. I want to make sure it's common knowledge that he's back on the streets. There's a strong likelihood that Mr Fox will try to take him out again, and given your spotty track record on surveillance I reckon he's got a pretty slender chance of survival.'

'Why don't you just shake the details of Fox's ID out of McCarthy?' asked Renfield. 'I can put the fear of God up him without leaving any marks. Leave me alone in a room with him. He'll fall apart in minutes.'

'Thank you, Jack, we're a Home Office unit, not the Stasi. I'll let you know if we need the electrodes.'

'Just offering, that's all.'

'Whoever killed Hillingdon took his overcoat and wore it to kill Cassie Field at the station,' said Longbright. 'That doesn't make sense. Dan, did you get anything off it yet?'

'There were no hairs, a few skin flakes, a couple of small oily patches around the collar. I'm expecting the analysis back shortly.'

'So,' said Bryant, 'any questions?'

'Yeah, plenty.' Meera folded her arms defiantly. 'But are there any answers? I mean, do you think this is over now? That whoever's been doing this has achieved his – or her – aim and finished?'

'Have you actually been in the same room as us for the last hour?' Bryant snapped. 'I've told you, these acts are premeditated, but we don't know to what end. Until we understand the killer's psychology, we won't be able to tell if it's over. We have to assume it isn't, and find a way of protecting all the potential victims.'

'Can I remind you that we've less than ten hours to wrap everything up?' Meera retorted. '*Everything* – your Mr bloody Fox, this subway vampire, the lot. I've already been out of a job once this year, I don't want to be back in the same situation again.'

'Then come up with something useful,' Bimsley suggested.

'We break in,' said Renfield.

'What?' It was Bryant's turn to stare.

'We break into the house in the square. Just smash a window and storm the place. Put the fear of God up them. We've got legal entitlement. You reckon somebody there is arrogant enough to think they've got away with it – they won't be expecting a surprise visit.'

'Apart from the fact that Dan already took the house apart looking for evidence, ransacking the students' rooms while they're still asleep is not an option I want to consider. First you suggest torture, now burglary. Why don't we just go out and shoot them all?'

'You come up with a better idea,' muttered Renfield.

'Mr Bryant, you're sure it's one of the housemates?' Bimsley asked.

'I know it is.' Bryant smoothed his hand across his desk, which was still littered with playing cards. 'The proof is shapeshifting right here in front of me. I can see it – I just can't identify it.'

'Then we stick to them like napalm for the rest of the morning, until one of them makes a mistake.' He looked to the others for confirmation. 'What difference is it going to make? We can't do any more here, and it's our last day. There's nothing else left to do.'

'Can I just say that in the entire history of the unit, this has been the most disastrous investigation you lot have ever attempted.' Raymond Land spoke up finally, adding his opinion in the most unhelpful way possible. 'It's like something out of *The Muppet Show*. I've seen better organized water-balloon fights. Well, it's over now. We're no further on than when we started. We're dead. Finished. Washed up. We might just as well all go home and do some gardening. On Monday morning we're going to wake up with no jobs to go to, and this dump will be turned into a Starbucks. It's the end of my career. Well, thanks a bunch.'

Everyone booed and threw paper cups at him.

41

THE TRENCH EFFECT

DS Longbright was taken by surprise when Georgia Conroy called; she had not been expecting to hear from Pentonville Prison's former history teacher again. 'You told me to call if I remembered anything else,' Conroy explained. 'It's only a little thing.'

'That's fine,' replied Longbright, searching for a pen. 'Right now I'll be grateful for anything.'

'Well, you know I said Lloyd Lutine wanted me to go with him to visit Abney Park Cemetery?'

'Yes.'

'I thought it was odd at the time, because he'd given me the impression that he'd hated his father. He asked me to accompany him because he'd just discovered where he was buried.'

'How did he find out?'

'I don't know. Maybe he checked the Council records. As I said, I turned him down because it seemed a bit creepy. Then he mentioned something odd. That his father wasn't supposed to have been buried there. It wasn't allowed, there had been a mistake, something like that. I'm sorry, it's not much . . .'

'No, I'm glad you called.'

Longbright thought it through. If Mr Fox's father had also been raised in King's Cross, Abney Park would not have been his local cemetery. But people could be buried more or less wherever they wanted, so why should it not have been allowed? Thanking Georgia Conroy, she rang off and took her notes into Arthur Bryant's office.

'I know we're supposed to be concentrating on the Mecklenburgh Square case, but can you spare a minute?' she asked.

Arthur peered up at her over the tops of his bifocals. 'Is it urgent?'

'You're doing a jigsaw, Arthur.'

'It helps me to think.' He gave up trying to fit a piece and sat back, turning it over in his fingers. 'Queen Victoria's funeral procession. Two thousand pieces. I wonder how many mourners in the crowd travelled by Tube that day to watch it pass? Dan Banbury thinks someone chose to murder Gloria Taylor in the Underground system because of the sheer volume of people passing through it. He says it's difficult to solve a crime in a public place because the site always gets contaminated.'

'He's got a point.'

'I thought the killer might be re-enacting some kind of historical event connected with the tunnels – after all, they've been there for a century and a half. All three deaths are connected to the railway. Even Tony McCarthy was attacked underground. Despite my insistence that everything has been premeditated, John has a theory that we're looking for someone who's acting out of sheer panic. I can't see the sense in that myself. Meera thinks it's a man who hates women, and Matthew Hillingdon just got in the way. Bimsley and Renfield think we should be looking for an escaped lunatic. Raymond's right, in all my days with this unit, I've never had such a disagreeably confused investigation on my hands – and yet I know there's an absurdly simple answer we've all overlooked. It tantalizes and terrifies me to think that someone else may die because I can't see something that's right in front of me.' He threw the jigsaw piece down in annoyance. 'What's your opinion?'

'I need to talk to you about Mr Fox.' She told him about Georgia Conroy's phone call.

'Perhaps it wasn't about the location of the cemetery, but the grave itself,' said Bryant, rolling up the jigsaw and sliding it into his desk drawer.

'What do you mean?'

'The only people who aren't allowed to be buried on Christian sites are those of different faiths, and suicides. Could he have been a suicide, do you think, accidentally buried in a Christian spot?'

'I suppose it's possible.'

'Suicides happen all the time in the Underground system. Mr Fox had a photograph of a London Underground bench on the wall of his bedroom.'

'Some kind of sentimental memory?'

'One way to find out. Give Anjam Dutta a call at North One Watch.'

Longbright eventually got through to the King's Cross security headquarters. 'Can you do me a favour?' she asked. 'I need a list of all the one-unders you've had at King's Cross, going back as far as records allow.'

'That would be about thirty years,' Dutta told her. 'We never transferred anything older than that to the new data system.'

'How difficult would it be to get me those?'

'Not difficult at all. They've all been logged in. Give me a few minutes.'

While they waited for the email, Longbright and Bryant followed the thought. 'Mr Fox asked a virtual stranger to accompany him to his father's grave, and he still visits the site,' said Janice.

'So the death of his father could have been the turning point in his life.'

Bryant's laptop pinged. Longbright didn't have the patience to wait for Bryant to fiddle about trying to open his emails, so she leaned across him and launched the document, quickly running down the list of names. Most of the suicides were marked with ancillary files containing brief police statements. It didn't take her long to find what she was looking for.

'There you go.' She tapped the screen with a glossy crimson nail. 'Albert Thomas Edward Ketch went under a train on November the eighteenth at 4:00 p.m., on the Piccadilly Line platform of King's Cross Station, the third suicide that year. Hang on, there's a witness statement.' She clicked through to the attached page. 'Witness told attending police she had spoken to a boy she thinks was named Jonas. She insisted he had been sitting with Albert Ketch, waiting for a train, but the child was never traced.'

'No child traced,' mused Bryant. 'A key witness. It shouldn't have been that difficult.'

'It looks like they didn't even try to find him.'

'No. No, they didn't.'

'Why not?'

'They didn't have time to look.' Bryant clambered to his feet and searched the stacks of books balanced on crates around the edges of his desk. 'They couldn't conduct a proper search, because later that day—' He pulled out a volume on the history of the London Underground and threw it open. 'You see what I'm getting at?'

'Oh no,' said Longbright softly.

Bryant stabbed a finger at the page. 'November the eighteenth, 1987 was the date of the King's Cross fire.'

'The boy's name was Jonas Ketch. The bench—'

'The place where he last sat and talked to his father. I asked Dan to run out the shots of Mr Fox's room. What did I do with them?' Bryant found the sheaf of photographs and laid them out. 'There it is.'

The photograph showed the missing picture of the red metal bench. 'It looks like the boy saw his old man commit suicide right in front of him. Just an ordinary metal Tube station bench, but the background of tiles – that has to be King's Cross before it was redecorated.'

'So he took the boy there,' said Longbright, 'sat him down and talked to him. Then he rose, walked to the edge of the platform and dropped under the wheels of the incoming train.'

'Jonas Ketch's father died just three and a half hours before the King's Cross fire. Hang on.'

Bryant turned the page of his reference book, glanced at it and said, 'No one was ever able to discover exactly how the fire began, but they think someone dropped a lit match down the side of the escalator. It was one of the old wooden ones, and was covered in grease embedded with bits of paper and human hair that caught alight. Thirty-one people died, and another sixty were seriously injured. There had been a number of small fires at the site before, but this one spread in a completely new way. The escalator had steel sides and the flames rose at an angle that created the perfect conditions for something called the Trench Effect. An intense blast of flame that turned the ticket hall into an incinerator.'

'You think it was the boy?' Longbright was appalled.

'After seeing his father killed, he burned the station down in an act of fury.'

'My God.'

'It fits with everything we know, and would explain why death means so little to him.' Bryant returned to the laptop. 'Show me how to do this.'

'Don't touch it, let me. What are you after?'

'The names of all the fire victims.'

The list of those who died that day was public knowledge, and it took no time to locate a memorial site. 'That's why he wants to silence Tony McCarthy,' said Bryant, sitting back. 'It has nothing to do with the time they spent together at Pentonville. There's a Jim McCarthy listed as one of the victims of the King's Cross fire. Tony McCarthy's prison file records his parents as James and Sharon McCarthy. Suppose when they first met, Mr Fox—'

'Real name, Jonas Ketch.'

'Ketch accidentally revealed a little too much of himself. Suppose Mac realized that as a boy Ketch had committed an act of arson.'

'Killing McCarthy's father in the process.'

'It puts the case on an entirely different footing. You'd

better make sure Renfield's there when Tony McCarthy comes out of UCH, and stays by him wherever he goes.'

'This is my case, Arthur,' Longbright pleaded. 'Let me do it, for Liberty's sake.'

'No, it's too dangerous. I want you to switch with Renfield and take one of the students.'

'That's not fair, and you know it. You owe me this.'

'Janice, your mother died in similar circumstances, trying to lure a criminal out into the open. Do you honestly think I'm going to let you risk your life as well? Put Renfield on it. I want you to stay right here, where I can keep an eye on you.'

Longbright stormed out of the detectives' room. Back in the corridor, she walked past Jack Renfield's office, stopping only to grab her jacket.

42

SLEIGHT OF HAND

'Hillingdon's overcoat,' said Bryant, wandering into the Crime Scene Manager's room, 'the oily patches are tobacco spray.' He looked very pleased with himself.

'How did you know?' Banbury asked. 'The results only just came back. I was about to come and see you.'

'The killer didn't forget the coat, he planted it.'

'What do you mean?'

'Someone in that house has been a bit too clever for their own good. The principles of magic: if you see the impossible happen, it isn't impossible. You've been tricked.'

'Sorry, Mr Bryant, I don't have the faintest idea what you're talking about.'

'In other words, you can only disappear from a moving train carriage if you were never on it in the first place.'

'Do you want me to get John before I go?' He made it sound as if he was offering to fetch a nurse for a rambling patient.

'No, go and keep an eye on – who did you draw this time?'

'The girl – Ruby Cates. Giles is covering for me until I get there. I'm going to make her take that cast off.'

'Go on, relieve him.' Bryant waited for the door to shut and turned back to Professor Hoffman's book of card tricks. Holding it open with his left hand, he attempted to shuffle a fresh pack with his right, and sprayed cards all over the floor.

Outside in the corridor, John May saw a ghost. The sight brought him up short and chilled his blood. Fearfully, he slowly backed away.

Liberty DuCaine was sitting on an orange plastic chair in the hall, reading a copy of *Hard News*. But that was impossible; Liberty's bodily remains had been poured into a City of London Crematorium urn on Monday morning.

May looked at DuCaine, and DuCaine gave him a friendly smile. 'I'm here to see Janice Longbright,' he said cheerfully.

'Is she . . . expecting you?' asked May.

'Yeah, I'm Fraternity – Liberty's brother?'

Now May saw the differences between the pair. Fraternity's eyes were a little more deep-set and thoughtful. He was bulkier, with a dense neck and arms like heavy copper pipes. The black gym shirt under his tracksuit said 'Full Contact Fighter'.

'Sorry, I'm a little late. Some kind of problem with the Northern Line.' When he rose, he stood a full head above May.

'Don't worry. I'll take you to her office.' May wondered why Henley had turned him down, if DuCaine had achieved good grades. Despite the guidelines set by the

Equal Opportunities Commission, physically imposing males were always useful on the street.

May pushed open the door to Longbright's office and found it empty, her coat gone. 'It looks like she's nipped out,' he said. 'Do you mind waiting?'

'No problem.' Fraternity walked around the room, taking it in. 'She said she had some information about my case. I appreciate the help.'

'I'll have to leave you here until she gets back. We're having a very difficult day.' May headed to his own office, and found Bryant on his hands and knees, picking up playing cards.

'I see you're hard at work on the investigation, then,' he said.

'I am, actually. I know how Matthew Hillingdon was able to vanish from a moving train. Obviously, I had a rough idea fairly early on in the investigation, but it only became crystal clear to me a few minutes ago. Would you like to hear?'

May waited at his desk while Bryant picked up the cards and clumsily attempted to shuffle them. 'On Tuesday night, Hillingdon boarded a train at Liverpool Street Station, went west on the Circle Line to King's Cross and was supposed to catch the last southbound Piccadilly Line train. It arrived on time in King's Cross at 12:24 a.m., yes? He texted Ruby Cates from the King's Cross interchange at 12:20 a.m., telling her he was heading for Russell Square Tube, a two-minute journey. The CCTV showed him getting on to the train. The next shot we've got is of the train pulling out. But there was another event.'

'What?'

'Hillingdon shut his coat in the door, so they had to

re-open the carriage doors. We don't know how soon after this the driver shut them again. Suppose Hillingdon ducked and ran down the carriage, getting off at the other end before the train left?'

'To go where? The cameras would have picked him up.'

'If you remember, there was one more train that night, leaving from the Northern Line platform three minutes later. The tunnel connecting the two lines was being retiled, and that camera wasn't working – Dutta told us that. So he hops on to the train, deliberately shuts his coat in the door, waits until the doors re-open, hops back off through the next set of doors, beyond sight of the working camera, and catches the northbound train.'

'Matthew Hillingdon's body was found in King's Cross, not at the far end of the Northern Line.'

'I didn't say it was Matthew who caught the other train, did I? Hillingdon was sprayed with tobacco somewhere in the station and left to die. The killer switched clothes with him. He put on Hillingdon's woolly hat and his ridiculous candy-striped overcoat, and ran for the train. The cameras picked up the hat and the coat. I mean, they could hardly miss, could they?'

'I know we only saw the figure from the back, but it looked like Hillingdon.'

'No, it *moved* like Hillingdon. Not a very hard motion to imitate, typical drunken student pimp-roll, feet at ten to two and arms swinging. And he was running, so the frames were blurred.'

'Then what happened to Hillingdon? If he'd been anywhere in the station, we would have seen him – oh my God.'

'Precisely. We *did* see him. He was caught by the cameras, and in the process became his own urban myth.'

'The Night Crawler.'

'Exactly. Not the ghost of a dead man, not a giant walking bat, and not a homeless person either. A dying student in a long black leather coat several sizes too large for him. He was pouring with sweat, so his long black hair was plastered around his head, and he was dying – crawling along the floor in the only direction he could manage – downwards. Disoriented and confused, barely able to breathe, he falls from the unused platform and hides in the cool darkness – but he manages to get the coat off and loosen his shirt collar before losing consciousness.'

'You think even that part was planned? That the black leather coat was chosen—'

'—by the killer to hide the victim. Probably, but what if it was somebody who actually knew about the myth of the Night Crawler?'

'That's something only the guards talked about,' said May. 'Isn't it?'

'No.' Bryant offered his partner a card. 'It's in a book called *Mind the Ghosts*. You brought back the paperback from the house in Mecklenburgh Square. It either belonged to Ruby Cates or Toby Brooke.'

'Or both of them. No, it can't be her. She's in a plastic cast. She's got a broken leg.'

'Except that Renfield didn't check to see if it was really broken. Tell me which card you picked.'

May turned over the card and studied it.

'It's the nine of clubs, yes?' said Bryant triumphantly.

'No. Mrs Bun the Baker's Wife.'

'Bugger,' said Bryant, 'I've mixed up the decks again.'

324

43

THE LURE

DS Janice Longbright arrived at University College Hospital just as Tony McCarthy was emerging, limping through the swing doors. He waved her away as soon as he spotted her. 'I just want to be left alone, OK? Don't come near me. I don't want no cops following me around all the time.'

'You'd rather have Mr Fox find you again?' asked Longbright, falling into step with him. 'Next time he's going to push that skewer through the soft underside of your jaw and up into your brain, assuming you have one. Is that what you want?'

'I can handle it.'

'How? Going to grow a moustache and dye your hair? Or have you got a gun at home? You'll need it, because he'll come after you again if you hang around his manor. Got somewhere else to go?'

'I can take care of myself.'

'You couldn't take care of a spider-plant, Mac. Don't you think the medical services are strained enough without them having to look after you?' She placed a strong hand on his skinny arm. 'I think you and I had better go for a little talk.'

'I've got nothing to say to you.'

'You already admitted you know Mr Fox's real identity.'

'No, I never.'

Longbright looked into his bloodshot eyes. 'Oh, you don't remember, do you? Did they give you a bronchoscopy?'

McCarthy looked blankly at her.

'Did they stick a bloody great tube down your throat?'

'Yeah.'

She knew they had; she had seen the equipment being prepared on the day she visited the hospital. 'It means you were dosed with a retro-amnesiac drug. You don't remember anything, do you? You were whacked out on meds, Mac, that's why you don't recall shooting your mouth off about Mr Fox. Or should we call him Jonas Ketch? Thought you were being clever, did you, giving us a few clues about a prison teacher, when all the time you knew who he really was?'

That brought McCarthy to a halt. 'You're doing my head in, I don't remember . . .' he pleaded.

'I think you should be asking yourself why I'd even bother to save the life of a grubby little junkie like you.'

'I'm not using any more.'

'Pull the other one, Pinocchio. The worst part about being you must be waking up every morning and remembering who you are. Not that you'll be waking up for much longer, with Ketch waiting to stick you.'

'What the hell do you want from me?' asked McCarthy, exasperated.

'Help me catch him and I'll save your miserable, wasted little life,' said Longbright.

It was 2:14 p.m. on Saturday afternoon, a relatively busy time at the King's Cross intersection, but today the Northern Line was seriously overloaded with passengers. Anjam Dutta set down his coffee and shifted his attention from screen to screen.

'We'll have to shut Staircase C ahead of the rush hour,' he instructed. 'And re-route the incoming Blacks across to Navy.' The safety and security team referred to the Tube lines by their colours when they were working at speed. 'What's happening out there today?'

He studied the two cameras trained on the main ticket hall. 'We've accounted for the Arsenal charity match and the Trafalgar Square rally – remind me what that's for?'

'Something to do with global warming,' said Sandwich. 'There's an anti-fur demo in Oxford Street, but West End Central's advice is that it'll be pretty small.'

'The traffic's still way up for a Saturday. You haven't picked up anything on the Net? Anyone running RSS feeds?'

'Local news, Sky, BBC, London Talk Radio, nothing unusual I can see,' said Marianne, 'but you're right, there's definitely something going on.'

'Keep your eyes open. If it gets any worse, we'll have to partially shut the station. This is really weird.' Dutta mopped his forehead and watched as a fresh surge of passengers descended the staircase to the ticket hall.

Janice Longbright wanted to get McCarthy off the street, so she dragged him into the New Delhi Indian Restaurant on Drummond Street, behind Euston Station, chucked him into the chair opposite and ordered spicy Thalis for both of them.

'I like this place because it's fast,' she explained. 'In fifteen minutes, when you get up from this table, you'll have told me everything you know about Jonas Ketch, or I'm going to take you into the kitchen and shove your face into the tandoori oven, d'you understand?'

'I don't know why you're so aggressive,' McCarthy whined, going for sympathy.

'It's your choice, mate. Talk, or this'll be the worst Ruby Murray you've ever had.'

'I'll give you what I know about him, all right? I could tell he was bang out of order, soon as I met him.' McCarthy fidgeted around on his chair like a child at Sunday school. 'All sensible talk and that, but crazy behind the eyes. Damage, see. You can't trust damaged people.'

Longbright figured it took one to know one. 'How did you meet him?' she asked.

'I was doing eighteen months for receiving stolen goods, he came in to teach English. A lot of the inmates ain't got English as a first language. I got volunteered to help him. He never said much, but there was this one day, he was showing the class how to write a CV for a job using some prepared examples. When the lesson ended he got off sharpish and left some stuff behind, just papers in a plastic folder an' that. I was going to put our answer sheets back inside and leave it on the table, honest.'

'But you had a look through.'

'Well I had to, didn't I? And I saw this letter he was writing to his old man. About a dozen different versions of the same thing, all slightly different, written months apart from each other, like he kept starting it and changing his mind about what he was going to say. So I nicked one, I figured he wouldn't notice. When I got back to my cell, I read it. So get this: it's a kind of history of his life, all the stuff that made him angry. His parents was always trying to kill each other. Finally his old man, this bloke Al Ketch, took the kid out of the house one morning after some big bust-up with his missus, and dragged him down the Tube at King's Cross, saying they was going away on holiday.'

'Keep going.'

'Jonas hated his mother, right, so he reckoned the old man was taking him off somewhere where he'd never have to see the old cow again. He was all excited about going away with his dad. So he sits down with his dad on a platform bench and they're talking about their plans, how they're going to go to Spain and get a fresh start, how it's going to be great for both of them. Then his old man gets all excited, striding about, ranting, and when he's finished, he calms down and tells the boy he's leaving. Not *they*'re leaving, *he*'s leaving. He's had enough of them both, and he's dumping the kid. And Jonas worships his old man, right, he can't do no wrong in the boy's eyes. He thought his dad was taking them off some place where they'd be happy, and it turns out the bastard is abandoning him. And while the kid is watching, the old man turns away, goes to the edge of the platform and walks – just walks – under the train that's coming in. The kid is halfway there, heading towards his father just as he goes under, and he gets covered in his old man's blood. So he runs off in a right state, and when he gets home, he finds his mum has killed herself. She's taken an overdose of sleeping tablets and choked to death on her own vomit. How messed up is that?'

'And then you ran into Ketch again at St Pancras Station?'

'That's right, and he didn't even recognize me, 'cause it was two years later and I'd lost a lot of weight, being off prison food and on the smack, and he gave me a couple of jobs to do, just pocket-money stuff, and I couldn't tell him that I'd still got the letter, and that night I went home and read it again. And it freaked me out.'

'Why did it freak you out?' Longbright asked as their food arrived.

'Because by this time I'd worked out the date, hadn't I? I mean, I'm not likely to forget it, ever. His father died on the day of the King's Cross fire, just like my old man, only my dad was in the station and burned to death, and his died under a train in the morning. And that's when I knew, see. That's when I knew who started the fire. He didn't have to say nothing, I just knew. I could see it in his eyes. Kind of horrified he'd done it, and kind of arrogant as well. Trapped by something caused by his anger, something so terrible he'd never be able to leave the area until he'd come to terms with it. But that's not possible, is it? I mean, something on that scale. I watched on the news as they carried the bodies out. Even the survivors were completely black. The effect those scenes had on me – I guess that's when I started playing up, you know?'

He started to cry, and the trickle of a tear became a flood, so that he was forced to blow his nose on his napkin and turn away from her, nuzzling the heel of his hand against his forehead. The gaudy red Indian restaurant had become a confessional. Longbright suddenly felt sorry for him.

'Here's what we're going to do,' she said, drawing his eyes to hers. 'He'll know you're out of hospital now. He's around here somewhere. He'll follow you home and try to finish the job. But you have a chance of staying alive. I'll stay close by you, and keep my team on alert. When he shows his hand and moves in, we'll get him.'

'Is that it? You really think I'm going to survive that?' McCarthy was rubbing his red eyes, a frightened child. 'He'll stick me, and he'll give you lot the slip again.'

'You want to end this, don't you?'

'I know what you're up to. You just want to get the arrest, you don't care about me.'

'I'll bring him in, Tony, I swear. And I won't let you die. We need to get him somewhere that's enclosed, with escape routes we can monitor. Somewhere that's always being watched.'

'Where?'

'The station. You're going to perform that stupid wide-boy walk of yours, shout at the guards and passengers, generally make a bloody great nuisance of yourself, and draw him back to the spot where it all began.'

'People could get hurt. You're crazy.'

'You have no idea how crazy,' warned Longbright.

44

REMOTE CONTROL

Arthur Bryant found Sergeant Jack Renfield in the filthy junk-filled anteroom that passed for the unit's reception area. 'What are you still doing here?' he asked in obvious irritation.

'Dan's been trying out his new radios,' said Renfield. 'But don't worry, I'm on it.'

'What radios?'

'We're short-handed,' Renfield explained, 'so he's been developing these close-range radio mikes.' He held up something that looked like a pen refill, curved at one end. 'He's been dying to try them out. They're like the security headsets bouncers use, but they've got a better range. During surveillance we can stay in contact with each other, and we can track everyone's movements on the laptops.' He turned his screen around and pointed to a number of red dots pulsing on a Google map of London.

'Do they work underground?'

'I don't know,' Renfield admitted.

'We're after a killer who operates in the Tube network, you flybrain. This is not the right time to start testing out Dan's toys. I asked Janice to get you to cover Tony McCarthy as he came out of hospital. Didn't she come and talk to you?'

'No. I saw her go out a while back. She didn't say where she was going.'

'Stubborn bloody woman! Has she got one of those things?'

'Yeah.'

'Then see if you can raise her. And get after whoever it is you're supposed to be following.'

'Nikos Nicolau. He's been sitting on his fat arse in an internet café in Tottenham Court Road for the past two hours.'

'And what if he suddenly disappears? Where have the others gone?'

'Dan's gone after the stroppy Indian fella, Sangeeta; Colin's got Toby Brooke; Meera's got the rich one, Fontvieille; John's covering Ruby Cates. Raymond's in his room having a massive row with someone from the Home Office.'

'And I know exactly what Janice is up to,' added Bryant. 'Find someone to cover Nicolau – use Raymond if you have to, he'll kick up a fuss but we need everyone we can lay our hands on. Find out where Janice is, and bloody go after her. If it turns out that Mr Fox is following them, she'll need all the back-up she can get. This has the potential to blow up in our faces. We're close now, so I don't want anything to go wrong.'

'We're close?' Renfield was surprised. 'That's news to me. Hang on, I've got Dan on the line.' He talked with the

CSM for a moment, then covered the phone. 'He just spoke to Janice. She's on the Euston Road with McCarthy in tow, heading east.'

'I know what she's up to. She's taking him back to the Tube station, where it all began. Your bug won't be any use there if they go down on to the platforms. Get to her first. Stay as close as you can, and keep in contact.'

'How can I if she goes underground?'

'I don't know, run up the stairs and call me as soon as you get a signal. You'll have to figure it out. I'll stay here. Someone has to keep an eye on you all.'

'You know me,' said Renfield, 'I'll have a go at anyone, but we could do with some more back-up than this.'

Just then, Fraternity DuCaine appeared in the doorway.

'Good God, you're not dead,' said Bryant, clutching theatrically at his heart.

'Yeah, I get that a lot. I'm his brother,' said Fraternity. 'Sorry, I didn't mean to make you jump. You don't know how long the DS will be, do you?'

'You could give us a hand while you're waiting,' said Bryant.

DuCaine shrugged amiably. 'Sure, no problem.'

'Good.' Bryant unleashed a gruesome smile. 'What do you know about card tricks?'

Anjam Dutta badly wanted a cigarette. He couldn't drink any more coffee. His nerves were on fire. Something very big and very bad was happening at his station. He had called his bosses, but all they could suggest was closing the entire interchange down. Dutta's eyes flicked from screen to screen, trying to make sense of what he was seeing.

'We've got a camera out on the Circle, Sandwich. Did you call maintenance?'

'Twenty minutes ago,' Sandwich told him. 'They're having trouble getting to their equipment.'

'I'm not surprised.' Dutta could see the problem: a knot of passengers blocking the path to one of the supply stores. Usually he could register travel patterns just by glancing at the screens. Football days were the easiest because supporters were helpfully dressed in their team colours. Other groups offered subtler clues. Rush-hour commuters knew their way around the system, and rarely strayed from their routes. They didn't queue for windows because they all had travel cards. Tourists stood in line for tickets and grouped around the two main maps. Schoolchildren, students, hen-night parties, clubbers aiming to arrive in time for cheap admissions, concert-goers – they were all easy enough to spot.

But this one had him puzzled. There was no pattern – just a massive increase in traffic, right across the station. Passengers of all types and ages were pouring in from every entrance, despite the fact that access had already been restricted. He checked the arrival times of the Eurostar trains and found no correlation there. The wall clock read 14:34 p.m. It was as if the rush hour had decided to start three hours early.

'What the hell is going on? I think we'll have to shut the East Gate completely.'

'We've never done that before,' said Sandwich. 'The BTP will be pissed off if you back passengers up on to the street.'

'The British Transport Police should be telling us about this, not the other way around. The Northern Line southbound platform is overloaded. They're virtually falling on to the rails.'

The system worked so long as the law of averages operated normally and only a fraction of those who held travel cards decided to travel at the same time. Today, though, it seemed as if the law of averages was on hold.

'So long as the trains keep coming in on time we should be all right, but if one of them gets a signal delay, we're screwed. Where are they all going? You'd better get everyone in here.'

Nikos Nicolau sat by the window in Costa Coffee, monitoring the messages on his laptop. They were climbing fast now. A few minutes ago they had stuck at 3,700, but suddenly they were hitting 7,000 and rising. There was a gullibility factor in people that you had to target by appealing to their vanity, he decided, as he posted another instruction. He figured the unit had probably sent one of their drones to keep an eye on him, but what would they see? An overweight geek sitting alone at his laptop in a coffee shop. He played on the cliché, because he knew it would blind them to his real nature.

Time for another post. He typed 'Thirty-two minutes to reach King's Cross'. Skipping through the messages, he felt like a chef adding flavours to a stew. *It needs something more*, he thought. *A fresh ingredient*. Looking at the original post, he had a brainwave. He re-coloured the words in day-glo greens, blues and yellows, then changed the font setting to 'Balloony', a script kids loved. Next, he dropped the message on to RadLife, a new social networking site targeted at tweens. *Damn*, he thought, *this is going to be so cool*.

He wanted to be there, but it was smarter and safer to handle the event remotely. This way he could keep it going right up until the last minute. Nikos wiped a patch of condensation from the window and peered out into the afternoon rain. *Watch me and learn, you losers*, he thought, hitting Send.

45

KILL PROXIMITY

Ruby Cates had unclipped the plastic cast on her leg and dropped it off at the University College Hospital outpatients' department. She emerged from the entrance a few hundred yards behind Tony McCarthy.

Now she was heading along the rain-battered pavements of Euston Road towards King's Cross Station. Her mind was racing. The police were suspicious. She had seen various members of the PCU lurking about outside the house, and for all she knew one could be following her right now. *That could work in my favour*, she thought, hopping between stalled taxis. *Things are getting seriously out of control.*

In the past week, it seemed as if the world had turned upside-down. Matt gone, Cassie dead. Everything that had seemed exciting a week ago had been wrecked or tainted. The true horror of what she had done was only now starting to sink in. *Get to King's Cross*, she told herself. *Put an end to it and get the hell out.*

*   *   *

Toby Brooke could see the man with no neck watching him in the reflection of the furniture-store window. He was wearing a black padded jacket and jeans, but couldn't help looking like a copper. He thumped miserably from one boot to the other and wiped the rain from his shaved head, but seemed fairly content, just standing there in the downpour like a dumb animal.

Brooke wanted to get away, but was running out of options. Everything had gone wrong, and he had a bad feeling about the way it would end. He thought about slipping into the store and leaving through the rear door, but knew it would not be so easy to shake off the man who was following him. The sight of a taxi with its 'For Hire' light glimmering through the sheeting rain forced his hand, and he hailed it, jumping inside before his shadow was able to react.

'King's Cross,' he told the driver, and sat back, turning to see if the policeman was managing to follow.

Meera Mangeshkar was five metres behind Theo Fontvieille, who was looking very unhappy indeed. *Rich kid*, she thought, *he's more upset about having his car nicked than he is about his so-called mate being killed. But where's he going?* Fontvieille had cut up from the house in Bloomsbury and was heading toward King's Cross Station. Tucked beneath his elegant Smith & Son umbrella, he was immaculately attired in a handmade suit and matching black overcoat. *Must be a bit of a shock for him, having to board public transport*, she thought. *Probably going to visit Mummy and Daddy's country pile.* Meera frowned, looking again. Ruby Cates had appeared behind him, near the overcrowded entrance to the Tube station.

The top of her spine tingled in alarm. Something was not right – all these people – what were they doing here in the afternoon? Crowds of them milling around, waiting to get through the station entrances. It just looked – dangerous. Cates was closing in behind Fontvieille, but had they even seen each other? From here it was hard to tell. Meera tried to get nearer, but the crowds pressed in.

Dan Banbury sat watching Rajan Sangeeta eat a salad in the UCL cafeteria. The student was idly twirling an alfalfa sprout between his forefinger and thumb as he scanned a paperback copy of Herman Hesse's *Steppenwolf*. *I've really drawn the short straw here*, thought Banbury. *This one's far too boring and studenty to be involved in anything dubious.* He sat back on the uncomfortable plastic banquette and waited for something interesting to happen.

'Keep going,' said Longbright, giving Mac a shove in the back. 'What's the matter?'

'This is his territory.' Mac was frightened now. They had stopped by the clogged Underground entrance and were quickly hemmed in by new arrivals.

'If you try to give me the slip, I'll leave you somewhere he can get at you and withdraw police presence, do you understand?'

'He knows I'm here. He always knows when I'm in the station.'

'He can't be everywhere at once, Mac.'

'This is his home.'

The crowd was still moving. After waiting a minute, they slowly descended the staircase into the ticket hall. So many people were milling around that the makeshift queue barriers for the ticket office had all been pushed back. They weren't descending to the platforms or using the tunnels, they were just standing there, as if waiting to be told what to do next. A cluster of BTP officers stood off at one side of the crowd near the security control centre, but they seemed uncertain how to act.

'Now what?' asked Mac, panicked. 'He could be anywhere, I don't know where to look. He could be creeping up beside us right now.'

'You're going to start making me nervous if you don't shut up,' Longbright warned. 'I want you somewhere with maximum visibility.' She pointed to the guards waiting to feed passengers through the unused ticket barriers. 'Go over there and start an argument with one of them. Tell him your travel card doesn't work and you want a refund. Tell him he looks like a warthog, tell him anything. Make it loud and be bloody minded – I'm sure that'll come naturally. Wait.' Her earpiece crackled into life. She listened to Renfield and nodded. 'Go.'

There were at least three other members of PCU staff in the station, but things had a habit of going wrong where Mr Fox was involved. Watching Mac thread his way towards the guards, the memory of Liberty DuCaine suddenly filled Longbright's head, and she turned around in alarm, half expecting to find a killer standing behind her.

46

JOKER IN THE PACK

According to the reports reaching John May, three of the five housemates were making their way separately to King's Cross Station, along with Longbright, Renfield and Tony McCarthy. Only Sangeeta and Nicolau were away from the site. Did that remove them from suspicion, or implicate them further? And why were the others all heading to the one place where the PCU was most likely to catch Mr Fox? *You're being paranoid,* thought May as he tacked through the stalled traffic. *Arthur's done it to you again, forever trying to join the dots where no links exist. It's a massive terminus, it's the weekend, and students are more likely to use public transport, that's all.*

The rain pockmarked the pooled tarmac. May darted under the station awning and queued to enter the station, several rows back from Ruby Cates, who was no longer sporting her cast.

What am I doing here? he asked himself angrily. *I swear, this really is the most chaotic investigation of my career.*

When I look at our methodology through the eyes of Home Office officials, I can honestly see why they're so keen to retire us. The unit's working methods confuse its own staff, so God knows what they do to outsiders. Arthur put his faith in me to close this quickly, but I'm damned if I can see how to do it. There's something missing that I'm simply not equipped to spot. And now he's back at the unit with his jigsaws and his playing cards, letting me slowly hang myself. It's as if he no longer cares what happens to the unit or to any of us.

He angrily pushed his way down the steps into the ticket hall, where he was spotted by Longbright. She shook her head at him. *No sign of Mr Fox.* But there was McCarthy, having some kind of arm-waving argument with a baffled barrier guard.

Looks like everyone's decided to travel today, thought May. He checked his watch; 3:39 p.m. *Not a very satisfying end to our careers – a dead officer and two unresolved cases.*

The problem with the students of Mecklenburgh Square was not one of culpability but motive. Without that, the investigation could never be resolved. It seemed to May that the suspects, the victims and the investigators had created a perfect deadlock. As the minutes ticked away, May patted the rain from his jacket, stuck his hands in his pockets and leaned against the tiled wall, watching and waiting as the human whirlpool swirled aimlessly around its vortex. There was nothing else he could do.

Arthur Bryant's office had started to resemble a magician's display room. Apart from the books of magic, there was now a working model guillotine and a full set of

Chinese linking rings on his desk. Several packs of cards were strewn over the floor, along with random items of evidence, including a number of volumes on the London Underground, the paperback edition of *Mind the Ghosts*, the students' opened laptops, Hillingdon's rainbow raincoat and a series of enlarged frame grabs of Tube train seats from a mobile phone.

At times like this, Bryant found it helpful to break confidence and discuss the case with a complete outsider, although he took the risk that Fraternity DuCaine might simply think him unhinged.

'You see, I keep coming back to the cards,' he said, spreading a pack across his desk. 'I can't explain my thinking to you, because I can't entirely explain it to myself.'

'Let me get this right,' said Fraternity. 'You see a connection between the playing cards and the death of a woman on a staircase?'

'Believe me, I know how that sounds. But the colours and shapes keep repeating themselves in my head.'

Fraternity looked more confused than ever. 'No, I'm still not getting it,' he said.

'Let me see if I can explain.' Bryant opened Professor Hoffman's manual of card conjuring. 'I've been trying to learn the system of finding marked cards that's recommended in this book, but I don't have a mathematical mind. One way of doing it is to locate imaginary points on the backs of the cards. Hoffman teaches you to superimpose patterns over seemingly random choices. If you're careful, you can divide the back of a card up into thirty different points. I look from the diamonds and hearts on the faces to thirteen photos taken of the Tube station seat covers, and every illogical cell in my brain starts to vibrate. But what exactly am I looking at?'

'I have no idea,' Fraternity admitted. 'We didn't do anything like this at Henley.'

'What happened to you there? Do you have any idea why you failed?'

'It couldn't have been anything that occurred during the training period. My coursework was good and I got on just great with everyone.'

'Then it must have been somewhere else. Where did they put you out in the field?'

'I did two weeks at Albany Street station. That seemed to go OK.'

'Just OK?'

'Well, until the end, at least. I'd been placed under some uptight dude who seemed like he'd skipped a few stages of his diversity training.'

'He had a race problem?'

'No, not that. The inner-city boroughs would collapse without a heavy proportion of ethnic staff. Besides, I got the feeling that if you really have issues you can get posted to an area where you only have to deal with your white brothers.'

'So what was it?'

'I was supposed to go for a drink with the team at the end of my last day, and my ex-partner came by unannounced. I was kind of embarrassed about that.'

'Why?'

'At the time, he was one of the principal dancers in Matthew Bourne's production of *Swan Lake*.'

'Ah. Yes. I can see how that would do it.'

'Look, he was between performances and wanted to wish me well. You wouldn't know—'

'You don't need to explain. Officers always know. Your mentor had championed you to the others and suddenly felt he'd lost face.'

'I guess that's a possibility.'

'And he was in charge of your field report. Why didn't you say something?'

'It would only have made matters worse. I didn't feel comfortable talking about it. And I had no real proof.'

'I can look into this for you. Do you remember the name of your senior officer?'

'Sure. He was a sergeant. A guy called Jack Renfield. I tried to get in touch with him one time, but they told me he'd moved on. They wouldn't say where.'

'I won't be able to retroactively change your report,' said Bryant, 'but if we survive beyond the end of the afternoon, I may be able to recommend you for a position here.'

Fraternity's smile was sunlight after rain. 'You really think that's a possibility?'

'It would mean confronting Renfield. He's at the unit, you see. Albany Street was angry about losing him to us, that's why they refused to tell you where he went. You think the two of you could discuss the matter civilly, without any bloodshed?'

'Could I hit him once, maybe?'

'All right, but first help me with the cards. What am I missing here?'

'OK.' Fraternity narrowed his eyes at the card backs, then glanced across at Professor Hoffman's manual. 'You're learning how to mentally mark cards so you can track them through the pack, right?'

'Right.'

'And you got these seat patterns. Why would anyone take pictures of those?'

'To track something – somebody – from line to line.'

'That's what I see. There are twelve underground lines, right?'

'Yes.'

'But you've got thirteen shots. This one isn't a line. OK, it's a bit out of focus but it looks like red polka dots to me.'

Bryant mentally slapped himself. 'That's a close-up of the dress Gloria Taylor was wearing when she died.'

'Man, that's a hell of a dress. She must have been the most noticeable woman on the Tube that day.'

'Of course – it made her easy to follow. She got on at Bond Street and changed at Oxford Circus. Maybe the killer was with her all the way. It's like tracking a playing card through the deck. He chose her because of the dress.'

'A sexual obsessive?' Fraternity suggested.

'Then why not simply touch her or try to strike up a conversation? Why push her down the stairs?' Bryant realized he could answer his own question. 'She almost left the station, then turned around and went back. She'd forgotten her daughter's birthday present. And then she was pushed because someone was angry with her. Angry that she didn't go through the barrier and leave. You track the card through the pack. But the card lets you down, and you lose your temper and knock the cards over. Everything else that has happened is because of that one moment.'

'It's a game,' said Fraternity, looking at the fallen cards. 'And someone didn't like to lose.'

'What kind of game has stakes so high that you'd actually shove a stranger in the back?' He looked back at the pack of cards, and the upturned nine of clubs. 'I marked that one so I could trace it through the pack.'

'Sorry, Mr Bryant, not with you.'

'You don't mark a card the second before you turn it over. You mark it right at the beginning, so you can keep an eye on it through the shuffle. The killer didn't put the sticker on Gloria Taylor's back just before he killed her. He did it so that he could prove that she was the marked card. She wasn't hard to keep track of in the Tube crowds, because of the way she was dressed. But he had to show someone else that she was the victim. Matt Hillingdon's mobile was missing because it revealed the marked card.'

'I'm still not getting a clear signal from you, Mr Bryant,' said Fraternity. Getting used to Bryant's way of thinking sometimes took decades.

'I need to run the security-camera footage from Monday evening at Bond Street Tube.' Bryant indicated that Fraternity DuCaine should grab the nearest phone. 'Then I'll know who killed Gloria Taylor.'

47

ROLL

Here we go, thought Nikos Nicolau, counting down the seconds in the corner of his screen. *This is going to be so damned cool. From team player to team leader at the touch of a button.* The screen counter had stopped at 11,353, but if even a fraction of that number turned up he'd have proved his point. The bait-and-switch site had worked like a dream, setting up a Flash Mob that would last for four minutes, the duration of the song.

He waited until exactly 3:00 p.m. then hit Play. A video of the band appeared onscreen, and the first power chord sounded. The band was called Snap Monkey (feat. Aisho DC Crew) and the song 'Perfect People' had become a club anthem two years earlier, because the band members had taught the movements of their supremely vacuous song to the inmates of a South Korean prison. Since then it had replaced Michael Jackson's 'Thriller' as the most imitated dance song ever to hit the Web. Even tiny kids in nursery schools knew the steps, which were a damned sight cooler than anything Michael Jackson ever recorded. And the best part was that he could get them to RickRoll* in the station without ever noticing the irony in the song's lyrics.

> Nobody can be controlled.
> Nobody can be patrolled.
> What we do is what we love.
> Nobody orders from above.
> Where we are is where we stand.
> The hottest lovers in the land.

And here he would be, controlling them through a broadcast to 11,353 iPods, BlackBerrys and assorted PDAs, beamed into the grand concourse of St Pancras International Station. He remembered the KissRoll staged there a couple of years back, two hundred lovers smooching beneath the disproportionately vast, tacky statue called 'The Kiss' that dominated the station atrium. But this was on a different scale entirely.

More importantly, it would bring an end to the argument he'd been having with Rajan and the others about pedestrian flow in public areas. Rajan had argued that the public could be persuaded to walk in non-instinctive directions if properly directed. Groups generally moved in broad clockwise circles, Nikos had told him, because the country drove on the left and people were used to driving clockwise around roundabouts. Customers entering shops usually headed left, circling the store and exiting from the

---

*Named after the singer Rick Astley, whose fans turned up at stations to perform his greatest hit.

right; it was the natural thing to do. But in countries where they drove on the other side of the road, the system was reversed.

The webcam feeds sent back by his viewers a few minutes earlier showed that the group in the station was automatically following a clockwise route. Social engineering only worked if the instructions didn't contravene human instinct. Certain rules held true whatever the circumstances; build a block of flats with lifts opening on to the street, Nikos had argued, and they'd be avoided by residents because the lift-space became the property of the street rather than the tenants. Design a public lavatory where the urinals could be seen from the pavement, and the British would be reluctant to use them. Deep-rooted beliefs in what constituted public and private spaces were hardwired into the human psyche.

But something was wrong. The café's broadband speed was pitifully slow, but as he checked the incoming feeds he could see that no one was dancing. The song was already past its first verse. What had gone awry? The chorus was coming up.

> *Gonna live like perfect people.*
> *Gonna love like perfect people.*
> *Live and love like perfect people.*
> *Live and love like perfect people.*

It wasn't exactly Rimbaud, but it felt about right for the duped drones down on the concourse. He studied the feeds again. Nothing. They weren't dancing. Why wasn't anything happening? The video was playing perfectly. He could see it on the site. He opened the site's admin page and checked the stats. He ran through the set-up and hit log, but found nothing unusual.

Then he saw it.

Although the destination was correct in the body of the site instructions, the Flash box he had created to run as a site banner was wrong. Where he had typed in the location of the event, a pre-logged template had set the destination to King's Cross Station instead of St Pancras.

He had forgotten that although the two stations shared the same complex, they were entirely separate termini. He had lost concentration for a moment and clicked through to the wrong place.

Breaking into a sweat, he toggled back to one of the video feeds and zoomed out to take in the whole scene. Instead of the great vaulted ceiling of the Eurostar terminal, he found himself looking at a cramped, tiled hall. He had sent his Flash Mob to the wrong station.

Christ. The concourse at King's Cross Underground was minuscule compared to the one at St Pancras. A sinking sickness invaded Nikos's stomach. He had instructed 11,353 people to meet there. Maybe some of them had figured it out and had made their way to the right meeting point, but what if the rest were trying to cram themselves into the small Underground ticket hall beneath the main station? The result could be a massacre, like the ones which occurred at Mecca or the Heysel football stadium; people could be crushed to death in the ensuing chaos.

Sweating violently now, he killed the video and wiped his trail, removing the online instructions, shutting down the website, clearing the computer's history. He was using his backup laptop, the one he had stored in his UCH locker, the one the police didn't know existed. If there was any comeback, at least he had bought himself some time – until someone ran a trace from the host.

He knew that he would have to go and see for himself. It would be like rubbernecking at a traffic accident, but he had to make sure that his conscience was clear. Slipping the laptop into his rucksack, he zipped up his jacket and ran out into the rain.

48

MAELSTROM

The scene in the station was becoming nightmarish. The crowd had started dancing but there was no space to move, and their synchronized movements had quickly fallen apart. A party of schoolchildren was disgorging from the Victoria Line escalator, but the hall was so crowded that they could not pass through the barriers, and had become trapped halfway. Children were screaming and crying. The staircases were ranked with passengers unable to move in any direction. A sense of barely controlled hysteria was breaking out in the claustrophobic hell of the ticket hall.

John May could do nothing but watch. Longbright and McCarthy were nearest the barriers, and he could still see Ruby Gates fighting her way towards the Tube escalators. Had she seen Theo Fontvieille nearby? And had either of them identified Meera or Colin? *We're all in trouble here if anything bad happens*, he realized. He called Bimsley.

'There's no way of getting anyone out, Colin, so they'll

have to force people down on to the platforms and get them to board outbound trains. Try and connect with the others. I want you all on this floor. If you go to a lower level I'll lose radio contact with you.'

'OK boss.'

Arthur Bryant and Fraternity DuCaine made their entrance into the station via a staff elevator that delivered them into the ticket office. Anjam Dutta was there to meet them. The security officer looked stressed but in control.

'We've got crowds backed around the exterior of the station,' he explained, ushering them through an unmarked door and walking them to the surveillance room. 'I'm trying to clear the exits but I can't close them, because I need to get people up first. We've never had a situation like this before. Usually only a tenth of the population should be travelling at a time. But we think we've found the source.'

'What is it?'

'Somebody arranged the staging of a Flash Mob in the station, but the induction site was pulled a few minutes ago.' He got a sweetly blank look from Bryant. 'It was a passing fad a while back. People click on a site that re-routes them to a different destination, and that destination sends instructions to laptops, mobiles and PDAs, telling them to meet in a certain public place and dance to music played out on MP3s. The craze died out after companies copied it to use as sales tools. We've got all our staff and the LTP trying to move the crowd. In general, people have lived through enough terrorist alerts not to panic, but they're getting pretty close to the edge right now.'

'We have PCU members out there tracking suspects,' Bryant explained. 'Our leads may be connected with the situation you've got on your hands here.'

'You're telling me there's a murderer crowded in there with the general public? You're supposed to be helping us, Mr Bryant, not making matters worse.'

Bryant looked up at the staff roster of security guards. Photographs of Anjam, Rasheed, Sandwich, Marianne, Bitter and Stone were arranged in a row on corkboard, their weekly duty roster marked beneath them in black felt-tip pen. 'They're all out on the floor right now?'

'Yeah, you can see Marianne near the Circle Line tunnel, and there's Sandwich, by the lift. Stone's over at the barrier.'

Bryant glanced back at the ID of the man the others had nicknamed Stone. He found himself looking at an earlier incarnation of Mr Fox. 'When was that taken?'

'Two weeks ago.'

Bryant checked the fine print beneath the photobooth shot. *Jack Ketch.* 'He sat in on my briefing session with the security staff,' said Bryant. 'Inattentional blindness. You have got to be kidding. He's been here under our noses all the time?'

'And now he's out there,' said May. 'Come on.'

The detectives pushed themselves into the crushing chaos of the crowd. 'Janice,' May called on his radio, 'brown leather jacket and glasses, to your right. Mr Fox is less than three metres away from McCarthy. You have to move the boy out of there.'

'I can't, John, we're stuck here.'

'Then we'll come to you.'

The Flash Mob song had come to a rowdy, ragged end, and the disappointed crowd was looking lost, not yet ready to disperse. Tannoy announcements were proving ineffectual in easing the constrictions.

Anjam Dutta could see the pressure points reaching maximum density. His mobile showed an incoming call from John May.

'We have to clear the hall fast,' said May. 'Can you open all the ticket barriers and leave them up?'

'There's an electronic override, but it'll lose the network a fortune. I have to have authority—'

'Someone could get killed if you don't. Just do it, Anjam. I'll take full responsibility.'

Dutta released the safety guards and punched in the code that released all of the barriers simultaneously. The crowd surged forward and poured through to the Victoria, Piccadilly and Northern Line escalators. The pressure in the ticket hall began to ease at once.

Longbright saw Mr Fox standing on the other side of Tony McCarthy, pushing his way between tightly packed bodies. 'Mac,' she called, 'he's right behind you. Run.'

McCarthy panicked, and instead of going up to street level, fled down in the direction of the escalators. Mr Fox broke his cover and set off after him.

Ruby Cates reached the barriers just as they opened. She was swept through with the crowd, but managed to pull free and head towards the southbound Victoria Line platform.

'Hey, Ruby.' Theo was on the step below her. He turned and grinned. 'I thought I saw you in the ticket hall. What was that all about?'

'Someone's idea of a joke. I'm surprised no one was squashed flat. Where are you going?'

'Oxford Circus. I want to buy some trainers. How about you?'

'Victoria. I'm going to Brighton.'

'Who you got down there?'

'Just some friends.'

'How long are you going for?'

'Probably just for the weekend. I need a break.'

'You didn't say you were going.'

'I decided when I heard about Cassie. There's so much awful stuff going on, the police are hanging around the house, everyone's on edge. I haven't been able to concentrate on anything.'

They stepped off the escalator together. 'I can't believe you didn't tell me you were getting out. I thought you were serious about us.'

Ruby looked uncomfortable. She turned the ring on her finger, studying it too intently. 'I've been thinking, I'm not so sure I want to be with anyone just now. I need some space to think. I'll call you from Brighton, OK?'

'What happened to spending more time together? Listen, I could come down with you, just for tonight. I don't have to go into town. I don't really need another pair of trainers.'

'No, that wouldn't be workable. I'm staying with these people I know.'

'Well, it seems like you're running away. Are you meeting someone down there?'

'No, of course not.'

'Then why is it I don't believe a word you're saying?'

The platform had become overcrowded. The guards were warning everyone to stand back from the platform edge as there was a train approaching.

'Tell you what. As a token of trust, give me that back.' He pointed to the diamond ring on the third finger of her right hand.

Ruby gave an awkward laugh. 'Actually I was going to

leave it on your bedside table this morning but I couldn't get the damned thing off. It's a little too small for me. This is my train.'

'Give me the ring, Ruby.' There was menace in his voice now.

She gave him a strange look. 'I told you, I can't get it off.'

When he grabbed her arm she was so surprised that she momentarily lost her balance, and was almost pulled under the arriving train.

Longbright could see Mac bobbing and shoving ahead towards the red and silver train that was just opening its doors. Mr Fox – she could only think of him in the identity he had used to kill – was closing in fast behind him.

Further ahead, Mr Fox was feeling a strange, cold serenity descending over him, a feeling that always seized him in the moments before he killed. He saw everything at a distance; among all those scurrying little people was the pathetic junkie Mac, desperate to escape, searching a way out like a Tube rat sensing a coming inferno. Sweat was leaking from his hairline down his sallow, diseased cheeks. He looked badly in need of a fix.

Perhaps that was the answer; perhaps the entire interchange needed to burn again, to sear itself clean in a rising tide of flame. But no, that wouldn't work now. Steel had replaced wood, smoke sensors and cameras lined the walls. And what would another conflagration resolve? The horror of the past could not be erased with a second atrocity. The memory of that terrible day could never be burned away.

Mr Fox allowed the silver skewer to slide down into his

palm. He felt its cool heft in his hand, demanding to be used. Killing could calm him.

But now the doors of the Victoria Line train stood open, and Mac was free to board. If he did, Mr Fox knew he would lose the opportunity presented by the crush of the anonymous crowd. He stamped hard on a woman's foot and shoved her aside, moving in to commit the act that would provide him with a temporary respite from the ever-present pain of remembering.

Just as he reached towards Mac, a tall young man stumbled into his path. The man was grabbing at his girlfriend's hand, trying to twist a ring from her finger, and the girlfriend had turned to slap him in the face. The crowd – mostly made up of old ladies, it seemed – pushed back with force, and suddenly they seemed to have linked arms, forming a solid barrier across his path. It was absurd, but he could not pass between them to reach his target. He watched, stalled, as Mac jumped to safety, moving nimbly between the closing doors of the carriage.

Now the young man was twisting the girl's hand and Mr Fox heard the snap of her finger, saw her scream, knew that some other drama was unfolding before him, but all he could see was Mac escaping, getting away to some place where he could talk to the police; and then he knew he had lost, lost it all, because of the old ladies and this damned man and his stupid lovers' tiff, and the needle-sharp point of the skewer had risen in his hand as if moving of its own accord.

He slammed it down into the young man's arm and pushed, shoved it through the artery above his wrist until the point emerged from the other side. But he couldn't get the skewer back out, no matter how hard he pulled.

The student released the girl and collapsed with a roar of pain. The pensioners before him were suddenly replaced with familiar faces, and he saw that he was surrounded by members of the Peculiar Crimes Unit.

The centre of the group slowly opened to reveal the crumpled face of Arthur Bryant, closely followed by John May. The most humiliating moment came when a woman, the big blonde detective sergeant they called Longbright, twisted the silver skewer from his grip and removed it from the victim, confiscating his beloved weapon.

From the day he watched the burning match tumble down the side of the escalator, a part of him had always prayed for this moment to arrive. With delicious anticipation, he waited to hear the words that would finally seal his fate.

Instead he saw Arthur Bryant look past him and announce, 'Theodore Samuel Fontvieille, I am arresting you for the murders of Gloria Taylor, Matthew Hillingdon and Cassandra Field.'

49

CHARISMATIC

'Two arrests before six o'clock,' Raymond Land was excitedly telling Leslie Faraday over the phone. 'They've done it! No, I've no idea how. Nobody ever tells me anything. Oh, really? Oh, I thought you'd be pleased.' Land found himself looking into the receiver, a dead line burring in his ear.

This time, Mr Fox found himself locked in a cell at Albany Street police headquarters, and there was no way for him to escape – not that he wanted to. On the contrary, he seemed almost relieved to be behind bars, as if somehow the memory of those painful years between his destruction of the Tube station and his return to killing had finally been laid to rest.

He refused to speak to anyone, and flinched when his features were recorded, fearful that his true face might be placed on display for all to gawp at. And gawp they would, for even as he lay in the corner of his cell, his jacket thrown over his eyes to shield them from the overhead lights that were never dimmed, the Home Office was leaking the story to the press.

Having been so protective of his true identity, Jack Ketch, alias Lloyd Lutine, alias Mr Fox and a dozen other names, would now face his greatest fear – exposure of his most horrific, shameful secret. Thinking back to the moment when he ran crying up the escalator with the burning match in his hand, he buried his face ever more deeply into the cloth of his jacket, savouring these last few moments of darkness, knowing that the blaze of publicity would soon obliterate him, as the braying clamour of morons began.

The PCU had dragged all the members of the Mecklenburgh Square household back to the unit's headquarters for a final showdown, and this time batteries of police recorders and cameras were there to cover the event. Theo Fontvieille had been stitched and bandaged, and was seated with plastic ties securing his wrists. The others found chairs or spaces on the floor where they could sit. The two Daves had been sent away, despite their protestations that they hadn't had time to repair the hole in Bryant's floor, but everyone else was in attendance, and it was Arthur Bryant, of course, who chose to take the centre stage.

'Well, it's been quite a week for all of us,' he said, looking around, his blue eyes shining, 'but tougher for some than others. Now that we're all together, I think we should dispense with formalities for a while and talk about what happened.'

'We should be taking separate statements from each of them, sir,' said Renfield, 'to prevent corroboration.'

'No, I think the only way to put this together is to hear everyone out,' Bryant contradicted. 'They're not in the mood to provide alibis for each other any more.' He turned to the students. 'So, let's imagine we're playing a game. I'll be the Bank. Although strictly speaking, Mr Nicolau, you should be the Bank, shouldn't you?'

Nikos looked awkwardly at the others, wondering how much he should say.

'Come, come, Mr Nicolau, this is no time to be shy. I imagine you were very excited when you came up with the idea for the game, weren't you? All those nights spent online could finally be put to some use.'

Nikos cleared his throat and edged forward in his seat, conscious of the police cameras recording him. 'Yeah, it was me who came up with it, but it was never meant to end up like this. I don't know what Theo's been up to because I had no part—'

'Let's just stick to the facts for now. We'll have plenty of time later to ascertain everyone's level of involvement. Why did you come up with the game? When did you first think of it?'

'It began in the Karma Bar,' he mumbled. 'A bunch of us were sitting around, and we were all complaining that we were broke.'

'We were talking about our student loans, and the rent and all the bills,' said Ruby. 'I was always having to lend the others—'

'Please, let's stick to the point,' warned Bryant. 'We'll get to you in due course. Go on, Mr Nicolau.'

'I said I thought we should try to make some money with online gambling. I knew a lot about statistics and had a few ideas for beating the odds. What I didn't know was that *he* – ' here Nikos pointed angrily at Theo, ' – had been gambling online for quite a long time. I explained to the others that the main problem was the number of players. You're more likely to die in a plane crash than win most lotteries, because there are too many punters participating. I said if we could just keep the number of players limited, we stood a chance of making some real money. So we tried out the game for a few weeks, just accumulating small sums. Matt – Matthew Hillingdon – was the overall winner. But we realized that in order to make any decent amount of cash, everyone would have to put a lot more in the pot.'

'Who came in on the game?' asked May.

'There were the six of us at first, but Cassie dropped out because she didn't want anything more to do with Theo. He had started sleeping with Ruby.'

'That's not why she dropped out,' said Theo quietly. 'She couldn't raise her share of the stake.'

'So there were five players,' Bryant prompted.

'Yeah. We each put five grand in, but it still didn't seem like enough if we were going for one winner.'

'You were all broke, yet you managed to raise five thousand apiece,' said May. 'Obviously the definition of "broke" has changed a little since my day.'

'My dad's brother owns a chain of Greek restaurants,' said Nikos. 'He's a complete idiot. On the same day of every month he takes a suitcase containing around £65,000 to his bank in Paris, all cash. He goes on the Eurostar. So on Monday morning I set up a Flash Mob in St Pancras Station to create a diversion, and while that was happening Theo robbed him.'

'It was like taking sweets from a very stupid child,' said Theo. 'He kept the bag attached to his wrist with plastic binders.' He held up his own wrists. 'I just cut them with kitchen scissors while he was standing there watching everyone dance.' He sniggered, looking to the others for approval.

'So then we had a decent stake to work with,' said Nicolau. 'Ninety grand in all. I wanted to find two more players to make it an even hundred, but Theo wouldn't let me. He really wanted to keep his odds of winning high.'

'Yes, this image you perpetuate of the bored rich kid isn't quite accurate, is it?' said Bryant. 'You'd clocked up some serious gambling debts, your last business venture – property, wasn't it? – had failed spectacularly, your car was repossessed – not stolen – and your family had cut you off without a penny.'

'You have no idea,' said Theo. 'I'd surrendered my savings, I sold my watch, my pen, everything I owned, and replaced them with fakes. You have to keep up appearances, after all. Some guys in Shoreditch were going to come round and break my arms if I didn't pay them by the end of the week.'

'Tell us what happened next.'

'Well, now that we'd raised a decent stake, we started playing in earnest,' said Nicolau. 'Toby had been the previous week's winner – five players, five days of the week – we drew straws to see who would get which day.'

'And it was my turn to play again on Monday,' said Theo.

'How long had you been playing?'

'This was week three. It's an elimination game. We decided that each player should have three lives. If you were knocked out three times, you'd lose your stake and be out of the game. And I had two strikes against me. The winner of each week got what we called living expenses, until the final overall winner was decided.'

'Of course, Toby had to flash his cash about,' Sangeeta complained.

'I think at this point you should tell us what the game involved,' said Bryant, striding about with his thumbs in his waistcoat like an old-time prosecutor. The image would have been more appealing if the waistcoat had not been held together with safety pins.

'We wanted to come up with something that wasn't just based on luck,' said Nicolau. 'We thought it should require some skill, bravado even. I was talking to a guy who worked for London Underground, and he told me about a game he'd heard of, a gambling dare you could play on the Tube. You pick a stranger, text the amount of your placed bet, then follow the stranger on their journey, and whatever they do scores you points.' Nicolau was warming to his subject, forgetful of the fact that the game had ended in a series of brutal murders.

'I laid down the ground rules. First, you send a photograph of the line you're going to play on – we'd taken shots of the seat livery in all the different carriages – then you photograph your mark – the person you've picked to bet on. To make sure there's no switching, you also put a sticker on their back to tag them in your pictures. Then you film the different things they do, like reading a book or listening to an iPod – all of the activities score points – and you send the results to the next player's mobile to verify them. Then you score more points for how many stops they travel, and if they get off at the station you've pre-designated, you win that day's pot.'

'We weren't allowed to talk to outsiders about the game,' said Toby, his head in his hands. 'I had to borrow the stake money from my uncle. I don't know why I got involved.'

'And with the aid of the robbery, you were able to up the ante,' said Bryant.

'It wasn't a robbery.' Theo was utterly dismissive of the idea. 'It was taking money away from a total creep who would have only spent the profits from his shitty little restaurants on gold bath taps and plasma screens for his stupid villa in Cyprus. And it was my turn to play. I went to Bond Street Tube and saw this woman in a bright-red polka dot dress, and knew at once that I'd be able to track her through the system without losing her, because she looked different to everyone else. Man, it was a total winning streak – everything I suggested she would do, she did. I sent the photos and texts to Matt's phone – he was going to be the next player – and told him that I staked her destination as King's Cross. I'm good at reading people. I was sure she would get off there, and she did. I followed her up the escalator to the ticket barrier, and just as she got to it, the bitch turned around and went back down.

'Well, in that one second I lost everything. Three strikes, I crashed out of the game, all because she wouldn't take another two paces through the barrier. I don't know what happened – I think I just nudged her in anger, I couldn't control myself – and I was amazed to see her fall down the stairs. She was wearing these really high heels. So I just carried on past as if I hadn't seen, as if it was nothing to do with me, and caught the first train that came in. I was in a suit and tie. Nobody looked twice at me.'

'Jesus, Theo.' Rajan and Toby were staring at him in horror. Ruby, nursing her broken finger in the corner, remained sullen and silent.

'You don't understand how frustrating it was,' Theo told them. 'It was kind of an accident.'

'Not if you pushed her!'

'Yeah, but I didn't mean her to die.'

'Let's move on,' coaxed Bryant. 'What happened after that?'

'I thought no one would find out, but when I got home I realized I'd sent all my photos to Matt. That woman was all over his phone. I had some time, though, because the story didn't get picked up and none of the others knew what had happened. I saw a way that I could still come out on top. Matt came upstairs and told me he had seen the pictures on his phone, so he knew I had been eliminated from the game. I made light of it, bluffed it out – I'm a very good poker player.'

'Yeah, he only lies when he opens his mouth,' muttered Ruby.

'On Tuesday night, I took Matt out for a drink with the intention of getting him hammered, although he was already half-cut when he turned up. We hit a bar in Spitalfields – there are so many around there and they're all so crowded that I knew no one would remember seeing us. I'd taken his asthma spray and switched it with one filled with tobacco tea. Then I gave him the spray and waited for him to get sick, but it took longer than I'd expected. Earlier that day I went around the Tube station and checked the cameras, and I could see that a couple were out, but I figured it would be more luck than judgement if I got away with it, because I wouldn't know exactly where he'd collapse. The most useful thing was that Matt trusted me.'

My God, thought May, looking into Fontvieille's dead eyes, *he really sees nothing morally wrong with what he's done.*

Theo was anxious to explain, and appeared to be enjoying

himself. 'It was all pretty simple stuff. I switched coats with him, then he started to pass out behind one of those great big caged fans they've placed in the tunnel entrance. I was pretty sure it was a blind spot and the cameras couldn't pick him up. And I'd been careful to keep my distance from him ever since we'd left Liverpool Street. I even sat on the escalators while he stood, so I wouldn't be seen. I heard the train approaching, so I left Matt and ran for it. I'm only an inch taller, and in Matt's hat and rainbow coat I figured I'd look like him from behind. I jumped on to the train but shut the coat in the door – I hadn't realized how long it was – but when the doors opened I had a better idea. I went to the other end of the carriage, got off and headed for the last Northern Line train.'

'You'd prepared a lot more than that, though, hadn't you?' Bryant suggested.

'Yeah, I'd taken Matt's travel card – we used regular tickets 'cause they can't be traced – and I left it in Toby's room. And I wrote Ruby's name in his library books, just to confuse things further. But the best part went wrong. Before I met up with Matt, I drove to the Buddha Bar with Cassie and made a big deal about leaving the Porsche outside. Everyone remembers that car because of the personalized numberplate. I wore my red scarf and made sure they all noticed me. I figured I'd go out, meet up with Matt and come back at the end of the evening, and everyone would be so wasted they'd tell anyone who asked that I'd been there all night. Only as I got out of the car, I locked my bloody keys inside it.

'Then I remembered an old trick. If you lock your keys in your car and you've got spare keys at home, all you have to do is call someone on their mobile from your mobile. You hold your phone about a foot from your car door and have the other person press the 'unlock' button on the spare keys, and it opens your door. So I called the house and Ruby answered the phone. I was kind of in a panic and I think she sensed that. Didn't you, Ruby?'

'Don't involve me, you scumbag,' she warned. 'Everything you said, everything you ever told me was a lie.'

'Hey, it's what I do.' Theo grinned at her. Incredibly, it seemed he was comfortable making jokes.

'Go on,' said May.

'I asked Ruby to help me unlock the car, and knew I'd compromised my alibi. So I thought to hell with it, and I asked her to say she saw me come home earlier than I did. I knew she was nuts about me, so I was kind of in the clear. I got to the bar to meet Matt – he'd already had a massive head-start drinking with some old mates from Nottingham, but he still wasn't drunk when we left. I had to wait a few minutes for the booze to kick in. I got him out of breath at King's Cross and persuaded him to use the spray, went back to collect the car and then headed home. I had the evidence from Matt's mobile, and no one would ever suspect a thing. Plus, it looked like the money would default to me, because the game was to be stopped if the next player couldn't take their turn. In this case, the next player had died – or at least, gone missing – I hadn't expected him to crawl off like that. There were two small problems I needed to deal with, though, because you guys were starting to sniff around the house.

'First, Nikos was still holding the cash, and I knew it would be found if the house was searched. So he came up with a good idea – he went to some jeweller's in Hatton Garden and used the money to buy a ring. You know what Jews are like, they see wads of money and don't ask questions.' He smiled ingratiatingly at everyone, making Longbright's skin crawl. 'And to keep Ruby sweet, I told her she could wear it – to prove how sincere I was, you know?

'Everything had fallen back into place. I mean, obviously we couldn't play on with you watching us, so the game was declared over. The others were angry, but like I said, we'd put a clause in the rulebook saying that in the event of a *force majeure* the last high score would take the pot. I could claim the ring and pay off my debts.'

'But they had no proof that you were the winner,' said May.

'Yeah they did, because I had the photos on my phone. I just said I didn't know where Matt had gone. I kind of implied he'd found out about me and Ruby, and had stormed off. But Ruby didn't believe me. And then Cassie figured it out.' Theo shook his head, irritated by the thought. 'Because you went to see her about the damned stickers. She knew one had been placed on the back of a woman who'd died on the Tube – you told her. And she told me she knew I was involved. That girl – it was one of the reasons we broke up – she could always see right through me. I asked her what she was going to do about it, and she said she didn't know. She wanted to talk to an old friend of hers, a lawyer. I knew then that she had to be removed. I followed her to Greenwich – I was still wearing Matt's coat because I'd put my black leather Marc Jacobs original on him and I didn't want to get my clothes dirty – but I didn't find a chance to get her alone. I kept trying to think of a way to kill her, but it was really difficult coming up with something good, you know?'

'You managed it, though.'

'Oh, yeah. I stayed outside the flat, watching as the pair of them got drunk, but I couldn't tell whether Cassie had told her about me. I couldn't see properly from outside. I wasn't about to kill the friend as well – I mean, where would it have stopped? But then Cassie went back to Westcombe Park Station, and there was nobody on the platform. It was too good an opportunity to waste. By this time, I could tell that your investigation was falling apart, because it was so easy to provide a vague alibi.'

'So you pushed her on to the line.'

'Well, I'd managed to kill a complete stranger just by nudging her, so I figured it should work again. I couldn't think how to guarantee that she'd fall, but then I saw the steel frame of the waiting-room door, and it was just like going to the gym.'

'And you implicated Miss Cates by leaving behind a piece of her plastic cast.'

'I thought that was a nice touch, yeah? I came up with lots of cool little touches like that, but I don't suppose anyone even noticed. I had to deflect attention away from myself, obviously. The last thing I had to do was get the diamond ring back from Ruby – it had seemed like a good idea to have her look after it. But then the little bitch did a runner and pretended she couldn't get it off her finger.'

'Who told you about the game?' Bryant asked Nikos.

'I was talking to some guard at King's Cross,' said Nicolau, 'and he told me about it.'

Bryant shot his partner a meaningful look, as if to say *I suspected as much.*

As the students started arguing with Fontvieille, John

May turned to his partner. 'All right, I give up. How did you get to him? What made you sure it was Theo?'

Bryant looked over at Fraternity DuCaine and grinned. 'Once we realized it was a game, the rest was easy. You see, it was a cheat.'

'What do you mean?'

'Fraternity and I looked at the players, then took a guess at the type of game they were playing. We saw at once that if it was something that required social skills, then the game was rigged. I mean, look at them. Ruby hobbling about with a plaster cast. Toby, a borderline stalker and a hopeless closet case, which was why he spotted Jack Renfield following him—'

'You mean he thought I was trying to pick him up?' said Renfield, utterly horrified.

'That's why he was so cagey about where he went at night,' said Bryant. 'So, Ruby was incapacitated, Toby was crippled with shyness, Rajan was downright unpleasant – forgive me, Mr Sangeeta, but you do lack social skills – and Nikos was simply unprepossessing. There was only one person in the group who strangers would truly be comfortable next to.'

'Are you telling me that was all you had to go on?'

'It made sense. Mr Fontvieille here kept on about his wealth, but it didn't ring true. Look at him – he looks like he hasn't slept for a month. So I ran a check on his car and found it had been repossessed, not stolen. We called his parents and heard about his history of getting into debt. And we checked the security footage at Bond Street Tube. Lo and behold, here was Theo, following Gloria Taylor down into the station. Once we had the basic idea, it only took minutes to sort out what had happened. We followed the joker in the pack. Then, when we saw the station besieged by fans of Mr Nicolau's website, I enlisted Dan's help.'

'What do you mean?' asked May, puzzled.

'Well, I needed to protect our staff, didn't I? We had two murderers both on the move in a tight, crowded space, so I asked if he could use the same technology to help us.'

'I downloaded one of Mr Bryant's databases and sent an urgent text to everyone on it. We thought they'd be in the area,' said Banbury.

'What was it?'

'Friends of the British Library. They're running a series of events just down the road.'

'Textiles and tapestries of the Middle Ages,' added Bryant.

'You mean Mr Fox was stopped by ladies from a *knitting club*?' said Renfield.

'They're tough old birds,' said Bryant, patting his pockets. 'I wouldn't want to mess with them. Well, I think it's time for a pipe. Can I leave you to finish up here? If anyone needs me, I shall be out on my verandah, contemplating the evils of the world.'

'All right, you lot,' shouted Raymond Land, holding up his hands. 'Let's have some peace and quiet. You might want to start thinking about your statements.' He wagged his finger at Fontvieille, who appeared suddenly exhausted. 'You're not so clever now, are you, sonny? You obviously reckoned without the sheer professionalism of a crack investigation unit.'

Land took a step back and vanished down the hole in the floor.

50

THE WAY AHEAD

The detectives were standing in the only magic shop actually situated in the London Underground system. Davenport's Magic emporium had existed for decades opposite the British Museum, but had now moved to one of the dead-end tunnels beneath Charing Cross Station. Few commuters knew of its existence – why would they? – but its crimson curtains hid a world of misdirection, deception and amazement.

Realizing that card tricks were not his forte, Arthur Bryant was shopping for something bigger.

'What are you looking for?' asked May.

'I'm not sure,' Bryant replied, looking around. 'Perhaps I could saw a girl in half, produce doves from unfeasible places or explode my landlady.' Alma was hosting a charity lunch for the women from her church, and he was keen to provide her with a magic act, whether she wanted one or not.

Daphne, formerly Radiant Lotus Blossom, assistant

to the Immortal Mysterioso (available for weddings, bar mitzvahs and children's parties) came over to demonstrate an illusion. 'How are you with rabbits, Mr Bryant?' she asked. 'I had to give up the old act because I put on a bit of weight and got stuck in the cabinet of swords a few times,' she confided, dropping a French Chinchilla into a glittery tube and running a sabre through it. 'You can do this with a small child, providing they're not easily moved to tears.'

'I don't think he should practise on anything living,' said May. 'They might not stay living for long.'

'And then of course the Immortal Mysterioso turned out not to be immortal after all. Bowel cancer. So I put away my spangly tights and came to work here.' Daphne held up the gold canister to prove that nothing had actually penetrated the rabbit. 'It works on cats, too. Especially if you don't like them. Could I interest you in X-ray goggles?' She pulled out what appeared to be a diving helmet with rotating spirals over the eye-holes. 'Very popular for mind-reading acts.'

'You always accuse me of being a bad judge of character,' said Bryant, poking May in the ribs, 'but Theo Fontvieille bothered me from the moment I met him. He was too gaunt, too energetic. He made light of everything, acting as if nothing in the world ever touched him, but behind the banter there was a terrified child, screaming in the dark.'

'That's true. The first time I laid eyes on him he left me feeling uneasy,' May agreed. 'But he kept his nerve, bluffed his way through and almost got away with it.'

Bryant shook his head sadly. 'I thought I'd finished my learning, but apparently not. Human nature is like an iceberg, mostly hidden from view. Imagine the terror of waking up every morning and remembering who you are, wondering how on earth you're going to get through the day.'

'You could say that of Mr Fox,' added May. 'Or even of Mac. All of them were haunted.'

'Well, those two were damaged by irreversible childhood traumas, but Theo – he's the most interesting. I honestly think he suffers more than any of them. Every time he wakes, he realizes afresh that he has no soul, nothing inside that really cares for anyone or anything. You meet people like him all the time, the desperate players trying to cut one final deal that will make them rich and allow them to keep their kids in private schools.'

'Perhaps I could just intervene?' said Daphne, trying to break up what sounded to her like a very depressing conversation. 'We've got something new in involving a blowlamp and half a dozen squirrels that will make your eyes stand out like chapel hat-pegs.' She ran its instructions seductively up her arm.

'Self-preservation is a very strong instinct,' said May. 'He was quite happy to murder his friends if it meant he would survive. It's almost as if he thought they wouldn't mind giving up their lives for his.'

'That's just arrogance,' Bryant replied. 'He honestly thinks he's worth more than the others. But at night the truth must surely rise to the surface and terrify him.'

'Put your finger in here,' urged Daphne with a faint air of desperation. It had been a slow morning. Bryant did so distractedly, and she slammed down the guillotine on two carrots and the detective's digit.

'I'm not so sure Theo has quite that level of self-awareness. He's the kind of man who'll go to jail and write endless newspaper articles about the experience afterwards. I wonder if that's better – choosing never to wake from the dream.'

'Life is all a dream,' said Bryant, smiling gently. 'A wonderful, wonderful dream. The object is to make everyone else who shares it with you as happy as possible.'

'An admirable sentiment,' May agreed, smiling back at his old friend. 'Come on, the weather's supposed to clear up this afternoon. Let's get out into the sunshine while we can.' He turned back to the disappointed magic assistant. 'Thanks for the demonstration, Daphne. I think my colleague is going to try a different act. Perhaps he'll take up tap dancing.'

They left the magic shop arm in arm, laughing.

BRYANT & MAY ON THE LOOSE
By Christopher Fowler

Londoners are losing their heads . . .

Tracking down a murderer in King's Cross, one of the busiest meeting points in Britain, would be a nightmare for any police force. The discovery of a decapitated body in a shop freezer points to this being a case for the Peculiar Crimes Unit. However, the team has been disbanded and retirement seems the only option left for its elderly detectives, Arthur Bryant and John May. But then a second corpse is found. And again, it doesn't have a head.

Something decidedly strange is upsetting the area's property developers too. The mystical image of a forgotten legend – seemingly half-man, half-beast, covered in deer skin and sporting antlers made of knives – has begun stalking construction sites at night.

With limited resources and very little time, but freed from the system and on the loose, the nation's favourite decrepit detectives and the PCU are back in business, searching for body parts and behaving disgracefully as they go in search of London's pagan secrets.

At the heart of the investigation lies the city's oldest mystery – who really owns London and its landscapes? As they close in on the truth, Bryant and May find they have made a very dangerous enemy indeed . . .

'Devilishly clever . . . mordantly funny . . . sometimes heartbreakingly moving'
Val McDermid, *The Times*

'Another triumph for the Peculiar Crimes Unit'
Independent on Sunday

9780385614658

THE VICTORIA VANISHES
By Christopher Fowler

A BRYANT & MAY MYSTERY

The London pub was once a haven, a place where anyone could sit with a drink and ruminate on the ways of the world. Not, it seems, anymore . . .

While walking London's backstreets one evening, Arthur Bryant sees a middle-aged lady, slightly worse for wear, coming out of a pub. The next morning, her lifeless body is found at the point where their paths crossed.

In itself disturbing enough, but there's a twist: the pub has vanished. Bryant is convinced that he saw the street as it had been a century earlier; however, having recently lost an urn containing the cremated remains of an old friend, could the elderly detective be losing his mind as well?

It soon becomes clear that the lives of a number of women have been cut short in London pubs. A silent killer is at work, striking in full view, and yet nobody has a clue where he'll attack next. As their new Peculiar Crimes Unit team goes in search of a madman, detectives Bryant and May find themselves on the pub crawl of a lifetime – and come face to face with their own mortality.

'Bears all the hallmarks of the classic British
mystery . . . but much funnier'
Guardian

'One of our most unorthodox and entertaining writers'
Sunday Telegraph

9780553817997

WHITE CORRIDOR
By Christopher Fowler

A BRYANT & MAY MYSTERY

Britain is gripped by its coldest winter in years. Blizzards sweep the country, trapping elderly detectives Bryant and May – *en route* to a spiritualists' convention – somewhere on Dartmoor. Not the place to be when, back at the Peculiar Crimes Unit HQ in London, one of the team has been found dead in highly suspect circumstances.

But as the snow thickens and temperatures plummet, things are about to get much, much worse for the two octogenarian policemen. For along the line of vehicles stranded on this desolate stretch of road prowls a killer – a deranged murderer who is edging ever closer to one particular victim.

With no official help at hand and armed only with their wits, woolly coats and a mobile phone with a fading battery, can Bryant and May solve two very different crimes in time to prevent the pristine snow being stained blood red?

'Quirky, touching, profound and utterly original . . . a gripping page-turner'
Peter James

'Invests the traditions of the Golden Age of detective fiction with a tongue-in-cheek post-modernism'
Evening Standard

9780553817980

TEN-SECOND STAIRCASE
By Christopher Fowler

A BRYANT & MAY MYSTERY

It was a murder tailor-made for the Peculiar Crimes Unit.

A controversial artist is found dead, displayed as part of her own
outrageous installation. No suspects, no motive, no evidence.
Only a witness who swears the killer was a masked
highwayman on a black horse . . .

In the face of others' disbelief, it's very much business as usual for
the octogenarian detectives Arthur Bryant and John May.
Then the perpetrator is spotted at the scene of his next outlandish
murder. It seems he's intent on ridding London of certain minor
celebrities while becoming one himself as the tabloids
begin stirring up 'Highwayman Fever'.

Baffled by a case that involves everything from bitter artistic
rivalries and sleazy sex to gang warfare and the Knights Templar,
Bryant and May know that, to crack it, they must use every
orthodox – and unorthodox – means at their disposal. Not least
because it looks as though these deaths are connected to a
decades-old killing spree that nearly destroyed the two
partners once before . . . and might yet again.

'Witty, sinuous and darkly comedic storytelling
from a Machiavellian jokester'
Guardian

'Atmospheric, hugely beguiling and as filled with tricks and sleights
of hand as a magician's sleeve . . . a genuine power to thrill'
Joanne Harris

9780553817201

PAPERBOY
By Christopher Fowler

Superman, Dracula, Treasure Island, The Avengers . . . when
you're ten years old you can fall in love with any story, so long
as it's a good one. But what do you do if you're growing up
in a home without books? Christopher Fowler's childhood
memoir captures life in suburban London through the
eyes of a lonely boy who spends his days between the library
and the cinema devouring novels, comics, cereal boxes –
anything that might reveal a story. But it is 1960, and
after fifteen years of post-war belt-tightening, his family's
not quite ready to indulge a child cursed with
too much imagination . . .

Caught between an ever-sensible, exhausted mother and a
DIY-obsessed father fighting his own demons, Christopher
takes refuge in words. His parents try to understand their son's
peculiar obsession but they fast lose patience with him – and
each other. As the war of nerves escalates to include every
member of the Fowler family, something has to give,
but do the tough lessons of real life mean a boy
must always let go of his dreams?

The memoir of a childhood at once eccentric and
endearingly ordinary, this does for storytelling what
Nigel Slater's *Toast* did for food.

'*Paperboy* is fabulous, and I hope it sells forever.'
Joanne Harris

9780385615570